A Knife
Well Spent

Also by Jackie Ivie

Heat of the Knight

The Knight Before Christmas

Tender Is the Knight

Lady of the Knight

Published by Kensington Publishing Corporation

A Knight Well Spent

Jackie Ivie

ZEBRA BOOKS
Kensington Publishing Corp.
www.kensingtonbooks.com

ZEBRA BOOKS are published by

Kensington Publishing Corp.
850 Third Avenue
New York, NY 10022

All Kensington titles, imprints, and distributed lines are
available at special quantity discounts for bulk purchases
for sales promotion, premiums, fund-raising, educational,
or institutional use.

Special book excerpts or customized printings can also be
created to fit specific needs. For details, write or phone the
office of the Kensington Special Sales Manager: Attn.
Special Sales Department, Kensington Publishing Corp., 850
Third Avenue, New York, NY 10022. Phone: 1-800-221-2647.

Zebra and the Z logo Reg. U.S. Pat. & TM Off.

ISBN-13: 978-1-4201-0165-2
ISBN-10: 1-4201-0165-X

First printing: October 2008
10 9 8 7 6 5 4 3 2 1

Printed in the United States of America

Chapter One

AD 1141

He was awake, he was moving, and he was in pain.

Rhoenne eased his step to accommodate the pain lacing his calf. It was more a shuffling stumble than a walk. He wiped a hand across his forehead and grimaced at the sweat beads there before rubbing them away on his tunic's edge. He couldn't prevent the shudder. He knew why. He was fevered.

He forced another step, another wince, and another quickly drawn breath. He couldn't prevent the signs of weakness. All he could do was make certain no one else knew it. That was why he was forcing one agonized step after the other onto a leg mangled to the point he was afraid to look at it.

Rhoenne stopped, listened, and sagged with relief. He could hear the sound of running water. His instincts hadn't failed him. Knighted at sixteen and awarded this fief at the age of a score-and-one, he'd made it a point then to visit every croft, every field, crop, every water source. It had been years . . . but he still remembered.

Rhoenne brushed the hair that many likened to a lion's

mane from his forehead before entering into the glade. There was one huge boulder, four large stones arranged like steps, and a row of overhanging willows weeping into the brook. It was exactly as he recalled—except for the strange figure straddling the waterfall that fed the brook. Rhoenne was so disappointed and frustrated he didn't bother to hide the weakness. He lowered his head and groaned loudly, letting every bit of agony pierce the sound.

The black-shrouded figure promptly fell right into the pool, showering everything, Rhoenne included. He kept from a major dousing by stumbling back two steps, before the motion became an all-out fall, slamming him onto the carpet of grass, and stealing every bit of air from his body.

"Oh! How could you?"

Rhoenne opened his eyes, started sucking for air, and glared at the girl who was screeching her words. It didn't work. She was angrier. And she had command of her breathing.

"You—you great big—oaf!"

She was standing beside him, dripping water everywhere, shaking what looked like a child-sized fist at him. Then she gave him the oddest indignity of his life. She stepped right up onto his chest and hammered her feet into it. Rhoenne had only a moment to grasp his luck that she weighed little and that she hadn't anything on her feet, before she was putting words with her steps as she stomped.

"I have to start anew! You've ruined everything! Dinna' just lay there with those big blue eyes and stare! Go! Move!"

The growl he gave hadn't much sound, but he had her off him and onto what scrawny buttocks she probably possessed, by grabbing and twisting her ankles and letting the spin make her fall. He registered that she had fairly shapely legs before she rolled back to her feet, pulling her sodden black mass of clothing about herself.

"So . . . you have a bark? I'm cheered for you. Now run

along, before The Lady gets annoyed with you." She'd punctuated her speech with heaven-sent arms. "Well? Dinna' just lay there after ruining my blessing ritual. I have to finish."

He bristled. It was rare, but he knew what it was. He knew what caused it, too. He'd never been treated like this. He pulled in a breath. He couldn't decide which pained him more at the moment; his chest or his lower leg. The leg won out. He held the bit of air he'd managed to breathe, and then let it out extremely slowly, since anything else seemed beyond him. The leg was definitely more painful, and it throbbed worse; due, no doubt, to how he'd been forced to move it as he fell.

That was her fault, he thought.

"Are you a dimwit? Why dinna' you say something? I wouldn't have been so angered at you. Come. Tell me why you've sought the services of the Lady of the Brook. I'll na' hurt you."

Rhoenne made fists as she knelt beside him and looked him over with strange-colored eyes. In fact, if he wasn't mistaken, she had one of green and one of brown. That was interesting.

She smiled then, showing two very deep dimples. Rhoenne stared. She wasn't as young as he'd first thought, nor was she uncomely. If he wasn't mistaken she was freshly bathed and clean-looking, too. His eyes widened. She was wearing a head covering made from what could only be his own vivid blue cloth, beneath her own wimple! No one outside the Ramhurst castle was allowed to wear it. It was his own command. He was still reeling from that revelation when she put an icy hand against his cheek.

"You're fevered. You came to me just in time. You ken? Take off this tunic. What is wrong with you now?"

Rhoenne didn't know what she was referring to. He was looking at her with as little expression as he could manage.

It was actually better that he didn't have use of his voice just yet. Otherwise, he'd probably be yelling.

"I canna' begin healing if I dinna' see the reason for it. Have you been ill long?"

She lifted the hem of his garment. Rhoenne tried not to move while she peeled it up, exposing his belly flesh to the early morning air. Despite his every effort, the bumps rose, making his shiver worse.

"This is na' good. You've size . . . and strength. How can a dimwit get so—so . . . fit? You're na' going to hurt me, are you?"

She dropped the garment and came back into view. Rhoenne barely held the reaction to how it felt to have the wet weight of the tunic join with his other ills. *Now she asks it?* he wondered. He shook his head.

"You ken me?"

He nodded. She sighed.

"Good. I'm known as the Lady of the Brook. I'm a healer. You look to need a healer."

Rhoenne nodded again, slower this time. He couldn't believe his luck. As strange as she was, he'd heard of far worse from those few gifted in the healing arts. He didn't waste time debating it. If she could heal him, mayhap he wouldn't take a switch to her when she finished. Maybe.

"I'm na' a witch. I want you to know this."

His eyebrows rose.

"I dinna' practice it. I never have."

He sucked for breath as she pulled up her skirts. Then she was splitting bare legs to straddle his torso, dampening him worse and making him shudder anew. Then she made it all worse by burrowing both cold hands well beneath his tunic and placing them directly atop his heart. Everything in him reacted; his heart stopped, his shuddering ceased, his breath caught. Then his heart decided it would continue beating, and rather rapidly. He was afraid she'd spot it.

Rhoenne watched her and admitted to himself that he'd slighted her on her comeliness. She was more than that. She was beautiful. She had arched black brows, long, perfectly spaced lashes, high cheekbones, and very full lips. He found himself wondering if she was in possession of all her teeth, and if they were in as perfect condition as the rest of her. He wondered what color her hair was, and how long, and how it would feel between his fingers.

"I canna' work if you insist on such thoughts," she whispered, stiffening her arms and sitting forward so that her upper body hovered above his.

Rhoenne flushed. He knew it, although he couldn't remember ever experiencing it before. He watched as she arched herself above his, catching the first rays of sun as the dawn broke over the biggest boulder. He caught his breath for an entirely new reason as light flooded her features.

She wasn't just beautiful, he decided, and wondered what word did fit.

"You've been injured," she said softly, moving her head down to match her gaze to his.

Rhoenne's eyes showed the surprise. He couldn't prevent it.

"You took a weapon in your lower leg. You have na' had it seen to. You're hiding it. You dinna' even clean it. You're very brave. . . . Or very foolish. It's poisoning within you."

His eyes went wider still. She winked. Rhoenne knew he had a full-out blush now. He didn't know how to hide it.

"You need na' fear me. I'm a healer. I have strange methods, true, but I can heal you. I swear it. Do you wish me to go on?" she asked.

He nodded.

"Are you a knight?"

He shook his head after a moment. She didn't look like she believed him.

"Dinna' lie to The Lady. I canna' heal you, if I canna' trust you."

"I'm not a knight," he replied in a raspy whisper. It was true. He wasn't. He was the liege lord. He had legions of knights serving him. He didn't say a word about any of that.

At his reply she hesitated. Rhoenne waited. She couldn't have known that he had a great, deep, resonant voice. It was notorious. He'd been described by it. It came along with the immense frame the Lord had gifted him with. A small voice would have been incongruous coming from him.

"You're na' a dimwit . . . are you?" she asked with very little sound.

He shook his head.

"You're na' a knight yet you've a battle wound? This is na' the mark of a learned, scholarly man . . . nor one using his wits, if he possessed such."

Rhoenne bristled. "I am not a dimwit." He couldn't keep the defensive tone from the whisper.

"Then why did you lose?" she asked.

Rhoenne's mouth gaped.

She grinned, bringing the dimples back into existence. "I dinna' have special powers. I'll na' stand accused of such." Her face clouded and her grin died.

He shook his head rapidly.

"That's good, for I'll na' be able to heal if you worry over the methods."

"I don't worry," Rhoenne whispered.

He didn't know if she believed him or not, for the enigmatic look she turned on him didn't tell him anything. The word came to him then. She was absolutely exquisite. Her skin was silk-smooth, her mouth reddened and lush-looking. He found himself hoping she had black hair that matched her brows; thick, glossy strands of it. She deserved the setting of his castle room, richly covered with tapestries and filled with gilded furniture.

"I already have all that," she said.

Rhoenne went stiff with the surprise.

She giggled and the stiffness went straight to his groin at the sound. There wasn't anything he could do to prevent it. That was unbelievable. He'd never had his body betray him to this extent. He tried bringing the pain of his wound back to the forefront of his mind. It almost worked. He was afraid he was rose red with the reaction.

"If I close my eyes, I have castles, servants, and silver. Anyone can. Close your eyes."

He didn't want to. He almost said it aloud.

"You have to mind The Lady. Right here. Right now. Otherwise. . . ."

She left her threat unfinished. Rhoenne closed his eyes. That was worse somehow, for she not only was clean-looking, she smelled like fresh-picked wildflowers. He pulled in a long breath and held it.

"You claim you are na' a knight . . . yet you've every mark of one. You're *nae* idiot, although you dinna' show much in wits when you entered my glade. I surprised you. You're na' easily surprised. All of that is strange. Verra strange. You've a battle wound, so you have been in a battle. If you'd won this battle, you would have had your wound tended to before now. You must have lost. You see the method of my knowledge? I weigh out what I know with what has to be. You dinna' even take out the weapon, I'm guessing. How can you pretend 'tis naught? You're very strong. You're very brave. You're very manly . . . *and* you're very foolish. Verra."

Rhoenne opened his eyes and lifted his head. She wasn't hovering over him anymore. She was kneeling next to his boiled leather shin-guard, the one he'd strapped tight to hold in the grotesque-looking, linen-swathed swelling below his knee. He wondered when she'd moved. He hadn't even felt it.

"I'm going to have to remove this Sassenach thing . . . and this hose. Will that be a problem?"

He wondered how she could ask such a question, when the answer was starting to distend the patch at his crotch. He groaned the breath out and lay back down. Perhaps if he pretended she was a man—and a fat, ugly one at that—he could stop such a reaction.

"I mean . . . I—I canna' just cut through it. Those you have been hiding this from . . . they—they would ken your wound. It would na' remain hidden. Your bravery would be . . . for naught. You do see?"

She was stammering and stumbling through the words. Rhoenne sucked in on both cheeks and kept any expression where she wouldn't see it. He guessed she hadn't had that reaction before. She didn't sound like a confident healer calling herself the Lady of the Brook. She sounded just like what she was; a young, beautiful, virginal maiden with a man at her fingertips.

Rhoenne groaned again. *Virginal*, he repeated in his thoughts.

"Forgive me. I try na' to pain."

Her face was back in view as she scooted to his side. He did the best he could not to let her see, or think she could see, where his thoughts had just been. He suspected he hadn't been successful and he moved his glance away before he reddened again.

"I canna' tend your wound like this. You must unstrap that leather shield piece and shed your hose. Will you need assist?"

"No." Rhoenne gave her the answer, before undressing himself. The act of rolling his own wet tunic back into place was checking his earlier reaction to her and the tremor of his frame was back. He couldn't help it. The material was wet, clammy, and cold. And he was fevered. He hoped she wouldn't spot the weakness and nearly shook his head at his own idiocy. She was a healer. Healers dealt with weakness.

Then he had his hands beneath the tunic edge, fumbling with the rawhide ties at his waist. He eased the garment down over his hips. That's when it got difficult. Rhoenne forced himself into a sitting position so he could maneuver his own clothing down. He didn't want her to assist with it and not only because he never let anyone see such weakness.

It was something more.

It was her.

He had trouble the closer he got to his wound. He couldn't keep the reaction hidden. He tensed. He sucked in each breath, only to ease it out with a groan of sound. He had to let the stoicism go. She was right. He *was* injured, he'd worn the hose for days, and he didn't want it sliced through, either—because he didn't want anyone else to know of his injury. He'd strapped the shin guard on for the same reason—and because it gave him stability enough to move. Rhoenne untied the straps with a vicious, efficient motion, breathing rapidly and shallowly the entire time.

He still had to shed the hose. That garment had been excellent for its purpose; keeping him warm and the bandage hidden. When he was finished, it was just a puddle of gray-shaded fabric about his ankles. And he was drained.

Rhoenne felt as wearied when he finished as if he'd just been on the list, battling. About the only good thing was he had the pain to a bearable level. He turned his head, met her gaze, and then his heart lurched—sharply and powerfully. Rhoenne had it hidden almost the moment it happened. He couldn't do anything about the flare of his eyes, the increase of his pulse, or the sudden tautness of his frame. He had to react slowly, and do what he could to keep her from seeing or guessing at any of it.

She looked away first, saying nothing, although the two spots of pink on her cheeks were telling him plenty.

Rhoenne watched her look him over. It helped mute the throb of ache he was ignoring. He was grateful he'd shed his chainmail hauberk, shirt, and the steel-grommeted leather gauntlets before seeking sleep last night. He was doubly grateful he'd left the sword named Pinnacle in the sheath at his destrier's side. If she knew who she really had at her fingertips, she wouldn't be looking him over with her lower lip caught between her teeth and a blush that was easy to spot with the growing dawn.

"I've been puzzling this . . . and you have too much strength na' to be a knight," she finally said when he just sat there regarding her, with hands resting on his thighs, which appeared to be the same exact position she was in.

He waited for her to finish surveying him, although it took some time as she slid her gaze back down to his boots and up. He was afraid his body could feel a touch that wasn't actually happening. He was very tempted to tighten the muscles beneath the skin she was looking at, too.

"You're certain you are na' one?"

"Do you wish me to be?" he whispered.

Her eyebrows rose at that. She finally shook her head and moved down to attend to his wound. Then there was nothing in his world but fire and pain and ache. The moment her fingers started circling and probing the bulge of bandaging around his calf, Rhoenne went stiff with the agony.

"This is going to pain," she remarked.

He had his hands splayed onto the ground behind him for support. It also made it easy to watch. He almost wished he hadn't as she reached in and pulled a small, curved knife from somewhere in the voluminous cloak she wore. She obviously knew her way about a knife was his thought, as she settled it into her palm and started slicing at the linen he'd wound about his leg not two days earlier, and the closer she got, the worse he tensed.

"You've taken a lance. I'll have to find the tip. It will na' be pleasant. You'll have to hold still."

He opened his mouth to tell her he already knew the whole of it but then she touched the red, swollen lump with her knife blade. Her action had him arching from the carpet of grass, while the ground absorbed the weight of his elbows. A hand on his belly was what sent him back onto his buttocks. Only by grinding his teeth together did he keep from giving any of it sound.

"You mustn't move. I have to build a fire. I need it to clean the water."

Rhoenne concentrated on her words. He had to. Otherwise, he was afraid he'd be sobbing. *She needs fire to clean water,* he repeated silently.

"It was na' clean enough even before I fell into it," she answered, as if he'd spoken aloud. "I also have to gather moss; and get my herbs . . . like burdock, amica, and a bit of roseweed. You're na' to move. I forbid it. You ken?"

Rhoenne had his teeth too tightly clenched to answer. He was beginning to wonder at his sanity. He had but one more day's ride before he'd be at Tyneburn Hall and in his own healer's hands. To think a Celt lass, calling herself the Lady of the Brook, could do better was a fool's prayer.

"You've na' got time," she spoke, divining his thoughts again. "The wound festers. You may lose your leg even with my help. If you dinna' believe me, question it when you arrive. Dinna' tempt fate or question what brought you to me. You need the gifts from a healer? I am one. I swear it on all the gods. I'll return. Dinna' move! I will be very angry if you do. I swear to that, as well.

"You dinna' want to see me when I'm angry," she continued. He watched her stand, gather the wet folds of her cloak closer about her, and look down at him. Then she sighed loudly. "You're na' a very good patient. I understand that about you. You've na' had anyone command you. You command others. I understand that, too. I do. I'll still be angry if you dinna' obey me. You ken?"

He nodded and kept his eyes on her until she disappeared. He'd never felt as defenseless and open to attack as he did then, sitting amid the grasses, with his tunic pulled down for modesty, his tights about his ankles, and no weapon handy. He was called the Lion of Ramhurst, yet had been brought to a state of vulnerability, and sat half-dressed, docilely awaiting the command of a child-woman weighing about a third of what he did. He still couldn't believe it.

Chapter Two

Aislynn's hands were shaking before she had everything gathered and she was beginning to doubt she could work on him. That led to questioning her own abilities and that wasn't good. She believed in her healing gifts and the extent of them even if she was the only one who did.

It took longer than she wished it to but that was because she hadn't a spark handy for a fire, or mead for him to drink. She knew he shouldn't face what she had to do in a completely sober state. That meant a trip home. Even at a full run, she didn't think she could get there and back before the sun moved. She decided time must be changing on her, however. The sun didn't seem to have moved as she fished two coals from the fire for a small torch and opened her father's ale keg to dip a wineskin out, careful not to awaken anyone.

Her arms were full, her breast was burning with the exertion of running, and she was half-afraid he wasn't going to be there when she returned, but he was.

Aislynn stood just outside the fringe of shrubbery ringing the glade she called hers and waited for her heart to calm. The Norman giant was still where she'd left him. He didn't seem happy about it. She watched as he plucked a

blade of grass and ran it through his fingernails to make
it curl. She took a deep breath, assumed her confident
Lady of the Brook image, and stepped in.

He looked up and stole her breath again with the clear-
water blue of his eyes. Aislynn swallowed and looked
away before he noticed. It was better to stay busy. She
knew he watched as she stacked a small pile of broken
twigs near the stream bank and tipped the coals onto it.
She fed grasses into it until the fire was strong enough to
keep going by itself. Then she set the small iron rack atop
it, dipped a pail full of water, and set it atop the flames.

The indecision over whether or not to heat her knife ate
at her, but she wasn't going to let him know. His wound
was trying to knit, it was full of poison, and it would be
easier to slice if her blade was warm. She opened the knife
into its half-circle shape and placed the tip in the center of
her blaze.

Though she knew he'd be watching her, it still made her
start when she turned and caught those blue eyes on her
as intently as they were. Aislynn looked down at the
ground as she approached where he sat. She couldn't believe she'd actually stepped up and stomped on the expanse
of chest facing her, but he'd frightened and startled her.
Nobody saw her at her morning blessing. Nobody. It would
start the whispers again. She assured herself it hadn't mattered. He hadn't even acted like it was of any consequence.

"I've brought ale for you."

She pulled the skin of it from where she'd tied it about
her waist and put it in the grass beside him where it went
to a bulge shape. "You may need it."

"I won't," he replied in that soft whisper of his.

Aislynn shivered. She wondered if he always spoke like
that or if he was doing so for a reason. She cursed her own
lack for not checking to see if he had further injury. "Have
you hurt your throat?" she asked.

He jerked his head slightly, his eyes widening with the same odd look he'd given her on several occasions already. She wondered why he did that, too.

"I . . . no," he replied.

"You possess a voice?" she continued.

He nodded.

"Why dinna' you use it?"

He shrugged. Aislynn's lips tightened. It wasn't her business but she could guess. He had an enormous, well-muscled physique. He was easily a head taller than she was. The lower leg she was about to work on looked larger than both of her thighs put together. He probably had a voice to match. It would be loud, captivating, and strong, just like he was. She instinctively knew that was why he wasn't using it.

"I understand," she said. "It will give you away."

This time his mouth dropped fully open. Aislynn nearly giggled. He was going to think she was a witch yet. She bent to check her knife. The blade tip was glowing red. She wrapped a bit of her cloak about her hand, lifted the blade, and walked over to him. He was very trusting, she decided, as she knelt beside him. He was also in the stiffest position a body could possibly be in and still be breathing. Aislynn put the blade against his skin and sliced.

Then she knew he definitely had a voice and it was massive, as his curse and groan filled the air. She ignored it. She had work to do. She was going to drain the pus-filled poison from him and then she had to find the lance tip he still harbored.

Aislynn put her fingers against his skin and lightly grazed until she felt where the metal had to be. It was lucky for both of them that it hadn't reached bone. She didn't think herself capable of extracting anything that deep.

She was beginning to think she couldn't retrieve it, before she had it, and the act of sliding it out was worse.

The blond man was quiet the entire time. He looked intent on drinking the wineskin dry. Aislynn looked his way once and then bent back to her task.

He'd not only been carrying the entire lance tip in him, it had binding still attached. Aislynn put it to the side of her and tipped his leg so he'd bleed freely onto the grass. Then she squeezed the wound until no more poison came out with the blood. He didn't complain. Another quick glance showed he was still gulping, although the ale was in danger of sliding over his cheeks with the speed with which he was drinking it.

Aislynn picked up his souvenir and her knife and walked over to the burn to rinse everything off. Once the lance tip was clean, she realized the obvious. It wasn't a keepsake. It was too dangerous. She dropped it into the water and watched the current rinse it away. Then she busied herself with crushing a palm-sized portion of brittle, dried orange amica flowers into the pot of water. She whispered as she did so, begging the water goddesses to assist with their healing powers.

When the pot was steaming the aroma into the glade, she knew it was ready. She needed it warm, not burning. Aislynn lifted it and turned to him. His eyes weren't as crystal-clear, they were a more vivid blue, with red-rimmed flesh around them.

"You had poison to your wound. I'm going to wash it. It should na' hurt. Worse," she finished.

"Don't stay . . . the work on . . . my account," he replied.

He was pausing through the words, not whispering anymore, and he had a deep baritone voice that made the air rumble. She knew why he hadn't used it earlier. It was very distinctive and very authoritative. Anyone hearing such a voice would immediately know the owner of it.

She frowned. He'd assured her he wasn't a knight, he certainly wasn't a Scot . . . *so what could he be?* she wondered.

He was too old to be one of their Sassenach squires. Which left only one thing: a mercenary. He was one of their paid killers. Aislynn wondered why she hadn't realized it instantly. Not only was he her enemy . . . he was paid to be one! That made everything she was doing so much worse. She should have known it the moment she met him. A man possessing all the muscle and scarring this man did obviously warred for a living. No wonder he hid his wound from the others. It would probably mean his death. She was shaking as she brought the pot over to him.

"What . . . is it?" He slurred the question with that resonating voice of his.

Aislynn turned her attention to rinsing the wound. She had to. She had to keep herself occupied. Aside from a quick intake of breath, her giant didn't give any outward sign of how it pained him. *Perhaps it isn't paining him,* she told herself, *since he'd just drunk a wineskin of ale.*

"Feels . . . strange. Like naught. What is it . . . you do?" he asked.

"Your senses must be blunted."

"You do . . . such a thing? You—your talents must be . . . in great demand."

"You drank yourself into it. I had little to do with it," she replied stiffly. The last of the water mixture had been poured on, leaving the flesh slightly white at the edges, before it started bleeding again. Aislynn frowned more at it. She knew she was going to have to seal the wound. She'd only done it once and that was to a stray dog—and she'd had her other knife. The cur hadn't even stayed around so she could see if it worked. She stood, looked for her blade, and then put it back in the fire.

"Why do . . . you heat it? A-again?"

"I have to burn you."

His eyes really were a perfect match to the sky. It was

especially noticeable as wide as he had them as he stared up at her. "Nay! Why?"

"To stay the bleeding. I've *nae* other choice."

"Oh." One word and he went from an anxious male back to a virile, handsome, enormous, and slightly intoxicated one. "Is it going to hurt?"

"Aye," she answered. "Everything I do hurts. It heals, too."

He nodded and was silent, watching her with luminous eyes that now matched the center of the flame. Aislynn looked away, put the comparison aside as more stupidity she didn't need, and picked up the knife. She moved the three steps to him quickly, before the blade could cool.

At the first touch, he arched his body and groaned again, louder than the first time, and filling the clearing with his deep voice again. Aislynn looked quickly about. Everything seemed to stop, the very air seemed to have silenced, and that made the stupidity of her actions even more apparent. *If the people accompanying him think him in trouble, will they come?* she wondered. She returned her gaze to him. There wasn't anyone or anything else to see.

"That . . . pained," he said, breaking the silence.

"Just as I warned. I'm na' finished," she was answering as she rose to look down at him.

"You're . . . not?"

"I have to sear the other side."

He made a sound suspiciously like a sob. Aislynn was afraid of verifying it. She rinsed her blade, twisted her lips at the blackened metal near the joint, and then shrugged before putting it back into the fire. It was a special knife; hers for years. It was one of her prized possessions. Now it was strangely tinted and used, but still prized.

If he'd suffered anything like tears, they were nowhere in existence as she knelt and pressed the blade to him the second time. In fact, he was looking at her with something indefinable. His expression sent shivers through her. Aislynn had to look away. He was too immense. He was too strange. Everything was. The entire morning was getting too large to absorb. She was going to be late at the mill. She'd be punished. And she was tired. That was especially strange. Aislynn never tired.

She hung her head and waited for the blade to cool against his skin before sliding it away. He was going to have a definite scar below his knee but there wasn't one sign of poison.

"I believe . . . you succeeded," he commented finally but with the same disjointed phrasing. "It isn't bleeding. You didn't hear . . . me cursing . . . much?"

"I dinna' have to," she whispered.

"Discard . . . it. I infuse suffering . . . with anger. Makes it . . . bearable. My. You did . . . well. It even . . . feels better."

"I'm na' finished," she told him. He went so tense next to her that she felt it. "Dinna' fret—it will na' pain. I'm going to wrap it with special moss. It will soothe. It will keep poison away. *Nae* one will know. You'll have full use of it again soon . . . then you can go back to your business of war and killing."

"W-war and—and—and . . . killing? Why . . . do you . . . say that?"

She should have bitten her tongue to keep from saying it. She spoke her next words to the grass. "You're verra large. Fit. Scarred. You kept a weapon in your leg for days ignoring the pain. Such things define what a man is and by your own words you're *nae* knight. I decide at what I dinna' know. I use clues. You've given me some."

"Unlike . . . all else you say . . . that one is not—not—not . . . it's wrong."

Aislynn looked up, caught her lip at the intent look on his face and looked away. "I—I have to get the moss," she stammered.

"It will be . . . most welcome."

She stood and moved to where she'd left the woven greenish netting, covered with a thick layer of lichen. It looked wet enough. It smelled of earth and loam and the strength of the spirits. She lifted a section between her fingers and thumb and approached him with it. Then she was kneeling beside him, placing the lichen atop the freshly cauterized flesh and holding it there.

"Lady?" he whispered.

Aislynn turned her head, moving her eyes up his tunic-covered chest, and caught his gaze. The moment she did, she knew she was in trouble. She forgot to breathe, every thought flew her head, and pinpricks of sensation tickled the area about her nose. She'd known he was disturbing, she just hadn't realized how much. She'd never felt this way. It surprised and stunned and terrified . . . and yet it felt wondrous, too. Aislynn knew there wasn't any such thing as love in the world anymore. The warring and killing destroyed it. There was no such thing as love, and there certainly wasn't such a thing as love at first sight. Such an idea was for those who believed in faeries.

"You've my . . . thanks." He stopped and licked his lips. "I'd pay . . . but I have no—no coin with me. I'll . . . have some sent. Tell me where."

Aislynn looked down and welcomed the embarrassing sting of reaction. *Love at first sight?* she wondered. It was obviously one-sided and he was stewed. She cleared her throat in order to answer as forcefully as the Lady of the Brook would. "You must forget me. That is my price. And my payment."

"What . . . if I say . . . nay?" he asked, filling the glade with sound again.

She didn't have a choice. She had to turn back to him and force herself to show nothing although the thudding of her heart was loud in her ears. "I'm a healer but I'm also Scot. I dinna' know what you are, but I'm certain 'tis na' Scot. You've Sassenach clothing and speak the Norman tongue. I'll stand accused of treachery if my actions are known."

He gave her a level look, then it wavered as he smiled. When he answered, his words were worse slurred. "N-not good enough. The only treachery . . . is to me. I'll buy you. I mean . . . your services. Now. Ride with me. Now. I mean, as soon as I reach the horse. Then. We'll ride . . . then. Away. I'll allow none to call you . . . other than lovely—I mean healer. Beauteous healer."

Aislynn gulped. "The only men requiring services such as I render are warring and killing men," she said softly.

"And men who live, breathe . . . get sick . . . and bleed," he replied, with a tremble to the words. "I'm surprised. You're young . . . for such a—a—a thing. Healing. That . . . thing. 'Tis . . . im—im—impressive."

The last was said as he lifted his injured leg and angled his head to look down the length of it. Aislynn found herself doing the same. She had to turn aside after the first glance though. With his limb raised as it was, every solid, rippled contour stood out. What morning sun was reaching through the willow above them was caressing every knotted muscle with light and shadow. He looked exactly what he was: a Sassenach warrior—and an extremely powerful one. She'd never seen anything like him. She didn't think she ever would again.

"Something . . . troubles you?" he asked.

He was having such difficulty with his words, he sounded drunk. And then Aislynn knew. He was weak from loss of blood. She'd done him a disservice by giving him the mead. She should have brought less. She looked back at him and did her best to keep the thought from showing.

"I must go. I'll fetch the wrapping. To keep the moss

against your wound. It should na' pain you as much. It
will knit well, given time. It may leave a vicious scar,
though. It will na' be pretty."

"Scars?" He rolled a sigh through his lips. "They don't . . .
bother me."

A warrior to the bone. She shrugged. "Then it will na'
trouble you."

"Besides I wear . . . thick woolens. For the clime."

He probably didn't mean to bring her attention to the
fact that his hose were about his ankles, leaving him as
naked beneath his tunic as if he wore a *plaide*, but that was
what happened. Aislynn started, pulled her gaze away, and
endured every bit of the heat that flooded her.

"I must ask you . . . something. I wonder how to pro-
ceed with it, though," he said, and he was back to the
whisper again.

"I'll fetch your wrapping."

"Wait." He reached out and caught her arm with one
hand. Aislynn had known she was slight in comparison to
him, but she didn't realize the extent of it as his hand
closed about her upper arm. She knew he noted it as his
forehead wrinkled. She was slender. She was considered
frail and sickly by everyone she knew. That was why she
wore a large, voluminous cloak.

"I would ask . . . a question. Will you . . . listen?" he
continued.

"You ask such, after making certain I canna' do otherwise?"

His lips twitched. She felt her heart do the exact same
motion.

"Do you have . . . a man? Mayhap . . . a husband?" he
asked.

Aislynn's eyes went huge. She couldn't prevent it. She
was very wary of the question. She'd just taken a Celt
lance tip from a very large, overpowering, and muscular

warrior. She knew him to be a warring and killing man, despite his claims to the contrary. It wasn't a far leap to think him capable of warring, killing, *and* the ravishment of females.

"Why do you ask?" She had to swallow to make the words.

He blew a sigh, feathering the blond wisps of hair at his forehead. "I don't know. Because you . . . are here. I . . . am here." He licked his lips. "I may not . . . come this way again. You know it. I know . . . it. Don't ask me the why . . . of it. You have healed me and I have no payment. I have nothing . . . save an ale-loosened tongue . . . and I think you've bewitched me."

Aislynn stiffened. It didn't stop him.

"Now answer. Have you a husband?"

"If I say yea, how will you know it for a lie or na'?"

She looked across the arm's-length he was holding her and met his eyes. He tipped his head slightly back and then he smiled, revealing perfectly spaced, white teeth. Aislynn knew then that she was in very serious trouble, as her heart felt like it dove to the bottom of her belly and started an ever-increasing pounding from there.

"If you tell me yea, I'll . . . be saddened."

"I . . . have *nae* man." The words were out before she gave time to think them. Aislynn wondered why she'd lost every scrap of sanity.

"Good. That is good . . . and just. And fair."

He was pulling as he spoke, using his other arm to bring her against him. For a man weak with loss of blood, stewed by ale, and enduring what he had, it was surprising how easily he handled her. She was making extreme trouble for herself by further contact with him, yet hastening toward that very thing. She might as well be running toward it. Aislynn ended up clasped to his chest, listening to his heartbeat, and feeling his arms enfolding her. His chest seemed molded for snuggling against, she decided.

"You'll receive payment . . . my little Lady of the Brook," he whispered to her mantle-covered head. "You've eased . . . pain, stopped . . . my bleeding, and ask too little. I would . . . change that. Now. Right now."

Aislynn actually registered what he meant to do, she just couldn't imagine it. Nothing in her experience could've prepared her. He put the side of his index finger beneath her chin and raised her face. His eyes were such an intense clear-water color, he was probably known for that, too. He was entirely too interesting, too handsome, and too intriguing. He was also holding her gaze as easily as he was holding her. Aislynn did everything in her power to break the spell but nothing worked.

"Hmm. I sought out a place to—to hide. Pain. Hide . . . suffering. Hide. I found . . . succor. In . . . the woods. This morn. You're . . . strange."

"I'm a healer," she replied.

He smiled widely, bringing small lines into place about his eyes. Aislynn noted them. It appeared he smiled. Often.

"True. A—a healer. With strange . . . methods and stranger . . . reasons. No healer does this for free. It makes light of . . . it. I would pay for your services . . . in another way, then. My way."

She didn't answer. Her throat closed off as Aislynn accepted her full measure of trouble. She hadn't lied. She had no husband, although the new blacksmith held promise of it, but what she was feeling while perched atop this Norman's lap was obliterating even Donald O'Rourke. Easily. If she wasn't careful, she was going to believe not only in love at first sight, but the next thing she knew tales of faeries would start coming true. She shook her head to clear it. It didn't work.

"What . . . is it?" he asked.

Aislynn felt her eyes sting with tears. She didn't know where they came from or why they'd bother her. She only knew they swelled, crested to her lashes, and then hovered there. She watched his reaction as he watched her. She knew the truth, too. He may be a Sassenach and a warrior, but he was no killer.

"You're very . . . beautiful," he whispered and bent his head toward her, blocking the ray of light as he did so.

Aislynn's eyes shut, pulled by something beyond her control as her lips pursed. She knew he was going to kiss her. She was going to receive her first one! She'd listened of them from her sister, Meghan. She dreamed of receiving one. She'd been so far off the reality it was amazing.

The man's lips were warmth and comfort, joy and delight, and then even more. Aislynn experienced each emotion as he kept his mouth against hers, breathed onto her nose, and then nuzzled her own lips apart with his. She felt, rather than heard, the warble of sound put into existence by his moan. She nearly joined him.

The entire morning's experience passed in the moments he kissed her, and Aislynn recollected each bit, with every heartbeat and every conjoined breath. She not only believed in love at first sight, she was well onto scripting her own faery tale when he pulled back, separating them.

Aislynn didn't open her eyes. To do so would make it too real. Too unavoidable. Too wrong.

"You're a . . . special lass. That's a shame," he said finally, and his voice had an edge to it, defying his inebriated sound.

Her breath halted. That was far different from his. The chest she was held against was moving her up and back down with the force and depth of his own breathing.

"Special is . . . bad. Very bad."

Her eyes opened wide. "It is?"

He nodded. "Makes everything that happens . . . worse."

If Aislynn had thought her eyes wide, she'd been

mistaken, as they opened to such an extent the morning air felt like punishment.

"I tell you this, so you'll know the why of what I do. Don't . . . take offense. I want . . . more. I want . . . you. But I . . . won't. I . . . cannot. I shouldn't have kissed you. Not . . . like that. 'Twas unfair."

He wasn't smiling now, and the lines his expression brought out were going to be the ones carving his face when he was an old man. They wouldn't detract from his features. In fact, he was going to grow more intriguing and handsome as he aged.

"You must rise," he said. "You must leave . . . and not look back."

"I ken that," she said with a voice that rasped.

"I won't take . . . you. I can't. I will not do that to a special woman. I would force myself only onto wenches paid . . . for the chore."

Aislynn blinked. *I thought him capable of ravishment?*

"I'll . . . think of another way to pay. Stealing a kiss . . . was not it."

"It . . . wasn't stolen," she replied.

His smile was sad and it was devastating at such a close range. Aislynn blinked again since moisture was making his image swim again. She didn't know what was wrong with her. She didn't like it. She felt, rather than saw him push her away, lifting her to her feet where she swayed on knees that felt as insubstantial as water.

"Who—what are you?" she stammered.

"I'm a troubadour," he replied. "And that's all . . . you need . . . know." And then he hiccoughed. Loudly.

Chapter Three

He thought of her all day, especially when trying to bring the remembered pain back. For two days every step of his horse had brought torment, now there was nothing save numbed relief. He'd been foolish to drink the mead, let his emotions rule him, and most especially to claim a kiss from her.

Rhoenne winced against the throb in his head, ignoring the men about him. The girl may be a virgin, but she had an innate gift at kissing, he decided, as he repositioned himself again atop his saddle. Such thoughts were a waste of time and energy. They weren't gaining him a thing. He shifted against the leather. He would welcome his hall, his bath, and a used woman; one that was barren and wouldn't lose her life birthing another Ramhurst.

"Your hall appears unwelcoming, My Lord."

Rhoenne lifted his hand, stopping the columns of men behind him. His senior vassal, Sir Harold Montvale, spoke the truth. There was no vivid blue banner with an emblem known as a *griffon passant*, waving from the tower, and no smoke rose from amidst the gray rock, either.

"'Tis early, still. Brent must be lazing."

"You wish as much."

Rhoenne flashed a look at the man speaking. Harold had
his confidence, guarded his back, and shared his sense of
humor. Or—as Rhoenne had often been accused—his lack
of humor. His frown deepened. His only choice was to
leave Brent Ramhurst at the head of Tyneburn Hall during
his absences. His half-brother by less than five months
had the right of liege lord as his heir. Unfortunately, he
also had the power.

"Come. We delay. Such an action could be costly to my
coffers."

"Fine his coffers instead. Or take it from his knight portion this time," Harold advised.

"Why? He's yet to pay back last quarter's penalty."

"True." The like-sized knight shrugged, moving the
chainmail with the motion. "He's also cost countless portions that you just forgave and tore up. He's too great a
penalty. Gift the king with his service and save your fief
from his influence."

"The king already has knights. And I never lost my fief."

"That's also true. I would hazard a guess that you never
owned it, either. King David doesn't have a Ramhurst at
his side anymore. Send Brent. His Majesty will be appre-
ciative. He may lord you beyond this earldom of yours. You
need more of these abrasive heathens to call your own."

Rhoenne turned back in the saddle. "Come. The ride
wearies on me as much as your words. I've a sup to eat."

"You've a sup to see prepared first," Harold answered.

Rhoenne ignored him and the vague twinge of unease
that settled between his shoulder blades. The Lady of the
Brook could probably help with that, too. She had small,
aristocratic-looking hands. More than once when she'd
placed them on him, the spot had warmed; rapidly and
markedly. The lass also had the ability to see right into a
person with those eyes of hers. She was the most lovely
thing Rhoenne had seen, and she hailed from one of these

heathen villages? Incredible. Especially if he factored in his brother. Brent was a danger to lovely maidens. He had an eye for beauty and a taste for taking vulnerability. The lass had shown sense to keep both hidden. She just hadn't hidden it well enough. Rhoenne nearly groaned at his incessant thoughts of her.

Tyneburn Hall was a motte and bailey castle, rising from the spit of land it straddled to lord over the countryside at its fore and the loch at its back. Rhoenne gave the signal and the men started down and then across the valley that Tyneburn's presence protected. Brent had better be in charge of the hall, or he'd feel Rhoenne's fist this time.

At the moat, he knew the truth. The castle wasn't welcoming anyone because there wasn't anyone but serfs in attendance. Getting one with acumen enough to lower the drawbridge made his frown deepen and his anger spark.

If Brent had gone on a foray, assuaging his lust and causing more havoc among unruly, cantankerous subjects—! The thought was enough to make the older brother set his jaw, work his teeth into pain, and cause the twinge of unease in the midst of his back to spread into all-out fury. And that was just from awaiting the drawbridge.

She was ready when he came for her; directly after sup; exactly as ordered. Aislynn squinted across the croft. It didn't work. Her caller was still the smithy, Donald O'Rourke. Aislynn sighed loudly. She'd known there was no such thing as faery magic!

Meghan shot her a look of pure venom, showing her jealousy. Aislynn turned the squinted expression on her little sister. That had Meghan making a sign to ward off evil, which had their mother stepping between them before anyone else saw.

"Good eve."

Papa answered Donald's greeting. Aislynn wasn't going
to answer anything. She pretended at shyness while they
spoke. It was better than the truth and the words of anger
and spite that she was choking on. That's what came of
being forced to go through with this . . . forced! That
blasted troubadour had soured her life and she'd only
known him one morn.

The smithy wasn't the problem. He'd shown his interest
in her from the moment he'd arrived two sennights past.
That interest was returned by the entire miller family . . .
until this morn. Aislynn swallowed around a knot in her
throat. It felt like a betrothal was being shouted from the
roofs already. She should be excited and thrilled. She was
neither. Donald was Scot, like them. He was strong. He
was healthy. He was employed with a skill. He'd been
granted land for his shop and his own croft. He was flesh
and blood. And there wasn't any part of him devoted to
poetry, or song, or anything resembling a troubadour.

Or anything blond. Or tall . . . with piercing, blue eyes,
a voice that halted her heart in mid-beat. Nor did he have
a frame made for snuggling against, molding to, clinging
to . . . while his lips sought out the very center of her. . . .

"Aislynn!"

Her head snapped up. It was Mother. She had Meghan
behind her and there was definite spite in her sister's eyes
now. Aislynn sighed again. *Faery magic and faery tales?*
she thought. *A pox on both!*

She turned for a shawl, taking as much time as she
could to smooth it about her shoulders. Then she was
wrapping it as loosely as possible to create volume. It
didn't help. She was petite. She was frail-looking. She'd
look like a twig next to Donald. She longed to pitch the
entire affair for her cloak, but knew she couldn't. This was
her punishment for being late to the mill.

It was specific, too. No cloak. No disguising attire. No

harsh words. No standoffish behavior. No arguments. Should the smithy offer for their eldest daughter, it was going to be accepted. Her wishes didn't matter. Her desires didn't count. Getting the eldest, strange, fostered daughter wed off was what counted to the miller and his family.

"Aislynn? Ready?"

Donald's hair was neatly slicked back and he wore a thickly woven, gray-colored *plaide*. He had a sleeveless doublet atop that was made from new leather, and the shirt beneath was knitted from muscle-encasing yarns.

Aislynn took one look before going back to her entwined hands.

"We'll na' be long," O'Rourke spoke above her head.

"Verra well. There's been *nae* understanding and *nae* bride price put forth. A walk about the village will be enough." It was her father talking. Aislynn wasn't saying anything; one way, or the other.

"As you request," Donald answered.

He stood at the stoop, his body holding their door flap open for her. She didn't look to verify it. She didn't look up at him, at all.

They set off. Somewhere a mongrel barked and the warm woodsy odor of cook-fires clouded small pockets of air about them in the late spring night. Aislynn still didn't look toward him. She didn't want to. No standoffish behavior? No harsh words? There had also been the admonition to keep any sign of her gifts hidden. Only Mother hadn't called them gifts. She'd called them curses from the gods. Aislynn bit her tongue, kept quiet and in pace with him.

"Shall we walk through the woods?"

She stopped at the first sound of his voice, then shook her head. She didn't know if he saw it.

"No harm in that, is there?"

What? There's every harm in it! she thought. She

longed to spit it out, but didn't. He knew. You didn't go into the woods for any reason other than the obvious. Bairns resulted from walks in the woods. Bastard bairns. She grimaced at the ground. They weren't even betrothed. It was ill-mannered and crude. She hadn't known that of O'Rourke.

"Well?" he asked.

"My father—" Aislynn said the words to the path, and gestured with her hand back to the croft. *No standoffish behavior?* she wondered. She was ready to run as fast as she could from him. That probably qualified.

Donald understood. His heavy sigh sounded it. "Well and good. We'll take the path, then. Will that do?"

She nodded, looked up, and paled. She felt naked with just a shawl. She rarely went out without her cloak. The look in Donald's eyes was the reason why.

She watched him swallow. At least he had spittle enough for that. Her throat was dry. She looked back down quickly, before any of the disgust transferred to her features. It wasn't due to Mother's admonitions, either. It was because she didn't know what Donald would do if he saw it.

"You're shy?" he asked.

She played along, lifting a shoulder in a semi-shrug. That was stupid. She knew it the moment the shift slid along a breast, outlining it, and nothing about the shawl muted or covered it. The sound of his grunt verified it for her.

Aislynn couldn't think of one more thing to do or say. She waited.

"Come. I have something to show you."

He didn't wait for her to agree. He reached for her upper arm, clamped his fingers around it, and started walking. Aislynn winced as he connected to a spot where Father had also gripped her. Men! That's all they were good for. Bullying. Fighting. Killing. Destroying. Maiming. Raping.

He was pulling her at a pace that kept her trotting beside him, her woven-twine sandals looking incongruous next to his calf-high leather boots. Then he stopped and dropped her arm. Aislynn fought the urge to rub at it. She didn't want him to see. If he knew he hurt her, he'd probably do it again. And wed with him? She'd rather try to spirit herself back to the faery-world her parents told her she'd come from!

"What do you think of my home?"

He'd brought her to the stable yard, no doubt to show off his blacksmith shop and his croft. And to prove his intentions; his ability to support her as a husband. He was also breathing hard.

"It's near finished."

"It's very fine," Aislynn replied, without looking at it.

Beside her, she felt Donald's agitation. "I've na' decided on placement of a loft, as yet," he continued.

What was it to her? Aislynn clamped down on her tongue to still the words. She was under orders. No argumentative or harsh words. The shivers running down her arms weren't pleasant. She should have known he'd mistake them.

"You're cold," he said.

Aislynn wrapped the shawl closer, proving her stupidity once again as her frame was outlined. That had him stepping closer. She forced herself not to back away from him. She'd decided that Meghan could have him. She'd never wed with him. She'd run away first. She'd rather roam the countryside; healing and existing on her own wits—regardless of how unsafe it was. Or perhaps she could search out the Norman mercenary. He'd keep her safe. He'd said he would.

The miller family could have the smithy for a son-by-law. They could give him Meghan. Aislynn wasn't marrying. She wasn't ever going out again without her cloak and her knife, and a thousand other things designed to keep men like Donald away from her. Just as soon as this night ended. *If* this night ever ended.

"I'll probably build a large one. Children require loft space."

Children? She replayed the word and stiffened at the same time. Now that was asking too much of her!

"I want lots of children. Lots. Sons. Strapping lads. To help with the work and keep me in my *auld* age."

He wasn't going to make it to old age if he kept this up! Aislynn clamped down on her teeth, releasing her tongue at the last moment. She had to. Anything else would unleash the harsh words filling her throat and choking her.

"I hadn't much to work with. Everything was charred. I had to clear and start anew. You should have seen it."

Aislynn nodded. It seemed to satisfy him.

"You're quiet. I like that. I think I like it a lot. Loud women argue and fight. You're na' like that, are you?"

Her jaw locked. She wasn't answering that. Not a sentence. Not a word. Maybe a curse. She considered that. It might work. She could curse him with a pox on his manhood. May it go soft whenever he wished to use it. *That* should keep him from worrying over arguing, loud women, and any need for a loft—small or large! She choked on the giggle and had to cover her mouth to keep it hidden.

"Come. I didn't ask you to walk with me this eve in order to bring up talk of mayhem and bereavement."

"I—" Aislynn didn't finish it. He didn't let her, either.

"We'll take a short way back."

He didn't ask. He simply gripped her arm again and started off. Aislynn kept pace, although she was striding two steps to his every one. The ground changed. She knew the difference immediately. Her eyes narrowed and her teeth set. He was taking her through the forest. He wasn't going to survive the harsh words she was going to release on him for this!

"Donald!" She growled out the name through gritted teeth. It didn't sound like her. He didn't appear to have heard it, either.

"'Tis a pleasant eve for a walk, I think. You agree?"

"Take me back to the path. Now. Right now."

"In time. I brought you this way for a reason."

"What? You touch me, and—!"

He burst out a laugh, stopping her. He laughed? *Well, why not, Aislynn? He's got you in the woods, you're as strong as a chaff of wheat, and there's not a soul to stop him. Why wouldn't he laugh?*

"You're verra comely, Aislynn. I noted that about you the moment I saw you. It was hidden . . . but I saw it."

She forced the first reply down. Harsh words weren't going to stop him. Maybe words of delay would. "You canna' do this . . . Donald. We're na' betrothed. Yet." She made her voice weak and shaky, and grimaced at the carpet of ferns at her feet, at how awful it felt.

"So? I'll fix the bride price tonight. We'll be wed at the next full moon. None will note if our firstborn is birthed early. None."

Aislynn gulped. "'Tis too . . . fast." And too horrid, and too insidious, and it was definitely too soon! Much too soon. And she was afraid she might already be in love. What a bother the emotion was . . . especially when the object of it was an unknown troubadour.

He answered by pivoting her right into his arms, bringing her against him before she could think to react. It was insanity to struggle. His limbs felt like trees and about as flexible. Aislynn's breath came faster and stronger and that only served to make his arms tighten. And he was still amused. She could tell by his chuckle, and the breath that was accompanying it, feathering across her nose and making her shivering worse.

"Remember I spoke of the attack that destroyed the *auld* smithy?"

He was asking it. Aislynn shook her head slightly. *He was asking it?* She had to get her mind to work. That was the only weapon she had. "Aye," she replied, finally.

"Well, I would join your sentiments . . . but had I been here, I would have helped burn it! To the ground! No Sassenach lord should rule us and *nae* blacksmith of Ramhurst should live among us! I hate them! All of them!"

"You hate . . . them?" She was stammering through the question but it wasn't for the reason he thought. It was because he wasn't giving her much room to breathe.

"I surprise you? Good. You dinna' think me soft like your father? Never! We must stand together and we must fight, and we must make certain *nae* more of the foreigners come! We're Scots! We should na' be ruled by Sassenach!"

"Dinna' do this!" Now she was struggling against him. Nothing much happened. It was as useless as she'd suspected already.

"We should make Scottish bairns, too. You and me. Now. Right now."

"Neart!" She got the one Gaelic word out; the one for strength and power; before he was lifting her. She knew what he was going to do. He was going to kiss her. Then, he was going to force himself on her and that would take every choice from her. Her curse on his manhood wasn't effective, either. It wasn't remotely soft where it was pressing against her lower belly.

Lips covered hers, sucking at her very life-force . . . and then they were gone.

It took a moment for Aislynn to realize her mouth was free. She'd been holding her breath, praying for unconsciousness. To be released was making her heart pound worse and her shaking intensify. She heard the sound of a throat clearing.

Donald was looking up, over her head. Then he swiveled Aislynn so that her back was against him. It felt, and probably looked like, he was using her body for a shield. She knew the reason the instant she saw them. She just couldn't believe they hadn't heard them.

There were ten of them. Ten knights atop their horses, separated by trees and yet joined by the slash of color across their mail. Aislynn didn't dare blink. She knew who it was instantly. Everyone knew. It was their overlord.

The men didn't move; only the breathing of their horses and flicks of sound from restless bridles being shifted betrayed their presence and their reality. Aislynn gulped. The Ramhurst was sitting, looking down at them, and all she could think of was his lust for women; any woman.

Aislynn felt Donald's left arm crushing her to him, holding her just beneath the breastbone as he lifted her. She didn't mind. As much as she detested it, she actually would have been molded to him without his help. There was only one thing worse than Donald: the man in front of her.

"Good eve, O'Rourke."

Aislynn watched as he pulled the chain head-covering called a hauberk from him, showing a thatch of medium brown hair, unshaven, wolfish-looking cheeks, and a nose that had been broken at some point, even with the protective nosepiece on his helmet. It didn't make his appearance more favorable, nor did it detract from it, since he looked like what he was; a battle-hardened man. He was stout, wider than Donald, and perhaps even than her blond giant had been. He had clear-water blue eyes . . . strangely, familiar eyes. Then he pursed his lips, narrowing his cheeks as he set the helmet atop his saddle pommel.

"I said good eve," he spoke again.

"Good eve, My Lord," Donald replied. Aislynn heard the rumble of sound through his chest, as well as felt it.

"You have reason to be about courting, rather than building? Or, should I say . . . rebuilding?"

"I was na' courting," Donald replied.

Aislynn watched the Ramhurst's eyebrows rise. Her own were probably mirroring it.

"He looked to be courting. I saw courting. Did any see different?" He turned to encompass his question to the knights about him. No one answered. He turned back to them. "Very well . . . since you were not courting this maid it will not matter that I shall escort her home. Come, lass."

He brought his horse closer to them and put a gauntleted hand down toward them. Despite the fact that Donald had her attached to him like a leech, Aislynn tried to back even more. She wasn't getting an escort home. She knew, very well, what was being offered.

"I promised her father I would see her home," Donald said.

"Methinks you should have hastened there, rather than dallied about in the woods, then. Wicked things happen when there are no observers."

He was smiling. It wasn't with mirth. Aislynn tried to curb every bit of fright and find her inner strength, but all she managed to do was bring the sheen of tears to her eyes. That sign of weakness, she could do without. She blinked them rapidly away.

"Come, maid. My horse grows restless and my men the same. I shan't harm you, or should you consider it harm, you'll be well compensated."

"I cannot allow this, My Lord. She's with me. *Nae* harm is to befall her. I have so promised her father."

"Then you should not have been kissing her, I would say."

"I was na' kissing her," Donald replied.

That reply got another raised brow from the man facing them. "He looked to be kissing her to me. What do you say?" He looked to the left and right of him again, as he asked it. Once again, none of the others answered.

"There are other maids," Donald replied, and his voice had a lower pitch to it than before. She wondered if he was stupid enough to challenge the liege.

"Aye. That there are. None near as lovely. How is it you have discovered her . . . and in less than a moon's time?"

"Allow me to pass so I can see her to her home. Find another wench—one of your own kind."

"I've already spoken for the chore and I don't like to be kept waiting. Cease this argument, and give over the girl."

"No harm is to come to her. I promised her father!"

"Harm? What harm is there to it? 'Tis no harm I would offer; only my love. I feel nothing but love for yon maid. Come. This encounter is not increasing my good mood."

He moved his horse closer. Donald didn't move, although the horse was sending prickles of gooseflesh down her body from its breath at Donald's ear.

"See reason, smithy. You've lived but a moon's time in this place. You don't know how it happened. It was so fast. The maid was stolen from you. Or, you can say she ran off. You can tell them Ramhurst has her. You will need no further explanations. Her father will know what happened. He'll know what to do. Send him to Tyneburn Hall if he wishes her returned." He shrugged, moving his chainmail with a slight clink of sound. "Most don't. Now, give her over. Now."

Although it was getting darker by the moment, Aislynn saw the other knights move a step nearer, closing in. Now she knew how terror felt. The earlier episode with Donald had been just a harbinger of it. She watched as one by one, they lifted their lances from the sides of saddles, until each one had it held, ready to pierce flesh and bone. Her heart was going to launch right out of her bodice with the pounding of it.

"You have to run, Aislynn." Donald's whisper had little

sound. She nodded slightly. Then, he spoke aloud. "You make a mistake, My Lord. The lass is na' even a maid. She may already be carrying another man's seed . . . or the pox. See reason."

"She is not a maid, you were not kissing her, you were not courting her, and yet you walk with her in the woods? I would not consider him as a husband with the words he spouts," he replied, looking directly at Aislynn.

"My Lord—" Donald began, only to be interrupted.

"My needs do not slacken, and I weary of words! Give over the wench or risk your arm."

It occurred to her that he might not have believed Donald's tales, but she had gone from being addressed as maid to being called a wench. That wasn't a good thing, either.

"Your brother shall hear of this, 'ere you continue," Donald stated in a loud, bold fashion.

"My brother? Ha! He's wearied from his continual battle with your kind and too weak to stay me. Go ahead, tell him. If you live to do it."

Aislynn had seen the man's real reaction before he could staunch it. He had a brother, and despite his words, the threat meant something she could use.

"Run, Aislynn!" Donald hissed it into her ear.

Run? she wondered stupidly.

"Perhaps you should wait until I have enjoyed the wench before you go telling tales to my brother. I should be granted the sin before I pay the penance."

Aislynn didn't realize Donald's arm had slackened. She was in shock. She had to be. *Enjoyed the wench?* she repeated to herself.

"Aislynn! Run!"

Donald shoved her from him, and that was all the encouragement she needed. She knew these woods. She knew the way home. She only wished she could outrun a man on horseback.

Chapter Four

Anger has a way of changing everything, Rhoenne decided, sometime into his second tankard of watered-down ale. It enhanced the scene before him until it was crystal clear and colored strangely about the edges with a reddish-gray haze. He'd ordered a boar quartered before it was put into the fire pit, to speed its preparation. He'd ordered the rushes changed and the linens aired out while it cooked. He'd even had to order water warmed for the knights' baths and his own. If he had a wife, it would have been her duty to see to such a homecoming. Or his brother's—if Brent had a bone devoted to responsibility and duty.

He scowled and diluted his tankard again, using the pitcher of water he'd pulled up and brought for himself. He wasn't quenching his thirst with ale. He wasn't partaking of the feast he'd ordered prepared. He wasn't listening to the tales of valor about their latest skirmish against his own warlike, heathen subjects. He was barely aware of the revelry taking place in his great hall. He had even forsaken replacing the numbing lichen, as the Lady of the Brook had instructed him to. His payment was the vicious throbbing of his lower leg. He knew why. He wanted the hunger. He wanted the sober awareness. He wanted the pain. He needed it.

His scowl grew. His brother hadn't tasted punishment in many seasons. The unkempt condition of his hall, the parade of angry fathers demanding payment for their daughters, the bastard Brent had produced along with the resultant death of the mother. . . . The constant harassing by Rhoenne's own people were the consequences. Rhoenne didn't need Sir Harold's words about it. He knew exactly what he had to do. And he knew he wasn't going to enjoy it.

He swigged another gulp, wondering why it wasn't taking the edge off the evening, yet knowing at the same time he didn't want it to. He rarely did anything without reason. Brent was going to be brought to him the moment he returned and Rhoenne was preparing for it.

The stir of doors opening caught his attention. He put his tankard down with a deliberate motion, lowered his head, and regarded the assemblage. What had begun as boisterous voices giving greeting was subdued quickly, he noticed, as his orders were given and heard.

"It appears the prodigal approaches. I'd give him no quarter, if it were it me."

Rhoenne slid his glance over to Sir Harold's chair. The knight winked back at him.

"Save your ire for your brother. He's earned it, not me."

"You brave much with such words."

Harold sighed heavily. "I've been at your side for a score, My Liege. I only seek to temper the anger. It's righteous, true, but Brent is your only blood kin, as I recollect?"

"You forget the lad, Richard," Rhoenne replied, scanning the grouping for his youngest sibling. He should have known Richard would be absent. Revelry and drunkenness offended the boy. As did every other manly pursuit, he reminded himself.

"Him? He is a mistake of nature, not a Ramhurst."

Harold's reference was not inaccurate, but it was distasteful. Richard had been orphaned from birth as had all the Ramhurst males. He'd been left in the company of women and ruined. Rhoenne had tried to change him, but it had been too late. Richard still ran at the sight of bloodshed.

"Richard has much of his mother in him. That doesn't change the fact that he's a Ramhurst. Same as I am."

Harold snorted. "You're amusing. Richard is half the man you are." He shrugged. "Mayhap . . . less."

Rhoenne blinked balefully. Then he returned to looking for Brent.

"Careful," Harold remarked, "your humor is showing."

Rhoenne sighed. "You've kept me company too long, Harold. Isn't there a wench or three available to satisfy your needs tonight?"

"None near as tempting as Fiona. You know she saves herself for you. If you have need, she's yours. More's the pity."

"Take her."

"There aren't many like her. Your requirements are too high."

Rhoenne moved his head again. He had a throbbing behind his eyes now.

His scowl probably showed it. It was blending in with all the other aches and pains he was encouraging. "Your meaning?" he asked.

"Fair of face, lush of limb, nails sheathed . . . barren of belly. Not many women in this cursed mist-land fulfill that. And lust. You require all that. Fiona has it. She's alone in it, I'm a-feared. Not that I quibble. I simply wouldn't enjoy my play at the cost of your own comfort. That is most against my knightly vows, I feel. 'Tis what a loyal vassal is known for, you know; knightly vows."

Harold's lips were quirked again. Rhoenne ground his teeth and added the twinge of ache in his jaw to the others.

"Fiona is still available to you," he finally said, from between his teeth. "I'll not need her tonight."

"You're inhuman. Send the wench to your chambers. Play. Sleep. Deal with your difficulties on the morrow."

"Difficulties?"

"These Celts are difficult to subdue and even harder to rule. You have taken on more than the cultivating and civilization of land with this earldom King David bestowed upon you. You have taken on the devil himself."

Rhoenne smiled slightly. "Scotsmen are like any other, just hardier. Sanctions mean little to them, punishments the same. I must learn another way to reach them."

"It's said their lances are sharper, too."

Rhoenne stiffened. "Your meaning?" he asked.

"I wouldn't know, of course . . . for I've yet to harbor one within my flesh. I must make a note to ask it of someone . . . more experienced in such things. If I chance upon one, that is."

Rhoenne sucked in on one cheek. "You're starting to bore me, Montvale. Always the same—speaking words and saying little."

"Little? I've untold breaths of words to speak on it. This earldom of yours is a curse and the subjects therein? Hate-filled and dangerous. As for women? Ugh. They're steeped in ugliness and deceit and filth. And bulk. I find them difficult to enjoy without the lights dimmed enough."

"Yet . . . Fiona is one of them."

"Ah, aye. The lovely Fiona. I can forget all with that one, My Liege. Should she grace my chamber, I sleep little. You should try it, too. Perhaps then no lance could stray into your leg, leaving this delightful vale in the hands of your brother."

"What lance?" Rhoenne said, in a carefully modulated tone.

"Perhaps we'd best see to your brother." Harold turned away and gestured toward the doorway.

Rhoenne's eyes followed the gesture. *"I* will see to Brent. Save your breath. And my ears. All saw the condition of my keep. All share the whispers of my weakness . . . even my own men."

"Send him to serve the king. I hear he's building again—a priory he's naming Jedburgh. That makes it three of the planned four of them. He probably needs stout noblemen with masses of brawn and a dearth of wits. That sounds like your brother. Send him. Such a thing will gain you gratitude."

"If I send Brent, I'll gain His Majesty's anger. Brent is a slackard and a lay-about. Should I send him to join in the building of King David's legacy, I'd reap naught but the king's ire. And if Brent were to do such a task, anything constructed will surely crumble."

Harold snorted again. "That much is true. We also have to consider King David's son, Henry, who is overseeing the thing. He probably doesn't stock enough wenches to service your brother."

"Speaking of—Fiona is still available to you," Rhoenne replied.

"Aye, but I'm needed more here, I feel."

"You waste your time. I'm not much company tonight."

Harold snorted. "You're never much company," he replied.

That comment got a smirk from Rhoenne. He lifted the tankard to his lips and took another draught. Then he pulled it away. They were giving him the signal. Brent was inside the keep.

"I know your game, you know," Harold said from his side.

"Game?" Rhoenne replied carefully.

"A bit of ale to fan the flame, a bit of pain to deepen it, and it will be Brent turn to rue the day's sport."

Rhoenne put the tankard down and swiveled his head.

"What . . . pain?" he asked, putting a slight edge to the last word.

Harold raised his brows. "Did I say pain? I've over-stepped myself. It must be your ale. It's hearty and brewed to a thick color; loosens my tongue when it shouldn't. Remind me to apprise your aleman of my compliments."

Rhoenne cocked his head back, hearing Brent's voice easily. He slid his chair back, preparatory to standing. "Brent!" he bellowed, the name stopping every other sound and movement in the room. Rhoenne wasn't spar-ing his voice. The reverberation seemed to be the only sound for a moment. He stood.

"Oh look. He's returned." Brent called it out jovially, his entrance filling the arched doorway with the sound of chainmail and boots.

"Aye. To an empty hall and an unguarded treasury! You have but the time it takes to reach you to speak your reason. Don't waste it."

Rhoenne put a hand to the surface and bolted over it. His movement had serfs, freemen, and knights watching with open-mouthed expressions. His reward was the agonized jar of barely knit flesh in his leg. He didn't give it thought. He didn't dare. They created a path for him. Brent had reached a good height but was still a hand-width below Rhoenne. The difference was made up with muscled weight, equaling his older brother in time. He was also still clad in his mail, with his sword strapped to his side, and gauntlets encasing his hands and arms to the elbow.

Rhoenne saw Brent's attire and ignored it. There wasn't a weapon to stop him. He watched Brent back a step, then another, at his approach. It didn't give him any satisfac-tion. Nor did Brent's knight's movements as they packed themselves together, forming a triangle, that shoved Brent forward to the tip. Rhoenne's scowl deepened. If his own knights tried such a self-serving move, he'd see them stripped of their titles and lands, and then he'd have them replaced.

"You left Tyneburn Hall with her throat bare and her belly exposed! Your reason?"

Brent opened his mouth then shut it. Then he shrugged a nonchalant gesture. Rhoenne's eyes narrowed.

"I gave you position in my household. I appointed you High Sheriff. You have the right of collecting my taxes and administering my laws. Were you away tallying, as I've asked you to do? Perhaps you were seeking justice for the blacksmith's death? Tell me that's what you were about. Or perhaps you forayed beyond the mense, hoping to secure the borders further?"

Brent didn't answer. He was looking toward the floor. Rhoenne's voice went soft, steely soft. "Or is it you've taken another maid? Will I have another angered father and his clan, thirsting for my blood, and the blood of all who call me lord? Don't you understand the consequence of such acts?"

There wasn't anything to be heard except that of the words dying when he'd finished. The room behind him might as well be empty, rather than full of revelers. Rhoenne narrowed his eyes and waited.

"I took no maid," Brent finally replied.

"What was it you were about, then?" He barked out the question almost before Brent had finished.

"We were just out looking for enjoyment. You are ever ceaseless with your listing of duties and tasks, chores and requirements. It was—"

Rhoenne interrupted him before the words became a full-out whine. "As my heir, you replace me! You protect and you defend. As my High Sheriff, you govern. That is no time for play. There is a fiefdom to secure for King David's purposes, and his alone. I can't raise an army for my sovereign from my own people! I can scarce move about without treachery at my side—and it's you at the heart of it!" He was shaking with the intensity of his own rash tongue and afraid it was being seen, too. That was what made his voice louder and harsher. Rhoenne had never spoken like he was speaking now. Sir Montvale was right. Even when it was watered-down, his aleman did brew a good stout mead.

"All you do is work, though."

His brother *was* whining. Rhoenne hadn't stopped any of it. He inhaled a breath and cursed the fire of it inside his own chest. "'Tis a bit of work securing a fief, brother. That's why it was entrusted to me. To me! The king could have lorded any other man, but nay. He lorded me. You know this! I will ask again, and only once more. Your reason?"

He waited, hoping Brent would say a challenge, so they could do this honorably and meet on the list. It wasn't Brent's fault his mother had been a serf, consoling their father when his own wife took sick with the child she carried. Nor was it Brent's fault that he wore the mark of bastardy. The younger man had always coveted what Rhoenne had. He didn't know the king, however. David could make a vassal of any man, including bastards—and he would have without remorse—if Brent had just earned it.

There was no way to teach such a thing! Rhoenne regarded him silently, wishing he'd heeded Montvale's counsel and waited, or at the very least, done this in his private chamber. That way his entire hall wouldn't be watching brother against brother, and the myriad of serfs, housecarls, and freemen wouldn't be able to carry further tales to their crofts. That was the reason he could scarce ride about without a guard at his back and at all sides.

It was too late to lament any of it, so he did the only thing he could; he pulled himself to his full height, put his hands on his hips, glared down at his brother, and awaited the challenge. Brent had fought well the one time he'd tried it. Rhoenne would accept eagerly. It might be what his brother needed. They'd each gained a decade worth of muscle and strength since they last met. It wouldn't be an easy battle, either way. Nothing happened except silence.

Cursed silence.

"You have no answer?" Rhoenne asked, softer than before, but it was still too loud.

Brent shook his head.

"Well and good. I'll answer it for you. A leader does not seek play and leave his keep exposed. You'll learn this. You're to take your men and see to it all are prepared for a journey. I have decided your punishment."

"I was only gone a night and day, Rhoenne," Brent said, with a pleading tone to his voice.

"Tyneburn needs a strong leader at its front, loyal to the crown. You need to find leadership. I've failed at teaching it. King David enjoins another construction. He sends his heir, Henry. A Ramhurst will serve on erecting this Jedburgh Priory. Prepare yourself."

"You want me to labor? To build? Surely that is too much, brother—"

"Brother? Brothers do not betray. Brothers do not shirk responsibility. God curse the day your mother birthed you into my life. Begone! And take your sniveling cowards with you."

Rhoenne swiveled before he'd finished. Then Brent did the unforgivable. Rhoenne didn't need to hear the gasps. He saw the flash that was his brother's gauntlet as he went for his sword. Rhoenne spun and sent a fist against his brother's jaw with enough force that he was launched backward into the knights who were supposed to be guarding his life with their own. Rhoenne's scowl deepened as he watched the tightly packed group of men split, letting their leader fall. All seventeen stones' weight of Brent Ramhurst quivered for a moment and stilled. Rhoenne didn't even look down. He pierced each and every one of Brent's cowardly retinue with what had been described once as his wintry-day's glare. He watched them shuffle.

"Get him to his room! Hie yourselves to your own. Prepare for your journey. Don't let me catch sight of any of you and ruin my mood further. If he wakes and argues, tell him I'll meet him on the list. He picks the weapons. He picks the time. We'll decide it that way."

He swiveled again and walked back to his chair, ignoring the look that was probably on Sir Harold's face, as much as he was ignoring the new ache that had begun in his knuckles to spread throughout his hand, and was now throbbing to his wrist. He also ignored the speculative glances he was receiving as well as the rustle of sound coming from the removal of Brent and his men from the great hall. He walked around the table, carefully blanking every bit of how it felt to continue putting weight on his leg from his features. He regained his seat beside Sir Harold and picked up his tankard again, using his left hand.

The entire room started making sound again. It was a fuller and even more boisterous noise than it had been before.

"I'd have let them see him drawing his sword," Sir Harold said slowly, directing his words to his own half-empty mug.

"Are you speaking for effect, or to hear yourself make noise?" Rhoenne asked.

"That way, none would think me guilty of attacking my own brother without provocation."

"A liege can be many things," Rhoenne replied.

"True. He can be brave. Strong. Decisive. He can spit in the face of agony as he does so."

"What . . . agony?" Rhoenne asked through clenched teeth.

"Strong ale, as I already made mention. It loosens my

tongue. Fiona is doing strange things to my pulse, My Liege. She's lovely. She's ready. She's begging you. Look."

"If she has need of a man, fill her need. As I already said, I've no use for her tonight."

"I beg you to reconsider. The woman sours if she cannot have you. All women do. I have no notion of the why. Women. Who can decide the why of how they think?"

"So? Choose another." Rhoenne shrugged, and pushed his hair off his forehead with his left hand, prior to refilling his tankard. Then he brought it to his lips. He put his mind to ignoring the throb of his arm, since the pain had moved to encompass his elbow, too.

"I'm trying to entice you," Sir Harold said.

Rhoenne choked on his swallow. It turned into a cough that ravaged his chest. He added that to his other ills. He had it under control before he looked at his closest knight. "You've the wrong shape for such a notion, Sir Harold, although I thank you, just the same."

The other man's lips twitched. "I would still have let them see why I threw such a blow. He was going for his sword. He was attacking your back."

"A liege can be many things, remember?" Rhoenne replied.

"He was attacking an unarmed man. You know it. I know it."

"He can't be a betrayer. None can think it, say it, or be allowed to see it. Had he unsheathed his sword, I would have had to banish him."

"You would have had to kill him. You know it."

"Only on a field of honor, Montvale. Don't over-speak yourself."

"So . . . you did the indulgent thing. You let his treachery go unseen."

Rhoenne's left hand tightened on his tankard handle. "It was my decision. I made it. I'll live with it."

"And had you done other, you would have had to find another heir. Or, God forbid, make the king find you a woman to wed with, accept your seed, and create one of your own. Pity."

Sir Harold was paying very careful attention to his tankard as he said it. Rhoenne felt the knot of nerve in his cheek as he clenched his teeth. Harold was right about Fiona, too. She had thick, light brown hair, a round face with a bow-shaped mouth, ripe curves, and a body that was perfection. She was making certain all noted it, too, with her display every time she moved. Rhoenne frowned. She shouldn't wear her neckline so loose or so low. It created problems with his men—none of whom would touch her, despite lusting for her.

"Take Fiona to your bed, Sir Harold, and spare me any more of your words. They're really starting to pale."

The knight looked him over. Despite his best intention, Rhoenne hunched his shoulders slightly at the unblinking attention.

"And allow you to wallow in drink-induced melancholy? I think not. Besides, she may not be enough. I have massive appetites . . . unlike you. Come, My Liege. Allow me to have her sent to your chamber. I'll even have her unwrapped for you." There was a long, distinct pause. "I wouldn't want to put that hand to the torment of having to undress the wench."

"What torment?" Rhoenne asked, icily.

Harold sighed heavily. "This ale is too much for my tongue. I will have to change to water, too. I think."

Rhoenne put his tankard down. "Your eyes are sharp, as is your tongue. I have more to do this eve. Drink would deter me from my responsibilities. Such is the mantle of liege, I fear."

"You are too noble," Harold said, sarcastically.

"I didn't say that. I have things to see to before I rest."

"Ah. . . ." Harold drew the word out. "You have another wench in mind."

"I didn't say that, either," Rhoenne replied.

"You must appease my curiosity. What wench appeals to your taste tonight?"

"Brent's," Rhoenne remarked with a slight smile to the word.

Sir Harold's eyes widened. "Brent has a wench? But, he said—"

"You don't listen well. Nor did you watch when he was first brought in. He has a wench with him."

"He has a wench?" Harold repeated.

"Aye. My guess is he stole her. He probably still has her bound."

"He stole a lass . . . and yet you still sit without mounting a rescue? You?"

"She's not a maid. You heard him. Perhaps she would have come willingly, once she knew the game. Perhaps not. That is what I go to find out."

"Not a maid, eh? Perhaps your luck holds and she is comely, too?"

"Have you known Brent to take an ugly wench?"

Sir Harold chuckled. The sound made Rhoenne's eyes widen a fraction.

"This is what I would have ordered for you, had I thought it. Go. Rescue this damsel. Leave me to the fair Fiona, who, although she is no maid either, has vast charms of compensation. She also has friends. Comely friends."

"Harold, you are rapidly losing my interest."

"Very well. Fiona is a fair flower of innocence and should she have friends, they are undoubtedly ugly and stick-thin."

"That is not my meaning, either. I speak more of Brent's wench."

"Ah. The lovely, captured flower. There's no need of haste there, My Liege. She won't need a rescue anytime soon. Her would-be lover is without his senses at present. That is your fault. You must take his place. You need to rescue her from sure boredom. Take her to your bed, instead."

Rhoenne sighed heavily. "I didn't say she was a would-be lover. I only said Brent had a wench. I would see to her. I don't wish her, or any other woman, in my bed. I've other uses for a bed tonight . . . like sleep."

"You're inhuman," Sir Harold replied.

"And you've drunk too much of this fine mead. Take Fiona to your chambers before you forget the why and how of it. Go, my friend. I'll see you on the morrow."

Rhoenne stood, tested his leg with his weight before striding purposely from the room, making certain none noted a limp, or how he held his hand close to his side to prevent movement. It was bad enough Sir Harold had seen through it. He didn't want anyone else knowing. He wasn't noble. He wasn't inhuman. He was tired.

Chapter Five

The man she feared was carried in. Aislynn stood in one corner of the filthy room they'd placed her in and watched. She didn't dare move. She was afraid they'd spot her. She hadn't been still. She'd wrenched an arm, trying to work it free, and had ended with it crooked at the elbow, making her look like an awkward one-winged bird. She was in the process of working it back before she ran out of time.

She would have tried getting loose sooner, but she'd had to face her own panic and fears first. In the darkened, smelly room they'd put her in, dampening fear hadn't been easily accomplished. She was afraid she looked it.

The four men carrying their burden dumped him onto his bedstead. There were more men following, bearing torches. Aislynn almost wished for the darkness again as heaps of discarded clothing, food trays, and upended pieces of furniture came into being with the light.

She moved her head, swaying the disheveled curtain of hair out of her face. The fact it was loose wasn't her fault. Her captor had wanted it that way. His hands undid the braids as they rode. Aislynn made a face at him. Then she noticed the lack of color to his lips.

"What's happened?" She asked it as she approached, managing shuffling, sliding steps that were the equivalent of the length of a half-foot. It was the only movement her strapped and joined knees allowed her.

"He took a blow." One of them answered.

"Turn his head! Now! Quickly!"

"What?"

Aislynn didn't think through her actions. If they hesitated, the man was going to perish on his own blood. "Turn his head now! He's got a mouthful of his own blood and is sucking it in with each breath. Do you wish his death?"

All nine of them looked down at the prone man. Aislynn rolled her eyes and scooted closer, so she could do it. She used her shoulder to roll his head to one side. All of them watched the blackish fluid spilling onto his blanket. "You see?"

"I—"

"Dinna' waste breath on your actions. Roll him. Pound his back! Now!"

"Pound his back?"

"He takes *nae* breath. You see? Dinna' just stand there! Tip him forward over his bed and pound!"

Some of her urgency got to them and the largest of them moved to help. Aislynn hopped backward, out of the way, as he shoved Brent onto his front. Then he slammed a fist into the man's back, splattering blood onto the blankets and wetting the dust on the floor with it.

"Again!" she hissed.

"But, he's—"

"He's without life if you dinna' get it back into him! Hit him again. He is na' taking breath. You have to remind him how to do it. Now pound!"

He slammed another gauntleted fist into Brent's back and all that happened was Brent's body moved on the mattress, making it creak a bit.

"Again! He wears his mail. He can hardly feel such slight tapping!"

The man she taunted glared at her, before turning to hit the body before them. This time Aislynn knew he used force. It sounded like he was cracking bones. It worked. All of them heard the weak cough, followed by a spasm of Brent's body. Aislynn gulped. She knew they all stared at her.

"N-now—" She stopped, before the tremor betrayed her. If she were going to assume her assertive Lady of the Brook mantle, she had to sound more like a confident healer and less like a frightened village girl. She cleared her throat. "Tell me what ails him."

Aislynn went to her knees to look over the unconscious man's face. The blow had worked. He was getting his color back. She didn't think it lucky for her, however.

"Bring a light closer," she ordered, since no one had answered her question. One of them held a torch aloft, where it shed more light. Aislynn's upper lip lifted as she watched vermin scurrying for the darker corners. She barely kept the shiver inside. *He lives with rats? Ugh!*

"What is it? Will he live?"

They'd misinterpreted her expression. Aislynn gulped and stood back upright, using the mattress with her crooked arm as a leaning post for the movement. No one offered help. If they had, she'd have shrugged it off. The fact that they hadn't made her lip curl worse. Brent's knights were an unchivalrous lot. Every one of them.

"I canna' tell that if I dinna' know what happened to him. Well?"

No one answered her again. Aislynn favored them with narrowed eyes and stifled her own gulp. She didn't like the way they were looking at her. Men didn't look at her like that. She rarely gave them the opportunity. Mother had spoken of how surprisingly lovely their faery-child was, if Aislynn stopped moving long enough for a body to get a good look at her.

Aislynn knew it was what was happening to her right now. The way he'd left her hair unbound and rippling probably made her look wild and untamed, and the tight straps about her were making every swell of her body apparent. She could sense the difference in the room and it stalled her breath. She swallowed. Her throat went as dry as barley dust. She was in a lord's chamber, deep in his castle, while his knights looked at her, lust written on every feature. Lust! Men and their lusts! She hated them even more than before.

She looked back down at the man who had caused her disarray and situation. He was creating havoc and he wasn't even awake. She set her shoulders. Very well . . . she couldn't change it. All she could do was keep their attention on him, and hope they had some valorous instincts hidden.

"Are you his knights, or na'?" she asked, in a sarcastic, loud tone.

"What?" One of them spoke. It was obvious he'd forgotten her question.

Aislynn slanted her head toward Brent. "He bleeds from the nose and mouth. You were leaving him to die if I had na' been here. What happened to him? I canna' heal him if fright holds tongues silent. Are you his men, or na'?"

"He took a blow," one of them finally said.

"A blow? Just one?"

The one who had spoken nodded. She could tell her plan was working as one by one, they looked from her to Brent. Aislynn swallowed. "One blow? Just one? With what? One of your Sassenach clubs?"

"A fist."

Aislynn gasped and looked at the blackish coating on Brent's face again. He was breathing smoothly and deeply now. "Was it a mailed fist, then?"

"Nay. It was bare."

"I have heard of the games you English play. 'Tis stupid and wasteful. Just look at the results. He may lose teeth and I suspect his nose is broken. I will need herbs. Spices. I need them fetched. Now."

The man who had pounded breath back into Brent jerked his head at another of them. "Fetch what she needs," he said.

"Why should I?"

The one who'd commanded it raised his fist at the other. Aislynn watched them. She was going to name him Brute and the other Weasel. The names fit. Brute had his helmet off and was in the light. She could see he sported dark hair, dark eyes, and slashes of black for his eyebrows. Still, in all, he hadn't been unpleasant to look upon, until a scar had scored across his nose and both cheeks, halving his face. Brute was an undisciplined, large, bullying sort. Most of them were. She knew that from the ride in. Not one of them obeyed willingly or without question. They obeyed because someone forced them to.

"Stay your blows," she said sarcastically. "You men use it too oft. I will tell you what I need *and* the why of it." She shuffled into the space between them, using her bent arm for propulsion.

Brute's fist slowly dropped. Aislynn turned, placing her back to him and looked up at Weasel. She'd rightly named this one as well, she decided. His eyes were closely set, and he had a thin, long, spiky nose. She didn't think he'd ever been pleasant to look upon.

"I need mistletoe and valerian for his teeth. Or you can bring dried linden flowers. Check the kitchens. I'll also require boiled water. A pail of it for his face, and at least six buckets of it for cleaning this hovel of a room. I need kelp or peat, as dry as you can find it. This is to stop bleeding. I will also need rosemary. It will prevent blockage of his nose while it heals. That should also stay his temper once he awakens and looks at the damage done to his face. Bring me mint, too. Four leaves of it." She stopped, afraid of her own impudence.

"What is this mint for?" Brute asked from behind her. Aislynn hopped as she turned to face him.

"For his breath. It reeks."

"You're a saucy wench. Brent has my sympathy."

"He'll need it. He will learn this soon enough. You will see this fetched—finally?"

Another jerk of his head and the door opened and closed. Aislynn caught the reaction of shivers and stanched them. She couldn't have another recurrence of panic! Not now. Not when Brute was looking her over as he was.

"You still have na' told me what happened," she reminded him.

"Then you don't listen. A fist. He took a blow. That's all."

"With this much damage?" Aislynn shuffled the six mini-steps over to Brent again. "And it was just once? Truly?"

"Aye. But once."

Aislynn's eyebrows rose. "So," she mused aloud, "he does have a brother he fears. And it looks to be with good reason."

One of the others nodded; his eyes wide and frightened. Aislynn looked at him. She was going to call that one Rabbit. The door opened again and then closed. She suspected they were slinking out, deserting their lord before they were put to his assist. She didn't check to verify it. She expected Brent's knights to be disloyal as well as undisciplined. What was interesting her was that Brent had a brother, and he was a force to be reckoned with. It was all she had.

"You must all fear him." She sneered as she said it.

"And with good cause. The man must be the size of his donjon and carry the force of a battering-ram in his arm."

"You make light of what isn't," Brute answered, his voice gruff.

"I make light of naught. I am deciding the where-all of your lord's injuries. You say it was a blow? I merely state that if this was one blow from a bare fist, then a man powerful enough to do such a thing actually exists. Furthermore, I'm surprised your lord received such a blow when he had nine, brave, strong men like you . . . guarding him. And yet none of you have the slightest mark."

"It didn't kill him," Brute said.

Aislynn could tell he didn't like her words or the long, drawn-out way she'd said them. There was a flush rising from the unshaven portion of his cheeks to stop at the scar-line. She had to duck her head to hide the smile.

"Well, it would have, without my help."

"That's right, wench . . . or should I call you witch? You saved him. Soon he'll be right as cake and wanting to finish with you. I hadn't thought you desirous of it a-fore. You must hide a lusty nature, although faith; there's not much hidden about you."

The one who spoke now had the aggressive, swaggering behavior that she'd noted during their ride firmly in place. Aislynn lowered her head and favored him with an upward cast, narrowed glance. She was going to name him Rooster. Unlike Brute, Rooster had always been pleasant to look upon. It was obvious he'd never taken any type of weapon to his face. There wasn't a mark on it. He was handsome and cocksure, from his dark hair and eyes to the muscular frame his tabard-draped mail wasn't hiding. Rooster was an apt title for him: all show; no substance.

Aislynn smiled widely, surprising them. She couldn't help her attire. She couldn't help the wild look of her. She couldn't help that she'd just been called a witch. She could use it, though. "Too bad the worst is hidden, Sir Knight. Why, the man who beds me, withers a-fore he's finished and then he stays the same. 'Tis a curse I bear from birth. I carry a mark. Is that what you wish?"

"Is that proof you're a maid . . . and the smithy lied?" Rooster asked.

Aislynn swallowed back on her own stupidity. It tasted slightly metallic at the back of her throat. She lifted the bent shoulder, trying to make it a seductive gesture. "As maidenly as any other lass. I'll be the last you bed, though. Dinna' you mark my words? Now, untie me. I have to see to your lord."

"Oh, I don't think so. I rather fancy you this way. I think my lord may have the same opinion, if he were awake and looking at what I am."

"Do as she says."

Aislynn gasped. She knew that voice. Every man within Aislynn's sight did, too. She watched the change. It was immediate and total. Her own eyes were probably just as wide and frightened. It was the troubadour from her glade, yet it wasn't. His voice was the same velvet-smooth timbre, although the strength and depth of it were awe-inspiring in the small room.

Rooster stepped forward, reaching for the dagger at his side as he moved. He slipped it under the binding at her elbows, then the one at her knees. Aislynn moved her arms forward, more to have something to clasp onto. Rooster had lost all his bravado. He wasn't looking at her any longer. He wasn't looking at anything except the floor.

"Now leave us."

It wasn't said twice. Aislynn watched them file from the room, all of them looking to the floor. The door's opening silhouetted him, then it shut. He was more immense than she'd suspected, from how he'd lain between her legs in the glade. She couldn't see more. The torchlight wasn't illuminating the area beyond Brent's bed and she wasn't capable of facing him, yet.

"Is any of that true?" he asked.

He was coming closer if the voice was any indication. Aislynn backed a mini-step, then another. Her action didn't please him. She could tell as he halted just shy of the light and breathed out a loud sigh.

"You dare fear me? Now?"

"I fear *nae* man," she replied.

"Then why do you back from me?"

She took a deep breath. "Because you dinna' tell me the truth. You're *nae* troubadour," she said to the floor.

"'Tis but one title I claim. I am anything. Ask me."

"Liege lord? *Sassenach* liege?" She tried not to give it any inflection but knew she failed.

He gave another loud sigh. "Aye. Liege. Lord Rhoenne Guy de Ramhurst. First Earl of Tynebury. Lorded to it by Scotland's King David. Norman by birth."

"The Lion?" she asked, in the silence that followed his voice.

"Some refer to me as such. I cannot stop it."

Her heart was hammering to her throat. She moved a hand there. *"La Bete Grande?"* she whispered.

He chuckled. "Great beast? If you've heard it, then it's still said. Such a title was earned from my prowess at Brittany. I demanded a high price for surrender. They didn't pay it . . . at first. It may also be due to my size. Or mayhap it's my temperament. I cannot say. Besides, at times such a title is apt." Torchlight fluttered down from the top of him, highlighting a sinister-looking nose and deepening the cleft in his chin.

"I may also have earned such a name from my tourneys. There are none I lose to. If there are, I have yet to be challenged by him. Some even refer to me as Avenger. It's said I fight as one. I am called all these things . . . *witch.*"

Aislynn curled her tongue into the back of her throat to stop another word.

"Since we have this between us, what of it? I have titles I bear. You have named some. There are more. A title does what it needs. It convinces and sways others. What of yours . . . my Lady of the Brook? Are you this witch they accuse? 'Tis not a far stretch. Healers are ugly crones or men of great years. I've never known one to possess great beauty and skill. Nor a healer who appears without warning and disappears with the same . . . just like this witch you're called."

He was accompanying his words with two more steps toward her, losing the light's illumination, save as a means to outline him. He wasn't wearing chainmail or padding about his form. His arms were still held slightly outward away from his form, almost as if the size of them prevented their closure. With such shadowing, he not only looked the size of a great beast, he resembled one. Aislynn gulped.

"Alas . . . my lovely; I am also a troubadour, just as I told you."

He was bowing as if they were at a king's court. Aislynn glanced that way, then back down. Her face was hot with the blush. She'd been kissed by the liege lord this very morn? And she hadn't even known it was him?

"You needn't fear me. You can see for yourself that I have not reached the size of my home, be it known as keep or donjon. Nor, I might add, am I about to."

"You . . . heard that?" she asked, and frowned at the timid-sounding words from a like voice.

"That, and the battering-ram reference to a blow from my fist. I enjoyed the listening. It showed wit to use such to control them."

"Words?"

"Nay, fear. Their fear."

Aislynn's eyes went wide on the dust at her feet. He was

this perceptive and she'd thought him a dimwit just this morn? She couldn't believe her naiveté.

"You listed titles and I believe you know the why of them. They inspire fear. You knew that and you used it." He was right in front of her. Aislynn took another step back, but he matched it.

"You needn't back from me. You need only say the words. Grant me your service and your fealty, and reap the rewards. Your every desire I would grant. Your every whim I would see to." His voice was lowering.

"I—" she began.

"Nay." He put a finger to her lips, silencing any desire to speak. Then, he moved it away. The spot tingled . . . burned. She almost licked at it.

"Don't answer yet. Not until you know the offer. I put it forth now. I would have you for my healer, just as I spoke this morn. I would protect you from further ravishment. By anyone. You would be *mine.*"

The inflection on the word started such a swell of warmth through her belly that Aislynn's eyes widened.

"You'd wear Ramhurst blue—legally and in full view. You'd sleep in Ramhurst linens. You'd be served. You'd be safe. There is no man to dispute it. Or, if he does, he can feel my wrath. You have already seen some of it." He gestured with a head movement over to where Brent lay.

"Is that all?" she asked.

She assumed he was smiling as he answered, since it sounded in his voice. "You would also have the duty of overseeing my household . . . and you would have the care of me. All of me. I would put myself in your hands. I have needs. I would have them seen to."

Aislynn's heart felt like it did a dive to the depths of her before resuming its position. She was choking, but he just kept talking through it.

". . . and start with this leg of mine."

She glanced down at the hose-covered calf. Then, she raised her eyes to the black holes that were his. "You dinna' speak of your hand, My Lord," she replied, finally.

He reached out with his left hand and took her arm, bringing her close enough she could smell the wood smoke, pine soap, and mead scent of him. That was just what one of her senses was experiencing.

"How do you know about that?" he asked softly, his voice a rumble of sound while his breath fanned her cheek.

"I have brought all she requires. I only have one bucket of water. I am no serf. They can haul more water if she needs more."

The door slammed open with a shoulder applied to it and Weasel stomped in, setting a bucket noisily on the floor. He took exactly three more steps before stopping, mouth wide as his arms opened, spilling her supplies.

"What is it you've brought?" The liege swiveled both of them to ask.

Aislynn was being held against him, where her cheek rested against his chest. From this hearing distance, his voice was a thing of immensity in one ear. She didn't hear Weasel's answer, or even if he gave one. All she heard was the door slamming and the liege's huge sigh. The whiff of air touched her head.

"That one reminds me of a weasel."

She started and moved her head to stare. He'd turned them toward the light and the look on his face wasn't sinister or fearsome. He looked more like he was hiding a smile.

"Don't tell me you didn't note it."

Aislynn caught the answering smile, probably giving her the same expression he had.

"So . . . you did see it. This is good. Such a thing binds us. You and me. The beast and the witch."

Aislynn stiffened. It was stupid, since her movement put her entire frame against his. Beyond a blink, she ignored how it felt as she glared up at him. "I'm *nae* witch," she said finally.

"I've said something to distract you from fear? Good. Come. Show me what you plan to do to my brother with these weapons you've requested."

Brother? Aislynn wondered at her blindness as he moved them back to the pool of light above Brent's prone form. There was a pile of herbs and a broken jar on the floor.

"You must unhand me," Aislynn told him.

He sighed, moving her with it. Her eyes widened. "If, as you say, I must do this, then I must. But only for the moment, I fear."

"I dinna' understand," she replied.

"You haven't given an answer. Without it, I have nothing. You'll escape me. I think you a mountain sprite, or a lowland faery, or an enchantress; one possessing uncommon beauty, and a heretofore unknown sweetness of smell. If I release you I have nothing." He released her and stepped back.

"You . . . jest." Aislynn choked out the words, and went to her knees to check the supplies and keep the reaction on her face to herself.

"I never jest," he answered.

"You flatter, then." Her voice was stronger.

"I never flatter."

"I tire of the telling. I am neither faery, sprite, or enchantress. I'm a healer."

"You didn't tell me I would ponder the methods of bewitchment you practice, though. You forgot to speak that part."

She gasped at the floor. "I've done naught," she whispered.

"Here. Cover yourself."

It was his short cloak falling onto her shoulders. Aislynn had a moment to enwrap herself in his smell, before she stopped.

"Make certain there are no escaped locks of hair. Cover that skin. Such perfection was meant to be touched and savored . . . enjoyed. You're a bewitching maid. Almost too much so. I'll not leave. I will give you distance. I will give myself the same."

He was speaking the soft words in an ongoing cadence of sound, making a sonnet of words. She could believe him a troubadour. She could believe almost anything of him. She focused on her supplies. It was all she could think of.

Weasel had broken the jar containing her herbs. The floor held the fragrant aroma. Aislynn picked up each linden flower petal, scraping them with her fingernail to release the aroma before mashing them in the jar bottom. Then, she moved toward Brent.

"What is it you do?"

"Make certain he does na' choke on his own blood," she replied.

He grunted. Aislynn ran a hand over Brent's jaw, feeling for the joints.

"What are you doing now?" he asked.

"Checking for breaks."

"I broke no bones."

"Nae? You loosened teeth and I fear his nose is broken. You must na' realize your own power." She was adding scooped water into the jar and mashing the linden flowers with her fingers into a paste.

"Tie the cloak more securely. Cover your head."

Aislynn glanced from the corner of her eyes at him. He was pacing; silently and stealthily . . . passing through the light before disappearing into the gloom. Reappearing. Disappearing. In a leonine fashion. *Prowling.* The word flashed through her mind.

"I will na' be able to see, if I . . . cover myself," she replied.

"I did not save you from ravishment only to practice it myself," he answered from the darkest corner.

Aislynn lifted the cloak over her head.

"What is it you do now?" he asked, with a rough edge to his voice.

She glanced at him and then back to her supplies. "'Tis linden flower and mistletoe to make a paste for his teeth. I dinna' know how many are loose. I am checking."

"What good is this paste?" he asked.

She shrugged. "It takes away pain. And lessens swelling."

"He cannot feel pain. He's yet to awaken from my blow."

"True." Aislynn dipped a finger of the herb mixture and filled Brent's lips with it. The liege had loosened four teeth that she found, two seriously. If the man gave them time to heal, they'd seat themselves again without trouble. The paste would help.

She finished and ran her fingers lightly down the bridge of Brent's nose. It was crooked.

"What is it you do now?" he asked.

"It needs straightening. It will heal faster and look better for him."

"What is it to you, how it looks?" His voice wasn't the same warmly embracing tone. It was cold.

Aislynn moved her hands to her lap and watched them. "The same I have for any creature in need; even a creature of prey. I know it will attack again, yet I still heal it. Because a gift is na' something to spit in the face of. 'Tis exactly as I did this morn. To you."

He didn't say anything for long enough, Aislynn had time to wring her hands, run them over her hips, tuck a lock of hair back behind her ear, and then glance in the direction he'd last moved to.

"Finish," he said.

She went onto her knees, put a hand on either side of Brent's nose, placed her fingertips along it and said the silent words of prayer. Then she was gripping his nose and wrenching it sideways, using both wrists. The result was an instant release of blood all over her. "Quickly! Hand me the peat!"

He was on one knee beside her, putting the crumbles of dried moss in her hand and pulling back the moment he did so. Aislynn forced herself to ignore it. Then she was packing the moss into Brent's nose, stopping the bleeding, and putting it back into alignment. Through it all, she was aware of the liege watching, his eyes boring into her.

"Have you finished?" he asked, when she was satisfied and sat back on her haunches to look at Brent.

She nodded. "It will heal well if he keeps still. I must make certain he rests without moving."

"You're coming with me. You're bathing his blood from yourself and finding suitable clothing. A serf can stay with him."

"I am a serf," Aislynn answered softly.

His voice lowered further. "Oh no. I don't know what you are as yet, nor do I know all that you are. Of one thing I'm certain, though. You're no serf."

Chapter Six

The liege carried her. She wasn't offered the choice when she'd finished with Brent but she didn't struggle. She was trying not to cause him further injury that she'd have to repair. His limp was only apparent when taking a step on the injured side, and that because she was in his arms. Aislynn had time to think through it before they arrived at his chamber. He had his lips sealed so firmly the entire time, they whitened. She glanced at him often, although he only caught her at it once. She'd been right about his hand, too. He was favoring it, for the one time he'd shifted her with his right hand, he'd clenched his teeth so tightly, a nerve bulged out the side of his jaw.

This man of muscle and strength and power hadn't one fiber of his being devoted to gentleness. He was demonstrating that with every step he kept forcing himself to take. *It was surprising he carried it in his voice,* she told herself.

They hadn't gone unnoticed. There were serfs trailing behind them and a large knight was walking beside them the moment they left the great hall.

"I see you found her. This the one? Brent's wench?"

"Leave me, Montvale. 'Tis of no interest to yourself."

"I would be the judge of that."

Rhoenne didn't reply and the man didn't act like he expected one. Aislynn swiveled her head further into the hollow below the liege's shoulder and tried to make herself as light as possible.

His breathing wasn't giving anything away. She wondered how much training he'd received in order to be able to do that. His leg had to be paining him unmercifully and his hand should be a solid throb of pain—if the blow Brent had taken was any mark. Yet, beyond the tight lips and clenched jaw, he didn't exhibit any of it.

Perhaps he should grow a beard to disguise even that. Aislynn tilted her head ever so slightly and looked up through her eyelashes at him. She ran her eyes over his chin, before answering her own question. He had a fine layer of white-blond hair covering his cheeks and a few sprouts of brown-tinted whiskers at the cleft she'd seen before. It didn't look like he could grow a beard.

Her lips curved. He looked down then and caught her.

Time stopped, ceasing to function. There was just her and him and the handspan of space between them. Aislynn licked her lower lip and then sucked in on it. She watched as he moved his glance there and then back to hers. Her heart stalled. He trembled slightly and his left hand tightened on her thigh.

"You'd stand a better chance of reaching your chamber, Rhoenne, if you walk *into* it, rather than *pass* it by," the large knight said in a long, drawn-out fashion.

The liege's eyes widened and he lifted his head. Then he swiveled back around to walk back three steps.

"Fiona? What are you doing here? I thought I told you to wait in my chambers. Mine."

"But, sir! You dinna'! You said—" There was a female voice answering him, but he interrupted her words before she could finish.

"Mine. Just as I made mention. I'll look for you there. And here is that Wesellen wench . . . *and* her sister, Mary. You didn't tell me about them, My Liege. For shame. Yes. Go. He'll not be needing you tonight. Go to my chamber. Have you any further women I need oust, Rhoenne?"

The liege had his eyes narrowed again and just looked at the knight, who had a quirk about his lips suspiciously like a withheld smile. Aislynn had the barest glimpse before he caught her at it, too.

"Take these old foodstuffs with you. Send up more! And mead! Lots of mead. Bring that, too."

"Why are you ordering my serfs about, Harold?"

"Because you're too enraptured with Brent's wench. Someone has to do it. If not, we'll starve."

"You just finished two trenchers of boar . . . and she isn't Brent's."

"Appetizing it was, too. But not nearly enough. Barely satisfied my hunger. Why, if one is to believe you, that's all I can hold on a feast night. Set this wench—who isn't Brent's—down. I would have a good look at her."

"She needs new clothing," Rhoenne replied.

"You have bolts of cloth for such a problem. Set her down. I would see what all this is about."

"She needs new clothing . . . *now.*"

"Now?"

"What cloth she wears is bloodied and torn."

"My Liege! For shame. You didn't tell me of the strength of your need. The poor lass. You should have had it seen to first. I warned you. Now, set her down. I would apologize to her."

"For what?" the liege asked.

"Your haste . . . and fumbling ways. There needn't be pain. I would have sent another wench to soothe the beast from you. I would, at least, have sent word up. No maid should have to deal with Rhoenne Guy de Ramhurst's lusts without a warning."

Aislynn knew her face was flaming red and her tongue felt swollen. She had no idea men spoke this way. She didn't know where she was supposed to have learned of it, either.

"Harold, your company pales."

"And yours bores. Set the lass down. Let her gather a fresh breath. I'm certain she's tired of your stench by now."

The Sassenach laird was trembling again. It wasn't visible but Aislynn could feel it along the arms holding beneath her. She didn't think it due to the knight's words. It had to be brought on by weakness. He was injured and he looked ashen. She suspected he'd fall in place before admitting to any of it, though.

"My Lord?" she whispered.

He tilted his head down a fraction and favored her with vivid blue eyes. Her belly twisted, her heart started hammering and she forgot what she was about to ask. She didn't like the feeling. She didn't know what to do about it. She didn't even know what it was.

". . . more than the two of you in this room for company, too! Oh good. The trencher arrives. And a mead cask! Thank the Lord for such favors."

Aislynn heard the sounds of revelry as the door opened; then silence broken by the other knight's movements. "You have thoughtful serfs, Rhoenne. Very thoughtful. What's her name? At least tell me that."

The liege's arms loosened and Aislynn slid to the floor to stand in front of him. She'd suspected the tremor was growing but it wasn't evident the moment she moved. She turned in the enclosure of his locked arms.

"Is she shy?" the knight continued his questioning.

"This is not a wench to be looked at, lusted after, or bargained over. Heed my words. I counsel you."

"You're warning me away? And haven't even let me see her, yet? 'Tis most unlike you, Ramhurst. Most."

"She'll show you herself when she likes. I've forced much on her already."

"As I already spoke on. Come, lass. Show yourself. The boar cools, my ardor heats, and time stalls. 'Tis not a good combination."

"Harold, I warn you—"

"And I'm heeding. At present," the knight interrupted him. Aislynn's mouth opened slightly at the obvious disrespect and the liege's failure to react. "My patience is on your behalf, so you should be properly grateful."

"My behalf? I tell you your company pales, you stay. I threaten and you ignore it. Leave us, Harold. I won't need you further."

"Who talks of your needs? I would look at this wench. I won't harm her. Why . . . I won't even touch her. I only wish to look at what Brent stole and you rescued. I'll not take further liberty. I wouldn't wish any damage done to your other hand should you seek to punish me, too."

"What damage?" Rhoenne asked, and it sounded like it came from between clenched teeth.

Aislynn hadn't been around men; especially large, powerful men. She listened to the voices escalate with words and intents and she hunched her shoulders slightly. The liege released her instantly. That felt nearly as odd as being in his embrace had. She walked until she was in the center of his room. She didn't know what else to do. She lifted her hands to the edge of the liege's cloak, carved an opening there, and tossed it back onto her shoulders. Then she turned her head and looked across the chamber and up at this knight named Harold. The flagon of liquid stopped on the way to the knight's lips, his eyes grew wide, and then he pulled his drinking vessel away.

"The devil take you, Ramhurst! She's . . . she—"

"I know."

"There's none to compare! Wherever did he find such a beauty? That skin! That hair! Where in this godless fief was she hiding? Have you secured a kiss, yet? If not, consider it yet another sign of your weakness, for I wouldn't have hesitated."

"What . . . weakness?" Rhoenne replied.

She tipped her head toward him, but didn't move her gaze from the knight called Harold. The man had put his drink down and was moving toward her, belying his earlier words. Rhoenne didn't change stance. Aislynn watched the knight approach until he was an arm-span from her. Then he stopped. She dropped her eyes.

"She appears overly small, Ramhurst. Dangerous, that. Hips well suited for dancing perhaps, but woefully little for receiving seed, and consequently, birthing the result."

Dancing? Aislynn repeated to herself, widening her eyes on the floor. *Birthing?*

"That won't be an issue with us."

"Truly? You don't desire this wench? You *are* inhuman. I should have known. Grant me first right, then."

Rhoenne sighed heavily. "She carries a curse. I heard it from her own lips. 'Tis enough to cool most men's ardor, mine included."

"This curse must be well-hidden, for this wench has been much blessed, I would say. Such perfection! Has she a frame to match? Tell me. The curiosity is making a liar of my patience."

Aislynn looked up then and caught his glance. He was bold, handsome, and he was big. Strong. And the liege wasn't offended at his speech? This was not going well at all.

"Ramhurst, I am most jealous. Has she a sister, perhaps?" The knight winked then, startling her. Aislynn looked down again. "God's truth, Ramhurst, but she appears virginal. Still. Such a jewel. How is it you possess such a treasure? You detest maids. You barely tolerate women unless your need is too great. Why you?"

"Because she's not what she appears to you."

"Truly? And how would you know this?"

The liege was moving as he spoke, until he stood behind her. She didn't check. She felt him. He was putting his hands beneath the hood where it rested on her shoulders. Aislynn slanted her head and shoulders slightly that direction to meet his look. The reaction of the knight before them was audible as he choked on his drink. Rhoenne looked away from her and back at his man. She didn't move her eyes.

"Well?" Harold asked.

"Well, what?"

"How would you know?"

"Know what?" the liege asked.

The knight made a frustrated sound. "How she appears to me."

"Oh. You've not ceased mouthing endless words over it. I'd have to be deaf not to know."

"You've lost your senses with the girl. *You.* Already."

The man holding to her caught a swift intake of breath. "Perhaps. Were you . . . in my boots, you would, too. Admit such and have done."

"Freely. I have already remarked on my hunger for the maid and now you seek to strengthen its grasp on me. My thanks. You're a true friend."

Aislynn giggled. She couldn't help it.

"She has a voice! And it laughs at me? I stand stricken. She isn't perfection after all. May she screech with a tone that hurts the ear and sport teeth that rot. That is my prayer for you, my lord earl. It is the least I can do."

"She has neither. Do you?"

Rhoenne looked down at her and closed what distance there was between them, placing her fully against him.

"I have been . . . known to screech," she stammered it.

He smiled and his eyes showed every bit of it this time.

Montvale snorted. Both of them turned to him. He'd moved back to his platter and was lifting a slice of meat with a large blade and then dropping it back. "At least feed the wench, Rhoenne. She can appreciate the bounty from your table. Alas, I have partaken fully. I couldn't hold another morsel."

"None asked or invited you to." He clenched his hands on her shoulders and Aislynn knew it wasn't an embrace. She was holding up too much of his weight. She had to lock her knees to keep from staggering with it.

"If I wait for an invite from you, My Liege, I would starve. So, tell me what the wench is to you and satisfy my curiosity."

"It's not as you . . . think and I tire of hearing . . . myself speak. Go. Now." The liege had to pause twice through the sentence.

"If I were not your most steadfast knight, I would be challenging you for her. Right now. You and me. On the list."

"You listen . . . to nothing!"

Aislynn's legs were wobbling beneath his weight and his breathing changed again, catching slightly before each inhalation. She didn't look up to see why. She already knew the reason. He was hiding weakness. It didn't change it. He was near to falling with it.

"Say something I wish to hear, then! Tell me the wench is yours and I'll leave be. And if she's free . . . allow me to speak my own offer."

Each breath touching her shoulder came out swiftly, and there was a long distinct span before he sucked another one in. He hadn't much time before he was going to fall right in front of them. She wondered if the knight speaking to him was blind or if he was the devious sort.

She glanced to his bulk again. If he was devious, it was going to be difficult to avoid him.

"She . . . is not available to you," Rhoenne said finally.

"Why not? Has she your offer?"

"Aye."

"Has she an answer to this offer? If not, I would put forth my own. I would see she had a belly burdened with child every—"

"You listen . . . poorly," Rhoenne interrupted him. He was fainting on his feet and his own knight was the man forcing it! Aislynn's lips set at such thoughtlessness. *Men!* she thought. *Leave them in charge and see what happens? Boasting and brawling and mayhem. That's what.*

"At least with me, she'd be warm in my bed and not set aside the moment I yearned for the comfort she would give."

"Mont . . . vale—" The name came with a gasp in the middle of it.

"Oh cease this!" Aislynn spoke up, stopping the unending barrage of words at each other. Harold looked down at her. She gulped and finished the words. "The liege does have me. I accept his offer. Right now. Right here."

He sighed hugely, lifting his chest with it. "Were I a wench, I fear I'd say the same. Who am I when compared to such a prize? I'm but a lowly knight, paid a scant portion per quarter, while he? He holds the treasury of Ramhurst in the palm of his hand and commands the fealty of thousands at the sound of his voice. Who am I against such odds?"

No one answered his complaint for a moment. Aislynn realized the liege was gathering strength to do it. She did it, instead. "Can you na' just go?" she asked.

"Leave? Now?"

Aislynn nodded.

"Have you bed with him?"

"Harold!"

The earl was growing weaker. That was the only excuse for the hoarse way he said the knight's name. Aislynn's eyes showed it before she could halt it. She was afraid the knight had seen it.

"Well, have you?"

"I—" Her voice ended. She didn't know what to answer. The man was impervious to words of rejection and the liege wasn't willing to show any of his weakness. It was a stupid situation that only men could cause.

The knight shrugged. "It would make little difference with me. I only say it to spare you the dishonor of harboring his seed and birthing a bastard."

"I'll meet you . . . on the list, yet . . . Montvale."

"And you interrupt on private words, My Liege."

Aislynn's eyes flew wide. The knight stepped closer to them.

"So, which is it, maid?" He reached out and lifted a lock of her hair. "If he has yet to bed with you, I may yet be in time. Accept my offer. Cleave unto me. I would offer marriage. The Earl Rhoenne Guy de Ramhurst cannot, even if he wanted to. He's a vassal to the king. He weds where the king chooses."

Aislynn could feel the reaction in the man leaning against her as he clenched his hands on her shoulders. "I already told you, sir. I am his. I accept. Now leave me to tend to his needs!"

The knight's face settled into a slight smile. Aislynn had to look away from the tenderness in his eyes. "Damn you, Rhoenne. You've won. Again. You'll be forever guarding such a property, though. I must warn you."

"Who . . . better?"

The second word barely made it to sound. Aislynn felt him weaving in place behind her. She watched the knight's eyes narrow. The liege hadn't been in time. His weakness was taking him down. Aislynn didn't know what the knight was going to do. She was afraid to guess what was going to happen to her.

The hands holding to her slipped and she was shoved aside as Sir Montvale caught the blond man just as he hit the floor. Her mouth gaped open as the knight hoisted Rhoenne over his shoulders like he weighed about the same as a sack of grain. She knew the lie of that. Her own shoulders ached.

"Clear off his bed," he said, using his head to gesture toward a curtained platform.

Aislynn was ahead of him and shoving the curtains aside before she lost every breath with surprise. Rhoenne Ramhurst had a king's ransom in jewels and gold heaped on his mattress, and beneath that, he had a mountain of silks, satins, and velvets.

"Quickly!" The knight hissed it from behind her. She pushed everything over the far side where it clanged and clattered as it fell. "Now, assist me with your new lord."

"How—?"

"The man keeps wealth in his own chambers. I've told him oft enough he should construct a larger treasury and post more guards, but he won't listen."

"I mean, how did you ken his weakness?"

"Oh. That. I've had his friendship since he was my father's page, with me at his side. He can't hide much from me although he does try. It took all my skill tonight to wait him out. It wasn't easy, either. You both thought me witless, no doubt."

"You were trying for this? You were na' offering for me?" She asked it before she could stop it. She couldn't stop the blush that accompanied the words, either.

He slanted a glance to her and his lips quirked. "Very few call me a liar to my face, wench. I forewarn you."

"I dinna' understand." Her body was suffering the same heat now.

"I meant every word I said. Don't force the issue. At least, not until he's well. Then it will be an even contest between us. Now help me."

He rolled Rhoenne off his shoulder and onto the bed, making it depress with their combined weights. Aislynn had to grab a post to keep from joining them in the middle of it.

"With what?" she asked.

He was shoving Rhoenne's tunic up and yanking on the tie fastenings of his hose. "These! His hose. He has a lance tip buried in his lower leg. He wouldn't let anyone know. He wouldn't even let anyone see to it. The leg may be festered beyond saving. Call the healer. Go! Now! Ask anyone!"

"It's na' there any longer," she replied. "I took it out this morn."

He stopped his motion, turned his head sideways to her and raised his eyebrows. "So . . . you're the reason," he said slowly.

Aislynn frowned. "The reason?" she echoed. Then she had to look away as he ignored her to peel the prone man's hose to the tops of his boots.

"He's had his mind elsewhere all day. Now, I know why." He was looking over the cauterized flesh of the wound as he spoke, so he missed her reaction at his words. Aislynn was afraid of it, herself.

"You did this?" There was a different look on his face when he looked over at where she still clung to one of the foot-posts. "You're a healer? You? That's what he was trying to tell me?"

She nodded.

"There isn't a sign of fever. What did you do?"

"Cleaned it, packed it with amica . . . seared it."

"You *burned* him?"

This Harold Montvale was a handsome man. He had a lot of depth and charm to every word. None of it was showing on the chiseled, stony face he assumed the moment he asked it. Aislynn gulped.

"I had to! To . . . stop the bleeding. He—he dinna' wish anyone to know about it."

"He seeks to save these heathens from the penalty of their own actions. If none know, then none can be charged and hanged. It was a Celt lance, wasn't it?"

She didn't reply although he waited for it. His lips twisted and he moved to replace the hose.

"Wait! There was moss for it. To stay the pain. He was to keep it against the wound. I dinna' ken why he's na' using it."

"I do. Go. Find this moss. Hurry."

Aislynn was already off the bed and searching. Everywhere in the vast room Rhoenne Ramhurst called his chamber there was either a wooden chest piled with jewels or spices, or a mound of sumptuous fabrics, or stacks of gold and silver coins. She'd never seen the like.

There was an old sack near the hearth. Aislynn recognized it instantly, and had the webbing of moss unrolling as she walked toward the bed.

"You took forever and look! He already moves! What kept you?" His voice was harsher, but that was due to keeping the prone man from moving.

"There's too much lying about. He has too much. Moss is hard to find amidst such riches."

"This is but a portion. One of the king's earls needs such a treasure. He has thousands of knights to feed, clothe, and mount on horseflesh, which must also be stabled. He has four strongholds to defend. He has enough at times for his needs. Barely."

Aislynn put the lichen onto his flesh. Then she stepped

back so the knight could pull the hose back into position and re-tie them. *Barely enough?* she wondered, looking about her.

"You did well. See to his hand. Quickly. We haven't much time. He'll be awake and seeking my head at the end of his sword if he sees any of this. You don't know him. Now! Move!"

Aislynn scooted onto the mattress and went to her knees beside the liege's waist. His right hand almost wasn't recognizable as one. Three of his fingers were swollen to double-size. He hadn't taken any of the blow with his thumb or small finger. She moved her attention to his left hand. She placed it, palm-upward, onto her lap and molded her fingers along each of his, searching for how it was supposed to feel.

"What are you doing? Cease caressing him and heal him!"

"I am healing him. It is na' a quick thing. I have to learn the structure of his hand. I will need the knowledge when searching for breaks. Hush now."

Aislynn closed her eyes, and ran her fingers along each of Rhoenne's, ignoring the tingling that went clear to her elbows as she did so. Before she was finished, she knew he was conscious. He hadn't opened his eyes, but he was semi-awake. She didn't know for how long.

She put his hand down and picked up his injured one, lifting it by his wrist. She placed it palm-upward on her lap and started the same movements along these fingers. Aside from tenseness in the body next to her, the earl didn't give any clue of his awareness, or lack of it.

"This is na' going to be easy," she finally said.

"Did he break them?"

"Nae. But he should have."

The knight sighed loudly. "It's all right, then?"

She shook her head. "He has damage to the fingers. I'm

going to have to pull at them. Hard. Swift. It's going to hurt terribly. He'll react."

"Perhaps we should get help."

"There's none better than me, Sir Knight," she said softly.

"Mayhap we should leave it be. Wrap it. Cool it with water—"

"If I leave it longer, he's in danger of deformity. Fingers that canna' bend, distort. I have to pull at them."

The knight looked greenish about the cheeks. Aislynn narrowed her eyes at him. "I am going to need a strong man to help me."

"I'm strong," he replied.

She looked him over critically. "I need more than that. Perhaps you should tie him."

"Tie him? To what?"

"His posts."

"What? Why?"

"He won't be able to control the pain. He will react. Every creature does."

"He isn't aware. If it will pain, then cease speaking of it and do it. I'm strong. I'll hold him for you."

"I am na' simply speaking of it. I am preparing his flesh for it. I have ever been doing so. You see?"

Aislynn held to the liege's first two fingers with her right hand, and then she wrapped her left hand about the third finger, and joined her hands together. She got up onto her knees to get leverage, took a deep breath, and then she yanked, as quickly and with as much strength as she could. They both heard the loud cracking as his fingers straightened. Then they heard the earl's yell and she was facing the solid fury of open, blue, crazed-looking eyes.

Sir Montvale wasn't strong enough. She should have known.

Chapter Seven

"God's blood! Montvale! What have you done?" Rhoenne Guy de Ramhurst was off the bed and moving, keeping his mind blank as he absorbed the agony. It was akin to having his entire hand placed into a flame and he flexed it into a fist over and over as he worked to keep the pain bearable.

Montvale was with him the entire time.

"And what are you doing in my chamber?" Rhoenne glared at the knight striding beside him. "You've wenches of your own."

"I was more needed here, My Liege," the man replied.

"For what?" Rhoenne asked sourly.

"To get your carcass onto the bed."

"What?" Rhoenne stopped, looked over at the girl as he squeezed his hand together again, which was helping to mute what had been searing pain, and then resumed his walk.

"Your carcass. Onto the bed. With the lass."

"I am not in need of assistance with that. I can't think of much I do need assist with. You may leave us. Now."

"I'm afeared you'll faint again."

Rhoenne came to an instant halt. Anger pumped through

him now, taking the pain to a bearable throb. He glared over at his knight and thinned his lips. "I never faint."

"Oh. My mistake." Harold replied easily, but there was a quirk to his mouth.

Rhoenne frowned in thought. "Very well, Montvale. I may have lost my senses for a bit. But it would be the first time."

"Agreed," Harold said.

They started pacing again. When they reached the side that held the narrow chasm that was an arrow slit, they swiveled, preparing for another cross of the floor.

That's when Aislynn noted something odd. The knight, Harold, was always staying between her and Rhoenne.

"And why hasn't the girl been bathed yet?"

Harold looked over at where she was standing, between the wall and the liege's bed, and that just made two of them doing it. Aislynn returned their even looks but it took an interminable amount of time while the sound of her heartbeat just got louder and louder until it filled her ears.

"I would lay the blame for that at your feet, Rhoenne," the knight named Harold finally replied.

"Mine?" Rhoenne was clearly mystified. He wasn't the only one. Aislynn knew she probably had the same expression.

"Aye. You didn't order it before taking leave of your senses."

"Must you?" Rhoenne asked.

Aislynn giggled and that had both of them looking back to her.

"The maid appears to find you amusing, Rhoenne. That is odd. Most lasses find you handsome of face, impressive of limb, and dead of emotion. None of them find you amusing. All of which is very bright of you, now that I think on it. You're a mystery. An untapped source. 'Tis no wonder they pursue you. Whereas I? I am open and willing and very available."

"Harold . . . I'm warning you," Rhoenne began.

"Again?" Montvale said.

Aislynn caught the giggle that time.

"You must tell me of this warning, when we again have time."

"I have time now."

"I believe at the moment you have other duties."

The blond giant sighed. It was a very visual sight. Montvale had been accurate. The liege was impressive of limb and handsome of face. The one thing he wasn't going to be was pursued by his Celt healer. That part she had control of. Mayhap.

"Such as . . . ?" Rhoenne asked.

"Ordering a bath for yon healer you have claimed. Or rather, the healer that claimed you. I don't know why women have ever taken you over me. Good thing you're immune to their charms." He stopped his words and gave Aislynn a look that showed his intent. The warning was for her. She nodded slightly. He smiled. "Ah well. Such is life. Were it me, I would order her a tub of warmed water, and I would do it before the clothing she wears is so stuck to her that you have to forcefully remove it."

"Montvale." This time the voice had a growl of sound attached to it.

"What?" The knight had the audacity to look innocent. "You wish me to stay and assist?"

"I think we should both leave. She can have her privacy, and I can have some peace."

"Peace? Well, why didn't you say so? You are ever mysterious, Rhoenne. Ever. Bide my words, maid. Does she have a name, or must I stay with lackluster titles such as maid and lass? Well, My Liege?"

"Aislynn," she replied. "I am called Aislynn."

"You've been well-hidden, fair Aislynn. I would satisfy my curiosity, if you will?"

She nodded.

"How is it that the brother managed to ferret you out? We ride far and wide, night and day, sennights at a time, and have never seen such beauty as you possess. Why him?"

Aislynn blushed. She didn't have to see it, she felt it by the heat reaching her scalp and making it tingle.

"Montvale."

"My Liege?" Harold replied.

"Aislynn doesn't need us for her bath. And you have wenches awaiting your attention. Come with me. We'll leave the girl to her rest." He tipped his head toward where she stood and pushed on his knight. Aside from moving a step to the side, it didn't look to have much effect.

"And where is it you go, My Liege?"

Rhoenne's joviality vanished. "To the chapel. As always."

"To pray?" The knight snorted, making it sound a curse word. "That is all you ever do. Such a waste. A beauteous maid, a long eve of play ahead, and you go to prostrate yourself before an altar. You are inhuman, Rhoenne. I said it before and I'll say it—"

"Would you just leave?" Rhoenne shoved at his knight this time and they both moved to the door. That's when he turned back to her. "I go to order a bath for you, Aislynn. Avail yourself of whatever you need. Whatever material, whatever jewelry. 'Tis what I promised. I won't be back this night."

"Nay. He'll be too busy being pious," Harold added.

Rhoenne sighed again. "Actually, I go to give thanks."

"For what? Stifling desire?"

Aislynn's eyes widened but she gave no further sign to any of it.

"Nay. For the gifts of a healer," Rhoenne replied, and

held up his right hand to flex it several times. They all watched it. He lowered it the same time that he moved his gaze to her. And then he smiled.

His knight had forgotten to mention the devastating impact of his smile, she decided, as the door closed behind them.

Summer's end . . . summer's set . . .

Images swam through her dream-world, alternately burning her before making her teeth clench on the chattering as the chills came. Aislynn shivered with it, warped with it, sweated with it . . . endured it.

"Wake up! Up! Why, it's nigh mid-morn and I've waited long enough."

It was a cheerful, loud, feminine voice. Aislynn forced her head to move, grimacing slightly at the sweat spot she was leaving on the pillow. She blinked. She shivered. She felt ill all over and knew it was the remnants of the dream, although she'd never had one like that.

"I want to see the woman my Rhoenne's keeping! Up!"

Aislynn swiveled to one side, although the voluminous velvet she wore didn't make the move with her. The door shutting was half of the noise the speaker was making. Then there was the sound of a trunk lid banging shut, the rustling of the drape being shoved aside, and the sound of wooden shutters being pushed open, letting sunlight in to flood the room.

"It's hard to imagine it, after all this time. You've little idea what a stir you've made. There's been talk of nothing else all morn. Come along, now. You can't stay abed all day, although chances are . . . you need to." The speaker chuckled at the end of her words.

"Go away," Aislynn said, speaking to the sweat-stained linen at her nose.

"Oh come along, it's entirely the natural state of affairs, although that Fiona is still screaming over it. She thought His Lordship was her very own personal property and she was getting quite big-headed about it. You don't have to hide from me, you know. I'm quite harmless."

"You're loud and annoying. You are na' harmless."

"Well!"

"Who are you?" Aislynn turned her head and asked it. The nightmarish dream was a portend of something. If she had time to ponder it, she'd know what it was. The woman's barrage of words, even if it was said with cheerful volume, was dispersing the last of the image and sending it out of reach.

"Old Rosie. Why are you wearing so much? And doing it so poorly?"

"What?" Aislynn asked. And then she remembered. She'd donned a length of yellow, sturdy-feeling material, wound it about her body until she ran out of it and had to use a brooch at her hip to pin it. Then, she'd found a dark length of velvet, used a blade to slash a hole in the middle of it, and that went for her neck hole. Then, she'd finished it all off with a length of rope that he'd had lying about, tying it about her middle, although it wrapped twice. She'd suspected the rope had gold strands woven into it. Glancing at it now, she knew it did. All told, she was probably wearing enough material to make a tent. It hadn't seemed so when she'd curled up against a rolled carpet. It was against belief that she'd slept in his bed.

"And that's velvet, isn't it? Much too expensive to sleep in, and probably miserably hot, too."

"Would you please go?" Aislynn repeated it.

"Not by an arrow's shot. I've been with the master from birth and I asked for the position of attending you. It's going to be a decided chore if this is all the welcome you have for me. So? What do you say?"

"You asked to attend . . . me?"

"As I've been saying."

"Then attend me. Go away."

The snort she made was raucous enough to come from one of the castle horses and it was probably twice as loud, as well. "I am going to serve you and I can't do it if I leave. 'Tis the lone way to stay abreast of all the goings-on in the castle. And I know everything that happens . . . or almost all of it."

Now that she was getting accustomed to the light, Aislynn saw that Rosie was an older woman with a large, gray knot of hair coiled atop her head, lines all about her face, and enough bulk to her frame to bow a horse's back carrying her. She was dressed in a servant's raw-linen mantle and hood, although she had it tossed back onto her shoulders at the moment. Her under-dress was of brown, and the braided cord about her middle didn't do a thing to define a shape.

"Is there a young Rosie?" Aislynn asked.

The woman considered that for a moment. "Nay," she replied, finally.

"Then, what makes you the *auld* one?"

"His lordship has a way with words. He called me such when he was a wee one and it's stuck."

"Lord Rhoenne? A way with words?"

"Don't tell me you haven't been the receiver of it. I'll not listen. Why, I've done enough listening, and we've not progressed beyond a greeting or two."

"You truly are my servant, then?" Aislynn asked. "Mine?"

"As I've been saying since I arrived. You're not just young, you're addled. That's it, isn't it?"

"I'm nearly a score in age, and I'm na' addled. What

I am is hungered, angered, and needing to think through something."

"Hunger I can fix. Just you stay right there."

Aislynn watched her open the door and speak to the crowd gathered there. She didn't see the size of it, but it was large by its swelling sound.

"Aye. I'll have her readied by sup and you can all get an eyeful then. Now, cease this and get us some breakfast. And then find other chores that don't take place outside His Lordship's chamber doors. What? The lass wants all. Eggs, fowl, pudding, bread, mutton, pie, sweetbreads. . . . You do, don't you?" She turned to question Aislynn, who shrugged. Rosie turned back to the door. "Now go! Hurry! We want the porridge warm and the mead cooled."

"I'll never eat all that," Aislynn said when the door shut.

The woman grinned. "Not to worry. I'll help."

"I dinna' need help with eating. I need help with directions."

"Directions? To where? And not in that attire. I'll be ridiculed from here to the king's newest priory."

"Why?"

The woman sucked in a huge breath, alerting Aislynn that it was going to be a long-winded reply. She wasn't disappointed.

"He entrusted the care of you to me. I'm very skilled with a needle. That was of prime interest to him. He wants you dressed as befits your station . . . at his side. I'm for disbelieving I actually asked for this duty. I would never live down the laughter if anyone sees your attire at this moment, but right now I'm wishing I'd just slept in and avoided His Lordship now that I've met up with you. He didn't tell me you had a sour tongue and a frame you were lief to hide away, since it embarrassed you. Am I leaving anything out?"

Aislynn watched the red face and couldn't prevent the giggle.

"And now she laughs at me! I've a mind to go ferret out

His Lordship and give him a tongue-lashing that will leave him cut and bleeding!"

"You'd do that?"

"None else in this household doubts me."

Aislynn gasped. "He'd listen? The Lion . . . the beast?"

"Beast. Hah. Peasant superstition and nonsense. I was his nursemaid. He's no beast. He's as gentle as they come."

"He loosened two of his brother's teeth last night," Aislynn replied.

The old woman grinned. "He didn't just loosen them, he took them out. With one blow. I saw it. We all did. I was ever so proud."

"They're just loosened. I know. I took care."

"You can take all the care you want, girl. Men don't always behave as they should. That Brent woke up with a mouthful of mashed weeds, and even when they told him nay, he spat it out, and with it comes two of his teeth."

"How could he be so stupid?" Aislynn asked.

"You don't know much about big, strapping men, do you?"

Aislynn shook her head. The movement ached clear through her.

"They don't take well to molly-coddling. They don't admit pain. They'll expire afore they ask an assist."

"That much . . . I ken," Aislynn replied finally.

"Then you should guess the rest of it. He's already out on the list."

"Who is?"

"The bastard."

"You . . . call him that?"

The woman shrugged. "Everyone does. We call things as we see them. And what I see is a wench, with little by way of womanly charms, keeping me from the chore of fitting her, by confusing me with words and questions."

"But such a thing would require a mind that isna' addled. True?"

The woman regarded her solemnly, then she smiled and raised her brows. "True. You've got spirit . . . and you're a tease. Both deadly to him. I should have guessed it. So! Where do you wish to begin?"

"Begin . . . what?"

"Your life at Rhoenne Guy de Ramhurst's side. He's claimed you. He's fighting Brent out on the list over ownership."

"Of me?" Aislynn was choking. It sounded in the question.

"Well . . . ownership of the whole fief. But you come along with it."

"You're na' concerned?" Aislynn was. Her skin was crawling with it.

The woman shrugged. "Of course not. There's no man alive that can best His Lordship, the bastard included."

"But it's too soon. He's weak."

"You think you drained him that well? What stuff and nonsense!"

Aislynn clamped her lips on the reply. Old Rosie didn't know about Rhoenne's injuries. Few did, which was just as he wanted it. Men! They truly were silly, stupid creatures, even if they were big, bold, and enough to take a woman's breath away. She blinked slowly to clear the image.

The woman made another snort. This one was colored with amusement.

"What is it now?" Aislynn asked.

"You. Daydreaming. I mention His Lordship's uh . . . and you went all star-eyed and wistful. I'm just mooning, myself. How well I recall it."

"You? And him—"

"Of course not him! I'll have your tongue for saying such a thing. Come to think of it, that might be an improvement. You've said little, and what bit it was, wasn't worth listening to."

Aislynn stared. Old Rosie stared right back. "You're my servant?"

The woman nodded.

"Well, what if I told you serving me required cleaning out Sir Brent's chambers? He has vermin there. I want them removed."

The woman's smile vanished. "I'm not a serf. I'm a freewoman. As such, I can march right out of here and never set eyes on you again. That's what I can do."

"So, what's stopped you?"

The woman huffed what was probably a reply, put her hands on what was probably her hips, and gave Aislynn what was probably a stern look. It didn't work. Aislynn felt more like giggling.

"It could be due to the fact that there's been nary a woman's hand in his affairs for so long, it quite took my breath away when I heard about it. Mayhap it's because I want the bastard's chambers cleaned out, too. Mayhap it's due to that Eldine's influence and how I want it changed."

"Eldine?" Aislynn repeated the name.

"His lordship's half-sister. She's a hand in all that happens, and it's not a good hand. I'd like to see you change that."

"How can I do such a thing?"

"Order that Eldine to work. Cease her . . . other activities."

Aislynn didn't want to ask, but she knew it was what Rosie was waiting for. "What other activities?"

"Eldine has the power in this household. She drinks to excess, she lays about, and she orders everyone as if she were the lady of the keep."

"She's his sister. You just said as much."

"Bastard sister."

"Another? Truly?"

"Aye. Ramhursts are lusty males. As you are already well aware."

Aislynn eyes were wide and she avoided looking anywhere but her hands. She was sweating again, too. It wasn't the dream. It was a blush.

"And if she had a hand in anything other than the procurement of females for the household—"

"She does . . . what?" Aislynn interrupted the tirade.

"Keeps the men busy. She's very good at finding and gaining lasses to serve their needs, which does tend to keep them from seeing things."

"Things?" Aislynn asked.

"Things such as unkempt stairs, cobweb-strewn storehouses, and gold that goes missing. That sort of thing. And all of this needs changed. And it's you I'm looking to see to it."

"Me?" Aislynn asked. "How am I to do that? I know naught of any of it."

"That's just why I accepted service to you. He's claimed you. That's a first, it is. Like as set every mouth gaping and not just mine."

"He canna' just claim me."

"Why not, pray tell? You're a serf . . . and you're Scot. And all that means is you're his . . . to do with as he will. All of you. Or as much of you as will be left once we get that velvet off of you. Come along. Hand it over. It's giving you sweats with the amount of it."

Old Rosie was right. Aislynn was sweating. She hadn't even noticed it. The freewoman wasn't right about what was causing it, though. She was sweating . . . and then she was cold. Her belly warned her. It was the dream.

"So, off with it. Now. I've a form to see fitted."

"I . . . feel ill." Aislynn panted.

"With as much cloth as you wear, it's not surprising. Here." She pulled the velvet over Aislynn's head, said more words about the misuse of good, golden drapery sashes. The moment it was gone, so was the sick feeling.

Aislynn lay on her belly, not even caring that the woman had handled her so easily.

"That's better. And you've shape to you, after all. My faith is restored."

"Faith?" Aislynn asked.

"In his eye. I was having doubts. Now, up with you. That hank of material isn't going to unwind by itself. I have to get you fitted. Then I have to get to sewing. I have to get you prepared."

"For . . . what?" Aislynn grimaced at the faltering way she asked the two words. Now, she felt weak . . . like her limbs weighed ten stone each.

"Your presentation to his household, of course! Do you listen to nothing? His Lordship wants you at his side, and he wants you dressed as befits your station. Richly. He wants all to know your position in his household. That, of course, elevates mine."

Aislynn rolled over, aching with the movement. "But, I dinna' wish this thing . . . this presentation." She said it to the carved wood that held up his canopy.

"Isn't it too bad that you're no freewoman like me, then? Come along. Up! We've got to get you readied. We haven't got all day, Well, mayhap we do, but the day's length isn't changing. If we tarry much more, I'll have to use cording to keep your bliant clasped about you."

"What bliant?"

The maid shoved a sound through her lips. "The one I've been sent to fashion for you!"

"I dinna' need a bliant. I need a shift. Of the same linen you wear."

"He's claiming you. He's giving you control of his treasury, his household, his affairs . . . and you want to be dressed thusly? You have all the wits of a faery!"

"I'm his healer. Nothing more."

"A healer? That's what you are? Well! Why didn't you say so? I've had this soreness in my feet. . . ."

Aislynn turned her head to watch as Old Rosie put the mass of velvet she'd folded on the floor and sat atop it, although it looked like more of a squat. Then she lifted a foot and started pulling at the lacing that went to her knee.

"You're na' in need of a healer. You've a need to stay away from the trencher table more."

"What?" The maid looked up from fussing with the leather strings.

"You've too much stone-weight to your frame. Your feet ache with it."

"Well! I'll have you know, I've an enticing frame. If it weren't for my many chores, I'd be gracing a different man's bed nightly, I would. There's not a man in the castle says different."

"I can believe that," Aislynn replied. "They'd be too afraid of the penalty of your tongue."

The maid put her foot down, smoothed her skirts back over her knees and looked over at Aislynn. "You're teasing with me, aren't you?"

"I am."

Rosie tipped her head to one side. "I begin to think that His Lordship has chosen well, after all." The maid huffed herself onto her knees and had to use the the bedpost to stand. "I've had the care of him since he was birthed. There's nothing he likes better than a little teasing. That must be what appeals to him."

"Lord Rhoenne? The Lion of Ramhurst? You lie. He's the death to mirth and merriment. I've heard tales."

"That's all they are, too; tales. I'll have you know that man loves a laugh. He's just had too little of it since our King David decided he'd make a grand liege, and most likely a fine husband for one of his daughters, once she has some age on her. It was different before. Much. Why, back then he actually thought the king had his well-being in mind with royal edicts and commands."

"King's edicts? Lording? You say too much and explain little."

The maid sat on the edge of the bed and swiveled her shoulder to look at Aislynn. "Well . . . I'll be telling you all, if you'll be handing over that length of yellow. I've got measurements to take."

Aislynn narrowed her eyes. "You're plenty crafty, aren't you?"

"All women are, love. It's ingrained. So. Are you going to hand it over nicely, or not?"

Summer's set. The words twinged as it went through her temples, and Aislynn put her fingers to both of them to stop the ache it caused.

"What is it? The light too bright for you? You'd best not be the sickly type. And if you are, they'd best hurry the fare. I'll fatten you up. We'll have you round and healthy just like Old Rosie in no time."

Aislynn grimaced, rubbed her fingers along her scalp, and looked at the woman with as little expression as she could manage. "I dinna' need fattening up. I need more covering. A cloak. Get me a cloak. We've work to do."

"Humph! As I've already been accounting over and over to you. A cloak isn't what you need. You need to break your fast with the food I've ordered and then you've got to unwind all that cloth from about you. Then you have to stand while I get your measure. That's what you've got to do."

"I need a cloak and a guide," Aislynn replied.

Old Rosie folded her arms. "Are you going to give me that tunic or am I going to have to wrestle it off of you? I'm warning you in advance. You'll lose."

"I have something to see to first. You dinna' understand."

"Convince me."

"You have a sickness in this castle."

Old Rosie stopped her words and her movement. "A sickness?" she asked.

"Aye."

The servant cocked her head to one side. "How do you know?"

"I'm a healer. 'Tis my business to ken such."

"We've still got to get you fed and dressed properly, before you even think about leaving. You can't go traipsing about in little more than a chemise and—"

"Are you going to find me a cloak or am I going to have to do it myself?"

Rosie planted her hands on her hips again and looked like she was going to argue. Then she opened her mouth and made it a reality. "I've prior orders to see to. I'll not allow you to leave this chamber until I've got your measurements, your selections of fabrics, and you've a full belly."

"We'll get to them as soon as I've seen to the one called summer's end . . . or perhaps it's summer's set. That one. He's ill. It's being hidden. Get me to him."

The woman blanched and seemed to waver in place, before it halted.

"What is it?" Aislynn asked.

"The youngest, Sir Richard . . . he has a—a companion . . . of sorts."

Aislynn narrowed her eyes. "A companion." She didn't ask it as a question. It wasn't one.

The woman nodded.

"And his name is—?" Aislynn waited for the maid to supply it, but she already knew what it was going to be.

"Somerset. He's the elder son of their last steward. His name is Somerset, Sean Somerset. He's Sir Richard's . . . uh—friend."

"He's ill, then?"

"Is it the plague?" Old Rosie whispered, making the sign of the cross as she did so.

Aislynn looked levelly at her. "And if it is?" she asked.

The door slammed open. Aislynn lost the ability to get more air as the mud, blood, and chainmail-covered mass that was Rhoenne Guy de Ramhurst walked in. He wasn't having the same problem with his air. He was breathing heavily, as if he'd raced the steps, which, with the rumor of his battling on the list, was more than any injured man should be attempting. The Lady of the Brook would be taking him to task over it. Aislynn was afraid she hadn't shut her mouth in order to do anything other than stare.

Both women watched as he sheathed his blade and put the scabbard tip on the floor and then he leaned on the support he made with the hilt, all of which made his right arm bulge distinctly. That's where she was looking as the black trickle of blood ran over it and dripped off his elbow.

Chapter Eight

You're injured?

Aislynn almost made the mistake of questioning it aloud as she pushed herself from the bed to approach where he stood. The length of material wound about her bent and swayed with each movement, hampering it. She didn't stop until his other hand came out to meet her abdomen.

"She doesn't appear dressed, Rosie." He was speaking to the old woman but he was watching Aislynn.

"True," the maid agreed. "She also is not fed. Serving her is a difficult chore. She's a very quarrelsome maid. You failed to warn me."

"Quarrelsome? You?"

He moved his hand from her belly and lifted a lock of her hair from where it was on her upper arm. Aislynn felt the shivers and couldn't believe they could come from the contact of just a gauntlet to her hair. She was very afraid they were obvious, and when his glance flickered to where the yellow linen was caressing her breasts, she knew the shivers were obvious. The shudder that accompanied the widening of his eyes was slight and gone the instant it occurred. But before she could marvel over that he was moving his hand to her chin and holding her face to move it, first one way and then the other. All that seemed to be happening to him was a deep frown, while her body was suffering the reaction of shivers all over. There was no shock, no anger, and no loathing . . . only shivers. Aislynn was disgusted with herself.

That, at least, was remaining hidden.

His frown deepened. "Her beauty hasn't faded, I see," he said finally. And then he dropped his hand. Aislynn watched. The wince was slight, as was every other clue he gave her, but he was in pain and hiding it. Again.

"Beauty like that takes years to diminish, my lord. Surely I taught you better than this."

He smiled slightly. "It's a shame. Truly."

Old Rosie made the sound resembling a horse again. Aislynn glanced in that direction. The freewoman still had her hands on her hips and was regarding both of them without expression. "After lamenting the lack, you now find there is a beauty from among your subjects. And all you can say is it's shameful?"

"You mistake me with Montvale. Those were his words."

Old Rosie smiled across at him, and it made her look beatific and beautiful and showed her love. Aislynn stared before she could stop it.

"What am I to do with her?"

"If you're asking me, it's obvious."

"Is it?" Rhoenne asked.

Aislynn moved her gaze back to him, knowing the mistake for what it was, but unable to prevent it. His eyes held to hers. Then he half-lidded them, shutting her out. It had the same effect. Aislynn was still rooted to the spot, trying to find her wits; and failing that, have the room open up somewhere so she could be swallowed whole by it.

"A man sees a comely wench and his wits leech right out through his ankles. I swear. Time and again I've seen it happen, and well? There you have it again. Right in front of me."

"What?" Rhoenne asked.

"You. And the lass."

"That's my answer?"

"She's a woman, my lord. You do what you always do."

"And that would be?" he prompted.

"Take her."

He turned his head away. "Take?" He croaked the word.

She shrugged. "What other idea have you in mind?"

He smiled, releasing the frown's hold on his features. "She's my healer, Rosie. That's why I returned actually. I took a hit. Not bad. Enough. I need it attended to. That is her use to me . . . her lone use."

"And the bastard?"

Rhoenne shrugged. A brightly hued color of blood slithered down the black one already drying on his arm. Aislynn glanced at it and returned to his face. He wasn't looking at her, but he knew where she looked. It was in the tightening of his jawline.

"He'll live," he answered finally.

"You let him live? Again? May the good Lord grant me patience!"

"He's my blood-kin and my heir. All know it."

"He's your curse. You're just too blind to see it."

"Rosie—"

"Don't take that tone with me, My Lord. You've a wound to see to and I've a sick man to attend."

His brow wrinkled. "You'd attend Brent?"

"Who said that? You know better. I'd let that man rot in place. I've got other men needing my touch. Ask your healer. She'll explain it."

He lowered his head then, catching Aislynn's gaze easily since she hadn't moved it yet. He didn't look re-motely wounded as his eyes narrowed, glinting blue fire through the lashes. Her own were wide. She couldn't close them. Her heart fell to the pit of her belly and started a pounding from there. She was afraid he knew all of it.

". . . leave you two to rot. That's what I should do!"

Rhoenne shook his head slightly and turned it. "What?" he asked.

Old Rosie made the snort sound again. "Other men needing attention. Men like that Somerset, although calling him manly is generous. I'll just leave the wee one here to serve you and get the castle healer to see to Richard's man."

Wee one? Serve? Aislynn couldn't believe she'd heard it correctly.

Rhoenne whirled, making the scabbard tip slide on the floor. "Somerset? You said . . . Somerset? Here? He's here?"

"Of course here. With Richard. He's the lad's companion. You recall?"

"But I had him banished. I left orders." His voice was still the same modulated tone but there was something different about it. Aislynn glanced, saw a flush starting to tint his neck and jawline, and then moved her gaze quickly away. Anything was better than standing mesmerized by the liege. Anything. She looked over at Rosie.

The old freewoman blew the air through her lips making them bulge. "'Tis true enough. You leave a lot of orders. All the time. And then you never stay to see them carried out. That is where you fail."

"My orders weren't obeyed? They were ignored?" Now, his voice was changing. There was a menace to the words and he was getting louder. He didn't look like he was weak at all. He was gripping his sword hilt and lifting the tip, too. Aislynn wondered if he noticed.

"Your orders are rarely carried out, My Lord."

"What?"

"You leave men in command that aren't fit for such."

Aislynn gasped at such an affront. Ramhurst looked grim. Everything on his features looked harsh and locked and dangerous. "Your meaning?"

Old Rosie laughed. "Don't try such antics with me, Lord Rhoenne. Save them for your enemies. And you've too many to count, most of which reside right here, beneath your roof. Treat them to your anger. Not me. I don't deserve it. I'm not the bad tidings. I'm the bearer of them."

"Where is . . . this Somerset? He isn't with Richard. I had it checked."

"East tower. Under veiling."

"Why?"

Rosie shrugged. "Ask your little healer. She knows."

"My Lord?" Aislynn looked at where she had gripped his forearm, which was exactly where he was looking, and then they locked glances. He didn't feel remotely weak.

"You shouldn't touch me. It's not safe." He was lowering his head a bit as he said it and his voice did the same thing.

Aislynn swallowed with a throat that was too tight, too dry, and too constricted to do much else with. Her next words sounded it. "He has a fever. Chills." She was going to lose the ability to put words together if she didn't move her glance. She wondered if he knew.

"Who?"

The way he said the word, put his lips into a pout. Aislynn looked there and wished she hadn't.

"Just bed the wench and get on with it! Lord! Must you tangle things worse?" It was Old Rosie.

"What tangle?"

He'd moved his gaze over her head again. Aislynn used the time to release her fingers from his arm. She was trying to make it an unnoticeable act. She didn't think she was successful.

"This tangle! You can't control your household, you

stay away too long, and then you add a wench with the beauty of this one into the mix."

"Perhaps I'll stay longer this time," he answered, and returned his gaze to Aislynn, so she'd have no question over his intent.

"I'll go see to Richard. You stay. Both of you. Bah! Men!" She was on her way to the door, when it opened inward.

And then there was so much confusion and noise it wasn't possible to be heard. Aislynn stepped atop a trunk before she was pushed over it. The bedchamber was as large as the miller's entire croft, but it wasn't designed to accommodate the volume of humanity being shoved into it. There were serfs at the forefront, laden with all manner of delicious-smelling fare. Crowding the hall behind them were knights covered with the same rain and muck the liege was, and there was more than one dog barking at the rear. Aislynn's mouth dropped open in surprise and dismay, and then Rhoenne bellowed a command to cease. The volume of it at such a close distance made her ears ring in earnest.

Everything stilled. Immediately. He had no right to think his commands ignored, she decided. Aislynn sucked in a breath.

"Is there a Richard Ramhurst among you?" It felt like she was shouting it. She hoped it was just the absolute silence the Ramhurst had ordered into being.

A hand went up. It belonged to a very slender lad with lace adorning the end of the sleeve. He didn't bear much resemblance to the laird. As he moved further into the throng, it didn't look like he bore any at all.

"You're treating the fever wrong," she told him. "You must use a paste made of dried calendula flower and use mead for your liquid. As dark with hops as you can get it. And as thick! You are to smear this on the chest. If you canna' find calendula, use hops alone. And you are na' to keep him covered! You ken?"

"Aye."

"When he sweats, he must be uncovered and allowed to cool. *Nae!* He must be forced to cool! Then you can cover him. See to it!"

She watched him start moving away. He was almost to the hall when she was shouting again.

"You there!" She was pointing at the serfs, threaded amongst the room. "You are to join yourselves into groups. Four strong. You are to get every *auld* rush from this keep. Every moldy one! Start at the top floor and sweep downward. This saves effort and time. Rosie?"

"Aye?" the woman yelled.

"Who would see to this?"

"Eldine," came the answer.

"Eldine?"

A hand went up. It needed washed, but the lack of calluses was easy to see. "See that water is boiled. Buckets of it. I wish to see every chamber scrubbed and washed. You are to start with Lord Brent's. I wish the shutters opened and the chambers aired as they dry. I will be inspecting. You ken?"

There wasn't the same response to this order. There was grumbling happening. Aislynn looked at Rhoenne, since standing on the trunk had placed her slightly above him. He nodded. And then he winked. Her knees wobbled, making a rattling sound of the trunk lid. She had to look away. He had too much power to affect her. No, that wasn't true. It was her fault. She *gave* him too much power.

"You fail in this and you'll answer to your liege! Now, do you ken?" She announced it as loudly as she could and every bit of argument stopped. There was the sound of shuffling. She moved her attention to the next problem.

"And this? What is all of this? Why are the contents of

the *panetrie* being hoisted to the laird's bedchamber? Take it back. All of it! Put the stews back on the fire and the breads back in the larder!" Aislynn felt the dismay in the room. She didn't care. She was discovering that having control of his household required wielding more power than she'd ever experienced. That was heady.

She watched as the knights went into a single file to press themselves to one side or the other to make room as the array of platters filed back out. Then she found her servant. "Rosie? You are to follow them and see that my orders are followed. They're na' to slacken."

The old woman nodded. Then she was clapping her hands behind them in a sharp cadence guaranteed to get results. Aislynn waited until they'd disappeared. Then she returned her attention to the rest of the room.

"And you! Montvale!"

He was of a large enough size, he stood out easily. He also had his hauberk shoved onto his shoulders, showing the thick thatch of brown hair she'd noted last night. He cleared his throat.

"Why must you also enjoin here? And bring hounds with you?"

"These are king's men, lady. Not hounds."

There was some laughter at his banter. Aislynn caught her own smile before it showed. "Send someone to see to the dogs. They belong in the stables or at the hearth. They do not belong at the heels of king's men."

She didn't know how he did it, but with a wave of his hand, the barking stopped as did the last of the grumbling. It was getting easier to breathe, too.

"Now, what is it you want?" she asked.

"The same thing they always want. Food, shelter, horses. Gold. Mostly gold, I admit. It's always the same with a royal command."

"Na' the king's men! You. And is there *nae* great room for receiving king's men in this keep?"

"Aye. That there is."

"Then see them escorted back to there."

He nodded. She didn't know how he commanded that, either, but he was especially good at it. Aislynn watched as the scarlet-draped men moved away.

"You are still here, Sir Montvale," she remarked.

He was grinning at her. "I have need of a woman, or three, again. Can you order that into being, as well?"

"Montvale." It was Rhoenne. He wasn't amused, if the inflection he gave the name was any indication.

"My Liege?"

"See to His Majesty's edict. Bear word to me."

"I'm actually here for another reason."

"Name it and have done, then."

It was Aislynn answering. Rhoenne's lips were twitching. She clapped a hand to her mouth. Montvale turned back to her and tipped his head slightly. He was openly grinning now. Aislynn moved her hand away.

"Well?" she continued.

"I've had a change of heart, Rhoenne. This wench of yours possesses a sharp voice, she issues orders like a wife, and she has a strange sense of what to do with drapery. She doesn't place it at a window, she winds it about herself. I am well rid of her, I think."

Aislynn glared at him. Rhoenne filled the gap with words that made her pinken.

"I own myself well-satisfied with her. My home was in need of a strong hand to be wielded in my absence. I didn't realize the extent of it until now. She did well."

I'll reserve judgment, I think."

"You dare insult her?"

Aislynn heard the sound of steel as Rhoenne pulled on his sword. Her eyes went wide.

"Insult? Nay. Only lick my wounds that I didn't see her first. I could have used her services. This reminds me. She needs to see to you."

Aislynn was silent. Rhoenne filled it with a bellow of the knight's name.

"Not in that way! You believe me capable of no other thought save those of the flesh? I'll address my words to yon lass. She has a more generous nature, she isn't crazed with pain, and I doubt she can heft a sword against me."

"She has no need. I'm her sword arm."

Aislynn saw the blade come between where she was perched and Sir Montvale. She couldn't take her eyes from it. It looked wicked . . . long and well-honed to a razor-sharpness that glinted in the sunlight. She forced her vision from the seductive weapon to Montvale. He was pale, and he was leaning back, but he hadn't moved. He was addressing his words to her.

"This man you call laird took a nasty blow. He wasn't to blame. He fought well. He's injured. This is what I came to speak of. He needs it seen to. It is much worse than he's stating . . . as usual."

Aislynn jerked her head over, following the line of the sword to Rhoenne's hand and from there to his closed expression. There wasn't the slightest tremble to his frame to betray anything.

"Badly?" she asked.

"A scratch." He hadn't moved his gaze from his knight.

"It was from a battle-ax," Montvale continued.

Aislynn gasped. Then she was off the trunk and at Rhoenne's side. She didn't need the knight's words to know the truth. There was a steady drip of blood falling from Rhoenne's arm, making a splash as it landed near his boot.

"Rhoenne?" she whispered. "Release him. Now."

His entire frame trembled and the blade with it. She

heard Montvale's sigh of relief as the sword lowered until it was scraping the stone floor.

"You'll rue this, Montvale," Rhoenne said, and it was spoken between clenched teeth.

"Oh, I think not. She has the frame of a goddess and the features of Aphrodite. Further, she has an iron fist. You seem to need one. I grant her free use of it. Especially on your head. All-in-all, I feel most satisfied. I don't have to stay and force you to your own healing. I already had that pleasure last eve. You really should take more care of your flesh, My Liege. Then again, it does keep you in an unclothed state while she does her magic on you. An enviable state. I'll bar the door as I leave."

Rhoenne hadn't said a word through the knight's banter. Montvale was at the door and shoving things with his boot.

"Should you still wish to kill me on the list over this, I shall grant the deed was worth it. Aislynn." He moved his glance to her, nodded, and closed the door behind him.

Chapter Nine

"Take off your armor."

"Nay."

Aislynn's eyes flared but she had it under control before he saw it. "Take off your chain. Now," she repeated.

"Nay."

"Take off this chainmail that you wear. And then we'll see to getting your shirt from you as well. I grow tired of speaking this."

"I'm not one of these serfs that you order about so easily."

"True. You are their lord. I am still telling you to take off your clothing, and do it a sight quicker than you are at present."

"Nay," he replied. And then he folded his arms. That movement flattened the broad flesh and muscle of his forearms against his belly, as well as made the blood find further paths to flow down. Aislynn watched as a wash of red colored the linked chains at his belly, slowly filling holes as it moved ever-downward.

"You have an injury. I would see to it."

"'Tis but a scratch," he replied.

"I am your healer. I canna' heal what I canna' see."

"And I still say nay."

"There are no observers to your pain," Aislynn pointed out.

He grimaced. "'Tis for that reason I keep all my clothing on my frame. And all of that drapery on yours."

Aislynn matched his expression. "You're impossible! You have pain and you won't allow me to see to it?"

"I have pain, true. But it is of such a nature, that you canna' be allowed to see to it. Or attend to it."

Aislynn took a step toward him. "You make *nae* sense."

He snorted, and then he responded with such a noticeable step backward, it was as if he were marching it.

"Men! You hide what I must see to do my work and then thwart me at every turn. Cease this and hand me that chain."

"You order others easily, I notice."

"When they require such. And it was by your own tongue it is so. Dinna' you grant me the power of your household?"

He nodded.

"Then hand me your chain. Now."

He shook his head.

"Must I fetch that Sir Montvale knight in order to make you?"

He tipped his head. Aislynn caught the slightest tilt to his mouth before it stopped. "Montvale would like that. He knows I'm too weak to give a full showing."

"What are you talking of now?"

"Montvale would take your offer. He would force me. He wouldn't win without much fight. I'm already depleted so he would win."

"All of which is words while you bleed! Give me your mail." Her voice was rising. She couldn't prevent it.

"'Tis but a scratch."

He was backing from her as he said it, and that put him toward the bed. Aislynn's mouth set.

"With you, My Laird, a scratch could be death. I dinna' trust your word."

"What?" Now it was his turn to stare as his eyes widened a moment. Then he had the reaction covered over.

"I dinna' trust you."

"Men have died by my hand for less," he answered, and his teeth were set.

"I am *nae* man. Now hand over your mail. Now."

He'd reached the edge of his bed and had bumped away slightly with the collision as he got there. It wasn't due to her chasing him, although it probably looked that way. It was due to the speed with which he was backing from her. Aislynn held out her hand, wriggled her fingers, and waited.

Rhoenne looked at the floor. He looked at the wall to his right. He looked back at the floor again. Then it was the ceiling, then the window to his other side, then it was over her head. Aislynn watched it. There was the most interesting pinkish flush rising from the edge of his hauberk to stain his lower jaw, too. He couldn't hide it. He was luckless with the sparse way with which he grew a beard, she decided. A beard would have hidden things like a man's blush.

Then he was glaring at her, his nostrils were flaring with it, but he was unclasping his arms and reaching for the hood made of linked chain. The hauberk went into her outstretched hand, and Aislynn nearly dropped it with the weight. She forced her arm to stay where it was but brought the other hand to help. He didn't move his eyes from hers as he lifted his injured arm, unclasping hooks from beneath it and showing more dark wetness on his side. She couldn't prevent the gasp as he yanked the chain forward and over his head.

The chain shirt fell the moment it went into her hands, and tore two of her fingernails as it did so. Both of them heard the links as it fell to the floor. It was impossible not to in the dead silence. It was only possible to hear her blood as it raced through her ears.

"Chain doesn't take well to such treatment," he said with a soft tone, unlike any he'd used thus far.

"I dinna' realize the weight of such armor. How is it possible to wear it as if it weighed naught?"

His mouth cocked into a half-smile with that. Aislynn had to clamp her teeth shut to keep from answering it.

"Because I am not a half-ling such as yourself."

Half-ling? She was glaring now. "Give me the tunic. Dinna' take such time over it, either. Now." She ignored the mound of bloodied mail at her feet, and stepped over it, placing her within arm-reach of him. The proximity was giving her trouble as a shiver raced her frame, centering right where she least wanted it—at each breast peak. He sensed it, too, if the increase in his breathing was any indication.

"This is not a good time . . . for this," he said.

"I'm your healer. You granted it."

"True," he replied. And then he crossed his arms again, only this time, the seepage of blood was quicker and darker and faster as it spread throughout the quilted cloth he was wearing. Aislynn watched it and set her jaw.

"Must I wait for you to faint of weakness again, a-fore I get you to obey me? Is that what it takes with you?"

"Obey?" He was as surprised to hear the word as he was to say it. It sounded in his voice. Aislynn couldn't stop the smile.

"Aye. Obey. You are to obey me. I'm your healer. I heal. If you dinna' obey me, you will na' heal. Simple. Now, cease this and give over the tunic."

Sunlight was piercing through the open window, sending beams to highlight him in slices of toned and tanned flesh. It was also glinting on the dark blood as it reached the bottom of his tunic and started dripping. Aislynn glanced there and her heart caught. Such a quantity was going to kill him!

"We haven't much time, My Laird. You'll bleed to death! And na' allow me to heal it? Now, cease this and take the tunic from your body or I'll call for Montvale to help me slice it from you! Now!"

"You continually call me this title—this laird. This has a meaning?"

"Laird. My term for lord. Now give me the tunic. Now." She stepped closer, and he actually arched away from her, bowing himself backward over his bed. He wasn't flushing anymore, either. He was pale. And he was trembling, and he was shiny with a filming of sweat, or the sunlight was lying as it embraced what flesh he was allowing her to see.

"This is not happening. I cannot . . . *will not* allow it," he panted the words.

Aislynn was right behind him, leaning forward, although the movement placed her at his chest level.

"You procured my services. You."

He gulped. She actually heard it. Aislynn had to catch the smile. Then she was reaching out with a hand and pressing it against his belly, compelling him down onto the bed. That way, maybe she could get atop him and force him to let her see the extent of his injury. All that happened was her fingers started tingling.

Aislynn pressed harder, the roping of muscles against her fingertips hardened, the thighs she was pressing against did the same thing, and not much else. Then there was something else, and her eyes flew to his with concern as heat and pressure and size grew against the region just below her breasts.

"Now do you see why you mustn't touch me?" he asked, pushing the words through clenched teeth.

She nodded.

"Then step away."

"I'm . . . your healer, My Laird," she whispered.

"I know," he replied.

"And you're injured."

"'Tis but a scratch," he replied.

The mass against her ribcage twinged, startling her. Aislynn gasped and pulled away, lifting her hands and everything else from him. She backed. He was breathing hard, he was in an arch that was impossible to imagine if she hadn't seen it, and he was in an all-out sweat. He was also very red along the collar of his tunic and everywhere else she could see. And he was very desirous of intimacy with her. Very.

Aislynn put both hands to her cheeks to stop the amazement, shock, and the response her body was experiencing. Every part of her felt awake and alert and sensitive . . . and full of craving. She didn't even know what it was she craved. She just knew it was a vicious want, almost too deep to fight. She curled her hands into knots, digging her nails into her palms at the same time, and wondered if it was the same for him. And he had an injury! She turned sideways to him and faced the window as if that aperture had answers.

"You should send the castle healer to me. I'll await him."

For a man suffering as she was, it didn't sound in his voice, she decided. "He sees to Somerset," she whispered. "By my orders."

"Then I'll wait."

"You wait and you'll die. You ken this."

He sighed heavily. "I keep telling you it's but a scratch. It's true. A scratch. Maybe less."

"Show me. Dinna' tell me. Show it."

Another heavy sigh. Then she heard the wood support of his bed creak. She still didn't look. It was all she could do to control her own body, preparing it to look. He was bound to have a gash, cleaving skin wide open, and she was feeling a sensation that had to be lust, or something close to it? What sickness was this? What demons have this much power?

There was a rustling. Aislynn closed her eyes tightly to it and tried to stop the sensation touching him had caused her. How much worse was it going to be when she had to touch bare flesh? She swallowed. She was the Lady of the Brook! She was confident. She wasn't interested in anything other than the furtherance of her experiments with herbs, spices, and mixtures. She didn't care about any man. Especially not this man. The lusts of the flesh were for her sister, Meghan, or other creatures too weak to fight it. Aislynn wasn't the same. She was different. She was—

He spoke, interrupting her thoughts. "There. Is this what you wished to see?"

She turned her head and the entire world shifted. The sunlight dappling the room carried too much warmth as her body broke out in a sweat to rival any of his. And her heart was lurching so heavily, she thought it might leap from her breast. Aislynn nearly put her hands there to halt it.

The Norman-bred laird was standing; he had a wadded, blood-filled piece of material clenched in his hands and held at his hip-line, hiding that portion of himself; he had sunlight caressing every fluid speck of flesh from the width of his shoulders, the roped texture of his arms . . . down to the wedge shape that led to his hips. And there was only a residue of dried blood on him.

"Lift your arm," she said.

He moved his right arm, lifting it above his head, his face twinging a bit with the effort, since there was severe bruising all along the side. That, and a long scratch. Nothing else. And it didn't break skin.

Aislynn crossed to him and reached out to see, before realizing her mistake. Her fingers weren't flesh and tissue and bone where they touched. They were sparks of sensation. She spread them wonderingly about his skin, shocking herself with the intensity of the tremor that ran her, and seemed to go from her right into him. She raised her eyes to his.

"It's a scratch," she whispered.

He didn't have one expression on his features. Anywhere. She'd never seen such a blank look. "I said as much," he replied.

"How is such a thing possible?"

"Goat bladder. Filled with blood. Prepared early this morn."

"Goat bladder," she replied. It wasn't asked as a question because it wasn't one. She wasn't comprehending much of what he said. Her fingers had given way to her entire hand, and she had both palms splayed open at his side . . . then one at his back, while the other one trilled along the denting and hills of his abdomen, learning the feel as it sucked in and out with his breathing.

"I had it tied . . . inside my tunic. Damn you for seeing."

"Tied," she repeated.

"Aye. My brother wasn't strong enough for his own challenge."

"Challenge?"

He was speaking words, his chest was rising and falling with it, and her hands were learning what that felt like. "Aye . . . and he has a terrible aim, too."

"He does?"

Aislynn wasn't listening. She didn't want the words to stop, or the breath to cease grazing her nose and lashes and cheeks. And she didn't wish to move away from the intricate pulsing of the veins along his arms and the sides of his throat. It felt as wondrous as it looked, and her fingers followed the pulsing ribbons to his chin, using it as the hand-hold to turn his head to her.

"You shouldn't touch me," he said. "Not like this. Not now."

"I ken as much," she replied.

"I made a vow."

"Why?" she whispered.

"Blast you, lass. May you rot . . . with the rest of your kind."

He said more, curses all of it, but he had her gripped against him, holding her drapery-wrapped form easily with just the one arm, and then he was nuzzling his nose along her hairline, whispering words of depth and strength as he went.

"I beg you to stay away . . . and you taunt. You tease. I tell you there is no reason for worry, and you insist. I beseech you to leave and you stay. I rail at you and you rail back. I am not made of iron."

Aislynn giggled. *"Nae.* 'Tis most definitely . . . na' iron," she replied.

There was a sparkle deep in the eye he tilted toward her. "You are a strange healer, Aislynn lass," he remarked.

"Aye."

"Very strange." Then he closed his eyes and lowered his lips to hers.

Aislynn was already pressed everywhere to him. It was impossible to get closer yet she tried, wrapping her arms about his neck for leverage and sliding her hips against his leg. Then she had her knees parted and her thighs pressed against one of his. She couldn't open her legs far enough to wrap around him. The volume of material precluded it.

It didn't seem to matter. The breathing at her nose deepened, alternately warming and cooling. Hands cupped her thighs, lifting her and pressing her against the throbbing lump of him, and holding her there while he shuddered, until it grew to a tremor that rattled the bedstead beside them with the strength of it. Then he was pulling away and looking at her.

Severe. His eyes were deep and ice-water blue, and they

were severe and tormented and sad. Aislynn met his gaze and felt her own eyes watering up at what she saw there.

"I have made a vow, half-ling," he whispered.

She held her breath. She didn't dare move.

"No women birthed a male Ramhurst without giving her life for his. I'll not tempt fate. I'll not kill a woman with my seed. Never again."

"Fate is there . . . to be tested," she returned.

"I'm not willing to risk it. Not now. Not you. You . . . ken?"

He used the Scot word. Aislynn didn't show that she'd heard.

"I'm not made of iron. I'm merely a man, but I'm a strong man. I have to be. I have to be strong enough to overcome temptation. Even the temptation of you in my arms. Right here. Right now. You understand?"

He was getting difficult to see with the amount of moisture her eyes were cursing her with. His face got even stonier as he watched.

"The cost . . . is too high, lass."

His hands eased their grip on her buttocks, and that lowered her back to the floor. It didn't matter. The floor had the consistency of mist beneath her. Aislynn wavered and actually wondered if her own legs were going to support her. It was bad enough being rejected. It was worse to know she'd forced the issue and how much he fought it.

She was free. She was cold. She had to rub her own arms for warmth the further she got from him and she just kept backing until she reached the wall.

"And now you know what only Montvale knows. I am not pious. I'm as lusty as any man. But I can't allow a joining between us. Ever."

She nodded. She didn't have a voice. If she tried using it, it was going to crack and then he'd have to prove that he was strong enough for the both of him. But at least he knew what he was fighting! Aislynn frowned at her own entwined hands and wondered why she couldn't feel them. That was strange.

"I wouldn't wish this morn bandied about," he said, with little inflection to the words.

Neither would she! She was close to crying with the shame.

She heard rustling of cloth, and clanging of links that she suspected were the chainmail of his armor. It would need to be rinsed. He probably had a squire for such things. She made herself think of mundane things. That was better than thinking he had to caution her not to say anything! Who was she to speak of this rejection to? *Auld* Rosie? Montvale?

"I would not want it thought that my brother has no aim, nor skill."

"What?"

She lifted her head and looked across at him.

He was pulling down a light blue tunic, covering over the span of lightly tanned and muscled flesh her fingers immediately itched to touch again. Aislynn swiped her thumbs along them, running the pads together to mute the sensation. It didn't work. This Rhoenne was more man than she'd ever come across, he was mystifying, and he was forbidden. All dangerous. All tempting.

"Brent. He enjoins the king's men. My sovereign requires men, supplies, gold. Were you not listening to Montvale's whinings?"

She shook her head, more to clear it than an answer.

He chuckled. "Don't let him know of it. He fancies himself an orator of great skill. He thinks his voice gathers women like bee to pollen. I wish him well of it."

"What?" Aislynn asked again. He made no sense. The entire morn had the same problem, and if she was going to stifle the reaction that just looking at him was causing her, it wouldn't be in her best instinct to continue doing it. She looked away. The window was safer.

"Brent and his men. They enjoin King David. I would not wish it spoken that my brother gave as poorly on the list as he did this morn. That was the reason for my goat bladder trick."

"What?" she asked again.

"He's my heir. He must have the respect that is his due."

"What if he's na' worthy of it?"

He sighed. She heard more clanking and movement. He was probably donning more of his attire, perhaps boots and a belt, and when she glanced that way, found it to be true, although he'd added an open vest atop his clean tunic. He hadn't tied the openings of any of it together yet, either. That was a view she didn't need to add to her musings, she decided.

"Find yourself something more suitable to wear. This day. I will not have you defined and covered with so little."

Little? Aislynn's lip quirked and she fought the instant feeling that had nothing to do with being rejected. He was having the same problem! He just hid it better. Much better. She was wearing more material than the bed.

"That's why I assigned Rosie to you. Fashion something. Something of power and authority. Something worthy of your position in my household." He was frowning again as he said it. Her minute glance told her of it. He didn't catch her at it as her eyes skittered away the moment he looked like he was moving his glance toward her.

"My position?"

"I don't speak lightly. You have full control of my household. I grant you the buttery, the treasury, and the armory. Speak with Richard of the holdings. He's my steward. You'll have all you require."

"I canna' ask it of you?" she asked.

"I'll not be available for such."

"Where . . . will you be?" And curse the impulse that made her ask that, with such a catch midway through it! Aislynn bit her own tongue, but it was too late. It was already voiced.

"I will be . . . wherever you are not. 'Tis safest. For both our sakes. When I see you next, be covered. You ken?"

The door was opening. He'd used the Scot word again, making her wonder if he even noted it. He wasn't waiting for her reply, either. He was slamming the door with a force that rattled the hinges, showing the angered emotion he was hiding. Aislynn regarded it for a long moment.

He was a master of self-discipline. That was obvious. He was strong; inside and out. He was also mystifying. Intriguing. Dangerous. Enticing. Fascinating. Bewitching. Male. . . .

So much male.

Chapter Ten

The woods had always had a certain fascination for Aislynn. Especially in the early morn with dew coating every surface and the sun just peeking through branches and leaves and shrubs.

"You go much farther and we'll need a guard."

She looked over her shoulder at Old Rosie. The woman was complaining more for the tiredness due to walking as far as Aislynn made her, since she carried so much excess weight. They hadn't gone far at all. Why, if she had enough height she'd still be able to pick out the chamber window that belonged to her now. Just her, since Rhoenne Guy de Ramhurst rarely graced his keep with his presence, and when he did so, he slept elsewhere, if he slept at all.

Aislynn mused about it as she went in deeper, sniffing at the fresh loam and earth smell, as well as startling several unseen things into a hasty flight from her, dusting her with dew. Such a thing as giving over the liege's bedchamber to a Scot healer was talked of but she didn't muse over it. She couldn't stop the whispers. She didn't actually care. She'd been faced with them her entire life.

"Aislynn!"

"Over here." She spoke more to the ground, since she'd

spied sprigs of the calendula flowers she'd been searching for. Tyneburn hadn't much of an herb garden, but she was gradually changing that. It was probably a good thing Rhoenne wasn't in his chamber. He'd not know of the little potted plants she lined his walls with, moving them to the window for sun, and then protecting them from the night cold until they sprouted.

"Every morn . . . off at the first sight of dawn, traipsing through woods in search of dirt. Rain or not. You're the strangest wench—Thanks Be to The Lord! There you are! Off by yourself and unaware of the dangers—"

"Hush!"

Aislynn lifted a hand, stopping the woman's incessant complaints. Strains of a voice touched her ear, making everything come to complete and total focus. She knew what the sound was instantly. She almost knew the location.

"I dinna' hear aught." The old woman said it as she squatted down in the long grass beside Aislynn.

"You have to be silent in order to hear anything, Rosie," Aislynn replied.

"Is this another of your lectures about the healing powers of silence?"

Aislynn grinned and ducked her head. She'd been at the castle a little over a fortnight. The entire keep smelled and looked so much cleaner it was hard to believe it the same dark, dingy castle it had been. It wasn't an easy task to keep it that way. She spent all day visiting every floor, checking for progress, and doing what Rosie called lecturing at anyone that slackened.

"Silence has its own beauty."

Old Rosie blew a snort over her lips.

"And you promised to listen for it more."

"Verra well. I'll listen."

Aislynn smiled slightly at the woman's use of Scot dialect. She did it often anymore. "Good. Stay here and practice. Pluck these. Keep the soil about the roots to stay the bruising. We need them for the castle garden."

"You dinna' need to tell me the method of pulling your weeds. I've been at your side every moment—and just where is it you are off to?"

The last was addressed to Aislynn's back as she was already moving toward the sound. She'd heard him holler. She'd heard his groan. She'd known when he was at the hall because she heard him. She had the depth and strength of his voice memorized. She'd never heard it lifted in song. The perfect pitch of it was impressive. Aislynn ducked beneath low-hanging tree limbs, parted heavy bushes, and snagged her skirts more than once on branches until she got close enough. The last steps were more a crawl of motion accomplished on her knees.

She was grateful for that stance as Rhoenne came into view. He was doing a series of movements against an invisible foe and he was using his sword as an extension of his arm for each motion. Aislynn caught her breath. Deep, throbbing notes were coming from his throat, accompanying the sword as it went above his head, then swung about in several melodic arcs of movement, before being planted into the ground, anchoring his leap to the other side.

She'd never seen anything to compare it to.

He was using words she didn't recognize, putting them into a cadence and volume that matched each of his thrusts. He hadn't been lying, either. He was definitely a troubadour.

He was also covered in sweat, making the dull gray tunic he wore cling to every bit of him. Aislynn could see the dark streaks of moisture as they reached the tan leggings he wore, as well. It wasn't surprising. If she were doing the motion he was while trying to swing the sword, she'd have expired of perspiration well before now. Aislynn clasped her hands and watched.

Rhoenne had reached a crescendo of sorts in his sonnet. He was still giving each note sound, but it was harsher when it came, more intense, and in greater volume. He was also lacing every bit of voice with a movement. First to plant his sword before him, the next time following a somersault of motion, landing on his feet in front of his sword. That was when the second word was given voice. The third came after he'd pulled his sword from the ground behind and brought it over his head to stick it in the ground again.

The second aerial was a cartwheel of sorts, using the hilt for stability. The moment his feet landed he was giving voice to another note. Then he was bringing his sword over his head, planting it again. This time he leapt it; brought it from between his legs; impaled it in the ground again. Catapulting his body over it. Landing. All orchestrated with his voice. And he was doing it again.

Aislynn forgot stealth. She forgot how to breathe. She was on her feet and walking toward him before he finished. She knew he was, too. It sounded in the last melancholic note as it died away. That was when he reached both hands for his hilt, locked them on it, and looked up at her.

He was breathing hard, moving the mass of muscle that was his chest up and down with huge gulps of air. Nothing else on him was moving. He didn't even appear to be blinking. Aislynn stopped when she got within an arm's length of him and looked up.

"That . . . was beautiful," she said with the softest voice she could give it. Anything else felt sacrilegious.

"You should not be here," he replied.

"Why na'? Is your meadow na' part of your domain?"

He nodded.

"And are we na' well within your borders?"

He nodded again.

"And . . . dinna' you gift me with care of all things?"

He didn't nod. He didn't say anything. He just stood there, sweating and breathing hard and letting the dawn light caress all of it right in front of her. Aislynn took a half step closer.

"Especially . . . this frame of yours?"

A tremor scored through the man in front of her. Aislynn didn't move. She was close enough she could feel the heat coming from him, as well as sense each breath as it touched her skin the moment it left his.

"You . . . have a grand voice, My . . . Laird."

He grunted in reply.

"But I dinna' understand the words. What is it you sing?"

"Frankish words. From Normandy," he replied.

"Of battle?"

He lifted one eyebrow slightly. It made an immense difference in the statue-like stiffness he'd been in. Aislynn smiled and kept it in place until his mouth softened to return it. He was still breathing hard, although the blond hair wasn't plastered to his head with as much moisture as before.

"Or . . . was it a sonnet of something else?" she whispered and tipped her head just slightly to one side.

He gulped. At least, that was what her senses put into place for her eyes to see. She didn't hear it. There was the greatest buzz in her ears, melding the sunlight of the dawn with the smell of green and the bottomless depth of clear-water blue eyes she was looking into. Looking deep. Making her entire body twinge with a lurch that had nothing melodic or graceful about it.

And then there was the sound of a great herd of beasts coming through the trees beside them, but it was in actuality Sir Montvale, breaking through branches. He was swinging his sword to clear brush and had his helm held in the crook of his free arm, and speaking loudly the entire time.

"There you are, My Liege! Upsetting all manner of life

with the abrasive tones you insist on yelling. And leaving your knights in your dust. Oh. I see you've found the healer. Good. Put her to use."

Aislynn didn't hear all of it and Rhoenne was reacting like he'd just been awakened. She watched as he narrowed his eyes for a moment before shaking his head and then stepping back from her. Two full steps.

"What?" He turned his head to ask it. Aislynn watched him do it.

"The Celt healer. You found her. Or perhaps it was she finding you. Whichever the way or why of it, you should put her to good use."

"What?" Rhoenne repeated.

"Her skills."

"On what?"

The knight snorted. "You, of course. I didn't think her skills available to others, although I'd not be amiss if she would—"

"Montvale." Rhoenne interrupted him.

"My Liege?"

"What are you doing here?"

"Searching for you. Finding you. And not for the first time, either. How was I to know you hadn't been knocked senseless? Or worse?"

"Harold," Rhoenne replied, with a slight warning note to the name. The other man seemed oblivious to it.

"I've been calling for you. I got no answer. Again. For all I knew you'd been beset by these bloody heathens—I mean . . . by your loyal subjects. How was I to know you were standing mesmerized into place by your healer? Well?"

"Harold." This time the name was said from between his teeth, if the sound of it was any indication.

"My Liege?" the knight replied.

"No one told you to search for me."

"Well, someone had to do it. It fell to me. I was the bravest."

"What?"

"Oh, very well. I confess. I lost the coin toss."

Rhoenne filled his chest with air and blew it out before he answered. Aislynn didn't move her eyes from the sight. She didn't know what his knight, Harold, was doing.

"So? Have you spoken to her of it, yet?"

"Of what?"

"You. Your inattention. And what it might cost."

Rhoenne wouldn't meet her eyes. Aislynn looked for that very thing. He was focusing on something above her head, and if she wasn't mistaken there was a slight flush on both cheeks as he sucked in on them.

"If there's a cost this morn, I'm very afraid it's coming from your knight portion, Sir Montvale," he finally said.

Harold snorted. "Always the same, aren't you, My Liege?"

"What inattention?" Aislynn asked, moving closer to where Rhoenne stood. If she wasn't mistaken, he caught at a breath and waited.

"My vassal . . . overstates things he shouldn't note or put into words," he replied. He still wasn't looking down at her.

"What things?" she continued.

Harold answered her. "Him. Losing thought. If I hadn't put my sword into play when I did, he'd have less blond locks to frame his head. Actually, I understate that. He'd not have much of a head left to hang blond locks from."

"Harold," Rhoenne said.

"You know it for truth. And we were in luck it was a friendly sword."

"How can a sword . . . be friendly?" Aislynn moved her gaze down and back up the wicked-looking length of his blade, and from there to the rawhide cross-hatching of his tunic fastening, and tried to make him meet her gaze.

"We were at practice. I saved him."

"Why?" she asked.

His knight blew out the sigh. "Why? Because that is what a vassal does, of course. Saves his lord. Aside from which, I've no desire to swear fealty to his brother and heir, Brent. You met him. Do you wish him as liege?"

"I dinna' mean that," Aislynn replied.

"That alone is reason enough to keep Rhoenne Guy de Ramhurst's head from being cleaved off his shoulders. I should think it clear."

"I meant . . . why was there a need?"

Rhoenne turned his head to look at his man. Since they were taller than her, she couldn't see the exchange of glances or what it meant. It was Rhoenne finally answering her, though.

"There's no need. There never was. Sir Montvale puts things into words that didn't happen and then he overstates. He does it oft. You'll learn that of him. If I allow him any time in your presence."

He looked down at her once through his speech, focusing somewhere on her lips, and then he moved his gaze again. Aislynn watched him do it and forced the shivers away. Then, he licked his lower lip. The reaction rocked her, turned her insides to fluff, her heart to an inferno, and the sting of sensation to her head made her eyes widen and her mouth drop open with shock. She was eternally grateful he wasn't looking. She didn't know what was wrong with her but she didn't want anyone else knowing of it.

"Come, Harold. We've interrupted Aislynn's morn enough with nothing but words. She has little time for nonsense. I know I don't. We've a meeting at Leiston. The blacksmith there believes he should get a like settlement to the miller over his loss of . . . services." Aislynn moved her eyes to his. He was looking for it. "You didn't tell me you were betrothed to him," he said.

"I wasn't," she replied.

He shrugged. "It wouldn't matter, little one. You already know that. A Ramhurst stole you. He'll accept what I offer. I already paid the miller handsomely. Your family didn't quarrel it. That was odd."

"I . . . was a foundling, my lord," she whispered. "Left on their stoop one eve. They may consider themselves in luck that I brought in gold."

He grunted. "Well . . . that explains their lack of sorrow. That, and the fact that they still have another daughter to offer his suit and be accepted."

"Donald is to wed with Meghan?"

"With what Rhoenne agrees to pay, that blacksmith could wed a queen."

"Harold!"

"What? I just want the foundling to know the worth you put to her services."

"She . . . already knows."

He moved his gaze directly to her and Aislynn was caught. Totally. Perfectly. She'd given love too slight of meaning, she realized, as the buzzing intensified and cut off sound. His gaze seemed to speak to her . . . fully. Totally. Heating her to an intensity that matched a flame center and spreading the warmth throughout her entire body. There wasn't any way to hide it. There wasn't anything she could do. There was just her and him, and eyes of such beauty and depth, the gods were probably weeping in envy.

". . . and he asks why I beg her service with this."

Harold Montvale's words were sarcastic and slowly spoken and made Rhoenne blink, breaking the intangible link she'd had with him.

"When all and sundry can see the problem."

"What?" Rhoenne turned his head and asked.

"You've a meeting to attend with men longing to stick blades, lances, and arrows into you, and what happens?"

"Nothing. Nothing will happen, either. They'll not harm me."

"Don't turn your back too quickly, then."

Rhoenne sighed heavily. "I believe a man to be good at his word and honorable. Unless and until he proves himself otherwise."

"And that is why you need me at your side, and the healer out of your thoughts. Such things lead to inattention."

"Harold!"

"Forgive me, My Liege. I have a loose tongue. You'll just have to take the amount from my portion. It will have been worth it. Trust me."

"What . . . did you just say?" Aislynn asked.

"Him. And you. Together. And his vow. The cost of it. I'll need a double portion this quarter to keep his head atop his shoulders and any Celt lance from piercing flesh. That's what I'm going to need. And mayhap another set of eyes. And ears. Can you arrange all of this?"

"I need another bit of silence away from your words. This is what I most need. That, and mayhap another swim in the loch," Rhoenne answered.

Harold nodded. "Agreed. Bid your lady *adieu*. I'll await yonder." He spun on the last word and walked from them, stopping when he got to the brush he'd cut an opening through and just stood there, waiting.

"My . . . Laird?" Aislynn whispered, stopping Rhoenne from moving. She had her breath already held for the locking of their gaze again. She didn't get it. He focused on her nose again.

"You suffer this . . . inattention? As he says?"

She watched him swallow. He didn't answer.

"Too?" Aislynn finished.

His eyes widened and he moved them to hers. That was

too much impact. Her breath fled her, taking her senses with it and making everything overly focused again. It was his knight returning for him and forcing him away. She watched it and all she was aware of was the rush of blood through her pulse, heating everywhere through her and making her long to burst into song.

"Old Rosie!"

The woman was snoring, comfortably propped against a tree with an apron full of calendula plants, still rooted with soil clinging to them. Aislynn smiled as she saw her. She knew exactly what the knight was speaking of. She just didn't know the cause.

Was it possible the liege was in love, too? With her? The thought alone was making her knees quake.

"Rosie!" Aislynn was on her knees and shaking the woman's shoulder. Good thing she hadn't swords aimed at her head, if her protection was the old freewoman.

"I was just resting, love. Hush a wee moment. You wear a body out with this walking, and plucking, and cleaning and scrubbing—"

"Tell me of the liege." Aislynn interrupted her and surprised her from her speech at the same time.

"What is it you wish to know, lass?" Rosie said.

"I wish to know of this vow he's made."

The old woman pulled back, pierced Aislynn with a look that made her go heated again, and this time she knew the cause as the blush heated her.

"And what is it you plan to do with such knowledge? If I give it to you, of course."

"I'd never harm him—if that's your question," Aislynn replied.

"You're a Scot maid, your kind has a death wish against

any lordling of any kind—even one as honorable as my Rhoenne. Why would I trust that?"

"Because I love him," Aislynn whispered.

The servant woman snorted and started tying up the ends of her apron to cradle the plant. "Join the legions of women with that issue, lass. My sympathies. The man's unreachable for you."

"He is?"

The woman didn't reply until she had her legs beneath her, and that took some time, a lot of puffing for breath, a bit of grunting as she used the tree for stability, but finally it was done.

"Look about you, lass. Have you noted the Ramhurst about you?"

Aislynn tipped her head to one side. She didn't answer.

"Rhoenne and Richard. The bastards, Brent and Eldine."

"So?" Aislynn replied.

"And not a mother to claim any of them."

"They've no need of mothering at their ages," Aislynn replied.

Old Rosie chuckled. That made her entire body move. "I dinna' mean that."

"You just used a Celt word."

"I dinna'!" Rosie replied.

"There! Again!"

The woman clapped a hand to her mouth, and that just released all the calendula plants to rain on the ground. Aislynn bent and was scooping them into her own skirts as the other finished.

"I'll na' turn into one of them! Cast my tongue off! We came to this land to teach civility, not change to heathen ways!"

"You just did it again," Aislynn pointed out from her position on the ground.

Rosie had a calculating look on her face when she spoke again. "You want to know of this vow or not, lass?"

"'Twas why I asked," Aislynn replied.

"Then cease tormenting me with your way of speaking. I come from a Frank household. Normandy. I dinna' speak in Celt ways, nor with a Celt tongue. I don't ken why you say I do."

Aislynn forced the giggle back as Rosie used the dialect yet again. "I'll na' speak of it again," she promised.

"Verra well. See that you dinna'."

Aislynn had her face turned away so Rosie wouldn't see it.

"So. You wish to know of his vow. I'll ask it again. Have you na' noted the fact that each Ramhurst had a differing mother?"

Aislynn sat back on her heels and thought. "I do now," she answered.

"Verra good. The Ramhurst liege believes the family cursed. No woman can survive birthing a Ramhurst babe. He's made a vow never to give a woman his child. Unless he's forced to by his vows of matrimony."

"He spoke of Ramhurst male babes. Why?"

"Eldine's mother lived through the birth. 'Twas chilblains that winter that took her. He'll not take a fertile woman to his bed. That's his vow. And that would include you."

"But . . . he's na' in charge of fate. *Nae* man is."

"You go tell him that. Go ahead. If you can find him. The man is stubborn, he is. Just look about you. You can see how stubborn."

"I dinna' ken your words."

"I just said it. He avoids his own keep. Why? Because he put you in charge of it. So. That should explain his stubbornness."

"You make *nae* sense," Aislynn replied.

"Can you find him? Well?"

"Find him?"

"Aye."

"I did find him. Just this morn. He's on his way to Leistonshire, after a swim in the loch."

"Well. That certainly explains your curiosity. Does he go to find cold water in which to swim?"

"He dinna' say," Aislynn replied.

Rosie grunted. "Trust me. It'll be cold. Poor man." She was snickering as she said it. "Come. Let's get these plants of yours potted. I've a hankering for this tea you tell me of. The one to relieve the soreness in my feet."

Aislynn followed her servant's bulk back to the castle, her thoughts not on the leaves she'd already harvested and dried. Old Rosie wouldn't know the kelp brew was designed to take away appetite and had nothing to do with painful feet. She didn't ponder that. She had to keep her vision on physical things, such as keeping her eyes moving. She had to stop them from closing for longer than a blink. She knew what awaited her if she closed them for too long; she'd see him and feel him again and be totally inattentive.

Which was a dangerous thing for Rhoenne.

Chapter Eleven

"You waste time. Endlessly. Again."

Rhoenne pulled himself into the saddle without assistance, although it felt like the hardest thing in a series of hard things that he'd done all day. His legs throbbed, the hands hidden by the gauntlets ached, the bruising everywhere on his frame was joining in. And all of that was overshadowed and swallowed and accompanied by the ache where he refused to allow.

He gave Montvale a sidelong glare, although the fellow was impervious as usual. He didn't know why, and every attempt to ferret it out had failed, but Montvale was to blame for all his body's ills at the moment. The man had come out specifically to find Rhoenne, and when he found him after a fortnight absence, the first thing he did was challenge him?

"I vow, Montvale, this time's the last you delay me. I've taken all of your foolishness I can stomach for one day."

"Foolishness? If I had strength left in my arm, I'd slap you with my gauntlet and challenge you again for calling me such a word. And can I help it? I'm a knight cursed with a head-full of your enchantress."

Rhoenne sighed. "She is not *my* enchantress. She is not

even *an* enchantress. She's my healer. We settled that this morn. Over a sword."

"Well . . . at the moment, she more resembles a wife, although you wouldn't note that, since you avoid returning to your own keep and haven't seen."

"Fiefs don't stay protected by themselves," Rhoenne returned.

"You should worry more over your keep. That is where it's not safe."

"Why?"

"Why? She has the rafters turned upside down and the rooms filled with lye and water as she scrubs. The entire place is in upheaval."

Rhoenne grunted.

"She sets the most wondrous table each night, too. You should see it. And taste it. Rather than work yourself into soreness each eve avoiding it."

"As well as borders. They don't exist without guarding, either."

"Verra well. Post guards. Leave them out here to enjoy camp cooking. You have a much better sup awaiting you. You'll still accompany me?"

"I am atop my horse, Montvale, and we are for the keep."

"Thank the Lord! And just wait until you taste her fare! The wench uses flavorings that melt the dish on your tongue. Your home is that much changed. You'll be impressed and pleased."

Rhoenne grimaced. *Pleased?* He doubted it. He was returning home but he wouldn't stay there and witness all the wonders Harold now spoke of. He didn't dare. He hadn't conquered the flare of heat throughout his body that rose every time he thought of her. Nor the pounding need that nothing tempered.

That was why he'd stayed away from her, practicing

battle with his men, riding his borders, hunting and then roasting his own fare. It was all to prevent what he was now hastening toward; seeing her again and being caught in the strange embrace of her gaze.

Rhoenne caught and passed the knight before they cleared the forest. It wasn't from skill or gaining a fresh wind. It was because some of his desire transferred to the horse and that gave him the edge. Montvale wasn't far behind when they rode to his gates, and across the drawbridge, escorted by a guard of men sent out to greet them.

The castle glowed with light, and a hum of humanity reached out a welcoming embrace. Rhoenne slid from his horse, tossed the reins to his squire, and looked about him, keeping the satisfaction so far hidden no one knew how it felt to experience everything he'd known Tyneburn could be. The wide doors leading to the great hall were open and calling their welcome to him . . . calling the same to everyone lucky enough to be granted entrance therein, as well.

Montvale was with him, after sliding from his mount in the exact same motion the liege used. Rhoenne reached for the hilt of Pinnacle, holding it against his leg, and watched Lord Montvale do the same with his sword. Then he was striding across his ground, up his steps and onto the flagstones of his own hall. That was where the shock stopped him so effectively, that the knight ran into him from behind with a force that moved him forward two more steps.

Rhoenne's eyes went wide as he devoured her. Despite the fact that it appeared his entire fief was there, watching. It was akin to when he'd lost his breath the first morn, and there wasn't a thing he could do to gainsay any of it.

"Oh, dearest God," he breathed the words.

"You see? What did I tell you?" Montvale chided from his side.

There were no less than five long tables paralleling

each other the entire length of his hall. They had benches gracing both sides, and were each laden with trenchers of steaming fare of roast boar, long beds of boiled broadbeans amidst cabbages, and everywhere were tankards of ale. All pointing toward the fireplace. That's where every eye went as if planned. That's where she was; the enchantress he'd put in possession of his keep. She was perched atop a cloth-covered, stuffed long stool, in front of the dormant fireplace, and even the blue of his banner seemed to point right to her. And she was surrounded by a bevy of nobles, vying with the king's court for spectacle. There was a very large silvered disk propped behind her table. From where he stood, it looked like someone had placed everything as it was on purpose.

Rhoenne stood there and fought his own body. Before his entire household, he was forced to find the fortitude to keep from racing toward her. He swallowed and heard the slightest of chuckles coming from the man at his side.

Aislynn's hair was undone, it was the texture and shade he'd known it would be, and it was rippling down her back and over the cushion behind her, shiny with the reflection of torchlight in the disk. There was a gossamer white veil attached to a jeweled circlet atop her head. It was intended to wrap about her black tresses, but she had it pushed to one side, rendering it useless for a covering. The same could be said of the pleated white silk of her bodice and the dress that seemed molded to her. Someone had fashioned a bliant of scarlet red, with a low, square, cutout neckline, framing the breasts, and then they'd puckered the edges to add lift and fullness to her bosom. It wasn't necessary. None of it was.

She stood, saying something. Rhoenne couldn't hear it over the roar in his ears. The others about found it uproarious, if the amount of laughter was any indication. He couldn't move. He couldn't think. He couldn't even blink.

The scarlet dress had been laced with the same color of ribbon and it was about her ribcage, defining every bit of her form for every person that was looking. It was obvious there wasn't one touch of enhancement to her attire, her hair, or her face. It was just as obvious, from the curve and shape of her bodice, and the linkage of her lacing that everything about Aislynn was natural and womanly and immensely pleasing.

Rhoenne took his eyes down her twice and then back, and knew he was turning the color of her gown. He was only grateful all of the torchlight in his hall seemed to be put there for her use alone. He was also grateful that he hadn't shed any of his mail. He needed it to hide the response he couldn't temper or deny or force away. He scowled and reached to caress where he'd pulled Pinnacle up from the scabbard with his reaction. At the sound of steel moving against the metallic trim, Aislynn stopped speaking, her eyes met his from the length of the hall, and Rhoenne lost his breath. Again.

Montvale nudged at him, forcing Rhoenne to steady his legs. Their presence wasn't going unnoticed and there was a path being cleared, from where they stood directly to Aislynn. There was also a change in where the populace appeared to be looking. They were focused on him. His scowl deepened.

"You need to approach, Rhoenne. They're awaiting that very thing. Look." There was a touch of humor to Lord Montvale's whisper.

Rhoenne slipped a glance at the man moving to stand beside him. "You planned this?" he asked.

"Planned what? You left instruction for her to clothe herself. Dress to her place. The place you entrusted to her. I had naught to do with that."

"She's dressed as a—a woman!"

"I believe she is one, Rhoenne," Montvale remarked dryly.

"But not like this! Not like that!" His voice was rising as he jerked his head toward where Aislynn and her retinue of nobles and knights watched.

"You granted her the oversight of your home. You gave her Old Rosie for aid in it. Rosie has a good eye. That woman can make a pig lovely to the eye."

"But not . . . now!" He was getting desperate. It sounded in his tone. Rhoenne had to ignore how the last vestige of conversation was dying down, making his whispering loud, no matter how softly he spoke it. He swallowed for time.

"I don't understand the trouble, Rhoenne. She is a woman. You've claimed her as yours, and she's done wonders with your home. What better way to greet the liege than with such a woman? You do see she's a woman?"

"I already saw her as that!"

"Then I fail to see the trouble. Go. Approach. She's yours."

"Damn you, Montvale. She's not my woman!"

"Of course she is. I heard it. I was there."

"She's my healer! Nothing more. Ever."

Montvale rolled the disgust over his lips, making a horse-like sound. "Only because you fought it. I think the reason is you dinna' ken the extent of it."

"I already knew of her womanliness!"

"But did you do anything about it? Or with it? Nay. Not you."

"Damn you again, Montvale. Damn all of you."

"Cease cursing me and claim your place. At her side. That's what they're awaiting. Go. Watch your step, though. There's tongues laying about the floor."

"We need to leave, Montvale. Now."

Rhoenne hadn't moved but it felt like he had. The room swelled in front of him and he took several breaths to right it again. He was sweating profusely, too. There was nowhere for it to go. He had a seven-day curve to the clothing beneath his mail, making it cling to his frame like it had been sewn there. It was a fit that nightly dunkings in a cold loch had only defined more.

"Leave? What? I don't see the issue, Rhoenne. It's all exactly as you ordered and put into play. Nothing less. No one did more than follow your own orders. Made from your own mouth. A month hence."

"I made a vow!" He wasn't shouting it, but he might as well be. His voice was hoarse, his hand trembled, and his vision was being tinged with the hollow thump of heart-beat, making a pulse of pain each time it tapped his temple.

"I think you need a woman's touch. And not just any woman's. Hers. You know it. I know it. She probably knows it. If you balk much longer, everyone else will probably know of it, as well."

"Not her! Never her! Damn you, Montvale. And then, damn you again. Where's Fiona?" Rhoenne's throat was dry. It made the words harsher.

"Surely you don't mean to do what it appears."

"Fiona!" Rhoenne called the name. No one answered.

"You can't do this! Nay. Not now! Not to her! Rhoenne . . . ?"

Montvale might as well save his breath. His plea wasn't being heard. Rhoenne was afraid of himself. He was afraid for her. He was afraid of the reddish haze he could actually see in the space between them. A space not one soul stepped into. The space making a line . . . right to her. There was only one thing he could do when faced with such roaring lust. Sate it. And quickly.

"Fiona!" Rhoenne sucked in breath and filled the room with sound at the name, interrupting Montvale's whispered words. He watched the table to his right where Fiona was as she jumped up. "Arrange a bath. In my chamber. And sup!

Bring a trencher. You there!" Rhoenne stuck out his arm and pointed at another wench he'd never seen before. "Assist her."

"But, Rhoenne—"

"Say another word, Montvale, and I'll bury Pinnacle within your shanks. In the morn. On the list."

"You can't just leave her there! Not like this. Look at how they act. You must take her with you. She's yours. Everyone knows she is. Everyone knows you claimed her. Everyone."

"See to her in my stead."

"What?" Montvale's voice rose. "You don't know what you ask!"

"Touch one hair on that head, or remove one scrap of that dress, and I'll kill you. Understand?"

"You truly don't know what you ask!"

"Take her from this room and do it before I change my mind. Go quickly. Get her to your chamber. Protect her."

"You punish me with torment, My Liege! You wish me to take her when all make note of it, and yet not take her, not touch her? Pray don't make this mistake."

"Do it! Suffer along with me. That is your punishment for playing games with my life."

"I did nothing of the kind! And I will not do this. She's your woman, not mine. I heard it from both of your mouths. Don't cheapen her in your own hall. I beg it of you. Don't make her a wench others can—and have tried to—have. Do something else. I beg you."

Harold was ashen. There wasn't a bit of color except his lips. Rhoenne watched as he wet them with his tongue. He let a pent-up breath out. Words went with it.

"Go to your chamber then. I'll bring her to you there. They'll not know. Only you and I will. Mark my words. I will kill you if you touch her. And I will very much enjoy it."

Harold looked at him, measuring him. Rhoenne watched as the knight sucked in on his cheeks and met his level look. Then he nodded.

Chapter Twelve

Aislynn watched the large knight watch her. It felt like they'd been doing it all eve. The only sound in his chamber was the fire crackling in the fireplace and the sound of his mail moving as he lifted his empty tankard to her in salute before putting it back down. She didn't break the silence. She didn't know what to say.

From the moment she'd attended the banquet tonight, she'd been on edge. Unsettled. It wasn't over the crowd swelling in numbers about her. She was used to dealing with the melee of supper in the liege's castle. Besides, all knew who she belonged to. It was more the liege's reaction when he saw it. It was the new dress Rosie had designed and the circlet about her head and the positioning of everything in the hall. It was for the reason it had been done: seduction.

She'd felt wicked and strange all eve, as she dressed . . . prepared. Bathing in warm scented water before donning lovely, form-fitting garments . . . anticipating the unknown as much as she was ready to welcome it. The crowd hadn't really been noticed. It was all for Rhoenne. To heal . . . and end his inattention.

Aislynn's heart had skipped when she'd first seen him

and then he'd called for her rival, the snipe-tongued Fiona? He called for the one wench that fought her control? That's who he wished for intimate company on his return?

Aislynn had silently cursed everything. Stupid man! He knew nothing of women if he could such! He knew nothing of his own half-sister, Eldine, and how she'd ruled his keep, allowing vermin and filth everywhere while she slumbered and lusted and drank herself into unconsciousness daily. He knew nothing of the fight Aislynn had undergone each and every day since she'd ordered Eldine into service, cleaning the hovel she'd created. He knew little of women and their wanton natures and argumentative tongues.

He was a beast. He was a rutting boar. A *poucah*!

She'd been cursing him in her mind but it hadn't worked. Especially when he'd moved, coming toward her and burning her in place with the locking of their eyes. Aislynn hadn't been able to stay any of her reaction. Her mouth had dropped open, her breath had caught, and shivers flew all over her as he'd just stood there, his height making him too immense to be ignored.

The liege hadn't said anything at first. He'd simply stood there, at the base of her table, running his eyes all over her revealed form until Aislynn longed to scream at him to stop.

"You do my treasures credit, Aislynn," he'd said finally, putting such sound into the room that it echoed with it, "and yet, there's nothing rich or pure enough to touch such perfection. Come. My room awaits. I'll show you what you're meant to touch."

He hadn't waited, either. He'd simply reached out and plucked her into his arms. Despite his covering of chest armor and the chainmail about his limbs, she could've sworn bare skin touched the same. Aislynn had to close her eyes to keep the scope of the feeling to herself. She was in a whorl of longing for what he was going to do, filled with wickedness, yet terrified at the same time. She knew what a mistake it would be for him to see any of it.

"Don't hold yourself so closely to me, Aislynn. I'm not strong enough to withstand you. Not yet."

His whisper had made her eyes fly open and her lips part.

"Nor would I gaze at me with such an expression right now. I'm not an inhuman beast. I'm a man."

"I . . . ken that." She'd sucked in on her lower lip after the words. She'd felt and heard his groan as he saw it.

Then his lips were on hers, sealing off thought and capturing her every breath. Aislynn hadn't much experience to match it with. There was no comparison as every nerve ending in her body sharpened and came alive.

"Damn you, woman! There's only so much . . . I can take!"

He'd wrenched his lips from hers. Then he was shoving a door open with his shoulder and moving across a chamber, and dumping her unceremoniously onto a strange bed.

Then he was gone. Striding back with purposeful steps and not one word said to either her or the only other occupant. The door had slammed behind him and Aislynn's eyes had met Lord Montvale's.

That had been when he raised his goblet for his first empty salute.

She watched now as he lifted it again and something caught her attention. He was hiding a wince. He was good at it for the wince was over the moment he made it and nothing else about him changed. Her eyes sharpened on him.

"You're hurt," she said, finally.

"Not enough," he replied softly. "Trust me."

"Explain."

In answer he shifted, stretching out legs that were the length of Rhoenne's as he crossed one booted foot over the other and lifted his empty tankard at her.

"Is that my explanation?" she asked.

"I have the care of you. I don't have the freedom of your form or the joy of your frame. Perhaps you'd best cover yourself. Please."

Aislynn reached for his headboard cloth and pulled part of the midnight blue velvet across her. "Is this better?" she asked.

He groaned.

"You would probably be more comfortable if you shed your armor. Would you like me to help you?"

"I want you to stay away from me. Far away. That would be most helpful."

"Why? I've done naught," she replied.

"True. I'd still prefer you over there. And me, over here. Covered over in all my armor. Just like it is."

"Are you being punished?"

His eyebrows rose but he didn't reply.

"I dinna' ken much about it, not having known men afore . . . but it's na' verra fair of him. He does na' even say why."

He gave another groan. Only this time, there was a painful note in it.

"Why are you in pain, sir?"

"If I pain, it's only to those parts dearest to me."

She frowned slightly. "Where?"

In answer he shifted, uncrossing his legs and then re-crossing them, with a different one on top. Aislynn watched him do it.

"Is that my answer?" she asked.

"Don't you need some rest?"

Aislynn narrowed her eyes. "You dinna' want to tell me, do you?"

"Nay. It's na' my place. Damn, anyway."

This time when he tipped a small barrel, he emptied some of the contents into his tankard. Aislynn listened to it and then watched as he raised it to her in salute, drained the entire thing, and then stopped for a breath.

"Are you thinking to dull this?" she asked.

"Nay. Drink doesn't affect me that way."

"Then why didn't you drink before?"

"Self-restraint," he replied, filling his goblet again.

Aislynn mulled that for a moment. "Then, why are you drinking now?"

He shrugged. "I thirst. And it's naught but ale. I've kept away for no reason. 'Tis the liege that cannot hold his ale, not me."

Aislynn giggled. "I've noticed."

"What?"

"I gave him a wineskin when I healed his leg. He was quite amusing once he drank it."

"I'll bet . . . he was." The words had a slight pause in the midst as he winced again. Aislynn watched for a moment and then spoke.

"If you let me assist with your mail, I'll heal your back."

He stopped the tankard from reaching his mouth and put it back down. "You're a sharp-eyed snipe, aren't you?"

"Are you denying pain, too? I dinna' understand you men. How can I heal if you're always hiding it?"

"I hide nothing, lass. I never did. As I already made mention, I'm practicing restraint tonight. Any pain is helpful."

"Well, cease that and let me assist you with your mail." Aislynn shoved off the bed and approached where he sat. The knight's eyes were wide as he watched her. "What is it now?"

"I'm not to touch a hair on your head or remove a scrap of that clothing," he replied.

"Truly? Did he say anything of me . . . touching you? Or perchance removing your clothing?"

"Oh, Lord," he replied beneath his breath.

"Well?"

He shook his head.

"Then there's naught stopping you from allowing me to heal your pain. Stand up. I'll help you with your mail."

"This is worse. I want you to know that."

"Why?"

"Because I make no secret of my desire for you. Nor, I might add, would I put a rein on myself if he hadn't ordered it so."

Aislynn stepped back. "Do I need fear you?"

"I don't practice ravishment. You needn't fear. He's your master, not I. This is my punishment."

"For what?"

"Setting things up. Fooling with his life."

"Old Rosie made this bliant on your recommend, dinna' she?" Aislynn said. She knew she'd surprised him when he pulled back. She smiled. "No wonder he's punishing you."

"He's inattentive. It might mean his life. I had to correct it," he replied, standing to tower over her and then he lifted an arm the size of Rhoenne's.

"Are all Normans this large?" Aislynn asked.

He snorted before he started to pull apart the little links beneath his arm holding his chains together. Aislynn bent forward to help, ignoring his intake of breath as she did so. He allowed her to assist, and it didn't take long for both of them to relieve him of his armor and mail, although he was the one who had to heft it to the table. Then he was pulling his tunic off and tossing it aside. When he was down to his sweat-stained chausses and tights, he stepped back from her, stopping her with both hands out.

"I'm inflicting self-punishment tonight, lass. Not torture. Leave be where we are." His voice was gruff and didn't sound at all like him.

She tilted her head and considered him. "Verra well. I can work. Lie down. On the bed. I'll join you."

"What?" His eyes went round again. "Nay. Never."

Aislynn giggled again. "Verra well. Lie down here then. On the floor. Beside the fire is best. The heat will be most beneficial. You'll see. I just have to put some weight in the proper place and everything will right itself. Verra good. Just like that. On your chest. How did you know?"

"Instinct and self-preservation. I'm not allowing you to be putting your body against mine—in that fashion. Not with my liege standing in the way. Damn him. To hell. And back. Twice."

Aislynn pulled back as he did a push-up and then several more, defining very well-muscled arms and a stout back for her.

"Now cease that and lie still; hands to your sides, head turned. Verra good. Now breathe in . . ." Aislynn's voice trailed off as she slipped from her shoes and put one stocking-covered foot on either side of him. Then she tipped forward and put a hand on either shoulder blade.

"Perhaps we should wait," he huffed, pulling another breath in. "Or get some witnesses."

"Hush," she replied and stepped up onto his shoulders.

They both heard the distinctive crack of bone shifting as her feet slid off his sides, making her land on the upraised buttocks, and that was the view Rhoenne got when he opened the chamber door.

"Montvale!" Rhoenne's roar sounded even larger in the smaller room, as it vibrated off the walls.

Aislynn was at Rhoenne's chest and holding to him the moment she could move. "Wait! It was I that touched him! I helped remove his clothing! He did naught! Naught!"

"You. Did. What?" Each word was enunciated loudly and clearly as he took a breath between them.

"He had an ache and I healed it."

"You did . . . *what*?"

Her words weren't soothing anything; they seemed to be doing worse. Aislynn clung tighter to his waist and tried to keep him from moving. It didn't work as her feet slid along the floor. "Please? You've got to believe me. He did naught!"

"What the lass says is truth, Rhoenne," Montvale said, in a long, drawn-out fashion.

"I'll have your throat, Montvale! I swear it!"

"Nae!" Aislynn cried the word.

"I hope you believe her soon, My Liege, although she says it poorly. You have to forgive that. She's a maid. Still. Maids don't realize how their words sound. Because they . . . just don't."

Rhoenne stopped. "Explain," he said and the one word rumbled through the chest she was pressed against.

"I take it by this display of yours, that the two wenches you requested weren't enough?" Montvale asked slowly.

"Enough for what?"

"Sating your ardor."

"I gave you time to explain," Rhoenne replied. "Use it for that."

"She already told you. I had an ache. Not a bad one, but like a thorn beneath the fingernail. It was in my back. Between my shoulders. I've had it since our last battle . . . I disremember which one. There are too many. The wench noticed it. God bless her, she's gone and healed it."

"Is this true?"

Aislynn felt his finger beneath her jaw a moment before he moved it, forcing her head upward to look at him. She nodded and he smiled in return, softening the blue of his eyes.

"She went and stood on me, Rhoenne. Right up on my back. The wench has strange ideas, but God's truth, it worked. I've lived with a twinge in my back for days and one bit of her standing atop me, it's gone. You should try it. She's light as a thistle."

Rhoenne didn't move from looking at her. "I have tried it. That's how we met. She wasn't curing anything at the time. She was angry with me. Much as she should be now." His words were softer spoken and the chest she was still attached to wasn't heaving like it had been.

"Shut the door on your way out, Rhoenne. It's been a long day and an even longer night. I deserve my rest. I think I've earned it this time."

Aislynn heard the request as if from a great distance and wondered how that had changed. Rhoenne hadn't moved. He raised his head and spoke over her back.

"I'll do you one better. I've sent Fiona. She's annoyed at not being able to pleasure and attend me, but she failed. Her emotion fuels her passion. Use it. We'll speak of this on the morrow."

"Go lightly, my friend. Handle what's given to you with the utmost of care. Very few are as lucky."

"I don't need such advice," Rhoenne replied.

"I wasn't speaking to you," Montvale answered.

Aislynn gasped and her eyes flew wide. Rhoenne saw every bit of it since he hadn't moved his gaze.

"I had it wrong. Curse me. I cannot be faulted for seeing what was hidden from all, can I?" The knight pulled in a breath to continue. "Rhoenne Guy de Ramhurst didn't need to see the prize in front of his nose, at all. It was the other way around."

"Montvale." The name was said without inflection of any kind.

"Think on my words or toss them aside. I give you free rein. But to do so, you'll need your own chamber, some quietude, and I would advise you to show a bit more of what you offer and less of the temper that comes along with it."

"You go too far!" Rhoenne's nostrils flared as he breathed in.

"You cannot challenge me, My Liege. You have your arms full of the enchantress and I need my strength to attend the women you send. Go. Show her all. Add to her suffering. We'll meet on the morrow if you still wish, but not early. I will need my rest. You see? No challenge was made yet all win. I should practice diplomacy at King David's court. What say you?"

"I say you talk too much. As usual."

Rhoenne turned, holding Aislynn to his side with one arm, while he turned the handle and opened the door. He sidestepped the rush of body that was Fiona. Sir Montvale caught her easily and lifted her from the floor.

"You can leave now. I have it well in hand, as you can see."

Aislynn started trembling as they entered Rhoenne's chamber. Since he hadn't moved his gaze, he knew of all of it.

Chapter Thirteen

The bedchamber didn't look the same. Or feel it.

Aislynn had her eyes on Rhoenne's chin as he pushed the door open, and then he set her down, waiting for her to get accustomed to her own legs again, and then he released her completely. She walked toward the center of his chamber, letting the sensation of warmth fill her. Then she was standing at the center and looking. Experiencing. Testing. Wondering. Thinking.

His fire was banked and sending out the barest golden glow, coating the rugs near it. There was one torch lit in its sconce, on the far wall, near his bed. There were the remains of a feast platter on his table, and a tankard of ale. She could tell it was still full by the glitter of liquid near the rim. She smiled slightly. There wasn't one sign that two women had been in there, nor was the space reeking with the smell of spent lust or passion or anything like that. There was a spattering of dark, wet spots near his window slit. She pushed a toe of her slipper against one and watched it smear. Water. He'd spent the time bathing. Eating. Stifling the same emotion she felt. The one she was vibrating with, alternately chilling and feeling fevered over. The same thing that was making him inattentive. The one he wouldn't appease.

"I . . . dinna' understand," Aislynn whispered.

"What?" Rhoenne's voice came from the area near the chamber door. She heard the bolt sliding into position with ears tuned for it and a heart that pulsed the moment the noise came.

"The women." Aislynn swiveled at the waist to look toward him. It wasn't possible to see him fully. He was in the shadowed alcove of his door frame.

"I shouldn't have sent them," he replied.

"Dinna' fash yourself," Aislynn replied. "All ken my position in your household. You dinna' harm it. Much."

"It wasn't that. Are you hungered?" he asked, and reached an arm to encompass the remains of his feast.

"Nae," she replied, softly, and then she turned completely toward him. It didn't make it any easier to see him, since he was still shadowed. It made it easier to be brave. Aislynn reached both arms up to the back of the gilded circlet atop her head and slipped the golden ring off its jewel peg by feel. Rosie had brought it from his treasury earlier and Aislynn knew exactly how it worked.

She lifted her arms higher, taking the tiara off, and with it came the gossamer white veil. The reaction was a choking sound from where he stood. Aislynn walked over to the fireplace, wrapping the material loosely about one fist as she went. Then she was at his stool and placing the wad of material and circlet on it. Rhoenne didn't say a word. She didn't know whether that was a good sign or not. Her hands went next to the tie just beneath her ribcage, where the scarlet ribbon ended. Her fingers trembled, but worked; first to pulling the knot loose, and then to spreading the lacing wide.

"Aislynn?" Rhoenne spoke from the spot he hadn't moved from.

She shrugged with one shoulder, and moved her hands to the tops of her sleeves. They'd been fashioned from woven flax and bleached to a white that matched her under-dress. Rosie had laced them on with little cords made of black satin, rolled into more ribbon. Aislynn busied herself with pulling the ribbon weave apart so she could take each sleeve off. She had to ignore the shivers as she did so, though.

"What . . . are you doing?" Rhoenne asked, using such a slight portion of his voice that it barely made sound.

"What you will na'," she replied, and turned her back toward him. It was easier to look at the red embers of his fire; warmer, too. She had to ignore the heavy quick breathing sounds he was making as she pulled the scarlet straps from her shoulders and let them slide down her frame.

Rosie had put her in a floor-sweeping length of bleached flax, woven of the lightest, thinnest threads so that when it was fashioned into her under-dress, it made a pour of material, sliding over every curve and caressing every portion of her. With the firelight behind her, it was probably next to useless as a covering. From the dark growl of sound coming from Rhoenne, she was certain of it.

"Why are you doing this?" he asked, in a chunk of voice that didn't sound at all like him.

Aislynn lifted her hands to her hair and lifted it from her shoulders. Then she swiveled to face him. "Because one of us has to do it," she replied.

"I've taken a vow."

She lowered her arms, letting the black tresses fall about her on the white sheath she wore. She took a step toward him and felt the flax material slide over her thigh to her knee. She took another, with the corresponding shift of material. Another. There was no response from his area, save a quicker intake of breath.

"You forgot one thing, My Liege."

Aislynn waited until she was within one more step of him to answer. She had her gaze fastened to the middle of his chest, and then moved it up. There wasn't any way to see what expression he had. He was tall enough the arch above his door frame shadowed his face completely. All she could see was the glitter of moisture on his eyes.

"What?" His voice was hoarse and came upon the exhalation of breath. It was followed almost immediately by another quick breath.

"Love," she replied, and got a severe groan for a reply.

"Aislynn . . . don't do this."

"Do what? I've done naught save taken some clothing off. To get more to my ease. Here. Let me assist you to the same."

She reached for the area of his belt. She almost expected him to step back, but he didn't. He didn't say anything, and he didn't stop her. She had to take that for acquiescence. He wasn't giving her anything else. His belt was latched with a spike of curved metal. Aislynn forced her fingers to cease trembling in order to unlatch it. She held on to the heavy silver disk for a moment longer than she had to, and then she opened her fingers, tilted her palm, and let it drop. The thud was loud in the chamber. He was solid, statue-like, and unmoving. A section of him was also starting to stir in the area just below his belt. Aislynn caught her lip as she watched that area of his tunic shift slightly, catching shadows from the torchlight.

She lifted her eyes up his chest and into the area where his eyes should be. There was no glint. She guessed why. He had his eyes closed, which was perfect for her, since it emboldened her further.

Aislynn stepped closer, holding back from touching him by a hairsbreadth of space that seemed to pulse with each flicker of light. And every breath she took. She looked back down and watched as each inhalation she made pushed her bosom closer to him, and that just made the lump of him enlarge, until it stretched his tunic forward and filled the space just below her breasts. All of which was accompanied by a series of tremors that went through him. Over and over. Defining his nipples through his tunic weave, and making the blond wisps of hair on his forearms easily discernible with each flicker of light.

"Rhoenne?" she whispered.

"Aye?" The answer was finally whispered back, and it sent a torrent of breath across her forehead with the force he gave it.

"Do you . . . desire me?"

There was a huff of air that was probably amusement, but sounded like a moan before he answered. "I should think it easy to spot, Aislynn."

"This?" She reached out and touched where the lump of him was shoving against her breasts, as if trying to cleave them apart with the growing size of it.

"Oh, dearest . . . *God*," he replied, saying the last word with such an agonized sound, Aislynn caught her own breath. It didn't stop her, however. It only made her more curious, and more restless, and more sensitive.

Her fingers spread, from the index finger she'd first touched him with, until she had three of them atop the hard part of him, and then she was adding her thumb, and pushing the tunic into a sheath, showing the size, scope and strength of what he was. And then she had to bring her other hand to assist.

"Ah . . . Rhoenne," she breathed.

"You must . . . stop, Aislynn! Now. Cease!" He caught his breath through the short words, and said the last two in a tone that was an octave higher than the others.

"What if I dinna' wish to?" she asked.

"I have made a vow! I don't vow lightly! I'm not made of iron. Damn you! Damn your kind!"

Hands that resembled iron grabbed her upper arms, and he used his strength to pull her hands apart, and then he was lifting her, and holding her in front of him, and baring his teeth throughout his speech. He had his eyes open, too, and they were blazing glazed-over anger at her. She didn't have to see it. She felt it.

"Is na' that too bad," she replied, and craned her neck forward, searching for and yearning for the kiss he denied her by leaning back.

"Why are you doing this for me?" he asked.

"I dinna' do it just for you." Aislynn accompanied her words with a lunge of her body toward him, and that had him moving a full step back, to keep his balance, and his distance from her.

And then he reached the door, thudding first his shoulders into it, and next his head as he craned back from her.

"You don't know what you do!" he said, and it came from between his teeth.

"So?" Aislynn swung out with her legs and on the return inward motion, had them wrapped about his waist, and shimmied herself closer until she was latched in place. From that position, she could use her thigh muscles to pull herself closer . . . closer . . . until the arousal he couldn't hide was firmly entrenched between her thighs. Then, she could tighten her legs at will, and feel the answering twinge. She did it twice to the most severe stiffening of his entire frame. Three times. Four. On the fifth gripping motion, everything on Rhoenne Ramhurst moved. The low growl of sound emanating from his chest was accompanying the movement of his wrists as he rolled them inward, putting her solidly against his chest, and then his mouth slammed against her.

Aislynn's cry didn't make much sound as her tongue parried every motion of his, her entire body ignited with flame, and shudders of anticipation filled her, trembled through her, and made it easy to cling like a leech to him as he moved. Every step of his slid her against where his arousal was settled, and that was making Aislynn whimper with need, desire, and want, and everything she'd been kept from.

"Rhoenne. Yea. Rhoenne." She said it over and over again in a cadence of wonder, amazement, and joy.

He stopped. Breathed deep; exhaled, and then sucked in another breath. Then he was twinging his hardness against her thighs, and moving his hips in an upward motion at the same time, tormenting her, teasing her, making her feel it, experience it. All of it. As much as the tunic and her flaxen under-dress would allow. . . .

"I am going to take you, half-ling," he mumbled against her lips, the words mixing with the sucking, slurping motions he was making. "Take you and make you mine. And I'm going to hate that you forced me to it."

"So?" Aislynn said it defiantly again.

His answer was intelligible as one. It was accompanied by his motion to slant her onto his mattress. Only it wasn't his mattress at all, it was the table. Aislynn gasped as the cold, hard surface met her buttocks, and then her spine, since he pushed her down onto it with the pressure of his kiss.

She didn't care. Her hands were filled with heaving chest and striations of muscles all over the tops of his shoulders, wrapping around to the back of his neck . . . his back. Aislynn shoved her palms into him, wrapped her fingers about lumps of muscle and clung, pulled, bruised.

His breath was labored and heavy . . . everything was heavy, and heated and sweat-filled, and then she felt his hands, reaching for, and finding the hemline of her under-dress, where it was shoved to her knees from the embrace of her legs about his torso.

She heard ripping, sensed air. Warm air. Cold air. All

kinds of air. And that was based on where he put the fire-like flesh of his palms, and then moved them. Over and over. Tearing material and shoving it aside, until the exquisite sewing at the neckline of her under-dress stopped the destruction he was doing to her sheath.

And then he was lifting his upper body. Standing to his full height in order to pull his tunic over his head, using vicious strokes of effort since the material was clinging to every portion with the sweat he was coated with. If she'd thought him beautiful before, it was an understatement. Shadows rolled all about his form, carving out valleys and hills of massive muscle and defining strength and hardness . . . so much hardness.

Aislynn whimpered again. Shimmied against him. Reached out for him. Rhoenne slammed both hands to the table top beside her head and leaned close. Eyes the shade of agate glowed at her, stunning and enrapturing her, and making her gasp for a breath he didn't seem to want her to have.

"I may never forgive this, witch," he hissed it at her, and then he lowered his mouth to a nipple, stuck out his tongue, and licked it.

Aislynn squealed. That had him chuckling throughout her cry, and that had more of the chill affecting every bit of where he was wetting. And that just made everything more pointed, and more grasping and more desirous, and more torturous. Aislynn had his head between her hands and was making certain he didn't move from where she wanted him. Not this time. She held him to her and experienced wave after wave of sensation, hot . . . cold. Rough. Intense. And then he was moving, sending his tongue down the center of her, to her navel, where he lavished attention . . . and then back up, bypassing where her breasts were aching for more attention, and ending with a gliding motion of suckling against her jaw. To her ear. Back to her chin and around to the other ear. Beneath it, to where he nibbled on flesh her hair usually had covered and protected, and making chills she hadn't a prayer of containing.

"Rhoenne? Please? Rhoenne? Please? Rhoenne?"

Aislynn was panting the words, and that just made him chuckle more. She tried lunging up, and that just gained her his hands on each side of her hips, holding her in place, while he did what he wanted to her neck. Her shoulder. And then her chin.

Aislynn's mouth was wide, gasping for air, and letting it go the moment she had any.

"Rho . . . enne . . ." She cried his name in two parts, making a keening note of the end of it.

Her answer that time was the movement of fingers along the backs of her thighs, wrapping about the flesh and using her like he would a musical instrument as his fingers played along, raising gooseflesh and tension and want and need and so much more, she pummeled at his back with it.

And then there was pain. Suffering. Fire. Shooting from where he was pressuring her innermost area to accept him, before arcing into her back and filling every pore with absolute torment.

Aislynn couldn't do it. Her eyes filled with tears, but her body betrayed her as it continued clinging to him, accepting him, and welcoming him into an embrace of blood, sweat, and pain.

"Vixen." He'd moved his mouth to her ear, slid his tongue along the edge, and filled her with whispers of sound, naming her things she wasn't, and all the while he was pushing himself further into her. Further. Deeper. Holding her in place and making her take him. As much of him as she could. Branding her.

And then he stopped. Everything. Even time. Throbs of pain were centered all about where he was semi-sheathed, and the fire emanating from there was contrasting to the chilled unbending surface of the table. Aislynn slit her eyes open, blinked the tears out of the way and met his gaze.

"You like this?" he asked roughly.

"I dinna' . . . ken the . . . pain," she whispered back.

"I haven't even begun yet, love," he replied. Then he smiled slightly, tipped his head, and nipped at her breast tip before taking the piece fully into his mouth and suckling deep, and thoroughly and with so much fervor, Aislynn went wild with it.

She forgot about the pain with the new sensations he was raising. She couldn't even bring it to mind, until he moved that part of him again, holding her with both hands and making her body stretch fuller . . . larger . . . accepting him, engorging him. Until his groin met hers. Fully. Totally.

He groaned long and loud, the part of him buried deep twinged, and Aislynn was screaming. Gripping tightly to him with arms and legs, and putting her muscles in an affliction of shudders as she felt it . . . felt the bubble of ecstasy erupting, rippling through her over and over and turning her entire existence into light and joy and wonder.

"My. My. Aren't you a wanton?" Rhoenne was whispering it to her nipple flesh when her breathing calmed, and her heart decided it would keep beating, and rapidly at that.

Aislynn couldn't bring him into focus at first. It didn't matter. Her entire world seemed filled with him. She didn't have to look to see him. And then he moved, taking her recent experience and turning it into so much more dreamworld. Her body flexed, gripped, sent the anger of it to the backs of her calves, and from thence to her ankles, and then, sending ripples of shivers through her back, to her scalp, making the wonder of it pierce straight through to her heart. Aislynn caught her breath . . . held the tremors close as her body shuddered to more amazement, more enjoyment, more thrill. And then it happened again. It was Rhoenne orchestrating it, too, sliding backward in bits of space before rocking forward again, over and over and over, gaining strength and length and volume to each thrust, and making little grunting noises with every single one of them.

Aislynn's heart stumbled, caught, pained her with the intensity of it as she watched him, experienced what he was doing, and gloried in where he was doing it. She hadn't known love felt like this.

"Aislynn . . ."

Her name was softly whispered and accompanied by yet another stroke, filling her body with him before taking it away again. Over. Again.

Time was filled with the sheen of fire glow on their fused bodies, the volume of curses and love-words he filled the chamber with, and the echoes of her cries of satiation. And then he increased it. Holding her in place so he could pummel his body into hers, rocking to a rhythm only he heard, and then he was lifting her into his embrace and heaving huge heavy lunges into her.

"Oh dear God. Oh . . . Lord! Oh . . . !" The last word was a cry of sound as he heaved into her body, shimmying and pulsing and doing little more than sounding very like he was sobbing as his body shuddered over and over, and then was still.

Aislynn was lowered to the table, where the cold embrace of wood was waiting for her. And he was pulling away, and stumbling once before falling to his knees. And then he was covering his face with his hands, and shuddering even more fiercely.

Aislynn had never felt more open and defenseless and bereft. Especially as it looked like the man on the floor was sobbing, or something close to it. She slid to the edge of his table and pushed off, although her legs weren't capable of holding her. She crumpled onto the floor right next to him and reached out a hand toward him. And then she was touching his shoulder and feeling him flinch away.

Everywhere he'd been on her body was still throbbing and pulsating, and thrumming in a cadence of sensation that made it difficult to avoid all of it, and what it had felt like . . . and he was flinching away from her?

"Rhoenne?" she whispered.

"Oh, Aislynn. Forgive me." He was mumbling it into his palms.

"Forgive you? For what?"

"What I've just done."

"You dinna' like it? What did I do wrong?" she asked instead, in a little voice she hated the moment it sounded.

He lifted his head and pierced her with eyes holding such anguish, her belly dropped with it. He wasn't crying, either. "Never say such a thing!" he said.

"Then why? Why would I forgive you for showing me such joy my body is still a-fire with it? Are you mad?"

"Oh Aislynn. I have just given you a death sentence. Oh dearest, God. Not you."

Aislynn went to her knees and looked over at him. And shook her head. *"Nae* God has the power to stop such a thing, Rhoenne. If you pray, at least speak the right words. And thank Him."

"For what? Killing you?" he asked, in a bitter tone.

"Nae. For love. The love we shared. That love." Aislynn said it, reached out to embrace him.

"That was lust, Aislynn."

She snorted. "Call it what you will, Ramhurst. I'll call it true. 'Twas love. And 'twas massive. Joyous. Is it like that every time?"

He lifted his shoulder in a half-hearted shrug.

"Well . . . it is?"

"Aislynn."

"What?" she asked, as innocently as she could. He was using his stern voice. The one he always used with his vassal, Harold. She caught the smile in case he looked over again.

"You make light of what isn't."

"I was just asking a question. I have na' much experience. I canna' wait for more, though. When can we do it again?"

Rhoenne moved his head and looked at her. He wasn't as anguished, if the way he'd pursed his lips was any indication.

"We don't," he replied finally.

"What? *Nae!*" Her voice was louder than she meant it, but he couldn't mean to deny her such beauty again. He just . . . couldn't.

"Aislynn, I meant it. I gave a vow. I will na' kill a woman with my seed. Ever again."

Aislynn tilted her head and regarded him and ignored what a strange conversation she was having after becoming his woman. The fire wasn't giving off much light at all, since it was down to a few coals. The torch was somewhere behind her, and that meant her body was blocking any light source for him. Rhoenne Guy de Ramhurst was in front of her, in complete naked splendor, and she couldn't even see it. Her mind had to do it for her.

"You are na' in charge of fate, My Laird," she replied finally.

He swiveled on his bare buttocks and gave her a good view of his broad back.

"What?" she asked with a challenging tone.

"I'm not discussing it further."

Aislynn sighed long and loud.

"And you're not to tempt me to it. Not again. I'll just have to be stronger."

"You're strong enough already," she replied.

He sighed then, and it made his body move with it. That was interesting to watch, she decided.

"In mind, Aislynn. Not just frame."

"I'm *nae* fool, Ramhurst. I ken exactly what you meant, and I still say you're wrong. Fate has in store for me what it has. You canna' change it. I canna' change it. And if you deny me this joy again, I may be forced to find it elsewhere. You ken that, as well?"

He wasn't remotely penitent when he turned this time. He was angered and large and turning blood-dark with whatever emotion he was trying to stifle.

"Over . . . my dead frame," he replied finally.

Aislynn leaned backward, putting her legs toward him, until she touched a bare thigh and her own toes immediately started tingling.

"Much better," she said.

"What?"

She crooked a finger at him. "Come here, lover man," she replied.

And was rewarded with his groan.

Chapter Fourteen

"Oh . . . dearest Lord!"

Rhoenne rolled from her, taking the coverings with him, and was at the long slender window looking out before Aislynn opened her eyes. And then she was raising them to the ceiling joists above. The man had been denying emotions and feelings throughout the night, even as he was deep into experiencing the "spell of lust" as he'd taken to naming it. And it was worse once his body had finished, and this guilt he claimed took over. Then it was all Aislynn could do to keep him at her side, teasing and whispering and soothing his skin with light touches, until he slept.

She pulled in a breath, used it to temper her first reaction—rejection and slight—and then she let the air out. Slowly. Reveling in how relaxed, content, and aglow she felt. Everything in her world had been rocked and changed. Especially her opinion. Normans weren't barbaric, crude, or filthy murdering hordes of *poucah,* at all. They were lusty, though. That much had been true.

She narrowed her eyes in contemplation of him as he bent forward a little to see more fully what his day held. Brawny, muscled, immense . . . and very fit. They were all of that, too.

And sweet. They were also apologetic, and full of remorse and guilt. If that was his religion, Aislynn was very grateful she'd been shown the ancient ways. The only gods she knew were the ones controlling everything, even the fates. She touched her flat abdomen in thought. Especially the fates.

"What is it?" she finally asked . . . softly, with the slightest touch of voice. That was the best way to approach the mantle of guilt and piety he seemed cloaked with when the throes of passion had passed: with womanly stealth. This man held the secrets to heaven on earth for her. She wasn't allowing his stupid vow to stay it! She'd use any weapon at her disposal. Even jealousy. Which he made easy. He was a jealous sort.

Aislynn smiled at the remembrance of how she'd used that emotion to get him back with her the last time. Just as the dawn had broken. Exactly then. And then she'd watched him for what seemed hours as he slept. On the side nearest the wall, curving about her in what was a defensible position if she ever saw one. No matter who ended nearest the open side, Rhoenne secured the back wall. She wondered if that was a trained maneuver, or one he simply assumed . . . which would say a bit about his character. She sighed.

He was such a beautiful man! Possessing eyelashes of a dark brown that swept his cheeks when he slept. Rhoenne Guy de Ramhurst was gifted with a truly beautiful face. One that should have sonnets devoted to it. Lost in slumber like he'd been, she could look as long as she wanted at his handsomeness. There wasn't a scar or mark on his face; nor a whisker. . . .

He moved, bringing her back to the reality that was his naked form being highlighted by the day-lit side, while shadows carved his buttocks and back into molded perfection. Aislynn sat up, went cross-legged, and studied him, as he was the elements. He needn't bother ruing anything. It wasn't a sun-filled day. It was a day of dripping rain, gray skies, and a moistness that, if she breathed deeply enough, sent cleansing feeling everywhere.

"'Tis day," he said finally, speaking to the opening he was looking through.

Aislynn snorted a breath. "True. A gloomy day. Raining. As it will for days yet to come."

"You predict the skies, too?" he asked.

"If it will get you back into my bed . . . aye," she answered.

He turned his head and was probably trying to look stern. Instead he just looked truly wondrous. Male perfection. On display. For her. Aislynn tipped her head to one side and sighed again, louder.

"Don't take that tone with me, wench," he said.

She giggled.

"And cease laughing. I have lazed about in a bed all morn."

"True," Aislynn replied. "Although I would na' have called it lazed. I would call it ecstasy and joy . . . and perhaps work. That's what you mostly did. You have worked. And I am a true taskmaster. I may need more."

He shook his head. "You're insatiable."

She shrugged. "Mayhap," she replied finally.

"I have to secure the fief."

"Today?" she asked.

"Every day!"

He gave the word emphasis as he turned, putting his hands on his hips and making Aislynn's eyes flare slightly. She'd take him to task about it later. If he was trying to be compelling, dominant, and forceful, it wasn't working. All he accomplished were wide eyes, quick panting motions for breath, and her nipples betraying arousal as well as they tightened. There was nothing to hide behind even if she'd wanted to. And she didn't. Aislynn leaned back onto her elbows, stretched her legs out fully, and watched as his eyes narrowed.

Dangerous. Lethal. Passionate. Feral. She watched his man-part stir with senses attuned to it and eyes looking for that very thing.

"You seek to delay me?"

"Nae," she replied.

"It won't work this time, Aislynn. I've stretched the bounds of God's mercy enough. I've enjoyed your body and taken my fill. I can withstand you."

"You are na' verra flattering, My Laird," she said, after a long span of time when he just stood there, taking deep breaths and then exhaling them out with enough force it was vivid. Eye-catching. Entertaining. She smiled.

"You don't need flattery. You're well aware of your gifts, and the extent of them."

"I am?" Aislynn asked without inflection.

"Oh, aye. And how to use such wonders . . . on me."

"Much better," Aislynn commented. "This is much better love talk, My Liege. Now. Come join me. I feel my *gifts* stirring, aching . . . wanting."

"Aislynn."

He was using his stern voice again—the one reserved for his men. She couldn't prevent the giggle.

"What now?"

"You."

"What about me?" he asked.

"You dinna' ken how to simply be. That is your trouble, my grand warlord. You have nae idea of the merit of rest."

"I can't rest. Sloth is a deadly sin."

"To whom?" Aislynn asked.

"All!"

"'Tis na' one of my sins."

"Heathen," he muttered.

"Christian," she gave a word right back and watched him straighten taller.

"You don't know the meaning of the word."

"Nor do I wish to! Why would I? I have better things. Do you na' feel it?"

"Feel what?"

"Beauty. Life. Wonder. Enjoyment. Rain, and the re-birth it brings. These things are not sins! They're steeped in the goodness of the earth and the passion of the skies. Look at it. Just look." Aislynn scooted to the edge of his mattress, rustling the straw filling, and stood. He watched her. "You canna' see what I speak of if you watch me," she said when he remained immobile, watching her and fighting his own response to it.

She knew he was, too, since everything on him stilled, making the ropes and striations of his muscling much easier to see, and his hands knotted into fists at his side.

"Aislynn," he said again, in his warning tone.

"What?" She was nothing save innocence and lack of guile. He wouldn't know what the inner woman was planning. She had a lock on his gaze as she walked toward him, skimming the surface of his floor with each footstep.

And then she was beside him, looking up at statue-like stiffness, except where he couldn't control. Aislynn dropped her eyes to the size, shape and glory of him, and then looked back up. And smiled.

"Wanton," he hissed.

She shrugged. "So?"

"We've not . . . even broken our fast."

"They brought . . . food," Aislynn replied.

"When?"

"As you slept. Why?"

He grunted softly. She didn't know what that meant.

"Food? You think of food . . . now?" She reached out a fingernail and traced a few of the bumps of his lower chest, where they moved from one into the other, like a weave of flesh-cloaked iron mesh.

"They . . . know I'm abed?" he said.

"Oh. *Nae.* Na' yet. But you soon will be." Aislynn tipped her head and glanced up at him through her eyelashes, and winked. The response was easy to feel, sense and see, as Rhoenne tensed even worse.

"Nor . . . have I given orders . . . to my men."

"So . . . order something." Aislynn moved closer, making it easier to reach all the male glory in front of her, skimming her fingers along tanned skin, lightly coated with beads that hadn't been there a moment earlier, and then the solid bulk of his arousal poked at her, stopping her.

"Or . . . der?" The word had a break in the middle of it, spoken at a higher pitch, as his entire frame pulsed and sent the motion of it right into her.

"You are their liege. You can order anything. Open your mouth and request it. You wish a fresh breakfast . . . perhaps a scone? Order it. You wish your men-at-arms exercising on your list? Say as much. You wish your armor polished? Order that as well. Whatever you wish. It will be as you say." She was whispering the words with her head tilted and experiencing every tremor he gave through the sensitive skin of her fingertips against his abdomen.

"I want . . . you to cease . . . this," he replied, breaking the contact of her eyes in order to look over her head. She wondered if it was to give himself the fortitude and strength to say something so foreign to what he really wanted, and a moment later knew it was as she curved forward slightly and his upper body leaned back a corresponding measure of space.

"Is . . . that an order?" She breathed the words across the immensity of chest he was showing her and felt the tremble in him from the one place she was still touching. And then she felt it harden even more.

"Damn you, Aislynn. Damn . . . !"

He didn't get the rest of his cursing out as his lips slammed against hers. The repast was forgotten, as was the dreariness of the day outside. Aislynn didn't even note the passage of time as he pummeled her body with his, bending her into contortions and sending all her senses into ecstasy. And when he reached his apex, and voiced the wonder of it into the chamber with his cries, Aislynn knew there was no greater joy available to her. None.

And if he thought this simply a spell of lust, he was very much mistaken.

Smoke alerted her nose, then flames did the same to her other senses. Aislynn opened her eyes, watched the mill burning, and screamed.

Nothing sounded.

Fire licked at the granary, smoking the labors of days into the night air, while the crackle of it ate away at the mill floor. Aislynn screamed again and there was still no sound to it.

Then it was Father opening the stable, smoke billowing from the door. *Even there?* Aislynn wondered. *In the stable? Fire didn't consume that rapidly, did it?* The shadow that was her father was moving, letting their prize goat from the building, and then he was falling.

Aislynn screamed again and again, until her throat couldn't contain more of them. Nothing changed. Her father was still being attacked. And then she saw the flickers of shadows; unclothed, muscled, frightening shadows.

A sound of agony and torment floated above the sounds of fire. Aislynn grabbed her throat, knowing they didn't come from her own throat. It felt too raw. She knew who it was making it, though—Mother. Horror gripped her tightly, suffocatingly, and there was nothing she could do.

* * *

Aislynn jerked awake, making the mattress beneath her rustle with the abrupt maneuver, her mouth wide and gasping for air, and her heart threatening to pound a way right out of her chest. There was no fire. The mill was still there and no one was murdering her family. It had been a dream, a horrid one. She'd never had such a dream. She wiped at the wetness of her face with hands that were still trembling.

"Aislynn? What is it?"

The warmth she'd been sleeping beside turned into Rhoenne, and he was just as large and strong and secure as everything else wasn't. Aislynn snuggled into his chest and the proximity brought recollection of passion, heat, and everything else.

"Tell me."

He had his lips against her forehead, making the words against her skin and sending flickers to the tips of every finger and the bottom of every toe, and making the shivers change to something very pleasant.

She shook her head.

"You have a bad dream?" His voice was seduction and bewitchment and nothing she should be listening to as it rumbled in the space next to her ear.

She nodded.

"You have them oft?" He was moving her upward, making the warmth of his breath slide along her throat.

She shook her head again.

"Tell me." He was requesting it against her shoulder, making tingles of sensation flit about her flesh and center where her breasts were held against him. "Was it so bad . . . this dream of yours?"

The breath from his words was gaining him exactly what a touch would have. She nodded.

"How bad?" he asked.

"Bad," she replied. The word didn't make much sound.

"Tell me."

"My family . . . was being murdered," she answered him. The sound came out as a rasp of whisper, making her throat hurt. She frowned.

His frame stiffened and then he lifted his head, taking all the warmth and secure feeling with him. "What . . . did you just say?"

"The mill was afire, my father was—was dealt a death-blow, and my mother was screaming."

"You have dreams like this a-fore?" He wasn't waiting for her answer. He was sliding from her and rustling from beneath the bedcovers to slide along the space between the bed and the wall. Then he was at a window, unlatching the long shutter, and flooding the chamber with what light the moon would part with.

"Well?" This time when he spoke, it was harsh.

He was standing in a moonlight shaft, looking like he'd been modeled of stone. Light was carving two slashes over his shoulders, shadowing everything into a statue of perfection. Aislynn sat up, clasped her hands to her breasts and stared. She forgot what he'd been asking.

"Well? Have you had such a dream a-fore, or not?"

"*Nae,*" she replied.

"This is not good. Get up. You're coming with me."

"Where are we going?"

"Make haste. Get dressed. Here."

He was tossing her a length of cloth that felt like one of his under-tunics, and after she tossed it over her head, that's exactly what it proved to be.

"I dinna' understand."

"I haven't survived more battles than I can count, and made it to an age approaching a score and ten without

some bit of instinct at play in my life. This is one of those
times. Come. No. Wait! We'd best fetch you a cord. Here."

He said the last because she'd moved from the bed,
making it obvious that his tunic, while it reached to her
ankles, wasn't staying on her shoulders well. He tossed
her a length of rawhide. Aislynn fumbled with tying it
about her waist, ignoring where he was pulling on his
chausses, and then his boots. She had to look aside.

"There are very few gifted persons in this world,
Aislynn. Very few. You're one of them. I don't question it
due to the mark you have on your hip, either."

At her gasp, he stopped. She didn't know what to say,
so she said nothing.

"Such a thing means little to me. Come. There's no way
to answer this by exact terms. I have to go by instinct.
Assist me."

He was lifting the length of chain that was his armor,
and tossing it over his head as if it weighed little, rather
than so heavy it bowed her legs.

"You're wearing armor?" she asked.

"I don't leave the walls without this mail. My subjects
have little love for me and we'll be outside the range of a
day's ride on horseback. That is the size of my *demesne*
and the range of my safety. I am also never out without
Pinnacle. This lady serves me well . . . and oft." He was
raising the sword and then he was sliding it into the scabbard at his hip. He didn't have the links beneath his arm
fastened. It didn't seem to bother him.

"This is what happens from a day spent in sloth.
Murder. Bloodshed. Pillaging. I was stupid to allow you
to dissuade me. Very stupid. And weak. Come! We must
waken Sir Montvale and the others. Now!"

She couldn't see his expression and if it matched the
tone of his words, she didn't want to. He had his hand
out for her. It looked to be a long way away.

Chapter Fifteen

The mill was still standing, as was the stable and the granary, and all of it was being breathed on by early morning mist, making it sparkle when the sun peered out. The ride had seemed to take forever, the perch in front of Rhoenne on his horse had been secure and comfortable, making it easy to ignore the dark shapes of night demons in the forests they'd journeyed through. Aislynn had even dozed with her head bent forward, supported on Rhoenne's left arm. When his horse came to a halt at the edge of the trees, she stirred and rubbed at her eyes, looking over the pastoral setting of the mill and outbuildings, and the fields covered in barley and corn, just as the dozen mounted men with them appeared to be doing.

"Our visit does not appear to be expected, My Liege." Sir Montvale spoke softly, from his position atop a horse at their right side.

"True," Rhoenne replied.

"Why . . . none even appear to be awake."

"True again," Rhoenne said.

"Such a thing is shameful."

Rhoenne clicked his tongue, but said nothing.

"It's obvious your subjects need further training. They

should know there is a proper way to greet their laird, should he decide to mount his knights and come calling in early morn. They should know it is with a full kettle of porridge and a bit of black bread. Such a thing is the proper greeting. It wouldn't go unappreciated, either. It certainly isn't with locked shutters and a fireplace that isn't even smoking."

"Harold." Rhoenne said the name without any inflection.

The knight had a smile hovering on his lips. Aislynn caught his glance and ducked back into Rhoenne's chain-covered chest.

"Had you asked, I could have warned you to visit when they awaken."

"Don't overstep, Harold."

"Forgive me, My Liege. I find my tongue loosens when I've been favored with a day of wenching and then denied sufficient sleep."

"I thought that was your problem with ale."

"You ever speak on my weaknesses. How am I to approach your lass with such a sad specimen as you continually portray me to be?"

"Approach . . . Aislynn?"

"With an offer for her hand."

Rhoenne sighed. "You talk nonsense. We're not here for such."

"Good thing. I'm fairly certain if you awaken one of your subjects for such a thing his answer will not be aye. He'll probably stick a field-prong in us."

"Harold, would you cease speaking nonsense?"

"Nonsense, he calls it? After awakening me and ten others, making us prepare for battle, and then forcing us to ride through the last of the night to reach the village mill so we can watch it awaken? If there is another word for such, I look forward to hearing it."

"My instincts have never failed me, Harold."

"Oh. This is an instinct-driven venture. I see. Much like your foray into our Battle of the Standard? That was on instinct, too, I recollect. Instinct to go to war with no winner."

"I was given Leistonshire over my loyalty, was I not?"

"That was a gift? You must learn better how to turn down such favors without incurring royal wrath. That would have been the smart move."

"Harold."

"You say my name like an argument that will assist with your version of events. You have no words of argument because you have no reason."

"I say your name in the vain hope it will allow me a moment of rest from your ceaseless words. That is why I say it."

Harold sighed. "Does your healer cook?"

They'd been sighted. The door was opening, and then a bundle was put on the steps. The door shut loudly.

"Oh, look. Your subjects have relented. They've decided to favor you with a gift. Riley! Fetch the bundle."

They all watched as one of them spurred his horse, galloped to the building, swooped low without breaking stride, and seized the bundle on the edge of his sword. It was impressive. Aislynn sat and watched it and knew how the miller and his wife must be feeling. They'd taken her in; protected her; sheltered her. She'd paid them back by shaming them.

She wasn't surprised when it was put on the ground and opened. It was her belongings, wrapped in the voluminous cloak she'd used when she was about as the Lady of the Brook.

"Your parents are sending your clothing?" Rhoenne asked.

She nodded.

"They don't welcome you?"

She shook her head. "They dinna' dare."

"Why not?"

She looked away, hoping it wouldn't sound in her voice. "Because I am a Ramhurst . . . wench, now. I canna' go back. They canna' welcome me. The entire village will know of it."

He sucked in breath on it. "That explains your dream and why such could happen. I'll post guards."

"They'll be safe, as long as they disown me."

"Perhaps. Perhaps not. Montvale! Hand up that bundle. See to gaining foodstuffs for yourselves. Post a guard."

"You'll not partake?"

"I have a bitter taste in my own mouth. I'll not be able to swallow. Report to Tyneburn when it's done."

"The meal?"

"Nay. The attack. There will be an attack on him. We have to protect them. Call more guards if you need them."

"How long must I wait out this . . . attack?"

Rhoenne looked down at her, touched her gaze and then held it. The sun was rising fully now, dispersing the last of the mist and shadowing every plane of his face. Aislynn licked her lips.

". . . time and again I am left with naught to do save await you two! Very well. We'll wait. All eleven of us, with growling innards and tired bones, while you gaze, love-struck, into each other's eyes. I still say you should walk your steed across this pasture and ask the man for his daughter's hand. *That* would gain you more than the posting of a guard. It might even gain us a bit of breakfast. I am not against that, at all."

Rhoenne's eyebrows lifted and his lips twisted, although he avoided making the smile. He looked over his shoulder, releasing her back to sanity and normalcy and everything that was hued with the off-white and yellow tones of the morning.

"Two nights. If there's no attack in that time, then my instincts have failed me."

"You'll not ask her father for her hand?"

"I haven't asked the king yet."

Harold smiled widely. "As long as you have that decided, I will do as you wish. Get Richard to draft your missive."

"What missive?"

"To the king. Alerting him of your stance. A-fore his daughter reaches an age of marriage and can be forced on you. Such a political alliance you couldn't decline. If I were you, I wouldn't tarry."

"Harold. None said anything about a wife."

"Well, someone should. Why, if these prickly subjects of yours knew your intentions were honorable, it would go far toward assuaging this hate they all feel for us. Aside from which, the lass has stolen your wits and turned you into a man capable of ordering wild midnight rides in order to watch one of his subjects awaken and start his day. Think on it, My Liege. Think hard! You'd have a beauteous bride—who happens to be one of them—a wedding ceremony that would be open and attended by all, and a bit of oil poured on troubled seas. For diplomacy purposes, it's perfect."

Rhoenne must be thinking. The line in his forehead was prominent as he looked over at Montvale.

"Besides which, she is the most beauteous in the land. She stirs your desires and your body. Admit it and have done."

"How would you know?" Rhoenne asked, in a cold tone.

"Because that's what she does to mine. If it's not the same with you, you're inhuman and made of stone—and yes, you can fight me on the list over my rash tongue, again, if you like, I'll still not deny it."

"What of the Ramhurst curse?"

Montvale rolled his eyes. "Bad luck doesn't make a curse."

"Bad luck? Five babes; six deaths. That is not just bad luck."

"Didn't she also harbor a curse? I heard it from Brent's men, when they weren't sniveling in their cups over the punishment you meted out. What of that curse? Was any of that true? Well? A curse is just that, My Liege. Words."

Rhoenne was looking down at her. Aislynn didn't look up to verify it. She couldn't. She was trying not to show how embarrassing either answer he might give would be.

"Harold, you're unchivalrous to ask such a thing."

"I am?"

"Any answer would impugn her honor or stain my own manhood at the same time. I beg leave of it."

Harold grunted. "Granted. Come, men. We dawdle when we could be filling our bellies with good gruel and dampening our thirst with heavy mead. If you think Lord Ramhurst's aleman a wizard with the brew, wait until you taste what a Scot is capable of. Come. I know of a croft near here, where the food is appetizing and the owner is not amiss to a pebble or two of Ramhurst gold to pay for it. Not you, Riley. You stay to guard. We'll bring you something."

Montvale was nodding toward them and Rhoenne replied in kind before turning his horse away.

The sun was rising farther, shedding a golden glow in a pattern of the hills at their back, making a snake-like line where the shadow was giving over to the light. Aislynn watched it from a position ensconced in Rhoenne's arms, and leaning against his chain-covered chest. She'd never felt so content, and couldn't decide why.

"As I recall . . . that brook of yours contains fish."

She nodded.

"Good. We'll follow it. If my memory is correct, that particular burn has a boulder at its head, spewing forth water."

That's what they did, for what seemed like hours, while the sun rose higher, the horse warmed to the point its heat was transferring to her thighs, making them sticky and itchy where they touched horsehair. It didn't seem to affect Rhoenne, and before the sun had reached its highest point, she felt the weight of his chin on her head as he used her for support to sleep. She knew that's what he was doing, too, as the length of breaths he was taking in the chest she leaned against increased and deepened, and the air of each of them feathered across her forehead and nose.

Sunshine-gold colored the landscape, making every hue more vivid, every smell more pungent, and every sound sharper and clearer, and with a definition that made it instantly recognizable as what it was. Aislynn sat, bowed backward into the man's chainmail-covered chest behind her, in order to hold up the weight of his head as he slumbered. She'd never felt so divinely happy, and couldn't decide the why of that, either.

The stream curved, molding itself into a pool, overhung with willows and grasses and speckled rocks, while all the water seemed to be spilling out from beneath an immense boulder at its head. There was more. The entire glen was in a pointed shape, looking like the boulder had carved its own way to its resting place out of the sides of the hill, and making any slight breeze deepen into a whirl of sound. The horse stopped, and the lack of movement must have been the reason Rhoenne lifted his chin and shook his head slightly to awaken himself.

"Ah. The fish pond. I did remember it."

With that, he put both hands on her waist and pushed himself off the side of his horse, before using the next motion to bring her off to stand shakily beside him. He proceeded to show her how to fish. He had to find the perfect, slender piece of wood, and while they were looking for it, they gathered twigs to start and then feed their fire.

Then he was requesting her rawhide belt, in order to strap
a dirk into place on the end of his stick.

Aislynn hesitated, and that had him asking if she wanted
to wrestle for it. Which got him the belt, and then he put
one end into the water to soak it before cutting it into two
pieces. She watched as he used the wet end of his piece to
tie it securely onto the fat end of his stick. Then he flipped
his pole, and held one end of the small, wet piece against
the handle of his dirk with his left thumb, pulled the tie
taut, and made it seem longer than it had started out, as
he worked at his makeshift spear. He should have put some
clothing on beneath his chain tunic, since the cloud-
interspersed sun was shadowing valleys of sinew and
muscle with his every movement, and highlighting arms
that she already knew would be useless to wrestle against.

Rhoenne went to a crouch and Aislynn followed, although she hadn't any idea why. He stopped at the far end
of the pond, his finger to his lips as he showed her. Where
he stopped had them looking like additional rocks on the
bank, while the sun sent their shadow over the ground
behind them rather than over the water. She watched as he
wound the dried end of the rawhide about his hand, then
he pointed to a silver fish, glittering beneath the water,
before slicing his spear into it. And when he yanked the
spear back out, there was a fish on the end of it.

He did it again, and on the fourth one, he asked her how
hungry she was, and looked at her with eyes that were reflecting the sparkle of sunlight-dappled water. If she had
an answer, his gaze obliterated it. And then he reached for
her, changing the dream-like sequence of everything, and
turning it into something very real and very exciting.

Metal links pressed against her linen shift, imprinting
the twined, oval loops all over both of them with the pressure of his hold. Groans fled his lips just before they
reached hers, and then they were echoing from inside the

caverns of her mouth. Aislynn squirmed against him, moving her flesh about the chains with a ripple of movement, and catching her breath whenever a link or its connector slid across the sensitive areas of her breasts.

"Oh, Aislynn . . ."

The act of speaking disconnected his mouth. Aislynn wasn't having any of it. Her body didn't belong to her anymore—it was back in the dream world she'd found and been residing along the fringes of, all day. The fish lay forgotten as Rhoenne pushed himself onto his back, taking her with him. Aislynn split her legs and straddled him to keep herself where she most wanted to be. That way, she could match the parts of her that were twinging and aching and in a world of want and need, against where he was denying her.

"This wasn't to happen again! I vowed—"

"Hush."

"You don't understand! We've gone too far! Too many times already! It's unsafe. Any more, and—"

"And you talk as much as your vassal, Montvale, does." She nipped at his lip to shush him and then she was sucking on his lips, drinking from his tissues, and gripping her fingers into his hair so he couldn't move.

"Nay, Aislynn. Not this. Not . . ."

His words ended when she flicked her tongue against his, making him lurch up and off the ground in a ragged movement of strength. The new sound wasn't a groan, but it was close, and it came from both their throats. A swell of sound rose to add to the bubbling of the water, the shy sweetness of a breeze and the rustle of grass along the shoreline. Aislynn started moving her hips, sliding them against where the leather patch of his chausses was hard and searching, and completely at odds with the man who was still mouthing denials.

Aislynn locked her lips to his, sucking what she could,

while her hands moved to the hard chain covering his chest, imprinting the weave onto her palms with the pressure she used to shove at him as she arched herself, while scooting into a crouch with her knees to either side of his hips.

Slickness coated her movements, hard breathing covered over her moans, and her own heartbeat was filling her ears with a thud of sound that thundered with the depth, rawness, and pull of unadulterated need.

He had his chausses tied with another strip of rawhide, and she worked it free with hands that were clumsy with her haste and lack of sight. Rhoenne didn't feel like he was in denial. He was holding to her hips, moving his hands upward and then back down, and sliding her tunic hem higher with each movement he made.

She had the tie open, the tops of his hose pulled apart, and him in both hands, and was cooing the sensation into his mouth. And then she was lowering herself, spreading herself about him, and crying aloud with the ecstasy as her flesh embraced him.

"Oh dearest God! Stop! Nay! Dearest . . . sweet—"

She stopped further words with her mouth, although the curve she had to go into was made difficult because his hands were trying to push her away, and she was using everything in her legs to make it impossible for that to happen.

"I'll not—I cannot! Pray, cease this! Cease!"

Aislynn opened her eyes to slits, accepted the anger he was looking at her with, the way his nostrils flared, and the way he'd gritted his teeth to lock his jaw as he glared at her.

"You fight this for *nae* reason," she told him.

"I'll not be the death of you!"

"You've *nae* power . . . to do so," she returned, although it was panted through two breaths, as she pushed herself

onto what portion of him she could reach, and then lifted
to do it again.

"I made a vow!" he repeated and it sounded like he
sobbed it.

"It was . . . na' necessary."

"I don't . . . vow lightly," he said, making the cords of
his throat bulge out with the force of it. Then he cursed,
and told her she wasn't just an enchantress, she truly was
a witch, and a lusty one at that.

All of which got him not the anger and fight he was
looking for, but her smile. Aislynn slid down further, embracing him deeper, and kept her eyes on his. She waited
until he looked and then she opened them fully, making
certain he'd note their color.

"Look at me, Rhoenne Guy de Ramhurst. Look." She
crooned the words, and they came out sweeter than they
should have, since his arms had slackened, allowing her
to embrace the entire axis of him. Deep. Throbbing deep.

She went into an arch to put her face close to his and
held herself there. And watched him. Enthralled. Like
always.

"Tell me what you see," she whispered.

"Lovely."

She pursed her lips, shook her head, and lifted her
upper body from him, running her fingers over the chains
still covering his torso, her fingers acting like the waters
of the burn as it splashed over bottom rocks, making
white-capped waves as it went.

She rocked when she reached an upright position and
accepted the lunging motion he made, in order to keep
him locked to her. Then she was moving again, sliding
back into the arch in order to get once again to the same
distance from his vision.

"Look again." She whispered it and reached out to lick
at his lips, wetting them, and then purring her satisfaction

as he loosened his hold on his teeth and allowed her tongue entrance.

"Oh, dearest God," he groaned when she finished her kiss and moved back to the span of space at the end of his nose.

"Look again. Closer. Look for what you dinna' expect."

"I cannot hold myself back much longer, Aislynn." He licked his lips at the end of his words, drawing her eye for a moment.

"Ramhurst. Look. What do you see?"

"Your eyes are both brown," he whispered.

She smiled, raised her brows and then she nodded.

"What does that mean?"

Aislynn wasn't giving him succor that easily. She moved away again, lifting to sit astride him again, owning him, glorying in him. She felt his hands moving again, his fingers sliding to her waist, and going from there to cup her buttocks, hold her to him, and keep her from making another movement with hands that felt like talons.

She snaked her way down again, across the chains, going into a slither of movement in order to bring her face back to his. Every motion made a corresponding lunge of his body as he shuddered along the water's edge, taking them dangerously close to the chill and the wetness.

"Give me what I want," she commanded when she got within an eyelash length from his eyes.

"I can't. Oh, God . . . dearest God." He was vibrating worse with his words.

Aislynn nuzzled his nose with hers. "You canna' hurt me, Ramhurst. Only the gods have that much power."

"But I *vowed* it! Dearest, sweet, God! No. No, Aislynn . . . no."

"Ramhurst. I love you," she whispered.

He jerked upward, seizing her mouth, while at the same time his hands tightened their grip, keeping her in position so he could slam himself into her, filling her over and over again until her cries of satiation blended with all the other sounds of the pond. And then he was rolling, holding her to him so he could put her before him on the grass, go to his knees, and elevate her for delectation and enjoyment and domination and the blood-pounding fury of a man who had been brought to the edge of desire and dangled there for too long.

Aislynn screamed, filling her lungs again and again with air, until the keening note of it was just a whimper of sound, and then the low, deep timbre of his cry came, as he held her to him and shuddered time and again, and then went completely still. Aislynn opened her eyes, and then she was reaching a finger and gliding it along a lone tear trail on his cheek.

"Damn you, Aislynn," he whispered. "Damn me and damn you, and then damn us both again. You're a witch. And I am in your thrall. Forever."

Aislynn's lips twitched, holding in the supreme joy, but that was the only part of her that managed it as everything else about her thrilled to it.

Chapter Sixteen

His home was aglow with light, making it a beacon amid the dark skies and spattering of rain the afternoon had become.

Rhoenne pulled in a deep, moisture-laden breath, filled with the scent from her hair, and held it. Just as he was holding her. Close. He had to, before the worry started up. His entire existence had been filled with a passion for more than he had . . . more wealth, more property, more titles, more power. He'd done all the king required in his quest for gaining and then keeping more.

There hadn't been any place for emotion. He hadn't allowed it. Rhoenne Guy de Ramhurst wouldn't allow anything to get in the way of his ambition, and then this little slip of a girl had managed it.

He watched the glow of Tyneburn beckon as they leisurely passed through trees, and wondered how he was supposed to put his defenses back in place. How was he to get the thirst for more acquisitions and power back, and the strength of conviction that came with it?

He knew he couldn't do it with Aislynn in his arms.

It wasn't until they reached the edge of the tree line that his senses alerted him. That wasn't welcoming light coming from within his keep. It was a melee of torches and men. Or his home was on fire.

Rhoenne groaned, lifted his chin from the perch atop her head, and tightened his thighs on his horse. The result was a surge of movement, sending them from the forest and into the cleared glen fronting his walls. They were spotted immediately, surrounded moments later, and then overwhelmed by the noise of hundreds of throats yelling.

The crowd parted slightly, giving room to move through them and thread across his drawbridge, and Rhoenne tightened his arm on Aislynn until they reached the sod of his courtyard. That's when he saw Richard standing at the main balcony. And with him was a group of knights . . . King David's knights.

Rhoenne's gut twisted, making him wonder how to get that under control as well. Ever since knowing Aislynn he'd discovered a wealth of weakness within himself that he hadn't known he possessed and didn't particularly like. It was better to be heartless and aware of only one thing— his quest for more.

Aislynn stirred in his arms, making everything feel all warm . . . hot. Heat shot from the space right below his heart and then down his limbs, making him tremble with it, and he wondered how he was supposed to get command of that response as well. He hadn't known this love emotion made a man weak. Nobody had warned him.

He shook his head, spurred his horse, and sucked in breath for a good yell.

"Richard!" Rhoenne used every ounce of voice the good Lord had gifted him with. The name he'd shouted wasn't intelligible as one, and garnered him little response. He spurred his horse forward, and forced a pathway through the crowd. He didn't have this volume of humanity living within his walls. He didn't know where his brother had found so many men. He came to a halt right below the balcony. That's when he was finally spotted and an order given for silence, which his drummers then guaranteed.

"Richard!" Rhoenne yelled it again.

"You've returned. Thank God. Send word to the others!" Richard had a large volume of voice for such a slender form as he issued a command. Rhoenne heard it with the same surprise it felt like everyone about him was exhibiting.

"Of course I return!" Aislynn was wriggling slightly in his arms. Rhoenne knew he had to let her go. He just didn't want to. Not yet.

"Then, come inside! We have much to discuss."

Rhoenne watched his little brother turn and leave the balcony, trailed by king's men, and couldn't help the slight drop of his jaw as astonishment set in. And then the pleasure and pride. He hadn't known Richard possessed leadership qualities, nor had he realized the extent of them.

He had Aislynn in one arm as he slid off the horse, and then he was whispering his request in her ear. She was safer in his chamber. Until he knew what had happened, and what was ordered. She nodded and he released her. He lost sight of her the moment he did.

Then everything on him felt cold. He was still affected by it when Montvale came through the crowd, pushing more than one fellow out of his way as he moved. He was trailed by men, their faces, arms and chainmail covered in rain-speckled grime and what appeared to be soot.

"Montvale!" Rhoenne made his voice loud enough to cleave the air with the throb of it. He had control of his emotions again. He felt it happening, and held the satisfaction deep, where it wouldn't show.

"My Liege." Montvale went to a knee.

"Rise."

The knight stood and regarded him solemnly. Black lines carved his face and sweat streaked it into a mask. From the glow of torchlight, it looked garish.

"And tell me what this is about."

Harold motioned with his head and Rhoenne walked beside him, up the stone steps of his entry and into his hall, where there was even more confusion. Such was the result of lazing about for a day and more, and allowing emotion to interfere with responsibility? Rhoenne looked about and frowned. And waited.

"Not yet. Your rooms," Harold whispered at his side.

Rhoenne shook his head. "Aislynn's there."

Harold sighed heavily. "Then an antechamber. With fewer listening ears."

Rhoenne led the way down one hall and into the space at the end of the hall overlooking the loch. The room he'd slated as a solar. When it was finished and had a door. It wasn't much, but it was private. Then he turned. "You left the mill unguarded? You disobeyed my order? Is that what this is about?"

"There's not much of the mill left to guard, although the granary's unscathed. As is the stable."

The knight stopped as Richard joined them. Rhoenne turned his head.

"What?" Richard asked.

"You usurp my place and then ask such?" Rhoenne asked.

Richard's brows rose. "King David's men arrived. You were missing. I kept them entertained with mead casks opened. And then he returned. Exactly like this, and with a cartload of bodies and a screaming wench with him. You expected different? You should have been here, then."

"What screaming wench?" Rhoenne asked.

"He over-speaks, My Liege. Neither the miller's wife or daughter were screaming. Crying mayhap, but not screaming."

"They were still seen. And heard. And creating havoc with every word. What was I supposed to do?" Richard asked.

"Order a force of men to get torches and start a war?" Rhoenne asked.

"I didn't do that. He did!" Richard was pointing up at Harold.

Rhoenne pivoted toward Harold again.

"There was no war intended. 'Twas a search party."

"For whom?" Rhoenne asked.

"You!"

"Me?" Rhoenne pulled back in surprise.

"Of course, you. Who else would command such loyalty? Not me. We survived an attack—exactly as you foretold, then we arrive back to the keep, sore and tired, and covered in filth that I have yet to bathe from myself—and meet up with a contingency of the king's men? And then find you're missing?"

"This was a search party . . . for me?" Rhoenne's voice stumbled. He couldn't help it. These Celts were assisting to find him? The possibility made his throat close off with more useless emotion. He had to swallow around it, and then he had to find his voice amid the same trouble. He didn't know what to do with all the sensations his body was betraying him with. He was overawed for a moment at the enormity of it. These Celts . . . were mobbed together in order to search for him?

"Don't let it pleasure you too much. These subjects of yours are not loyal. But they're more willing to find you alive and well, than get the alternative."

"Which is?"

"Brent," Richard supplied.

Both men looked to him. Rhoenne felt the bubble of satisfaction dissipate. His features were probably showing every bit of it, and that wasn't like him, either. He rarely showed emotion of any kind. He wondered when he'd lost control of that aspect as well.

"So, tell me," he said finally, as both men just looked at

him, making him feel weak and awkward and very strange. "Why would a search for me be necessary? You saved the mill. The battle was won."

"You may have foreseen this battle, My Liege, but you forgot one fairly important detail. You forgot to warn us that they'd be a Gallgael clan."

"You're certain?" Rhoenne didn't know how to respond. Everyone feared the descendants of the Picts from the most northern Highlands. Everyone. Even him. Now. Rhoenne kept the knowledge of that fear inside, and sent another curse to this love feeling he was suffering from. He couldn't afford to be weak and indecisive. Not with Highland Gallgaels attacking his fief. And king's men at his table.

"Aye. And they're a truly barbaric race. There's not a length of cloth between them, and they attack with little more than their bare hands. Without warning. And with stealth, cunning, and bravery. We took three of them for you. Their blue-painted carcasses are on a cart he's told you of. Beyond the gates. I'd have taken down more, but they ran off into the woods and escaped. I didn't have enough knights to follow."

"What of the miller? You say naught of him."

"Safe within these walls. Perhaps you should have journeyed back to your keep rather than play with your lass. You could have welcomed him and his family, yourself."

Rhoenne pulled in breath to answer. It burned. Then Richard answered for him. "Finish and cease the insolence," Richard said.

Rhoenne glanced over at his brother and the lad looked up at him without shrinking. He nodded and turned back to Montvale.

"Answer him," he commanded.

Montvale grinned, making his teeth look very white

against the black of his face. "Leistonshire will need another mill built, but that's the extent of it," he replied.

"How many did we lose?" Rhoenne asked.

"None."

Rhoenne nodded. "I see. You did well."

"We did well because we had advance knowledge of it. Exact knowledge. Odd, that. I'll not ask the why of it. I can guess."

"You'd be wrong."

Harold's eyebrows rose, making little, black lines etch his forehead. "You entertain an enchantress in your chambers, put her in charge of your affairs, and now you know of attacks before they occur? Such a thing will be talked of."

"Stop them."

"You cannot command what people talk of." It was Richard interrupting again. Both men turned toward him.

"Go on," Rhoenne said finally.

"Rumor feeds on itself. To try to stop it would only make more noticeable what you don't want whispered of. Trust me."

Rhoenne met Harold's look. The knight's brows rose, and he shrugged. "What have you have in mind?" Rhoenne asked.

"A celebration."

"A celebration." Rhoenne said it with no inflection.

"Aye. A feast to the victory and your safe return. Send your hunters out to bring down deer, elk, a boar or two. Open more casks and let the drinking begin again. Do it quickly, a-fore they talk more."

"Of what?" Both Harold and Rhoenne said it at the same time. Richard looked from one to the other.

"The miller doesn't claim Aislynn as kin. It's being whispered she's Gallgael clan and that's what they wanted. I don't know why. Something about a mark. A chain mark.

That's what they say. Loudly. To everyone. I don't know what it means, nor do I care."

Rhoenne gulped. Both of them watched him do it. He didn't know how to hide it.

"These Celts have heathen ways, Rhoenne, but your brother gives wise advice. Send hunters out. Order a feast. Get many hands busy. They need something to do rather than talk superstition and incite fear."

Rhoenne turned.

"And give command of it to your brother."

"Richard?" Rhoenne looked over at the lad he'd insulted and ignored for so many years. The look on his face must have spoken for him.

"You see another brother? Of course, Richard. The lad makes sense, has shown great leadership skill, and you have more important things requiring your attention."

"Such as?" Rhoenne asked.

"King David has sent a messenger. For you."

Aislynn took her time preparing. Old Rosie had attended to her, chattered on about events and gossip, and it was surprising how quickly she could get her bulk about the castle when she was chasing after serfs about their new duties. According to Rosie, the great hall was scrubbed and shined and aired out, and fresh rushes were scattered about. The trencher tables were groaning with the supply of breads and fruit. The fireplace spits were turning all manner of game meats. It was going to be a massive celebration.

Aislynn wasn't preparing for the festivities. She wasn't attending. Rhoenne had sent word with Rosie. Aislynn was preparing for when he returned.

A tub had been sent up and set in the middle of the room. It had been filled with boiled water, but it had since cooled. Aislynn tossed rose petals into it and let the scent fill her, soothe her, and work at relieving the nagging pressure that was a knot at the center of her lower back. She hadn't done anything. She'd had a dream. It had been terrifying, but that's all. A dream.

She rolled the soap bar in her hands, making lather that slid down her arm with the volume of it. She had no ability to foretell the future. No one did. It was a coincidence. It had to be.

The door opened. Rhoenne entered, pushed the door closed with his back, and then tipped the bolt down without even turning around to make certain of it. Aislynn let her eyes devour him. He hadn't changed. He hadn't done one thing to prepare himself. He was wearing the chain shirt and his leather chausses, and he was still taking her breath. She closed her eyes, and suffered a shiver that had nothing to do with the temperature of her water.

"What are you doing?" he asked finally, in a raspy tone that didn't sound at all like him.

"Bathing."

"Why?"

She opened her eyes. "A bath arrived. I'm making use of it," she replied.

"It was for me."

"Oh. In that event, I'm assisting you."

His eyes went wide and then narrowed. She knew what he was doing. She knew why he was doing it. She also knew how useless it was. She watched as his entire frame did the same motion to ignore her until he looked solid and still and inanimate again. She looked back down.

"I'm not staying."

"I ken as much," Aislynn replied, keeping her voice as even as possible. She was very proud of it. "You have a feast to attend."

"I don't join that. I may need to attend the king. In Edinburgh."

"Now?"

"On the morrow. Once his men have rested and I have heard his edict," he replied. "I won't have a choice. 'Tis what a vassal does—obey his lord."

"You are to him . . . as Sir Montvale is to you?"

"Aye. I've pledged fealty. As such he has my respect, loyalty, and friendship. I've been with him since he became Viceroy of Scotland and came back here. He wants to bring civilization, culture, and status to this land."

"We're already civilized," Aislynn replied.

"You haven't seen a Gallgael to think that."

"You're seen one?" Aislynn moved her gaze from her soaped hands to him. "Truly?"

"More than seen one. I've fought at their side. At the Battle of the Standard, three years past . . . almost four."

"This is the battle Sir Montvale described? Where nobody won?"

He smiled with half his mouth. "That would also mean nobody lost, although King David had his hands full convincing his court it wasn't a loss."

"You gained your fief from it?"

He looked at her. "Leistonshire. I was already given a large land grant for my service at David's side in Normandy and England."

"And now . . . you've killed Gallgaels. Is that why you journey to his side?"

"I go if I'm ordered to. I normally avoid it. There's too much arguing at court." He was bending forward, reaching his hands to the floor, and letting the chains slide off him, until there was a puddle of metal at his feet. When he stood back up, there was nothing on his upper body but muscle, sweat, and slight, thin streaks of scratches from wearing armor with nothing beneath it.

"Arguing?" Aislynn asked around the instant dryness in her own mouth.

"Noblemen have naught to do save argue and their wives practice fancy dress. I don't enjoy it. And I have too much unsettled here."

"Then have . . . him journey here."

Rhoenne smiled then. "The king rarely ventures from Edinburgh."

"Why?"

"He hasn't time. These arguments I spoke of? He settles those that warrant his time, from those rich and lucky enough to have the opportunity to be heard by him."

He shoved his hips forward as he leaned against the door. She watched him toy with the rawhide tie at his waist as he watched her. Such a view made her next words garbled and indistinct. "Rich? Lucky?"

"His chancellors are the men to see if one desires an audience with the king. They aren't immune to a gold-greased palm. If that doesn't work, you can tag along with a nobleman granted access to the king's inner chambers. That takes luck."

"I dinna' like the sound of that."

"A beautiful woman such as yourself would probably gain an audience with little more than a glimpse of her face."

"I like the sound of that less."

"It's impossible to settle all arguments, Aislynn. I'm sure he'd choose which ones to hear, but that takes away from the time spent hearing them, so he pays chancellors to decide."

"These chancellors. Are they easy to spot?"

"Are you planning on attending court and requesting an audience?"

"I'm trying to understand," Aislynn replied.

"They're very easy to spot. They fancy dress better than the ladies do."

"Nae!"

He chuckled. "King David disdains rich clothing and

appointments, unless he's hosting another noble. He prefers hunting attire. I've rarely seen him in his crown and robes."

"So . . . should I need to find him, I look for a plain-dressed man?"

"One look at your face and you wouldn't have to look anywhere. His majesty would spot you. Anyone would. I just spoke on it."

"Am I to await your return?" Aislynn asked.

Other than a swift intake of breath, it didn't look like he'd heard her, or he was being very careful to make it look like he didn't hear her.

"Well?"

"Aye," he replied finally, although it was so softly said, if she'd made any sound it would have obliterated the word.

"You have to be certain, My Laird," she said.

He groaned a reply that didn't have a decision to it.

"Are they afraid of me?"

"Isn't it enough . . . that I'm afraid of you?" he replied, evenly.

"You are? Why?"

He sighed. "Because you're . . . blessed."

"Blessed? I carry a mark. I have healing skills. A knowledge of herbs and scents. Nothing more."

"Nay. There's more. Much more. It frightens me . . . and it draws me."

She started rotating the soap in her hands again. "I had a dream. It wasn't real," she replied, finally.

"You saw what happened; exactly as it happened. Mont-vale told me."

Aislynn couldn't halt the shivers. "It was a dream."

"Then dream! Tell me of the next attack! And the next one. And the one following that. Help me put a stop to it! All of it!"

"I dinna' have that much power, Rhoenne," Aislynn whispered.

"You cannot hide it from me."

She didn't answer. He didn't seem to be expecting one. The torchlight was flickering from the wall sconces, glittering on the froth and making prisms of color dance about. She put her face close to it, pursed her lips, and blew gently, releasing a cascade of bubbles up into the air.

"You have a dark poetry in your soul, Rhoenne . . . and you have a secret. That must be why you call yourself a troubadour." Her voice lowered, making the words sound like a caress. She watched him watch her.

"And you speak riddles."

Aislynn took a deep breath. "You have a lover's soul. Buried. You've kept it hidden and locked away for so long . . . you dinna' even ken how to use it." Her voice dropped to a whisper of sound and she went to her knees, to make it easier to rise.

He groaned hugely, filling the space with the resonance of his voice and making everything stop for a brief moment of time. Aislynn whistled softly, at length, and waited until he looked toward her again.

"Are you still afraid of me?" she asked.

He didn't say anything for the longest span, and then he nodded, crossing the barrier of steam and space and making it feel like he was right next to her. She caught her breath at the sensation.

"Do you ken why?" Aislynn lifted her hands again and blew gently, releasing bubbles into the air again.

"Oh, dearest God."

Aislynn stood slowly, making the last of the bubbles pop as they came into contact with her skin. He was making gulping noises as she stepped from the tub, lathering each leg as she did so. He'd gone to making choking-type sounds as she crossed the floor toward him, put her hands about his neck, and then she melded her body to him, wetting the chausses with soap and darkening the material to a darker gray than it had looked to be when he'd danced with his sword in them.

Rhoenne was shuddering, but wasn't doing anything to help or hinder her. Aislynn got bolder, and started rotating her hands about his chest, running her soaped fingers over the ridges and planes and mounds and bumps of him. Then she was making her breasts follow the same path, all of which was gaining her groans from him and a tremble he couldn't deny.

"You think me an enchantress, My Laird?" she whispered, when her hands reached the waist of his hose and toyed along the edges of it, following the seams where they met flesh, and twining outward when a particular muscle forced her fingers to go that way.

"Aye," he replied, finally.

"And you find this . . . bewitching?"

"Aye," he said, again.

"Anything else?" She was rubbing her belly along the leather patch at the front of his hose and enjoying every lurch and jump and movement that he was making.

"I enjoy the way you . . . assist with my bath," he replied. And then he had her enveloped in his arms, his lips on hers, and everything on him speaking of his love.

But not once did he say it.

Chapter Seventeen

He was gone when Rosie came, loud and cheerful as usual. Despite his warning to stay in the chamber, Aislynn couldn't do it. Rosie would be telling her the story the moment it happened, but Aislynn wanted to know what their King David was requesting without getting it from someone else's lips. She already knew it was bad. Rhoenne may have known it as well. It had remained unspoken, but she'd guessed the reason he made the messenger wait.

It didn't matter what she wore, as long as it was donned quickly. She didn't care if it was one of her work shifts from the mill. She didn't care that there wasn't anything on her feet. She wasn't caring that she only had time to tie her hair back. For once, Old Rosie wasn't chiding her over her lack of decorum, either. Aislynn knew why. If they didn't hurry, neither one of them would know what was happening.

The great hall was filled with humanity: some sober; some not; some still eating; and some were snoring on benches. It was impossible to stay there and observe anything. Aislynn hung behind Old Rosie's bulk the moment they got to the room. It was difficult to hear. It was almost as hard to see. The rain-filled daylight wasn't doing much but denting the ceiling of the room through high windows, and what torches were still alive were but embers. Rosie grabbed Aislynn's arm and pulled her over to a narrow flight of stairs.

They reached the balcony reserved for minstrels and troubadours, overlooking where Rhoenne was already in place, perched in a huge chair, as if he'd been there the entire time overseeing the festivities. There was a cleared space on the floor directly in front of him, making anyone unlucky enough to be so close have to look up. It was imposing. It was meant to be.

Rhoenne was in a Ramhurst-blue tunic, beneath a silver-embroidered doublet that he wore open to show the large, hammered links of the chain about his shoulders. He had his broadsword in a scabbard strapped to his side; a row of skeans about his waist; heavy, silver armbands on each bare upper arm; leather knee pads called *cops* on each knee; and calf-high, black boots. He wasn't wearing hose. He was massive and muscular and strong and virile, and all of it was arrayed to be as impressive as it was. He'd taken her breath away when she first saw him. He still did.

Aislynn's eyes found him the moment they reached the perch, well above the hall, and that was only after they'd pushed their way through the throng already gathered there. From there she could watch him, with a quirk to her mouth and a sigh on her lips.

Then there were three long, deep booms, coming from a stretched-skin drum, making the air reverberate and the balcony tremble. Aislynn went to her knees, wrapped her fingers about the railing posts, and leaned forward, as everyone else seemed to be doing.

"Lord Rhoenne Guy de Ramhurst, First Earl of Tynebury!"

It was Richard announcing it, and he was using the all-encompassing voice he'd demonstrated he possessed yestereve.

"My Lord."

The emissary was bowing after he spoke, his rotund shape as unmanly as the high-pitched voice he'd used. Aislynn snorted her amusement. The still-drunk revelers below and to each side of her hadn't the same inhibition. There was laughter and chuckles, and then Richard was yelling for silence.

The room settled back into a low hum of sound. The emissary unrolled a large rolled document he had in his hands and started speaking again. He said something about coming on behalf of the king, but, at the first words, snickers became chuckles which became laughter, and then Richard had to yell for silence again.

"Give it to my brother to read," Rhoenne said, in a loud, bored voice, after the room quieted again.

"It's written in court script, My Lord," the man replied, sounding more like a complaining woman than a man whose presence was supposed to represent the majesty of a king. Aislynn wasn't the only one with that thought as the sound of laughter swelled again.

Rhoenne lifted his hand and the room quieted. "My brother reads all sorts of scripts, dialects, and languages. It's what he excels at. Give it to him. Now."

"But . . . this is most against court rules."

"Everything I do is against court rule." Rhoenne leaned forward, bumping his sword against the chair arm and looking menacing, even from a distance so far above him. Aislynn felt the thrill just watching him gave her. She could see it echoed in the sighs and movements of the crowd below. "Richard? Get the edict. Read it. Let's all hear what my king is requiring of me this time."

The man might have balked further, if Sir Montvale hadn't been escorting Richard to his side. Then the entire scroll was unrolled and Richard started speaking, and everything on her went blessedly numb. There was something said about the king's titles, how he was King of Scotland, Viceroy of the same, the Earl of Huntingdon with manors and castles through eleven counties in England. Then there was the listing of his accomplishments, although there were a few snickers when it came to the Battle of the Standard. The parchment started listing the three border priories he'd had built, one of which—Melrose—had already been exalted to the status of an abbey. There was a listing of the king's ecclesiastical accomplishments, the monasteries, the gifts to the churches and foundations of the country that was Scotland. Richard had to stop for a breath then, while everyone else seemed to hold theirs, and the next thing listed was the reason for the missive. King David was putting forth his own daughter as a bride for the Earl of Ramhurst. Before Richard could start listing the lands and titles that would confer upon Rhoenne as her dowry, he was already standing, glaring down at the man, and saying nay.

Aislynn didn't know what happened after that. It was numb and it was dark, and Rosie was the only thing of substance in her immediate world. She held to the old woman's hand, walked down the same steps, and was back in the hall before she realized what was happening. The room was louder than before, Richard was reading the entire edict again, word for word, and each one was burning into her breast and finding its way right to the base of her spine to join the ache that was already there.

The same thing happened at the end of it, too. Rhoenne loudly said no in no uncertain terms, and then he was cautioned on what would happen should a vassal thwart the king in such a fashion. Aislynn thought it was Sir Montvale leading the list of caution, but she couldn't be sure. She was too numb.

* * *

She was still in that state when Rhoenne reached the chamber, well into eve. He had probably argued. It wouldn't change it. Nothing did. Noblemen who went against the king were imprisoned, their lands were forfeit, their titles were stripped, and their clans were scattered. She had her hands to her ears over the litany taking place in her own mind, and then the door opened and shut, the bolt fell, and everything went perfectly focused and clear.

Rhoenne didn't look toward her and Aislynn stood from the bed. He didn't say anything. He walked to his table, pulled off his vest, unfastened his row of daggers, and then pulled Pinnacle from its holder, and set it atop the table where it caught and held the firelight. She watched as he lifted the chain from around his shoulders and put it atop the sword, where the thud of it was followed by a waterfall sound of metal links against steel.

"You've heard?" he asked.

"Aye," she whispered.

He turned a face as haggard and old as any she'd seen, and there was a film of moisture coating the bright blue she loved. She moved. Rapidly.

"And that's all you have to say?" he asked just before she reached him.

"'Tis a . . . great . . . match."

"True."

Then Aislynn had her arms about his back, put her forehead against him, closed her eyes, and breathed into the space between his shoulder blades where her nose reached.

"If . . . I'd not met you." He had his hands to his face now, locking her arms into the embrace with the pressure of his forearms against his upper arms.

"You must take your case to the king," she whispered.

"He won't hear it. I haven't a glib enough tongue, and I'll be in disfavor before I reach Edinburgh."

"Send Richard. He has a glib tongue. He'll create the luck."

"It wouldn't matter, Aislynn."

"But you're one of his favorite earls. You've been at his side, fighting for him, learning with him. You told me some of it. He'll listen to you."

"I'm thwarting him now. He'll order me put in irons if I don't agree to his choice. That's the cost of going against a king."

"Then see the queen. She'll have influence."

"His queen died. Years ago."

"Then see one of his chancellors!"

His bowed posture was frightening her, as much as his disenchanted tone and the defeated look of him. He was already giving in. He just didn't know how to tell her. She took a breath and made it easy for him.

"You must obey his edict, then. You must tell this emissary you will do it."

He snorted. "Nay. And do you know why?"

She shook her head. He removed his hands from his face and twirled in her arms, giving her a very good look at the light behind his eyes, and a glow she'd never seen before.

"Because I'm not the same man. King David will soon hear of it. Not until I heard the edict did I realize it. I won't do this, because there's one woman I will wed. One."

"You canna' do this—" she began.

"I've already done it. And I'll continue doing it." He swallowed, and went a pink shade along his tunic collar. "Because . . . I love you," he finished.

Her eyes were huge. He grinned when he saw it.

"You . . . love me?" she asked, choking midway through the question.

"If you'd look within, rather than with your eyes and ears, you'd already know. You were right. You hear me? I love you. Only you. Forever. There will be no other woman at my side, with the right to be there. I don't care what any number of kings decide and decree and write."

Shivers were flowing from her temple to her toes, over and over, and making her tremble with such intensity, he felt it.

"And when such a time comes that I hold our own son in my hands, I hope he will realize the bravery of his mother in giving him life. Between us, it will come to pass, too. You'll see. No curses. And no more edicts. Agreed?"

Tears filled her eyes, making pools at the bottom, before overflowing onto her cheeks when she blinked them into existence. She knew what she had to do. She only hoped she was strong enough. "I canna' allow you to do this," she whispered.

He snorted again, louder than before. "No one *allows* me anything. No one stops me, either. This is my creed and standard. For years."

"I can be your mistress."

"And have my children labeled bastards? I think not."

"I . . . there may be no children."

"Aislynn. I've already argued until I have no voice left, and all I received for my trouble was a pained throat and words ringing in my ears. I've listened to this royal emissary, to Sir Montvale, Richard. I've even listened to Eldine, since she'll share in my disfavor once it becomes known."

"What . . . will happen?" she asked.

"Censure. Fines. Seizure of property. Angry messages of protest. Arrest orders. Do we care? Let it happen. I have my instincts and your gifts to assist me, your caresses to blanket me, and the conviction of love to guide me. I can't fail." He sucked in another breath. "I never fail! King David needs to remember that if he tries force. I've fought at his side, I've protected him from blows, and I've never lost. Never. I've rarely even been scratched."

"You took a lance tip," she reminded him.

"'Twas a chance hit, and I thank God that I got it. It brought me to you. If I hadn't received that lance, I'd be signing my life away to my king and sovereign and allowing myself to be wed to a thirteen-year-old lass."

"She's verra young. She might even be pleasant to look at."

"With the castle at Fordingham as her dowry, she's very pleasant already. Just not to me. Brent can wed her in my stead. I'll put him forth. Perhaps His Majesty will allow such a union."

He had her lifted in his arms and was twirling, making the room whirl, and spin, and then he was lowering her, making everything right again.

The castle was galvanized overnight. The liege seemed to be everywhere at once. The entire walled estate hummed with activity. Aislynn still received sly glances from under lashes, but ignored them. She had Rhoenne's comfort to see to and a home to create. She didn't waste time worrying over baseless superstition. She knew the best ways to change such a thing were familiarity and time. Familiarity was in her hands and Aislynn made sure to be a common sight throughout the rooms. Time was the gift Rhoenne was giving her, by his constant presence at the hall. He rarely left the walls.

She wasn't vain enough to think the liege's presence was entirely due to her. She reasoned it was the change he'd wrought in her countrymen. He no longer patrolled his borders, fighting for possession of his fief, because there was no need for such. He had no dearth of clansmen to choose from for his household staff, or to grant Aislynn for her chores. Each day seemed to bring more of them to his castle.

And then everything changed.

* * *

"Have you nothing to say to this latest? Again? No answer to send?" Sir Harold's voice rang through the chamber. Rhoenne turned a baleful expression to him. Exactly like the one he'd used the day before.

"There's naught to say. Words beget more words. Action begets action."

"Then act!" Harold replied.

Rhoenne shook his head. "The king sends words. He won't act. Have courage, my friend."

"Courage? In the face of treason?"

Rhoenne stopped polishing Pinnacle for a slight moment before resuming the long slow strokes on a sharpening stone. That was the only hint he gave. "Go lightly with your accusations, my friend," he replied finally.

Harold sighed loudly. "Call it other, then. Give me a different word. I'll use it," he remarked finally.

"Our king won't risk a war. He doesn't dare. He'll lose this portion of the Highlands. He's no fool. He's a diplomat. Diplomats require patience. Words. Time. You worry over naught."

"Naught! He is threatening action this time, My Liege! It's been weeks of talk and he's finished talking. You know it. This latest missive came with garrisons of knights, mounts, squires, pages. So many they now have possession of the *demesne*!"

"You expected less?" Rhoenne slid a thumb along Pinnacle's blade as he sharpened it and watched his reflection in the polished steel.

"I expected you to keep to your vows. This is what I expected!"

Rhoenne stiffened. "I've found something stronger than fealty to my sovereign. Much stronger. Do you ken what it is?"

Harold rolled his lips. "This love emotion you continually spout. Tell me something I don't know!"

"'Tis true, Montvale. I am in love. Deeply. 'Tis an odd emotion . . . love. Powerful . . . and yet weakening at the same time." Rhoenne sighed. "When you gain it, you'll understand."

"God grant I never suffer it!"

"You should be on your knees begging for it! 'Tis that wondrous, Sir Harold. Vast. Consuming."

"You'll risk all for it?"

"Without thought! I'd risk all I have! That is how deep my love is for Aislynn. That . . . and still more." Rhoenne's voice had deepened as he spoke, filling the chamber with sound. Harold was silent as the reverberations faded.

"When we start dying for your love . . . will you listen then?"

Rhoenne chuckled. "Ever the doom and gloom it is with you, Montvale. You should have more faith. Nay. You should have some."

"In what?"

"Me. You. The power of words. Yours. I finally heed some of them, and look at the dissension you gift me with."

"For once, I am at a loss, My Liege. What words?" Harold asked.

"'Twas your idea to wed with her. Remember?" Rhoenne pointed out.

"Back then you had the choice. Now you have none! We have none! Must you be so blasted one-sighted?"

"Harold," Rhoenne said.

"Is love a good exchange for loss of honor? Well?"

Rhoenne flinched slightly and sheathed his sword. Then he turned back to the fire, giving Harold a view of the back of his head. It looked like a dismissal and it was.

"That question is for me to decide," Rhoenne finally

answered the fireplace. "I hear everything you tell me, my friend. I just chose not to listen."

"There is no speaking with you!" Harold was at the door, pulling it open with force enough to make a breeze.

"No, Montvale. There is *nae* arguing with me," was the reply.

Aislynn rounded the corner, her arms full of honeysuckle. She was just in time to hear Harold Montvale yell something unintelligible and to watch as he slammed the liege's chamber door behind him so hard, it cracked right down the center of it.

Then he turned to her. "What do you want?" he said with a softness that didn't match his expression.

"I . . . I brought honeysuckle."

"Why?"

"The scent calms the air, and alleviates . . . worry." Her voice had dropped. She felt her smile do the same.

"There's but one thing that will calm this. And it isn't little flowers."

Aislynn looked down.

"Have you a moment?" he asked.

"A . . . moment?" She was stammering, because his voice had changed as well as his demeanor. That, and he'd taken several steps closer to her, shrinking the space and making her clutch the wildflowers in her hands until the stems bent, coating her palms with their odor.

"To walk. To talk. I need to speak with you. Come." He didn't ask again. He put a hand on her elbow to pirouette her and started back down the hall.

"To . . . talk?" she asked, when he paced her down the hall, past door after door, before opening one and leading her into a room. He found what he was looking for with an alcove of space that had little purpose beyond intimacy.

Then he grabbed her arms, pulled her close, and lifted her to his level, face-to-face. It wasn't to kiss her; although her heart was already hammering the reaction if such a thing happened. It was to make certain she was the only one to hear him. She felt the breath on her cheek as he exhaled. Sucked in another gulp of air. Exhaled it again.

"Do you love him?" he asked finally, his face looking like he smelled something unpleasant.

She nodded.

"Words, lass! I want to hear words, and I want to hear them from your mouth. Now. Right now. You hear?"

She nodded.

"Do you love him?"

"Aye," she whispered.

"How much?"

"I dinna' understand," she replied.

"How much?" He shook her slightly. They could both hear the sounds of her slipper toes sliding along the floor, since he was dangling her just above it.

"More . . . than I can say."

He eased her back to the floor, and put one hand to his head to push the hair off his forehead. "The king won't release him from the betrothal. Do you know what that means?"

She nodded.

"Words, lass!"

"Aye," she replied.

"You can't."

"I do. He told me of it."

"Did he now? Did he tell you all of it?"

She nodded. Then she licked her lips and said the word.

"He can't have told you all. If you knew the whole of it, you'd not still be here waiting for it to happen!"

"But . . . I love him." Her voice was breaking. She watched him flinch.

"More than life itself?"

Tears glittered on his eyes. That had to be what was coating them with moisture and making them reflect nothing except a gray wash of color that changed with the light whenever he moved.

"Aye."

"Look at me when you say it!"

He was hissing the words, and even said in a whisper, they were frightening. She did as he asked.

"Good. Your eyes are both brown. He told me that signifies a lack of guile. You never lie if both eyes are brown. Truth?"

"He . . . told you . . . that?"

He nodded and looked over her head as somewhere in the rooms and halls behind him another door opened and then shut. Aislynn could see the pulse pounding in his throat, through the cords of strength and muscle that he possessed.

"Would you die for him?" He turned his face to ask it, surprising her.

"What?"

"Would you die?"

"Die?" Aislynn repeated.

He looked like he wanted to shake her, but didn't. "Does he mean more than life itself or not?"

"I'd die for him," she replied.

"Good."

"Good?" she repeated.

"Your eyes are still brown."

She blinked; inhaled; blinked again; exhaled. The scent of fresh honeysuckle and crushed stems and what had to be the male smell of Harold Montvale filled her nostrils each time.

"Why do you ask such . . . things?" she asked.

He licked his lips. "You've heard we suffer the king's

knights now? You've heard how they accompanied the latest message? And how they encamp about the grounds just outside the walls?"

She nodded. "Aye," she said when he frowned.

"How about the others?"

"Others?"

"Farmers, villagers, maids. Serfs. Freemen. Others. The castle is being overrun with them. You note any of that?"

She nodded slowly.

"How about the animals? You notice a surfeit of animals entering the castle yard and never leaving?"

"Animals?"

"Goats, pigs, cows. Milking-type animals; animals that are good for their meat. You see any of that?"

She shook her head.

"Words, lass!"

"Nae," she replied.

"Good. Brown eyes. Let's try again. You notice grains pouring in? Corn. Barley. Oats. Sacks bursting with it. You note any of that?"

She shook her head. Then she said it.

"How about the well-digging, then? You notice that happening?"

Aislynn wrinkled her forehead. They'd been digging over near the garden. She didn't know what it was for. "By the garden?" she asked.

"Good lass. Think. You know what it all means?"

She shook her head. *"Nae,"* she replied, when he seemed to expect it.

"Siege." He whispered the word and it still swept through every hair on her head, lifting it.

Aislynn's mouth dropped open and the honeysuckle fell somewhere at her feet. She'd been obtuse and blind. Rhoenne was preparing to survive a siege!

"That's right. Think it through. Do you love him enough to die for him? Enough to perhaps kill all of us for him, too?"

She gulped. Her mouth was too dry to make the motion and it ended up scraping her throat. *Foolish Aislynn.* The sly glances she'd been receiving from everyone wasn't baseless superstition—it was what her presence meant: siege and the fear that came with it. She'd been sightless, naive, trusting.

"What . . . can I do?" she whispered.

"Plenty. You're the only one that can, too."

He lifted her again, cradling her this time against his chest and whispering in her ear to make the words less brutal. "If you weren't here . . . and if you two didn't love each other to such a vast extent . . . and if he weren't a vassal to the king, there would be no need for all of this. Any of it."

"But . . . I do love him." She couldn't stop the tears that filled her eyes and then overflowed, until they found their way to her mouth.

"Do you love him enough to save him?"

"Aye," she replied after a long moment.

"Even if it's from himself?"

"Aye," she answered again.

"Even if it feels like you're cutting your own heart out as you do so . . . and killing everything you hold most dear?"

She wasn't the only one crying. Aislynn pulled away and looked up at him, took in the trail of a tear down one cheek, the nerve pulsing out one side of his jaw, and the sneer on his lips as he held it all inside.

"I dinna' know . . . if I can do that," she replied.

"Good." He said. "Your eyes are still brown."

"That's a good thing?"

"You're truthful. If you thought you could do it, you'd be heartless. And that you're not, are you, little half-ling?"

Her heart twinged at the endearment only Rhoenne used. "What . . . did you just say?" she asked.

"Do you want to save him from himself?"

"I am na' in charge of such a thing!" Aislynn was hissing it now and she was struggling, and all that happened was his hands tightened on her, sweat broke out all along her back and scalp, and not a whole lot more. He was waiting for her to calm before he spoke again. But at least, he was breathing hard.

"Do you love him or not?" he asked.

She licked her lips. "Aye," she whispered.

"Then save him. Give him back his honor and his life. You're the only one that can."

"I canna' run. He'll find me. He'll bring me back. He'll ken why."

"I know," he whispered back.

"He'll never let me go."

He sighed heavily. "There's one reason he'd let you go."

"There is?" she asked.

"Aye." He licked his lips. "Betrayal."

He had to be able to feel her heart as it reacted to the word, pumping blood and anger and red fury with every painful thump. She fought him then, trying with everything at her disposal to get free. All that happened was he had her legs locked between his, her arms got pinioned to her side, and then he was hissing words at her that she had no choice but to listen to.

"You think I find this any easier? Listen, Aislynn! I'd rather slice myself open than do what I have to do. You've got to be at that stage with me in order to help me. You've got to see it. You've got to do it! You've got to make him see it and believe it! You've got to!"

"You want me to betray him . . . with you?" Her voice wasn't holding the words very well, but she knew he heard what they were.

"I'd do anything to save him. I meant it. I'd die for him. I'll commit betrayal for him. I'll turn my dearest friend against me for this lifetime and all that come afterward. I'll give up my hope of heaven for him. I'll live with the guilt and I'll die with it. That's how much I love him. Now . . . it's your turn."

His words were slurred with the agony of saying them. He wasn't holding her anymore. He didn't have to. He had his head on her shoulder and was shuddering through the pain of what he had to do.

"I canna' do it! I canna'! Please dinna' make me! Please!"

"We won't have to actually . . . do it," he replied. "We only have to convince him that we are."

"I canna' do it. You dinna' understand how it is—"

"I'm the only one who understands, half-ling. The only one. Now decide. How much do you love him? Enough to save him?"

"I have . . . to go now. I have . . . to think."

"I know," he said.

"How much time do I—," she lost her voice on a gulp, ". . . we have?"

"I can give you tonight."

"I only have one more night?"

"He won't listen to me! He's set in his course. He's in love. He thinks it armors him against all foes. Can you change his mind?"

She shook her head.

"We're already closed off at two gates. Once the portcullis goes down and the drawbridge is lifted, no one goes anywhere. I don't know when he'll order it. Soon. We haven't much time."

"I dinna' . . . ken." Aislynn didn't have a voice left. He still heard it. For a visionary she was a complete failure.

For a woman in love, being asked to do the impossible, she had no choice but to be a success.

"I only wish I didn't know."

"There's . . . *nae* other way?" she asked. "You're certain?"

"Think. Spend tonight thinking. Meet me at dawn. West gate. 'Tis the lone one we still own. Bring a change of clothing and a cloak. Wear sturdy boots."

"Dawn?"

"We need daylight to get as far as we can. He's going to be vengeful. He's going to want blood—mine. I'd want it, too."

"What are you going to do?"

"Me? I'm going to go get drunk."

"Is that wise?"

He put a hand to his eyes and wiped at his eyes with his thumb and two fingers, scrunching everything as he did so. Then he looked back at her. "It isn't bright. None of this is. Tell him of my love, too. Will you do that for me? Somehow?"

"You ask too much!"

"I know. So do you." He released her and shuffled away.

Chapter Eighteen

She had one night to do the impossible; memorize and store away and say good-bye to everything that mattered anymore. And that everything was waiting for her when she got the courage to open his chamber door.

Aislynn had run from it at first. She'd gone back to the fields, thrown herself headlong into the honeysuckle, and waited until she was calm enough to face him. Then she'd washed her face with water from the burn they wouldn't be allowed outside to enjoy once this started, wrapped courage about herself until it felt like a cloak, and finally, she'd decided she was ready.

He knew something was wrong the moment she opened the door. Aislynn pushed it closed with her back and felt the slight give in the center from where it was now split. Rhoenne had been at his fire, contemplating the flames and waiting for her. He rose when she appeared, and Aislynn kept from blinking with a sheer act of will.

"What's happened?"

She shook her head.

"Something's happened, hasn't it?"

She shook her head again, watched the furnishings of his room swirl into a wash of design and color, and then blinked, sending it back to normal. If this was going to be her last memory of him, it wasn't going well.

"What's happened to your face?"

She smiled shakily. "A rash," she replied. "I selected . . . the wrong greens."

One of his eyebrows lifted and he lowered his jaw to pierce her with his gaze. A sea of noise flooded her ears in a large whoosh, making it impossible to hear a thing. Then it too died away, becoming a memory as her heart-beat took over, pulsing in her ear with a crescendo that increased the longer he just stood there, looking at her.

"Your eyes are both green," he said, finally.

Aislynn blinked and looked away.

"You have so many facets. So many layers. It's fascinating knowing you, every day, in every way. It's something I look forward to until my dying day. Do you know how that feels?" He asked it softly, coming close enough that he didn't have to give it sound, if he hadn't wanted to. She would still have heard it.

She nodded. Her voice wouldn't have worked enough to answer. Her throat wouldn't have let it. Even the breath she took shuddered. Her eyes remained dry, staring at the wooden enclosure of his bed that had seen so many passion-imbued nights, and pleasure-filled days! She trembled with another breath.

"Come away from the door, love. I had them prepare a feast for us. I felt like celebrating."

Food was going to stick to her mouth and make her gag. Wine might be useful. She looked at the center table hopefully. If he had wine, she might be able to get a sip or two down her throat. Aislynn envied Sir Montvale his freedom from this. She wished she had the same.

"What . . . are we . . . celebrating?" She stumbled through the question.

"My brother, Richard, has encouraged the Stewart clan to meet with me. It's more than I dared hope."

"Meet with . . . you?" she asked.

"About politics."

"Politics." She repeated the word with the same lack of inflection he'd given it. She was nearly to the wine cask, and the full goblet he'd already poured. It was looking like her salvation the nearer to it she got.

"You don't really wish to know, do you? It's nothing but senseless arguing, and dusty, dry words spoken by dusty, dry men."

"Why do you need . . . the Stewarts, then?"

"Because two large, influential clans are always better than one. Especially when dealing with royalty."

"He's na' going to accept a substitute groom . . . is he?" she asked. She had the wine goblet in her hand, then to her mouth, and was slurping the bitter liquid so rapidly his eyebrows rose.

"I didn't really think he would."

The wine was gone from her goblet. She put it down and picked his up. She had it almost to her lips before she asked the question. "Why did you offer it, then?"

"Because messages and emissaries do what is required of them. They transport offers back and forth, and that takes time. I needed time."

He watched her drain the second glass. It went down much easier than the first had, and put a nice haze on the entire scene. She blinked and watched the bedroom meld and waver.

"Time?" she repeated.

"Everything takes time, Aislynn. Everything. Close your eyes."

She didn't want to. The images in front of her were too interesting and absorbing to want to shut them off.

"Go on. Close them. Listen. Open your other senses. You know how. You've always known. You showed me."

Aislynn watched him weave, growing larger; then smaller; then larger. She blinked. It was a trick of the firelight. It had to be.

"Go on. Close them. Trust me."

She closed her eyes, finding them heavier than they'd ever felt before.

"You're acting very strange this eve," he said.

She told her body to stiffen, but nothing obeyed. She felt like she was swaying in place. She reached out to grasp where the table had been, and there was nothing there but him. She spread her fingers wide, discovered it was a thigh, and held on to it for balance.

"Strange?" she answered, finally.

"It's a new facet to you . . . a mysterious one. You're like a jewel, always different, no matter which angle you think you're looking at. It's always different, always strange. Deep, dark, bottomless—strange. Do you know of what I speak?"

She shook her head.

"Try harder."

Her forehead wrinkled. She tried to open her eyes, but they weren't obeying. That was strange as well.

"Do you know what I'm doing?" he asked.

She shook her head.

"Exactly what you do to me."

She gasped and stumbled, and he put his hand on her shoulder to stabilize her, making a center for her world. Then he had her within his arms, his chin resting on her head, and her head pillowed against the strength and size and power of his chest.

"I can hear your heart beating," he whispered. "It's like a caged bird, and about as desperate."

"Yours is na'," she replied, turning her cheek into his chest so she could hear it better.

"Describe it," he requested.

"Thick, strong, steady, powerful . . . constant, deep, harsh."

He chuckled, obliterating the sound she'd been describing with the depth of his humor. Then it died away, leaving the pump of his heartbeat behind again.

"Do you know how right you feel in my arms?" he asked.

She forced her eyes to remain dry. Shuddered with it. She couldn't do a thing about the catch in her breathing before she had it under control again.

"Do you know how empty it feels if you're not there?"

There wasn't anything on her that would stiffen, although she sent the command. All her body seemed capable of was clinging to him; resting against the massive chest of his and listening to his heartbeats as they continued their steady, undimmed thump of sound.

"And do you know what I'll do to make certain that never . . . ever happens?"

She knew exactly what he'd do, no matter how many lives it took, or how much it damaged . . . even if it were irrevocable, irreparable, and irreplaceable. The sorrow came then, spreading from the area at the base of her spine and moving outward, mercilessly changing every pore in her body into ache and pain and loss, and making it seem impossible for him not to feel it, too.

He slipped the ties of her shift apart, while his lips trailed along her forehead, down her cheeks, and over to an ear, as he mouthed ceaseless words of pleasure, and ecstasy, and everything a troubadour might say. She clenched her teeth, commanded her eyes to remain stone dry, forced her body to be open and giving and warm, and winged a prayer to the heavens that he'd not have a clue to what she planned.

* * *

The dawn was tinting the sky pink, yellow, and a shade of light blue that closely resembled his eyes as she walked across the garden lawn, careful to stay on the stepping stones, so her path wouldn't be so noticeable. The morning dew was wetting the bottom of her skirt, making the material and the longer grasses cling to her ankles, and making her wish she'd donned thick boots, instead of the flimsy shoes. She hadn't another choice. These were the only ones she could reach without Rhoenne hearing her.

Montvale wouldn't like that. She frowned. He'd told her to meet him at the west gate. She had to believe he'd know the only way she could sneak out of the castle and get there was through the garden. Any other place, she'd be spotted.

"There you are!"

Hard arms grabbed her to him, and she only thought about struggling before going limp. Sir Montvale was facing banishment just like she was. She was going to need him. Kicking and pummeling and screeching wasn't going to get them what they needed. It would probably get him killed.

At least, he'd be spared the starvation of a siege, she thought.

"You move too quickly! He's na' even awake yet!" Aislynn said.

"And I think you're a horrid accomplice."

"What?"

"If he's not on your trail, I don't know the man. Besides, I had Old Rosie to assist."

"Are you crazed? You did what?"

"She's awakening him at this moment. Just in case your departure wasn't enough to do so."

"You canna' involve her! She canna' keep a secret!"

"And if you raise your voice much higher, nothing about this will be secret. Come! These grounds have a path."

"So?"

"Goes right to the stables. I found it the other day."

"You wish a path to the stables?"

"I'm going to need access to my horse, and I'm not going to have much time to saddle him a-fore I need him. Here."

He walked her into a stand of trees, sheltering and private. There was a flat white boulder in the center of it. There was a blurred appearance to the clearing, since the pre-dawn light was glinting off the dew still coating the air. It looked magical and not at all what it was about to become.

He picked her up and put her on the boulder. Then he opened his cloak.

"Prepare yourself," he hissed.

"For what?"

Sir Montvale put his hands on his hips, looked up at the sky, and groaned heavily. "I've a head that wants to leave my shoulders, a scene to set up, and a naive wench with stupid questions. What else do you think? Open your cloak. Spread your legs."

Aislynn was going to do worse than that. She was going to lean forward and heave her belly's contents all over the long grasses that were trying to climb the sides of the white boulder. That's what she was going to do. The morning air was cold, coating her cheeks with a chill she had to keep wiping at. It also made her hands clumsy, and her fingers stiff and uncooperative. He had to help. He had his tunic rolled into a wad of material about his upper chest, showing he had an impressive array of muscle in his abdomen, the tie at the center of his chausses was undone and he had the leather patch askew. There wasn't a sign of anything hinting to wanting to do what he was pretending to do.

He shoved the cloak over her shoulders, fussed with the ribbon tie of her bliant before he had it opened, and spread apart, and then he had to rip her neckline, baring her breasts from the material, where the chill did even worse things to her, making everything go solidly frozen and suspended in filth and deceit and falsehood.

"Heave your skirts up, lass! Now! Now!"

His panic transferred to her hands, making her shaking worse, and it was next to impossible to bunch the material to her waist and even harder to splice open her legs. And before she could scoot down to where he was gesturing to her, there was a roar of sound so loud, so abrasive, so hate-filled, and so awesome, that their glances locked—wide and afraid—for an infinitesimal moment, before the fury that was Rhoenne Guy de Ramhurst penetrated the trees, swinging Pinnacle in front of him.

Aislynn leaped right over Sir Harold, vaulting over one shoulder and landing on her feet at the last possible moment. They all watched as the sword stopped a fraction of space into her flesh, since her palms had clapped onto the flattened blade directly in front of her bosom. She didn't even feel the wounds it was making.

"God *damn* you, Mont . . . vale!" Rhoenne's voice went from solid rage to a sob sound on the last syllable of the name.

"Forgive me, My—" Sir Harold began.

"Forgive you! I'd have put a sword through you if you weren't a coward hiding behind skirts!"

"It wasn't the woman's fault."

"She's not a woman any longer. She's not even a wench. She's a whore."

"Cease that, Ramhurst. We got carried away. Things happen."

"She's a whore. Proven this day. That's what she is."

She'd never seen a look like he was giving her. She

knew it had pain at its base, but she'd never looked at such wintry-cold hatred. Aislynn's eyes filled with tears no matter how viciously she sent the order not to. The pain in her back hurt so badly, it owned her every thought. She stiffened further, making her breasts more prominent, and she watched him glance there. Then he looked straight through her and sneered. She'd rather die than live through the look he was giving her. She tightened her hands on the blade in order to lunge forward, finishing the blow he'd been about to give and making it reality.

They must have known what she was about, for Sir Montvale had her elbows from behind, yanking her arms free of the sword, while Rhoenne let the tip drop to the grass. All of them saw the blood coating the edge in the morning dew. She couldn't even feel it.

"Get out of my sight. Both of you. Now."

"But My Liege, think! The woman can stay. I'll go."

"Both of you. Now."

"You don't have to marry her."

"Marry her? I don't want any woman that betrays me. Feel free to sell her services yourself, Montvale. To anyone."

He was turning away, his back and shoulders stooped and defeated, and Montvale snaked an arm about her, stopping her from running to him, going to her knees, and begging him to listen to what they'd done and why.

Then he was gone, and if it hadn't been for the steady dripping of blood from her palms, the pinprick of it that was welling right between her breasts, and the shocked stillness that descended all about them, she would've had difficulty believing it had happened. Aislynn heard the sound of ripping cloth, but her eyes didn't see anything beyond the space where Rhoenne had gone.

"Stupid lass. Give me your hand. Here."

She moved her eyes to him and watched him flinch. He

had white all about his lips, and looked suspiciously like he was about to sob.

She lifted one of her hands. There was a deep cut scoring the flesh, and she watched his lips tighten as he scrunched her hand into a cup shape before he bound it.

"Give me the other one."

There was an identical line scoring the other palm, just as deep, and just as bloody. She still didn't feel it.

"This is not going to heal easily. You're going to have to keep your hands from moving . . . to the extent you can." He said it, when he had both of them strapped into bound fists of linen he'd ripped from his own tunic hem.

She nodded. Then she fumbled with her shift, finding a way to hook her thumbs into the material and pull it over herself to shield and cover her breasts again. She didn't spare a thought to the drop of blood that started spreading the moment it touched the material. She had to wait for him to tie it for her.

"You shouldn't have done something so brave," he said when he finished, and pulled her cloak over her shoulders again.

"But he was going to kill you."

"Do you think . . . that's going to be worse?"

He turned from her then, went to his knees, and retched with the sound of sobbing accompanying it. Aislynn looked over his head at where the sun was trying to peek through the trees. Nothing about it felt warm. Nothing felt anything, anywhere, on any part of her. It was only by concentrating that she could feel the abrasive ache in her back.

He'd finished and was back to his feet, although she could see he wasn't just wiping his mouth, he was mopping at tear streaks on his cheeks, and ducking his head in the event she noticed.

"Come along. We've not got much time."

"Where . . . are we going?"

"Anywhere. We have to be gone before he gets to thinking and starts following."

"There's naught for him to think. He's labeled me a whore now. He won't follow."

"And you don't know your man. He'll follow." He was walking in front of her, stopping at the edge of the glade with a hand about her, putting her behind him before proceeding. She knew why. He was protecting her.

His horse was standing by itself, at the side of a stack of hay, just off the stable yard. That way, they didn't have to enter where there might be an observer, such as one of the king's knights, or a squire.

"You're going to have to ride in front. You can't keep a grip, otherwise," he said, when all she did was stand and look unseeingly at the horse.

"I can walk," she replied.

He was probably rolling his eyes. She didn't see that, either. She was observing and remembering the look Rhoenne had given her, and suffering through it each time. It was sending rivers of sickness all over her frame, and making her wobble in place. It didn't change. She still had to remember. It wouldn't go away.

She knew he put his hands about her waist and put her on the horse, directly in front of the saddle. She had a moment of ache, while her body recalled another time, and another horse, and another ride. Then it was gone.

"You truly think he'll follow us?" she asked, when they reached the main road and he went straight across it and into the wood on the other side.

"I know he will."

"Why?"

"Because nothing about this makes sense, except what it is. I just have to keep him from finding us."

"Why?"

"Because you let me live."

"You expected to die?"

He blew a breath across the top of her head. "Not only expected it. Needed it. I had to. That's the lone way this would work, and stay what it is."

"What will it matter now?" she asked.

"One look at us and he'll know the truth."

"Why?"

"I'm pale as a court lady, and you haven't ceased crying since he left the clearing."

"I am na' crying."

He snorted the answer. Aislynn reached her bound hands to her own face, and ran a bare arm along her cheeks, wetting them with the tears, and she still didn't believe it.

Chapter Nineteen

By mid-afternoon the pain had reached her elbows, and by the time Sir Montvale found a shelter for them to rest in, it was to her shoulders and making her regret having arms. Aislynn fell into his when he reached for her and barely kept the moan from sounding as he carried her to the deserted croft he'd found before setting her on her feet. The conical dwelling was matched against a hill, which formed part of the roof, showing how well-hidden it was, as well as being very easy to heat and keep cool.

"I'll find wood. We'll need a fire."

"Will anyone mind . . . that we use this place?" She whispered it.

"I'd ask, but it appears the owners left in a bit of a hurry. Here. It's last year's sup." He lifted a kettle from the fire pit and tipped it toward her.

She grimaced but said nothing.

"My thought exactly. I'll go to the burn, take some sand and see if I can get to the bottom of this. If I'm in luck, I'll hunt you a rabbit or two. Will you need help?"

Her shoulders were hunching forward with the agony. She didn't dare speak. The only words would be more moans. She shook her head.

"Good. I'll return."

She didn't watch him leave. She didn't blame him if he left her. She went to the bare raised shelf they probably used to sleep on, fell onto it, and tried to cease breathing. Aislynn didn't know there was pain worse than heartache. It didn't seem possible; nothing anyone had ever written or sung about had ever said so. It certainly didn't seem fair.

Her hands felt like they were on fire, and the flames had climbed her arms, gone over her shoulders, reached her back, and found the place that would hurt her the most— the small of her back. Aislynn was in an arch of stiffness when the door opened again.

She didn't have time to hide it.

"What is it, lass?"

His voice was care and concern and sympathy. Aislynn looked at him with eyes that weren't having any trouble seeing. Lines of suffering were etched across Harold Montvale's face, too. She had no right to add to it. She turned her face to the wall.

"Give me your hands. Damn. Hell-fire. Bloody hell. Stupid wench. Why didn't you say something sooner?" His curses got more colorful and said more vehemently as he unwrapped each blood-soaked bandage. Then, they stopped. "It's festering," he announced when he got the linens off.

"I ken . . . as much," she whispered.

"Tell me what to do."

She shook her head.

"Damn you! Tell me what to do!"

"Nothing," she answered.

"If you do nothing, they'll get the black flesh. They'll rot . . . you'll rot. It's a horrid death. I've seen it. Tell me."

"Nae," she replied.

He shook her. He got right up on the shelf, straddled her, put his hands on her and shook her. Aislynn watched it with wide eyes that didn't have a tear left in them. It was Montvale that looked close to it.

"You're going to tell me how to heal them, and you're going to do it now!" He said it through shudders of breath that matched his hands.

"Why?"

"Because I'm ordering you to!"

"I dinna' follow orders from you," she whispered.

He stopped, looked down at her, and snarled. "You're going to help me heal these, and you're going to live, and you're going to suffer through each and every moment of each and every day. I'm going to make damn certain you do! Do you know why?"

She shook her head.

"Because you didn't let me die when I needed to, that's why."

Aislynn narrowed her eyes. He wasn't crying. He wasn't doing anything other than looking at her. "I dinna' wish to live," she said, finally.

"You think I do?" He lifted his hands from her then he was lifting himself. She heard him over at the fire-pit, striking flint, sparking a fire. She smelled the flame as it reached the wood and caught. Her nose twitched. She turned her head and looked at him.

"I will need thistle tops, fresh water that I can boil, and honey," she said finally.

He looked over at her. "Honey?"

"Follow the bees. Find a hive. Come back when it's done."

"What are you going to do while I'm gone?"

She sat up, although everything pained at that movement. "Dinna' fash yourself. I'll be waiting."

He stood, looked her over, and nodded. "What a pairing we make. The witch . . . and the dishonored knight. They should sing a ballad."

She bit her tongue to stay the retort. He knew nothing

he'd done was dishonorable and she knew she was no witch. He was saying it to start an argument. It was the first of many.

They supped on rabbit soup with small onions, since he didn't have enough daylight to find other vegetables and greens to add to it. He was also nursing three bee stings on his upper arms and one on his chin, but he'd brought her honeycomb. Aislynn watched the fire until it became coals. Sir Montvale was already asleep. She could hear the even breathing that came of exhaustion. She was at that state, too. She should have been as dead to the world as he was. She had only herself to blame that she wasn't.

Her hands were wrapped again, holding her flesh into place, after she'd opened the flesh that was trying to mend and had him pour the herb-enhanced water on them. She hadn't made a sound of pain; not even when he'd poured honey onto her palms and layered strips of torn material from his tunic that were taking it to an immodest length.

Sir Montvale had massive, muscled thighs in his own right, and his new tunic length wasn't disguising any of it. Aislynn could see he was the match to Rhoenne. He was a very handsome man, if one hadn't seen his laird before-hand. He didn't stir her senses, or make anything on her body react, either. He was also argumentative.

He'd argued with her over the water temperature. He'd spent words of anger on the light layer of warmed honey. He'd been especially verbal over how she wanted a this-tle in each layer of her bandage. He thought it was self-punishment and was against allowing such a thing, since she'd prevented him from having the same gift.

She smiled softly, watching him slumber in the center of the dusty floor. The thistles were to draw out poison. She whispered the prayer with each of them he'd put in place, using the Gaelic language that no knight raised in Normandy would have knowledge of. He'd also been wrong. The thistles weren't for punishment; the lack of lichen was.

She could have instructed him to scoop moss from the bottom of his water source, and she could have steamed it in the fire, to make the right consistency to pack against her flesh. She could have done more to take away what was turning into hellish pain. She hadn't. It was better than dealing with the heartache that it was covering over. Sir Montvale had been right. It was a gift.

A sennight later, there wasn't anything strong enough to mute it, and Aislynn suffered a pain in her heart that radiated through every limb, turning her entire existence into one, huge ache. She didn't even hear Sir Montvale's continual complaints anymore. The man was a horrid traveling companion. He was also wearing only the neckline of his tunic, since he'd used all of it on her bandages, before starting on her shift hem. That was when he'd first started berating her over not packing another one like he'd asked her to.

Aislynn glanced over at him. He might be wearing only a cloak and chausses, but he was a very virile, large, physical specimen. Any woman accompanying him should be sighing in appreciation over what flesh he was displaying and tanning to a dark brown color, rather than looking through him and wishing he was another man, entirely. It was actually quite interesting to watch every motion he made transfer across the sinews beneath his bare flesh. She wondered what it would be like if Rhoenne were at her side, rather than the acid-tongued knight, and had to stop the thought the moment it occurred. She couldn't handle the memory.

Sir Montvale's temper flared from the moment he awoke each morn, all through each day, and he'd been especially verbal and complaining when he'd ripped at her tunic with too much strength, opening the entire left side, clear to her sleeve. The shock at seeing her mark and the desire at seeing her nakedness had been so clear in his wide, open gray eyes, that she'd shrunk back from it, covering over what he'd seen. Then she'd watched his look change, replaced by such inner horror and hatred, that he rained curses down upon her head, both their heads, and on every other soul in listening distance, as well.

He was especially vicious when this night started falling, and there wasn't any shelter in sight. It was his own fault. He was going north. Anyone could have told him that once he reached the mountains and glens and lochs of the Highlands, there wasn't going to be a deserted croft available to them every eve. They had actually been in luck that they hadn't caught the attention of a clan of Gallgaels.

She looked over at where he walked at the head of his horse, since he'd given her the saddle. He'd used an entire morning telling her a horse couldn't carry their combined weight forever. The horse would be spent and bowed at the back and worthless when they really needed it. Then when she'd told him she'd gladly walk and had slid from the horse to prove it, he'd spent the rest of the day haranguing her of it while he walked at her side, and neither of them rode.

He was impossible to please. He was difficult to tolerate, and if she didn't recognize the self-hate that came out with every word, she'd have been screeching her reply, rather than just nodding, shrugging, or saying nothing; all of which got her more words of argument.

"We'll have to bed down in the woods. I don't see a shelter."

"Verra well," she said.

"Verra well," he mimicked, saying it with a high pitch to make it sound more like her. "Everything is fine, Sir

Knight. Anything you do is welcome. I'm a pious, little thing, with few ideas of my own, and no likes or dislikes to voice."

"Why are you saying this?" she asked.

"Because it suits me to do so," he replied, quickly. Too quickly. Aislynn set her lips, realizing she'd stepped into what he wanted most—argument.

"Maybe it makes the days pass swifter, and nights the same. Maybe you should cover yourself more. Maybe you shouldn't flaunt your body to me with each and every step of *my* horse."

"I can walk," she replied, softly, and reached with a sur-reptitious hand to hold the sides of her shift together, going so far as to lift her left thigh slightly, to tuck it beneath, and cover over what he was referring to. The bandaging on her hands was two days old now, crusty with dried honey and filth, but she didn't want it replaced yet. If that happened, he'd be ripping at her shift again. The thought was frightening.

"I can walk," he mimicked.

Aislynn set her lips. That made him angry, too.

"And you can stop ignoring me! I've said ceaseless words about it, and all you do is look at me with those large eyes of yours and agree! Whatever I say, you agree! Do you realize how difficult you make this?"

"Aye," she replied.

"You see? There you go again!"

Aislynn giggled.

"And you can cease laughing at me! I'm not a man used to such. I'm used to feminine appreciation, not a woman who ignores me! Day after day, night after night. What do you think me . . . a statue made of clay?"

"Nae," she replied.

"That's it! Enough, I say!"

He yanked on his horse's reins, making the animal's

head turn sharply. Then he was at her side and glaring up at her with hard, gray eyes.

Aislynn's own widened.

"You're going to get off that horse, and you're going to spread yourself, and you're going to make me see what this is all about! You're not going to have the choice, either!"

"You'd . . . rape?" she whispered.

His eyes narrowed. "It won't be rape. It will be what's due you! What's been coming for days now! And what's fair for what you've done!"

He was pulling her off his horse. Aislynn's heart caught in her throat, closing off any ability to scream, even if she had the desire to.

"Fight me!" He was holding her against his chest, and that portion of his body was heaving and sweating and shuddering.

"I said—fight me!"

He'd slammed them against the ground, shoving the breath from her body, and sending the burn of her backache into a scorch of pain. She couldn't fight him; not when he was holding her down with a left arm across her chest, nor when he was shoving her shift up with his right hand, sending his fingers along her naked side, and making her gag. She couldn't fight when he was unfastening his groin tie, releasing himself.

"Why don't you fight me?" he asked, huffing the words through his teeth.

"Because you canna' rid . . . yourself of pain . . . by giving it to me," she replied softly, and reached with a hand to soothe a lock of his hair away from his face. "I will na' fight whatever you do, Sir Montvale. I will help you. If this is what you need, I will help."

He was softening, and it wasn't just his features doing so as he looked down at her. Then he collapsed, gathered her

into his arms, and rolled to his side. He started shuddering. "Why didn't you just let me die?" he asked, sounding
like a little bairn was speaking the words against her neck.

"Because I dinna' know how bad it was going to be. I
still dinna'."

He took another, trembling breath. Her chest sank and
rose with it. "I would never have raped you," he told her.

"I ken that," she replied. She took her other hand and
threaded it through the long, lanky strands of hair that
reached the middle of his back. "Aside from all that, I
wouldn't have let you."

"You can't stop a man bent on rape, Aislynn."

"I can turn it into something different than rape. I can.
I have that much power."

He lifted his head and looked into her eyes. "I'm afraid,
Aislynn."

"Me, too."

"I don't know what's happening to me."

She nodded.

"I'm not fond of myself anymore."

She nodded again.

"I don't want anyone else to be fond of me, either."

"Well, I'm fond of you," she replied, and smiled.

He gave her a stone-faced look. "I just tried to take you
and hurt you, and you still say so?"

"I ken the truth, Montvale, and that you did what you
had to do. I ken what you sacrificed to save everyone. All
of them. I ken it. I did the same. You can hide it from
everyone else mayhap. But not me."

He blew the reaction to her words. "Rhoenne was right.
You are bewitching," he said finally.

"Well, I think you are noble and honorable, and I'll
never cease thinking so. There is naught you can do to me
that would change that."

"Nothing? Even this?"

She raised and lowered her eyebrows several times. "You're a very handsome, masculine fellow. I dinna' think you can rape any woman. All she has to do is get a good look at you. She'll melt in your arms."

He lowered his chin to favor her with a look. "You're not helping."

This time her smile showed teeth. "And you are heavy, we have a supper to see prepared, and beds to create. This is na' helping, either."

"Well . . . we've succeeded in getting you off the horse. It's a start."

He was lifting himself, using his arms to push away, and defining everything his tunic would have covered over, if he still wore one. Aislynn watched him as he looked at her. She didn't cover anything.

"You're a very beautiful woman, Aislynn. Forbidden. Tempting. Seducing with your form and then possessing a man with that devil mark of yours."

"And you call the Celts a superstitious lot?" Aislynn sighed. "I dinna' ask for such. Especially this beauty. 'Tis *nae* gift, but a filthy, dirty trick of the gods and goddesses to make me suffer. More. Always. Daily. Without end."

"Now wait. I didn't rape you," he replied, defensively.

"I was thinking of . . . Rhoenne." Her voice caught, she felt her back twinge, and her stupid eyes filled. She knew he saw it.

"He didn't mean it, Aislynn. He was in shock. He was enraged. He was vengeful. Jealous. He wasn't thinking through what he said."

"You canna' make this anything other than what it is. I know the truth. You saw his face. I saw his face. His . . . eyes."

"And I know my liege. He's already thinking it through and regretting it. He's probably already trailing us. Why do you think I go north?"

"You're hoping a confrontation with one of the Highland Galwegion clans from Galloway will help you put an end to this life."

He pulled back and stared at her.

"I must warn you. You're going to fail at it."

He looked down at her. He didn't say a word. Day was turning into twilight and still there was enough light to see his expression. Aislynn nearly giggled at the surprise evident all along him.

"I go north, because he will think I go straight to Edinburgh, rather than round-about aimlessly," he replied finally.

"Edinburgh?" Aislynn sat up and arranged her shift over her legs.

"That is what any sane man would be doing."

"You're taking me to Edinburgh." She looked up at him when she said it. It wasn't a question.

He shook his head. "How do you know I go there?"

"You are a sane man," she answered.

He grinned. Her heart stumbled slightly. That surprised her enough to gasp, and that made her back pain twinge. She had to look away.

"I know it will take longer, but the results will be the same. We'll be in His Majesty's court, and that's only fair, since it's his fault we're in this position in the first place!"

"Verra good. Blame another. It helps."

"With what?"

"Directing hate."

He didn't answer for so long, she had to look. He was frowning.

"What are we going to do once we reach Edinburgh? Do you have enough gold to grease palms? And if you do, will the king see us? And if he does, what will you request? He got what he wanted. He won't know the part we played unless you tell him. You won't tell him, will you?"

He snorted. "You've been quiet for days, and now you have to pester me with questions?"

"Answer one of them, at least."

"I don't have much gold at all, and what I have is spent on my manor over Stropshire way."

"You have a manor?"

"Knights have manors. I have one. It's small. I like it that way. It's easy to keep up."

"You have a manor," she repeated.

"And I have a squire to keep it clean and prepared for me, and I have a bit of land that even supports my horses."

"You have horses?"

He sighed hugely. "All right. I have one other horse. It's not much in comparison, but I'm a lowly knight, not a liege."

"What are you going to do once we reach Edinburgh?"

"Get a new position with another laird. What else?"

"You can do that?" she asked.

"Knights change allegiance all the time. There's no dishonor. And I'm very good at warring and killing and other knightly pursuits. I can command a large portion for my service, and I will. I only lose to one man. Ever."

Aislynn watched his face cloud over. She felt the same thing happening to hers.

"There are numerous positions in His Majesty's ranks that require my skills. I might get a chance to show some of them and that should get me a position with the Stewart clan, or the Ballilol, or even a Bruce. Ramhurst is not the only powerful clan in Scotland, you know."

"What is to happen to me?"

"You should be able to catch His Majesty's eye with little trouble. Your future shouldn't be in doubt."

"What if I dinna' wish to be a royal mistress? What would you have of me, then?"

"King David is a widower. He has no queen. Whoever

warms his bed has his ear. You certain you wouldn't wish the position?"

Aislynn looked away; watched the myriad of trees about them as the night fell further, making it look like one dark curtain surrounded them, blocking the space. Then she looked back up at him. "I would be mistress to only one man. And, since that will never happen, I'll have *nae* man unless it is as my husband. What have you to say to that?"

He put his hands along his hips again, defining them, and puffed out his chest with the size of his breath. "I suppose you could just be the wife of this knight, and that would make you mistress of a small manor near Stropshire."

Aislynn smiled. Then, she was grinning.

"Come." He reached a hand for her elbow and helped her rise. "We have to change your linens and rewrap your hands. We could also use some of those flat cakes you made. I'll get wood for a fire. I'll find water. I hope we still have honey. It's difficult to find a hive at night."

"I'm going to need more cloth and I need you to rip it for me . . . and from me."

"As much flesh as we are displaying, it's a good thing you have my proposal in hand and have accepted already."

"I've accepted now, have I?" she teased.

He swung her to face him, lifted her by her upper arms and put his lips against her cheek. "Until a better offer comes along—aye," he answered, and then he put her back down.

Aislynn's shift stuck to his leather patch. She had to pull it away, and both of them heard it rip.

"You'd best guard that cloth, Aislynn. There's not much protecting your virtue from me."

"And even less protecting yours," she replied.

"What are we going to do when we're both naked?"

"Join a Highland clan from Galloway," she answered, and that got her his answering grin.

Chapter Twenty

Aislynn saw what a Gallgael looked like, and it wasn't what she'd expected. Rain filled the dream, blurring the forest, dancing from leaf to leaf, streaming straight to the ground when the treetops allowed it, and making every droplet a sound filled with menace, fear, and death. Mist hovered around the undergrowth, adding height to the vegetation and opacity to the width.

There were two of them . . . identical. Both handsome men, with the same flowing, dark-red hair, the same black beards, the same massive muscles and short, thick limbs. They had a length of material tossed over one shoulder and secured to their waists with a length of cord, forming a frock that covered their loins; front and back. Aislynn narrowed her eyes, focusing on the material. It was woven with thick strands, almost all the same color of gray, but there were differing strands, too, darker in shade, interwoven; to make a plaid of muted color.

There were more men behind them, stirring the mist with the volume of legs, and making a cauldron of fog that made it difficult to see. There was a log on a shoulder, an axe on another . . . a recognizable saddle.

Aislynn screamed but no sound came. One of the

brothers swung his arm forward, splitting the whiteness with the severed head he was carrying by its distinctive, long, brown locks . . . locks she'd held to . . . locks she knew. It was Montvale's severed head.

"Aislynn?"

Aislynn sat straight up, into Sir Montvale's arms, panting the horror, and shivering with an evil that no amount of blinking, wiping, and crying would send away.

"Dearest heaven. Sweet goddesses. Somebody!" She lifted her head and sent the prayer to the sky above her, and felt the first raindrop touch her nose, then another on her eyelid, her cheek . . . her lips.

"Aislynn? What is it?"

"We have to go." She stammered it between teeth that were still chattering. "We have to go now. Now. We have to go now."

"Now?"

"Right now." She was on her feet, shaking the shift back into place against her legs and holding out her wrapped-up hands. "Now."

"Where are we supposed to go? And, why now?"

He was still sitting where she'd left him, rubbing at the sleep in his eyes, and frowning.

"Dinna' argue! We have to go now. Out of the woods! We have to go back. Anywhere! As long as it's na' here!"

She was near hysterics and only keeping it at bay with severe will. The dream had been in a forest, but that was no proof the attack hadn't happened elsewhere. Aislynn checked to either side; every side. Everything was calm. The horse was still standing where he'd been hobbled, placidly munching on grasses, there was a slight murmur of a breeze as it ruffled leaves above her, and Montvale was finally on his feet, brushing twigs and grasses from his chausses and looking at her with his argumentative look.

"Dinna' argue it. Get the horse saddled," she said.

"You should await a wedding ceremony a-fore ordering me about," he replied.

"Get the horse saddled and get us out of this wood or I'll do it for you."

"With those hands?"

"With my teeth if need be!"

"Allow me a moment to relieve myself first."

He was rubbing his belly and yawning, and looking like a man awakened from a deep sleep was supposed to. He didn't look remotely rushed or hurried. Aislynn went across to him and punched him right in the abdomen, where his muscles only made her blow bounce and her un-healed palm sting.

"What did you do that for?" he asked.

"We're going to be attacked," Aislynn hissed.

"By who?" He looked to either side, and then back at her.

"Gallgaels. They're going to catch us. Move!"

"How would you know?"

"I dreamt it!"

That had him lifting his head and hooting at the sky, all of which had her hand cocked to hit him again before she remembered all that happened was she got the pain from it.

"Na' so loud! We've got to go. Now! Right now!"

"I'm not allowed a moment to relieve myself?"

Aislynn sent the frustration through her teeth. "Take a moment. Hurry!" She was frightening herself with the rapid pace of her own breathing and the increasing speed of her pulse. She tried for calm. She tried reasoning with herself. The mill hadn't been attacked immediately. It had happened later. They had time. *Please give us time!* She sent the prayer to the sky; to her gods and goddesses; to his God . . . to anyone that would listen.

The bushes rustled to the side of her, making the cry of fear lodge in her throat and stifling her voice the moment it got there. Her eyes went huge as the greenery parted, and then Montvale came out of them toward her. Aislynn nearly cried the relief aloud.

"All right. I'm awake. What did you want such a thing for again?"

"We're going to be attacked. In the night!"

"Not tonight?"

"I dinna' know."

"You woke me from a solid sleep to tell me . . . you don't know?"

"Please dinna' argue. Get your horse saddled. Hurry!" Something convinced him, for after a shake of his head, he went and got his saddle.

"I know, old man. Vicious wench. Won't even let a body get a little rest before she's making your ears burn and swatting at you like you're an animal of burden. I'd best re-think my marriage proposal."

Aislynn rolled her eyes. "You'd best hurry, if you prize that hair and that head of yours. That's what you'd best do."

"They're going to take my hair? Now, that's totally savage and against the rules. I'm right fond of it."

"They're going to take your entire head! Canna' you listen?"

"I'll be beheaded? Really? Me?"

She nodded. Her voice wasn't adequate to describe it.

"That doesn't sound like a Gallgael. They like to slice a man open and take out his innards. Woman, too. They don't like heads."

"Trust me. They like yours."

"Interesting. What else did you see?"

"There's two of them."

"You're making me run from two men? You have little faith in my abilities, don't you? I'm sorry if I'm not the great war beast that Rhoenne de Ramhurst is. Me and my Destiny have still taken our share of spoils. Haven't we, lady?" He'd pulled his broadsword from the scabbard against the horse, and kissed the steel before putting it back.

"Will you cease this and get ready? There were more than two! I meant there were two leaders."

"How could you tell?"

"I dinna' ken how. I just do."

He shook his head. He was putting the saddle on, though. "You have vivid stories and useless words, and expect everyone to leap at your dreams."

"I dreamt of the mill," she replied, softly. "I told . . . Rhoenne of it." She couldn't help the catch in her voice. She could only hope Montvale didn't notice it. "He believed me."

"You dreamt the mill?" He was finally serious, and looking at her with a frown between his brow.

She nodded.

"We have time, then."

"I dinna' know how much, though."

"Get up." He didn't wait. He put his hands on either side of her waist and put her up. He didn't join her.

"You need to ride, too," she said.

"We spend his strength and we're not going anywhere. I'll walk. We have time. Describe the men. The leaders. If I get to them, the others may flee."

"Large men, short."

"Large or short? Which is it?"

"Muscled. Strong. Short."

"Go on." He was awake now, if the tense line of his shoulder beside her was any indication.

"They have red hair, dark red . . . and black beards."

"Ugly men?"

"They dinna' look ugly," she replied.

"Handsome men?"

"I dinna' say that, either."

"Well, are they or aren't they?"

"They're handsome. Na' as handsome as . . . Ramhurst."

"Or me?"

Aislynn looked up again, caught a raindrop in her eye for her trouble, and looked back down. "They are na' as handsome as you, either."

He grunted, accepting it. Aislynn had no idea men were vain. Nothing about Rhoenne had been. She scrunched her forehead. She didn't think anything about him had been vain. Then she remembered. The first time she'd met him; the lance tip; the scarring beneath his hose. He wasn't remotely vain and he'd every right to be.

"What else?" Sir Montvale asked.

"What?"

He sighed heavily. "We're expecting an attack at any moment, and you forget what I'm asking? These men. The leaders. Anything else distinctive?"

"They're the same. Twins."

He stopped. The horse stopped. He looked up at her, and the movement sent the spear tip that was aimed at his jaw into the horse's neck instead.

Pandemonium ensued. Aislynn shoved her knees into the horse's side as he reared, making it difficult for Montvale to get Destiny out of the scabbard. He was lifted into the air as he did so, and then the horse was falling over, taking Aislynn with it. Montvale leapt them both, swinging as he came down, taking a head off with the movement, and giving the most horrid cry as he did so.

Then there were men everywhere; yelling, screaming, grunting men. The chill of the air was turning their breath into puffs of white fog, coating bodies and making it difficult to spot Montvale. The only thing she could count on was his voice. He was as vocal as they were, and he was taller, with a wider range of motion. He was also gravely outnumbered.

The horse fell in such a slow motion, Aislynn was off and on her knees at its side before the body bounced to a stop, locking the bottom of her shift beneath it. She yanked, pulling her wounds awry as much as she was ripping material, and landing on her buttocks when the material finally gave.

Then she was leaping obstacles, not looking at what they were to get to Montvale, and when she did, he was standing with so many spears against his throat and chest, he looked like a reversed quill-pig.

"Albanaich!" Aislynn screeched the war cry, and then she followed it by calling on the gods and goddesses of her ancestry, using the Gaelic language they understood, and then she was berating them, challenging them, and commanding them to bring their twin leaders to her. Now.

More than one spear pulled back slightly, leaving a bleeding laceration where it had been nearly imbedded in Montvale. Aislynn kept screeching, racing through all the curses she knew, gathering breath after breath to do so, until she was shoving aside men and spears, and then she was at Montvale's front, and pushing the last of the spears aside.

"Bring me the black-bearded ones!" She yelled it, tossing her arms out to include all of them. "The identical ones! I call on you!" She put her hands in two specific directions and pointed, and was the only one not surprised when that's exactly where the men came toward her from.

"Lift me!" She hissed it over her shoulder at Sir Montvale. He didn't hesitate. He raised her onto his shoulder, parting the shift to the center of her legs, and putting the mark she'd hidden since birth right at their line of sight, since Montvale was a good head taller than any man there. She heard the murmuring, saw the head shaking, felt the trembling in her body that she couldn't deny, and then the place at the small of her back that had been paining and annoying her since she'd betrayed Rhoenne did a very strange thing. It dispersed, sending heat to her head with such swiftness she broke out in a sweat.

"You know of us? How?" One of them asked it once they had parted through the throng and stood below her.

"I see things," she replied with a voice that hadn't any weakness or trembling to it. "I saw you. Both of you."

"You have the god-mark." One of them pointed to her hip.

Aislynn didn't move her gaze from his. She moved her bandaged left hand to where the links began and ran it along her waist and back behind her where it disappeared.

"Aye," she replied, returning her hand forward. "What of it?"

He grunted, turned to his brother and said something she couldn't hear well enough to decipher.

"What are you doing with him?" He pointed at Sir Montvale.

"He is my husband," Aislynn announced.

Both of them put their heads back and laughed heartily.

"This does not look good," Montvale whispered from beneath her arm.

"Him? You wed up with him?" One of them asked it.

"Aye. He's the strongest. The largest. He is a warrior beyond any of your own warriors." Her taunt had them stepping closer. Aislynn glared right back.

"This looks even worse," Montvale whispered. She dug a heel into his side, at the waistline of his chausses to warn him.

"He's a foreigner. A Norman," one of them said with derision.

"How many of you did he take down just now? One man. One blade?"

She sneered it and listened to the grumbling. Then there

were some nods. The looks she got now had more respect to them.

"Five. *Nae,* six."

She nodded, raised her eyebrows and pierced them with the look. "And you took down a horse. One horse. One. I would say he is the best warrior."

"Come."

They gestured, making it easy to understand what the word meant.

"Where are we going?" Montvale asked.

"With them," she replied.

He sighed, raising her with it. "Am I required to be your horse while we do so?" he asked.

She choked. He was going to have to be. Her legs were feeling the reaction. If he put her down, she was going to fall.

"What do they want?" He was whispering more words.

"I've confused them. I know what I'm na' supposed to know."

"Why did they let me live?"

"Because I claimed you."

He swore. She was lifted with the strength of it. "I wish you'd cease doing that. I'd rather be dead than a captive of Gallgael."

"You ever hear of them taking captives?"

"Nay," he replied.

"Then what makes you think they are now?"

"What are they doing, then?"

She shrugged. "I have value. They're interested."

"And me?"

"You're a great warrior. They canna' dispute it. That's what made them so angered. They'll probably want to test you further."

"That's wondrous. My thanks."

"I would na' worry over it. You are a great warrior. I have faith."

"Can't you just let me die?"

"Nae," she replied.

"Why not?"

"Because someone has to get my unborn son to his father when his birth kills me. That's why."

She thought he was going to fall for a moment as his knees wobbled, and then straightened again. His hands at her buttocks tightened, too.

"Why didn't you tell me?"

"I just did," she replied.

"You're certain?"

She snorted for an answer.

"Thank you, lass."

"For what?"

"You have just given me back my purpose. I swear, on my miserable life, that I'll get the child to Rhoenne. I'll explain it. I'll make him see. I'll not rest until it's done. You have my word."

Aislynn allowed herself to sag.

They became Donal clan, and it only cost Montvale four slices of his flesh and a small bit of scrollwork at the top of his cheek, just below one eye. He'd earned that, and Aislynn watched the appreciation they gave his skills with satisfaction. Thanks to the Ramhurst curse, she was going to get her death wish. Montvale was not. He'd get a clean slate once he delivered the bairn, though. And all it cost him was two scars across his abdomen, one on his thigh, one on his left lower arm, and a facial, moon-shaped mark that made him look sinister and rakish, and not at all the man of humor he was. It was comfort enough.

They spent the entire autumn season with the Donal clan. Aislynn was in no hurry to go, and Montvale was learning everything from another perspective. He could now toss a spear better than all but one twin, he could out-throw any with a hand ax, and he was no slacker when it came to the placement of arrows, either. He had a healthy respect for Highlanders now, and since none of them could beat him at any kind of wrestling, he had their respect back, as well. He told Aislynn after one particular win, that he would always beat a shorter man at arm, or leg, wrestling. He had the benefit of leverage. There was only one man he ever lost to. She didn't doubt it and she didn't remark on it.

She gave him her full attention when he required it, which wasn't often. He was in demand in other places, and other beds, too. Aislynn turned a blind eye to any nocturnal activities. She had no claim on him, and once she'd told him of the bairn, he'd gone out of his way to be chivalrous and teasing and protective of her and nothing else.

When the snows came, Montvale loudly announced it was time for them to leave. He'd waited until the fire-smoke from breakfast had been cleared, and the sleeping benches were put away before he said it. The others in their house smiled and nodded and agreed with him.

Far from being uncivilized, they were a structured, well-organized clan. They had simple rules: survival first; everything else after. She'd been told of their tempers and of their flair for fighting, but she'd seen little of it. Of course, she was in with the women and there wasn't much to fight about. Food gathering, preparation, and making cloth took too much time. Montvale could probably tell her more if she asked. She didn't. It was enough that he had more scars and the other men clapped him on the shoulders as if he were one of them. He was telling her he was winning every contest, and she believed him.

Aislynn and Montvale had been guests of the Donal twins. They'd been given space in the large, round, stone-sided house to call their own; they'd been accepted in, and told to stay as long as they wished; and they'd been left to their own amusements ever since. And then Montvale made his announcement.

Aislynn stood up from the center of the other women weavers, put her hands on her back to straighten it out, which made the rounded swell of her baby more prominent, and went to him with only a stumble of hesitation. Her feet had gone to sleep, since she'd had them in the same position all morn, and she swayed from her left to her right and back again, while she waited for him to tell her why he'd decided to leave now.

"We have to leave a-fore the glens are snow-locked and Edinburgh grows into a dim memory I can scarce recall. I'll na' have an easy time getting that bairn away come spring, if I dinna'."

Aislynn smiled up at him, lifting her hand to shield the light. "You've picked up the speech."

"It's *nae* wonder. I've only uncivilized savages and fast-tongued wenches to speak with for months now."

"Show me these fast-tongued wenches. I'll set them a-right. There's better things to do with a specimen such as yourself. Things that dinna' require talk."

He grunted and returned her smile. "Gather foodstuffs for the journey. I'll arrange a sled. Pack well. There may na' be game available. Gather more cloaking, too. If we arrive in Edinburgh wearing what we're wearing, we'll be arrested on sight, probably dumped into the dungeon, and then charged with crimes of a low nature."

She looked him over. He had a length of material called a *plaide* tossed across what was now one extremely tanned and muscled shoulder. There was a thick belt on his hips, holding the kilt to him so the drape just grazed his knees. It should have been longer, but he was much taller than the usual and required a longer weave. That was her fault, for she was responsible for his clothing, and despite listening to the other women's suggestions, she'd not gotten it right, yet. And he had Norman-designed and constructed boots on his feet, looking like they could use a replacement before much longer.

"You look full-dressed, Sir Montvale," she finally remarked, "for a foreigner living among Donal clan, that is. You look just right."

"Well, you look like a woman of easy morals and fast virtue. Especially with this bairn already trying to get out like he is."

He pulled her into his arms easily and patted the large, round ball that was making it difficult for her to walk. He did it often, and the babe always reacted, as if it was showing off.

"Tell him . . . I wish him named Harold," she whispered, when he looked again at her.

"I'll be lucky if he does na' strike the name from every record of the time."

"You must learn to talk as fast as one of these wenches, then."

"Aye." A shadow fell across his features. It was gone a moment later. She knew what it was, though. Dread. He was welcome to it. She was grateful she didn't have to face Rhoenne Guy de Ramhurst ever again. She didn't envy Montvale that chore.

The Donal clan didn't have a horse. None of the clans possessed them. Aislynn and Montvale said good-bye to those that needed it, and left the same way they'd arrived; by walking.

The hard leather of his boots crunched through the snow, making a path of holes for her to use by lunging from one to the other. She made a game of it. It helped while away the time.

Five weeks later, it was no longer a game. It was a never-ending series of steps that she forced her feet to keep making, no matter how her back ached, or how many antics the bairn did within her. Then, there came a time when she begged for a rest too often, and he lost his patience with her, told her to hide by the side of the road and wait for him. When he returned he'd bartered his prized lady, the sword, Destiny, for a sway-backed horse, which was all the black-smith had available to part with.

Montvale didn't remonstrate with her over it. He had a tight-lipped look to his face that forbade any argumenta-tive or sympathetic words over it. He told her why when he stopped and made camp that night. He didn't want her birthing the bairn on the road, with no wet-nurse in sight. He'd had no choice, and he'd had only one thing of value left to him. He was grinning as he described how the blacksmith nearly went for his own sword when Sir Mont-vale had first approached, since he looked like a heathen, and was acting like one, too.

Aislynn had laughed at his description, and told him she'd make it up to him somehow. He asked her to keep the bairn where it belonged until he had her at his manor, and that would be thanks enough. He could order another sword made, or he could take a bit of gold and buy his own Destiny back. He just didn't want to be stuck with a newly birthed lad and no wet-nurse in sight, since he hadn't brought a bonny lass from the Donals with them.

When she reminded him that he was going to have the same trouble no matter where the bairn decided to enter the world, he replied that there were plenty of new moth-ers who would serve, and that's what he kept a squire around for, procuring things like that. And then he asked her to cease pestering him with her fast tongue and allow an over-worked, swordless knight a bit of rest.

Aislynn found the most comfortable spot against her bundle of clothing, propped herself into a reclining posi-tion, and joined him in it.

Chapter Twenty-One

"I thought you said you had a small manor." Aislynn said it with her tongue in her cheek as they topped a rise and looked down at all the humanity that was in one small place. Even with the light snow that was falling, it was easy to see there were rows of striped tents, horses bunched together in fenced-off areas, and an air of festivity that reminded her of a fair. It was almost enough to make her forget the nagging twinge that was accompanying every sway of the horse.

"I appear to have company." Sir Montvale stood higher than the horse at its head, which would have been inconceivable on his war horse. He put an arm about the animal's neck and looked over the same area she was.

There was a very large tent directly in front of a two-story house that probably constituted Sir Montvale's manor house. The tent had a long pole in front of it, and if she narrowed her eyes, she could see that the standard atop it was a dark color with an emblem in the center. She couldn't tell what it was, or what color, but there was a sinking feeling inside her at what she suspected it was.

"I wasn't aware that I'd put my land out to be leased."

"Montvale."

"I know that tone. Dinna' tell me you need a rest . . . again."

Aislynn favored him with a look that should have frozen him in place. It didn't. Instead he turned, crooked an elbow, leaned against the horse's head and grinned.

"It's him. Ramhurst," she said.

"Really?" He swiveled his head and looked over at the tents. "How can you tell? Can you see the flag from here? I canna'."

"I dinna' have to see it. I ken it's him."

He turned to wink at her. "I wonder what he wants."

"He's been here some time."

"Aye. And in that time, he's churned up good grazing land, and made a muck out of my fields. I'll have to take it up with him when I reach my home. *If* I can reach my home."

"I canna' go with you. He'll see me."

"You're big with his bairn, wearing little more than cloth strips, it's snowing, and you expect me to leave you out here? I'll have you know, I'm a knight of the realm. I'm chivalrous, honorable, gallant, noble—"

"Large-headed," she added.

"Damn him! I've been dreaming of a soft bed and a warm fire, and now he denies me because he's decided to lay siege to my own house! What man lays siege to an empty house?"

"Maybe it isn't a siege."

Montvale favored her with a look from beneath his eyebrows and lashes. Snow was starting to cling to them, making it more effective. "I'll have you know I recognize a siege when I see one. I just wish he'd waited until I got in the house before sealing it off. Blast him!"

"What are we to do?"

"Well . . . you're going to find a nice sheltered place and keep hidden. I'm going to act like I have a lot more possessions on my person than a sway-back nag, a bit of cloth, and no sword. I'm lucky I have the most important thing. If it weren't for that, I'd not give myself much of a chance of reaching the edge of the tent-line, let alone my own stoop."

"What is that?"

"I have the information he wants. Now . . . here you go." He huffed a bit mid-sentence, as if she'd gained so much weight he was in danger of dropping her. He did it all the time, anymore, so she just shook her head, just like she always did.

He didn't put her down this time. He carried her all the way to a series of three rocks that had an overhang of ice and snow, making a cave-like interior. He kicked the loose snow away, until he reached ground, then he set her down, as gently as possible. Aislynn winced.

"The bairn?" he asked.

"Just my discomfort with carrying him. He's a large bairn."

"Bairns have a way of doing that. They tend to take after their sire, making them difficult to birth—!" He stopped and gulped. "Forgive me. My mouth moves faster than my wits at times. I dinna' mean that."

She smiled, but it probably looked as sickly as his did. They both knew she had a death sentence. She, for one, was ready to welcome it. "If you make me start crying, I'm going to melt my own snow cave," she whispered.

"True. Think on that. It won't be for long. I'll be back for you, or I'll send my squire, Stephen. I swear it. If I'm not back for you, I'll be dead. Before nightfall. Look for me or Stephen."

Nightfall? she wondered. She was already trembling with ground chill. She was going to be as frozen as the snow overhang atop her if she had to wait that long. She didn't voice any of it. She watched as he walked away from her, swaying a bit in his Highland cloth, his short cloak, and not a bit more. She had no right to feel cold. She had all three of her woven dresses on, with the sides overlapped for warmth, and the old Lady of the Brook cloak over the whole.

Montvale disappeared over the hill. She knew he was mounting his sorry excuse for a horse and preparing to ride down into his own property. He looked more like a beggar than the owner. She giggled at the thought. Then she went to a crouch and followed.

Rhoenne was pacing great strides that took him around the tent and then across it, over and over, in a random pattern of frustration, intensity, and worry. He didn't have anything in his way. If he felt ready to fall from exhaustion, he'd roll out a pallet and collapse on it. If the walls became too restrictive, and his need for release too strong, he'd open the flap and start running, until his lungs were ready to burst, and his legs shuddered with the chore of holding him up.

Those times, he'd turn, walk slowly back and then it would all start up again. He'd done it so often, he knew the size and extent and layout of Sir Montvale's land better than the knight did, himself. Rhoenne had his largest siege tent. It gave him more room. He'd ordered it when the weather grew vicious enough that any forays across Montvale's land ended up soaking him to the skin and making him feverish with something besides the fear.

The tent door moved, alerting him, and he swiveled on his heel, a hand to Pinnacle's hilt, and glared at the slight, dark-headed squire that stood there. He'd seen him before. It was Montvale's servant. He'd been the lone one there to receive Rhoenne's demands when he'd first arrived, and he'd been the one listening when they became requests, and finally, entreaties.

"What . . . is it?" he asked. He had to clear his throat after the first word to get the rasp of sound to make sense.

"Sir Montvale has returned. He's requesting—"

Rhoenne was shoving past him and to the front steps, before the lad finished. Then he was racing the halls, covering all three rooms on the lower floor, glaring at Sir Harold, before racing his stairs, three at a time. He checked all three rooms upstairs twice, opening each door, and bellowing her name until his throat was raw.

His steps were hollow sounding as he went back down the stairs, slower than he'd run them, and re-entered the middle room. Rhoenne set his jaw, steeled his gaze, and put a rein on his temper as he glared at Montvale, who was still standing in the exact same location, looking like he hadn't taken one sip from the mug of ale he held in his hand. The fire flared at the force Rhoenne shut the door with. He sucked in breath to calm himself and make sense of what he wanted to say; he let it out. Again. His heart thudded with each repeat. Again.

Sir Montvale put the tankard down on his table as if that's all he had to do all eve.

"Where is she?" Rhoenne asked, through teeth that were clenched so tightly he snarled.

"Who?" Montvale replied.

Rhoenne pulled the sword, hearing the steel slide against the leather and then the grommets at the top of his scabbard with the motion. He took a step forward and leveled the blade directly at Montvale's chest. "You know who," he said finally.

"I'm unarmed."

"Fetch your Destiny. Meet me like a man this time."

"Alas, Ramhurst, I have lost my Destiny. 'Tis fitting,

no? I *nae* longer need a destiny. But she served me well. I'll miss her."

Rhoenne filled his chest with air; exhaled it; and then filled it again. It wasn't tempering his reaction. It was only making his chest burn worse inside. "Where is she?" he asked again.

"I did what I had to. I traded her."

"You . . . what?" His voice cracked. He couldn't help it.

"I bartered her for a sorry sack of bones that went for a horse. I had to. My feet ached."

Rhoenne's eyes misted over. He tried to tell himself it was hate causing it. He knew different. He blinked it away. "Tell me the direction and the sum."

"Why?"

Rhoenne's eyes widened a fraction as Montvale lifted a slice of bread from his supper tray to his mouth and munched on a crust. He forced himself to calm, and concentrated on the racing pulse that was filling him, canceling out the burn in his chest for the vaguest fraction of time before it started up again.

"Why? So I can fetch her."

"You wish to retrieve my sword for me? That's noble. Considering." Montvale had finished chewing, and he had a slight smile on his mouth as he lifted the tankard again.

Rhoenne took another step toward him.

"Threatening me isn't going to get you what you want, Ramhurst."

"Where is she?"

"We're not speaking of my Destiny, are we?" he asked, softly. He still had a quirk to his lip, making Rhoenne's fingers itch to strike it off.

"You know who I'm speaking of and you know why. Waste words on those that like the sound of them. Tell me where she is."

"Perhaps I bartered her . . . also."

Rhoenne couldn't halt the verbalization of his cry, although he hated himself for making it the moment it left his throat.

Sir Harold wasn't smiling any longer. "That is what you told me to do with her, isn't it? Sell her . . . services?"

"You *sold* her?" Rhoenne tried to keep the tremor from the words but he knew the knight had spotted them, when he took his time lowering the tankard. It was for show. There wasn't a sign of liquid on his lips. Rhoenne watched him lick them.

"If I did, what would you do then?"

"Exactly as I have done already. Ask the sum and the direction." The sword tip lowered. Montvale was right. Silencing him wasn't going to get him anything.

"Why?" Montvale asked.

Rhoenne flinched. He knew the knight saw it.

"That's between the lass and me," he replied finally.

"I see."

He watched as Harold took another bite of his crust, waited until he'd swallowed it, and then watched as he took another. Rhoenne forced his heart to accept the man's rhythm; paced himself to match it. It was making a vein throb out in his forehead. He knew it because he could feel it.

"You can't use it for vengeance," Harold finally spoke again. "And you should have learned that by now."

"Use what?"

"Emotion."

"I can use whatever I wish for vengeance. That's what it's for."

Montvale sighed heavily. "What would you revenge?"

"Betrayal. My dearest friend betrayed me. Me! For his own lust. Or perhaps he betrayed me on lack of faith. Either way, it was betrayal. Deceit. Disloyalty. Treachery. Call it any word you care to, it still reeks of the same."

Sir Montvale paled. He covered it by looking down at the tray as if selecting another delicacy to tempt him. Rhoenne watched as he toyed with his food. He looked up. The gray of his eyes was slick and hard. "All spoken of the man involved. What would you revenge on the woman?"

"That's between the woman and me," he replied.

"I've watched you sway mounted, warring men, with the force of your words. I've seen you mesmerize whole rooms of nobles with the sound of your voice, until everyone stops to listen to what you say. I've observed you seduce women with the slick depth of your whispering. I know you have the gift. I've seen it. I was jealous of it."

"What of it?" Rhoenne snapped.

"I dinna' understand why you dinna' use it now. When you most need to."

"You want courtly words? Is that what you're saying?"

"Nae! I want everything to return to a fine, clear summer day. Early this same year. When all I had to worry over was the lance my liege had taken in his leg and his refusal to admit to it. That's what I want! Your turn."

"Ask me for something I can grant."

"Very well." Montvale had picked up a slice of what looked to be venison. Rhoenne could have verified it, but he didn't care. He watched as the man shoved the entire slice in his mouth, chewed it, and then swallowed it. He had to. He had no other choice. "Grant me answers."

Rhoenne nodded once.

"What would you have of the woman? If I ken where she is? And if I could see her fetched?"

"I don't foretell the future."

"You'd hurt her?"

"Pinnacle thirsts for your blood. Aislynn is safe."

"There are some hurts that go deeper than sword blades, Ramhurst."

Rhoenne ran his left hand through his hair, shoving it off his forehead with a rough gesture. "How much longer must you make me ask it?"

"This is asking?"

"You wish me begging?"

"How long did it take you to come after her?" Montvale asked, fishing through the food on his tray again with his index finger.

"That same morn."

The knight smiled shallowly. Then he looked over at Rhoenne. "How is your young princess bride, anyway? Does she satisfy you in the wedding bed?"

"God *damn* you, Montvale!" Pinnacle was raised again and pointed unerringly at the knight's throat. Even from the span of half the room away, he watched Montvale lean backward.

"You have the same temper, I see."

"Did you sell her, or not?"

"What is it to you?"

"I'm going to kill you, Montvale. And no woman's going to be around to save your soul this time. Coward."

Montvale snorted and spaced out every word of the reply. "Well, you'll need to wait until you ken where she's at. Will na' you?"

Rhoenne snarled; ground his palm into Pinnacle's hilt until the gold and silver of it felt like it warped with the pressure; and then he made the conscious effort to turn it and slide it back into its scabbard.

"Better," Montvale said.

"Did you sell her?" Rhoenne tried again.

"Answer me first. Where is your young princess wife?"

"I don't have a princess wife."

Montvale pulled in a breath at the surprise. Rhoenne felt the satisfaction at watching it. He knew then, the feeling that Sir Harold was gaining with this torment. And he knew there was only one man that could stop it: himself.

"You fought the royal edict? Still?" Montvale asked, in a soft voice.

"I answered the edict. I gave His Majesty the answer he wanted. I still don't have my bride."

"Why na'?"

"She died. His Majesty has sickly daughters."

"When?"

"The messages probably passed on the road. What does it matter?"

Sir Montvale probably shouldn't have tried to take a drink from his tankard, Rhoenne thought, as the man choked on his swallow, and had to put his vessel down to gasp for breath. "You never . . . had to protect the castle . . . from siege?" Montvale stumbled through the words.

"I had only to put food into some of the king's garrisons, stable their horses, and then send them on their way."

Sir Montvale looked like he was going to be ill. Rhoenne watched as what had been a healthy, tanned shade went pale, and then he regained some of his color back, although he was still looking at his food platter. "Will you tell me where she is now?"

"She's close. She's safe."

The words were garbled, but he understood. Rhoenne took a huge breath of air and held it. Then he let it out. It wasn't working. The burn in his chest was telling him of it. There was no relief.

"You truly dinna' have to protect yourself from a siege at Tyneburn?"

"Nay."

"So. You decided to lay siege to my manor house here at Stropshire. Was that your plan?"

"I want Aislynn. I want to talk to her. I *have* to see her!"

"Why?"

"That's between her and me. No one else."

"She's na' the same lass."

"You didn't sell her. You just admitted as much."

"I did?"

"She's close. She's safe. From your own mouth."

Montvale smiled. "Verra good," he said, softly.

"Let me see her. Send for her. Do what you need."

"I dinna' think so. You go too fast."

"Too fast? It's been an eternity of waiting. I know. I've been here doing it."

"Who's overseeing Tyneburn?"

"Does it matter?" Rhoenne asked.

"Nay. I'm just whiling away hours while I join you in your wait."

"Why?"

"Because . . . maybe she's na' as close as you think. Maybe she's verra far away. Maybe she'll never be close again. Maybe she's already wed. . . ."

"Nay!" The cry came from the bottom of him this time. He was shaking with it. There was nothing he could do to keep it hidden.

". . . to me," Montvale finished.

Rhoenne looked to the floor, swallowing over and over, on the wash of anguish he'd die before he let anyone else see. He forced himself to find hate; forced himself to accept loss; forced himself to kill every bit of everything he'd ever felt for the man sitting in front of him. And for her. He was very afraid he was failing.

"Are you going to answer me, or na'?"

Rhoenne lifted his head, claimed the roar of sound rushing through his ears, and when it crested and withdrew, he had every emotion back where he wanted it— under his belt. He thanked God silently with his mind and his heart, then he answered with a part of him he didn't know he had. To his own ears, he sounded different. He watched as the knight heard the same thing.

"What was the question, again?" The different Rhoenne asked it.

"Who is overseeing Tyneburn?"

"Richard."

"You selected the brother—who is half a man—to oversee your fief?"

"He has Old Rosie to give him backbone. She has him to give her wits. It's a good combination. I should have seen it years before."

"What of your heir, Brent?"

Rhoenne thanked God for the inanimate voice he was still able to answer with and the strength that was starting to flow from the depth of him. "Brent Ramhurst has his own property to oversee. He serves His Majesty at Jedburgh and has earned a tract of land and a title. He's changing. He's maturing."

Sir Montvale was gazing at him with a very long, considering look. Rhoenne remained emotionless and dead-feeling. It was better than the alternative.

"Interesting."

"Are you going to taunt and tease all eve, or are you going to give me what I seek?"

"What if I canna'? What if she's wed?"

"Then her husband is a dead man."

"Perhaps he's already . . . dead." Montvale spoke softly, his voice saying something the words hid. Rhoenne frowned.

"Words. Always it's the words with you! Give me Aislynn. Give me the direction. The time. The faith!" His voice rang out in the room.

"Perhaps I'll make you earn it."

Rhoenne waited while Sir Montvale started rolling up

his sleeve, and then he watched him roll up the other one. He eyed the knight.

"All I need to do is return to my tent and await her arrival."

"How do you ken that would happen?"

"Although you've turned into a man of such little faith that he'd betray his own sworn liege, you're still the man I've known since we first met on a field of honor when we were children. Children! And that man wouldn't allow his wife to stay out in such weather as this."

"You think na'?"

Rhoenne shook his head.

"Good. I was beginning to think I'd have to talk all night a-fore you'd admit to it."

"Admit to what?"

"That I'm still the same man."

Rhoenne didn't change expression. He just watched. The knight was pulling up a bench at his trencher table, and then he was flexing his arm, showing sinew and strength he hadn't had before.

"Come. Sit. Face me."

"Why?"

"Because I'm challenging you."

"To what?"

"Wrestle. For the information."

"You'll lose. You always lose."

"I always lost . . . a-fore." Montvale's voice dropped on the last word. "I dinna' think I will, now."

The door opened, letting a servant into the room. Rhoenne glanced at the cowled, hunched-over figure and dismissed it from his mind. He pushed his broadsword to the back of his hip while he straddled the opposing bench from Montvale.

They were a like size. They were a like build. Rhoenne had always had superior strength, but he'd been spending months with worry and fear as his bedfellows. Montvale had Aislynn. He'd gained bulk. He'd gained strength. He'd gained something else. He had confidence.

He heard the servant moving about, saw the shadow behind him, and put her from his mind. He had to put everything into the contest in front of him and he knew it. If he failed, he'd never learn where Aislynn was. Montvale would go to his death with it.

Rhoenne shoved his sleeve to his elbow, baring the wrist circlet of silver he'd had designed and crafted to match the mark on Aislynn's hip. He watched as the knight glanced there and recognized what it was. That made his lip curl, his heart start pumping blood through his body, and his mind to go crystal clear. He swiveled the circlet into position, gripped the other's hand, and waited.

It was like moving a castle wall. Sweat slicked their hands, muscles bulged out, sounds of endurance and agony and effort came with every breath from either of them, and still neither hand moved, either way. The servant woman put something on the table beside them.

Rhoenne ignored it as he was her. His breathing got deeper, matching the cadence of his own pulse, and he felt himself moving forward slightly, making Montvale grunt and react with a renewed vigor that came from within. Rhoenne was going backward. He was losing.

He heard the sound of a tankard falling and glanced over at her clumsiness. That's when he saw her palm as she reached to pick it back up. There was a long, reddish scar scoring her palm in half.

Raw elation slammed to the top of his head, filling his eyes, making his gut clench, and sending strength that had Montvale's hand on the table with a slam of noise. Then Rhoenne was on his feet and reaching for her. The sound of the bench falling wasn't as loud as her gasp.

Chapter Twenty-Two

"Leave us," Rhoenne said.

"This is my house," Montvale answered.

"Leave us," Rhoenne commanded in the same low tone that was sending crescendos of shivers up her back and making the baby do antics within her.

"My house. And that woman . . . may be my wife."

Aislynn had given away the lie with the slightest widening of her eyes. She didn't know if Rhoenne saw it or not. Nothing on him gave her a clue. He looked wonderful. He looked masculine and immense and impressive. He also looked soulless, empty, and even worse than the last time she'd seen him. She couldn't keep the chill look of his gaze and dropped hers to his chin, bare-looking in comparison to the bearded Montvale, and from there dropped to his chest. He hadn't lost an ounce of weight, he was still broad-shouldered, well-defined, and everything a man who had just been tested and found superior was meant to be.

Everything about him was superior; in every way. Her cheeks reddened. She moved her eyes away and focused on the table, where the empty tankard still sat in its up-ended position.

"I said leave us."

"Aislynn?"

Her eyes filled and she blinked it away before either of them saw it. She knew Montvale was giving the decision to her. She just wished he hadn't.

She nodded.

His sigh was her answer. It was one of disgust. She looked further down, at the mound that was her child, dressed with three layers of Highland *plaide*, and covered over still with the Lady of the Brook cloak. She blinked a tear into existence and watched it fall onto where the upper cord was tied, just below her breasts.

"Look at me, Aislynn. I have words to say, and I need to watch you while I say them."

She shook her head.

"Why not?"

Because she couldn't handle the look in his eye! The look she'd created. The dead look. Not for one more instant of time. It was slicing right through to her and making the pain in her back worse than anything the child's weight caused.

She shook her head again.

"How will I know you lie or not, if I can't see your eye color?"

She was swaying and there wasn't anything there to save her. Aislynn reached out blindly, connected with the trencher table, balanced herself with it, and then she forced her knees to stiffen.

"I'll na' lie," she whispered.

"You haven't heard what I'll say."

Her heart twinged. The babe responded, kicking so swiftly, she gasped and put a hand to the side of her belly to support the movement.

"The babe you carry . . . it is a boy-child." He didn't ask it. "And he's mine. Mine. Ramhurst."

She gulped and tried to make words to answer; any answer. She had to respond with a nod.

"He belongs to me. He's my heir."

There was emotion in his words after all, and it went right to her core. She didn't dare guess what it was. The bitter taste at the back of her mouth was warning her. She lifted her eyes for the slightest moment. He had a frown between his eyes and hardness everywhere else. She had to look back down.

"And I demand him from you. Right here and right now."

"Now?" she asked the table.

"Your husband will not keep him from me. Nothing will keep him from me. Do you understand?"

Aislynn looked up then, hated herself for it, and had to watch as he meshed and faded into the room about him with the wash of tears she refused to give existence to. His expression didn't change.

"You will hand him over the moment he is birthed . . . to me. To make certain of it, I'm taking you."

Hope flared in her belly, rose up through her breasts and rested in her nose, making it run so swiftly, she had to sniff.

"I'll not leave Stropshire without you. You'll be escorted to Tyneburn and kept under heavy guard once there. You understand?"

She was going with him. He was taking her with him. That's all she heard. That's all she knew. Aislynn blinked and watched his image distort into something so vile she didn't recognize it.

"All I wish from you is my son. If we're in luck, his birth really will kill you and save me the trouble of it."

She gave away the reaction. She knew it as her entire body endured the shock, making her knees bend, her body sag, and the babe went absolutely still as she went to the floor, scraping her knees when she got there.

"I'm known as the Avenger for a reason, Aislynn. I give no quarter, expect none, and never, *ever* forgive. You knew this. Both of you. *God damn* both of you now for making me prove it!"

He was probably still watching her. Aislynn didn't see it. She held her hands over her face, and tried to live through it.

They'd crafted a swinging cot for her in the bottom of one of their small wagons by placing two tent poles together and stretching tightly woven material between them. They'd also carved slick, flat pieces of wood to replace the front wheels, so it would glide easily over the snow. Then he'd had them connect her sled to his horse. All of this, she saw the moment he sent men to escort her.

Montvale was accompanying her. He didn't look like he wanted to, but he had no choice. He'd claimed her. He looked like he wanted to be anywhere other than astride his other horse, several placements back from her, and treated as a pariah among his own. It was easy to pick him out. He wasn't wearing the heavy fur cloaks the others were. He was still in his Highland *plaide*, exposing large, bare muscled arms, and he still had a full beard, too.

The journey to the Ramhurst fief took eleven days longer than it was supposed to. Aislynn had the first argument between Montvale and Ramhurst to thank for that information, and then she ceased listening to their bitter words, thrown with the accuracy of knives. Rhoenne was stopping as often as he decreed necessary, to see to the health and well-being of his heir. He was also setting up a tent every night and getting rest. He wasn't doing anything to harm his son. He was going to carry her everywhere she needed to go, and that took an act of will beyond Montvale's comprehension, if his first words were true.

They'd stopped the first time, within sight of Stropshire, although it had taken the entire morn to get that far. It wasn't Aislynn's fault. The snow was belly-deep on the horses and making the going difficult. Her sled bounced, and slid, and skipped along, on top of every obstacle, and came to a perfect stop each time Rhoenne halted his horse.

That stop had been the worst. Rhoenne was off his horse, hip-deep in snow and yelling for Montvale to move to the front and assist him. Aislynn hadn't known until then, that he meant to assist him with moving her. She struggled to a sitting position from the reclining bed they'd made for her of furs, quilts, and blankets, and told the Laird of Ramhurst that she was used to doing for herself.

Cold, hard blue eyes had answered her before he opened his mouth. He informed her she was carrying his property, and she was not to do it any harm, and that meant walking in deep snow. She was being carried to relieve herself, and he ordered Montvale to do it.

Sir Harold had been on the opposite side of her wagon, smiling broadly, showing white teeth amidst his beard. He'd folded his arms and asked for one reason why he should.

"Because you're her husband!" Rhoenne had replied.

The others had busied themselves with their own needs, and then to seeing to parceling out flats cakes, salted venison, and little, wrinkled, sweet nuggets that proved to be dried berries. They were all acting deaf to the words being flung across her body. Aislynn only wished she had the same luxury.

"If I'm her husband, she can walk by herself." Montvale had regarded Rhoenne with an inscrutable expression.

"She's carrying my property!"

"Ah . . . now there's a problem for you. How to keep her from damaging the property within, while appearing to have no concern for the vessel. I dinna' envy you the quandary you have set for yourself, Ramhurst."

"Carry her. I command you."

Montvale's lips quirked. "You're *nae* longer my liege, Ramhurst. You sent me from such a position, remember? I'm with you to guard the woman who might be my wife. It's a good thing I am, as roughly as you speak to her."

"Are you going to carry her, or not?"

"Cease this! I can walk!" Aislynn was struggling from the blankets, and then hard hands seized her, stopping her with the pressure of them.

"You'll do nothing to harm my son. Nothing."

"I've walked a-fore," she whispered.

He sucked for breath, put an arm beneath her knees and one behind her back and lifted her, taking her close enough to his chest that she could hear and feel his heart through the layers of clothing and furs they wore. That was matched by the heavy breathing he was sending over her nose, and the way he tightened his arms, making it impossible for her to even think of struggling.

"Please . . . dinna' do this," she whispered.

He didn't answer. He was looking over her head and he had his teeth clenched, making his jaw tighten enough to pull the cords in his neck taut. Aislynn moved her view from that back to where he was doing his best to pretend he hadn't heard her; his mouth.

"You'll be carried. You will not strain yourself." He glanced down at her, met her eyes and something happened. She watched as he licked his lips, drawing her gaze for a moment, and then she went back to his eyes.

"Always this happens. I might as well be by myself when you two look at each other. This is going to take a supreme act of will beyond my comprehension, Ramhurst. I dinna' envy you, at all. Na' at all."

Harold had sent his laughter after the words, since he was already turned and was walking back to his mount. Rhoenne had grimaced, tightened his hold further, and carried her into the trees. It hadn't ended there, either. He'd waited for her, and then he picked her up in the same fashion and carried her back. Aislynn tried to tell her body to hate it. She sent the command to detest the feel of being held against him. It was useless. She didn't have to wait for her increased pulse to tell her of it, or the sweat beading her upper lip, even with the frost stinging her throat with every breath.

"I'm truly going to enjoy killing him." He muttered it as he got back to her wagon, and lifted her gingerly over the side railing in order to place her back into the cot. She didn't look at him again. She couldn't. She was afraid. She knew what she was afraid of, too; the next stop.

Each night, Rhoenne had his tent erected, warmed, a bed piled with furs for her, and then he carried her into it, and set her on it. He had a look of stone about him as he did it. Aislynn watched it, and on the third night, she did something so horrid, her entire body went stiff with the surprise.

That night, she reached out and put her palm against his cheek as he was setting her down. Rhoenne's response was immediate and vicious. He yanked himself from her touch, looked at her with those steel-cold eyes, and told her to never do that again. Ever.

Aislynn would've cried aloud, if her throat could make the effort. As it was, she clasped both hands to her bosom, held them there as if it would protect her heart from further damage, and forced herself to live through it.

Then it got worse. On the seventh night, he drank.

Aislynn was getting lethargic with the lack of motion he forced on her, and lying about all day, while trying to find sleep all night. It wasn't doing her body any good. She would've told him of it, but if she looked like she might be speaking to him, he'd turn his back on her and leave. The only time she had him in a position when he'd have to listen was when he was carrying her, and every time that happened, her body gave her too much trouble on how his closeness felt to get her mind, or her lips, or her voice to do anything like creating sentences and speaking them.

Then came the seventh night. He'd settled her into her bed and looked aside as she tried to get comfortable. Just as he did each night. Aislynn shifted and tried to find a decent position. The only way was either sitting so she could breathe, which made it easier for the bairn to move about and make her miserable; or she had to lie on her side with her legs slightly bent, so the bairn could create the same misery. She'd just finished the flagon of water he gave her, and was handing it back. She didn't thank him. The only times she tried, he'd looked away, and set his jaw. She quit trying.

Then he decided to change things. Aislynn didn't know why. He was on his haunches beside her, waiting for the cup. He bumped her fingers when she handed it back and she watched his lips tighten. Then he was lifting the round flask at his hips, unstopping it, and drinking a healthy draught of ale.

Aislynn was watching him when he brought his head back down. That must have been what started it, for he put the plug back into his bag without looking. He had his eyes on her, and she returned the stare.

It had started snowing during the day, blanketing the men, the horses, her wagon, and making everything look like a magical winter kingdom again. It was also making everything still and silent; even more so, once the tent flap was tied and they were sealed in together. Aislynn's pulse rose in her ears, trying to take over, as all he did was stare.

Then he opened his lips and asked one word. "Why?"

Aislynn narrowed her eyes to make it easier, since she was afraid to blink, in the event the ale-softened look she saw was changed.

"Why, Aislynn?"

"Why?" She echoed it. He didn't know the power of his gaze, when he had it softened and looking as hurt as it did.

"Did he offer more than me?"

She swallowed. *"Nae,"* she answered finally.

"Is he more manly?"

"Nae," she replied again.

"Stronger? I know he's had you with the Gallgaels. He dresses as one and he bears one of their marks. He probably saved you from them. Such an experience should have been mine!"

"He dinna' save me," she whispered.

"I envy him the experience, and I hate him for creating that in me again. Do you know how that feels? Envy?"

She shook her head.

"Did he say sweeter words? Is that why you wanted him?"

Her heart pulsed. She put a hand there to stay it. It didn't help. It still felt like he had Pinnacle at her breast and was pushing with the blade. She had to shake her head again.

"Then why? Is he a better lover? Is that why?" His voice lowered, as if he hated himself for asking it. Aislynn's eyes filled with tears, and they were such a useless emotion, she hated her own body for giving them to her.

She shook her head.

"Your eyes are both brown. Damn you." He opened the wineskin and took another long swallow of his ale. Her throat made the same motion.

"I've gone over it a thousand times. I still cannot see it. He has never beat me. Never. He's ever tried, though. I always best him. Always. Except with women. I must accede the victory to him there."

"I—"

He stopped and waited. Aislynn didn't know what she'd been about to say. It was impossible to think when he came closer, scooting right next to her and lifting a lock of her hair in his fingers to rub it into the many strands that it was.

"He has a tongue that spouts falsehoods and flattery, and he beds women like there's no end to them. All the time. Sometimes several a night. Sometimes all at once. I know. I gave up tallying. I don't think even he knows the number. That contest, he wins. Is that why, Aislynn?"

He looked up at her, with a quizzical expression that had nothing cold or sober about it.

"Rhoenne." His name croaked. She told herself it was because she hadn't used her voice. She knew it was a lie.

"He must be better at loving women. That must be it."

"Stop this."

"Women swoon over his words. They don't know it for the falsehood it is. I do. I mean . . . I did. I don't understand this. Help me to understand this."

"Sir Montvale is na' the man you are," she whispered.

"I know! He's better!" He lifted the wineskin again; drank again; and then favored her with the watery-blue look she'd fallen in love with first.

"Nae, Rhoenne."

"He must be! You took him over me!"

He couldn't hide the pain that was eating at him. Not when he wasn't sober. Aislynn put a hand out, hesitated for a moment, and then placed it on his cheek. She watched as he leaned into it, and then he turned his head to place a kiss on the line of scar tissue there.

"Rhoenne?" she said, softly.

"I loved you. You know that."

Aislynn caught her breath.

"I fought the word. I fought what it meant. I lost then, but you know that. You were there."

"Dinna' do this." Aislynn swallowed. "Please?"

"Why not? Does he have prior claims on your time?"

"Because this is na' you talking. This is the ale loosening your tongue."

"Not true. This is the man, the one I call the troubadour. The man you betrayed and then destroyed. The man that only surfaces when ale flows, it's dark outside, and there's nothing for company in a tent in the middle of a blizzom, other than a whore with beautiful black hair, eyes of separate colors, and a tongue that spouts lies and deceit. Does he feel the same, Aislynn? When he takes you . . . does he? Well? Does he?"

There was nothing loving about him, and his fingers had clenched on her hair, drawing her up slightly, or risk having it pulled out.

"Nae," she replied, finally.

"Damn you. Damn you. Your eyes are brown. Still. Damn you. Damn both of you. To hell. Damn you. Damn."

The curses wouldn't stop as his other hand went behind her neck, his fingers spread over the back of her throat, to force her head up into a curve. Then he had his lips on her throat, his tongue against her skin, and the curses were doing more than helping him alleviate the hate. They were cooling the wetness he was leaving there, and making a trail of ice all the way to the bottom juncture of her jaw.

"So beautiful. So tempting. So lovely."

He was murmuring other love words and making every part of her weak and pliable and full of want. And then the words changed.

"So vile. So evil. So cruel. So . . . cursed. You are accursed, Aislynn. As am I. I suffer from your curse. I wither. I have no desire. I can no longer even bed a woman. Any woman."

His words got harsher in the same manner his breathing did, as he continued to mouth them to the side of her neck and the space below her ear. Aislynn tried to pull back, to get away from the spate of hate that was coming from him. It didn't work. He was on his knees, he was stronger, and then he was nibbling at the bottom lobe of her ear, and changing any pleas for mercy into cries of desire. It had been too long. It was too poignant. It was too sweet.

Aislynn had her head arched up, her eyes narrowed on the top of his tent and her breath coming in little panting whiffs of air. Tingles were flying about her body, centering in her breasts and then starting a throb of reaction in her core that had her moan attached.

The hand at her hair moved, coming around the other side of her face, and lowering her jaw so he could look her in the eye. Aislynn recoiled at what she saw there, but she wasn't fast enough to stop from hearing.

"Look at you. You cannot even be faithful to *him*," he said. Then he shoved from her, tossed on his cloak, and stomped out into the storm.

He didn't stay to see the damage he'd done. He didn't come back. He didn't see how the sobs shook her, taking her right off the pallet and onto the floor, and making her clutch the bairn her body harbored, while he kicked his displeasure at the ripples of her emotion that skimmed her skin and roved her flesh, over and over . . . and over again.

Chapter Twenty-Three

Aislynn used to live in a dream world of her own invention. It helped her through the worst of her growing years and she found it the only possible place to be during the nightmare that was this journey. She had to go there every time they called a halt, and every time Rhoenne came near her. It was the only way to stop the tears during the day. There was nothing that worked at night. The only thing she could manage was to sob silently on her pallet, so he wouldn't hear. That way, he'd never know.

He didn't have to know what she was thinking as she compared the fur around his head to a cloud, or the blond tips of his eyelashes to the flash of a butterfly wing. He didn't have to know any of it and his frown had no ability to change any of it, either.

"Something's wrong with Aislynn," Ramhurst said. She heard it.

"There's a lot wrong with this. Perhaps you should have noted it long a-fore this."

"You're her husband. You do something."

Montvale's laugh interfered with her dream world. Aislynn blinked, saw the sun was reflecting off new snow, blinding everything and everyone, and then she smiled softly again as it muted.

"You're the one inflicting the damage. You do something."

"When this is over, I'm going to kill you, Montvale."

"When this is over, you're going to *try*. There's a lot of difference to those two statements. You should think it through."

"You have words of wisdom for me now?"

"One can only give wisdom where it'll do some good. Some ears are too closed for such."

"You closed my ears when you betrayed me."

"I canna' continually pay for a crime I dinna' commit!" There was a shocked silence following his exclamation.

"So, now you're going to tell me I didn't see what I saw?"

There was a heavy sigh.

"He dinna' wish to do it, Rhoenne," Aislynn said softly, from between them, stopping the barrage of words for a moment. "Truly."

"Every man wishes to. This one was born ready. And willing. He just has to find ready females to satisfy his lust. You were easy. You were available. You were lusty. You were his match. Evil. Both of you."

"Now cease that, Ramhurst, or I'll be calling you out."

"Not until the bairn is birthed! Then we'll meet. I'll carve you open and dance on your innards, but not until I have my son in my hands! Killing you first may harm that."

"Describing it isna' helping, either. Look."

She didn't know what they were looking for. She wasn't doing anything other than watching the sun flit through the trees and touch the dunes of snow that were carving the glen they were in.

"Aislynn?"

One of them was saying her name as if they cared. She ignored it.

"You've done something to her, have na' you? Damn you, Ramhurst. Isna' it enough that you'll have me? Isna' it enough that you gave her a death sentence with your seed? What else can you want from her? What else is it going to take?"

"I want her to know how it feels. I want her to know what she did to me. I want someone else to know the pain and humiliation and disgust."

"Trust me. She already knows it. She's always known. Why do you ken she just lies there, willing herself to die?"

"Because it's easier than facing what she's done."

"It's because she's willing to do what you need her to do in order to take away your pain. She was willing to do it for me. She's willing to do it for you. She *is* doing it for you."

"She's lying about, looking at naught, and pretending. That's what she's doing!"

There was another heavy sigh. "She's a healer, Ramhurst. She heals. Even if the injury doesn't show, she heals it. Canna' you see that?"

There was silence for a bit. That was odd. When Montvale came near her wagon, there was never silence. There was a constant barrage of angry words. Aislynn tipped her head and listened for a moment. Then she smiled. It was a wonderful silence.

"She knows you want her death. And that naught else will satisfy you. So, she's helping you gain it."

"What ale loosens your tongue this time, Montvale?"

Another loud sigh. "She's giving you a living death! She's taking all the abuse, all the anger, and all the hatred you spew at her and she's na' fighting any of it! You ken why? Nay? I'll tell you why! Because if she's absorbing it, and living with it, and holding on to it, then maybe you're releasing it and na' having to live with it! That's what she's doing. Canna' you see any of this?"

"Well, do something! She's your wife."

There was another heavy sigh. "If I told you that was a lie, would it change any of this?"

There was a short silence. It didn't last. "Nay."

"Why na'?"

"Because liars tell lies. I used to think you spoke false-hoods to make things easier. To be helpful. Now, I know the truth. You lie because you lie. Simple."

"You dinna' ken anything, Ramhurst. You let your hatred think for you, and your bloodlust act for you, and since hatred will only dissipate if it's tossed, she's allowing you to do the tossing at her, so she can take it from you."

"There is nothing you say that I'll believe."

"Rhoenne, you are a beast. All the way through."

"I know."

"I hope you can live with yourself when this is finished."

There was a long pause. Aislynn stiffened between the shoulders so she could listen to words that were going to feel like a blow.

"So do I," he said, finally.

Old Rosie met them on the steps, she seemed larger than before, and she was louder. Then she added to that. She was angry. Aislynn lay against the pile of furs at her back and watched the woman's temper without emotion.

"That's no way to treat a Ramhurst bairn! What's the matter with you men? Get her up. Get her walking! Do you want a stillbirth?"

"The bairn's fine. I've carried her everywhere."

"God save you, My Lord. You've done it wrong. She's got to have strength to her legs and health to her belly. I may be too late to save them! Get her up!"

Aislynn didn't move. Rhoenne had to lift her, raising her slightly to get her over the railing, and then he was walking through the entranceway with her. She noted he was taking her up the staircase to the chieftain's chambers as if it was the normal order of things.

"I tried to tell him of it," Montvale said from behind them.

"Stay your words and get me some cold water. A bucket-full. Now! Melt some snow! Now. Stupid men!"

"The bairn's going to be fine," Rhoenne said.

"A weak lass canna' bring a child into the world. She's got to be strong! She's got to be stout! She's got to have some weight to her, and na' look like a stick with a large cocoon settled atop it! Set her on her feet, and get out. Both of you. She can't birth a Ramhurst male looking like this!"

"How do you know it's a Ramhurst male?" Montvale asked.

"I've seen the look of them. Now go. Get the snow."

Aislynn stood in the chamber that she'd found so much love in, and swayed in place. Her legs were trembling with holding her, and she moved her hands to her child, surprising herself with the size and volume and weight of it. Then she had ice-cold water tossed on her and was sputtering and screaming and shaking with shock and surprise.

"That's better." Old Rosie had her hands to where her hips were supposed to be and was waiting for Aislynn to finish screeching before she spoke.

"Why did you do such a thing?"

"Because you already had the look of death, and I'll not lose another woman to the Ramhurst curse. Come along now. Peel those scraps from your frame and let me have a look at you."

"I'm big, swelled, and ugly. What's to look at?"

"Not exactly. I only wished you were big, swelled, and ugly."

"What?"

The outer layer was already coming off. Aislynn hadn't had her clothing removed in so long, the garments felt like they were permanently attached together.

"And I want a bath. Your Lordship!" Rosie opened the door and yelled it. Rhoenne must have been waiting in the hall for he was there almost before she finished the call.

"Will the bairn . . . ?"

"Order a bath. A big tub, with a small amount of water. Knee high . . . on her, not you."

"We don't want a lot of water?"

"Warm water brings on the pains. We don't want her laboring too soon. Make the water lukewarm, too. Order that."

"Let me see her."

"If you don't do what I ordered you to, and do it quick-like, I'm going to have a large section of your scalp removed, and I already know how fond you are of that hair. Do we understand each other, Lord Ramhurst?"

"I'm being berated by my own servant?"

"I'm her servant. Remember that. I serve my mistress. Now, get what I ordered. And send up a sup; a huge sup. Order those garments brought up from wherever you sent them. And you'd best not have destroyed my handiwork. I spent days sewing tunics for this lass."

"Storage. They're in storage. I gave the chore to Richard."

"Don't stand there telling me where you put them. Go and fetch them! Now! Do you wish to see your heir alive or not?"

"I do."

"Then get your hindquarters in action, and fetch what I require. Men!" She finished the exclamation by slamming the chamber door. It wavered a bit in the center because it still had the same crack, Aislynn noticed.

"As for you, My Lady? Well, let's just get another layer of this off of you. What is this? Sackcloth? Have you been in a monastery? That would explain why His Lordship couldn't find you."

"He could na' find me? He . . . looked?"

"Of course he looked. He was crazed with worry. All of us were. You up and disappear and you take that Sir Montvale with you? I'm surprised the man still has his head. His Lordship was ready to take it off. Not that he said so. He's as close-mouthed as an old friar."

"How do you know, then?"

"I know because I raised that lad. I know when he's troubled. I know when he's been kicked in the mouth. He had that look about him. He's been worried sick. Sick."

"He didn't act sick."

"If he was looking anything but sick, then it was an act. I know my lad. He was gut-sick and full of pain. Pain that he turned to hate. He probably showed you the hate. That's a Ramhurst for you. Trust me. It isn't hate. It's covered-over pain. They'll never admit pain."

"Never?"

She nodded, like it was nothing to upend Aislynn's world. She'd forgotten that facet about him. He hid pain. He always hid pain.

"Well, don't just stand there with your mouth open. Tell me. Where did you hide yourselves?"

"We've been with . . . a clan . . . of Highlanders."

Rosie's eyes went wide. "Nay!" she replied.

Aislynn nodded.

"That explains the heathen look of Sir Montvale, although he does look rather manly, strutting about in the dead of winter with nothing on save a tunic and boots. He doesn't even wear sleeves."

"The Gallgaels are verra manly."

She snorted. "Well! I may have to go around his chamber and have a look-see a bit later. I could stand an eyeful of a manly fellow. I might decide to favor him this eve, too. He has the look of a man needing a woman."

"He'll na' be given his old chamber."

"He'll be lucky if he's given a stable with one meal a day. That's how much he's welcome. I know Rhoenne de Ramhurst."

"He'll give him . . . a chamber," Aislynn remarked.

"What makes you so certain?"

"He thinks we're wed."

"What? Now, why would he go and think such stupidity as that? There's not a man that compares to His Lordship and he knows it. There's no way a lass would wed anyone else, once she caught his eye. You didn't do it, did you?"

Aislynn shook her head. *"Nae,"* she said.

"Exactly as I said. Now, where does he get a fool idea like that, then?"

"Sir Montvale told him so . . . or he wanted Rhoenne to think it. I'm guessing that's what happened. I was na' there. I dinna' ken for certain."

"Men! Sometimes I don't think their heads are worth the space it takes to hold their hair to it."

Aislynn giggled.

"You really were with the Highlanders, then. Manly fellows?"

Aislynn nodded.

"They grow full beards, like that Sir Montvale has?"

Aislynn nodded again.

"And they wear naught more than the one strip of cloth?"

"In the winter. They wear even less . . . come summer."

Rosie licked her lips. "I might decide to favor Sir Montvale with a bit of my time, for certain. I'd like a visit with these Gallgael fellows. Less than that strip of cloth?"

"Oh, aye, and the women as well."

"No!"

"They saw my mark. They call it a god-mark."

"Lord have mercy on us all! You let them see such a thing?"

"My shift was ripped. It wasn't my fault. I had to protect my hands." She lifted her hands. Rosie's eyes went huge.

"Sweet heaven, lass! Those are sword scars, or I'm not a living, breathing! What devil sliced your palms?"

"You dinna' wish . . . to know," Aislynn replied.

"If it was Montvale, he's going to rue the day. I'll take every lock of hair off his head, and give him a fair shaving to top it off. And I'll use a dulled skean!"

"It was na' Montvale. It's na' important. It happened. It's over. It's all over."

"Now, don't go getting that look to yourself. I'll douse you with melted snow again. I swear."

"What . . . look?"

"Like there's nothing left to live for."

Aislynn's eyes filled. "There is but one thing left to live for." She looked down at the distended belly that was Ramhurst's future and cradled it beneath both hands. "And after that . . . there's naught."

"You've got the melancholy. That's what's wrong here. It's normal for a lass so near her time. Here. Let me help you with this cord." She was trying to untie the strip of braided rawhide that had kept Aislynn's open-sided tunic to her body beneath her belly. Rosie had to put a dirk beneath it and cut it free. Then, she sliced along the neckline in order to peel the last layer off.

The bairn looked enormous. Aislynn's eyes went wide as she ran her hands over the size of herself. She had no idea she'd gotten so large.

"Does he move oft?"

"He used to," she answered.

Old Rosie frowned. "How long ago?"

Aislynn joined her frown. "I dinna' recollect. Is that bad?"

"It just means he's biding his time, gathering strength. It's na' an easy thing to get birthed, lass. For him, either."

Aislynn closed her eyes and shuddered through the reaction. It was almost over. She almost thanked her gods again. She was leaving all the pain and agony that was this world, and it was going to be soon. She'd been telling herself for months that it was a just and right penalty for what she'd done, but now that it was on the horizon, she felt and tasted the fear.

"How much time do . . . I have?" she asked.

"Well, I'd have you lie on your back and get a good measure of it, but I don't want you on your back until you can't stand being up on your feet any longer. That's the problem with these men. They've done everything wrong. And that Rhoenne Guy de Ramhurst is the worst! Ever since you disappeared, he's been doing everything wrong; everything."

"*Nae* man does everything wrong," Aislynn said softly, defensively.

"Well, that man does. About the only thing he's done right is get you to me in time for the birthing of his son."

There was a knock on the chamber door.

"Perhaps he's changing, and has done this right, too. Into this robe. I'll see to everything. And they better have sweetbreads with them. Done this morn. Flavored with pig rinds and such. Tasty." She opened the chamber door and started waving. "Don't just stand there. Get the supplies in here. Tub? There. Buckets? Into the tub. Food?"

She looked at Aislynn, who was standing, wrapped in a Ramhurst blue robe, that felt like softest down against her bare skin.

"Put the food by the mistress. Quick-like! I'll report your actions to the sheriff. Richard levies fines for laziness."

Aislynn watched as serfs poured into the room, setting up a tub and an array of food that made her mouth water.

"Richard?" she asked, when the last bucket had been dumped and everyone left.

"Rhoenne named him sheriff. He has his ways, although manliness is still not one of them. Come along, lass. Get a bite or two in your frame and then hunch onto your knees in this tub. We've got a season of filth to scrub from you, and it's not going to float off."

Aislynn did as requested, although she had more than a plateful of sweetbreads down her before hunching onto her knees in the little bit of water Rosie was allowing her. It felt good, and she breathed the sigh of relief as the evening turned to night and Rosie made her climb the stairs twice before letting her sit back, too exhausted to get near the bed, even if it was beckoning to her from her memory and teasing her with the man who should be sleeping there.

It felt good, and right, and well-organized, and clean, and efficient. It felt like a home that a small lad could be born in, raised in, and grow up into a strong, healthy specimen the image of his sire. It was all she could have asked of her gods; all that she'd hoped for her baby. She wondered if she dared ask more of his God. She was too tired to go to her knees, but she winged a prayer to all that might be listening, asking for health, and safety . . . and time.

Most of all she asked for time.

Chapter Twenty-Four

She got a sennight of days and nights of time, then she got an eighth day, and then a ninth. The twinge that had dogged her for months started becoming something more than a backache, as it turned into what her world was going to become on the tenth day. Aislynn woke up, like she had been for over a week now, to the sight of Rhoenne's empty bed, a dull, sunless dawn, but with a strange nagging suspicion that something was wrong.

She rolled onto her hands and knees, catching her breath at how strange it felt when the baby rolled within her without moving. She stood. The catch of pain at her back came again. Aislynn ignored it as she always did. The walk to his long window took longer than usual. Either that, or time was changing. That was odd, too.

For nine days now, she'd walked ceaselessly, then she'd been forced to eat. Then, she'd had to walk again; eat . . . walk again; eat. Old Rosie had her on a regimen. She was beginning to think the woman wanted Aislynn as fat as she was. The walk to his window was finally accomplished. It had her panting with the exertion. Old Rosie would be frowning over that. Aislynn was frowning over it. Her legs were as shaky and weak as they'd been when she first arrived, and didn't resemble the limbs Rosie was making. That was strange, too.

There was a light snow falling. It was supposed to be spring, but winter wasn't giving up easily. Aislynn watched snowflakes as small as dust floating in front of her, taking their own sweet time to reach the ground. The twinge came again, radiating outward from the small of her back. She put both hands to it and arched upward, taking some of the ache away. That's when her water broke.

Rhoenne walked into Sir Montvale's chamber without knocking. He had Destiny with him. It had taken days to find it and had come at a pretty price. He waited until the knight looked up from the drunk he'd been creating. He dropped the sword onto the table where it clattered against the man's tankard.

"You brought my sword. Oh, dear, sweet lady. How I've missed you."

Rhoenne's lip curled as he watched Harold pick up the blade, and run his hands along the flat edge, before lowering his face to kiss the steel. The man was still wearing his Highland attire; he reeked of drink and sweat, for he hadn't been known to order or take a bath since they arrived; and he hadn't sought the bed he'd been given to sleep in, either.

"It isn't a gift," Rhoenne informed him.

Sir Montvale stopped his caress of the metal and looked over and up at Rhoenne.

"What is it then?" he asked.

"What you need for my challenge. And your death."

"One or the other, Ramhurst. You canna' have both."

Rhoenne didn't answer. He lifted his sword, Pinnacle, put the tip beneath Harold's chin to raise it a fraction.

"Do I get time to sober?" the knight asked.

"Are you ever in that state?"

"Some days." The knight shrugged. "The nights? Never."

"You get the time to wash your face and don decent attire. I'll not have it said I killed a Highlander. I have enough troubles."

"You never asked me what happened. You ken that?"

"Why would I ask a liar? All I receive is a lie."

The knight's eyes narrowed. "Would you join me in a drink first?"

"You attempt a cheat? Already?"

"Cheat? I haven't any need of such. I bested every Gall-gael. I can best you. I just wanted to wash the taste of these words from my mouth a-fore I gift you with my throat. You owe me that much, at least."

"I owe you nothing."

"I've protected your life with mine, Ramhurst. More than once."

Rhoenne regarded him for a few moments. He moved Pinnacle away and watched as the knight's chin stayed at exactly the same angle he'd placed it in. "You're sober enough," he commented.

"That is a problem. Join me in a drink. I'll remedy it."

"You know I'm a poor drunk. Drink dulls my senses. Slows down my reactions. Changes me. You know this."

"It makes you human. You could use a bit of that. Aside from which, it will even the odds." He shrugged again. "Either that, or slit my throat as I sit here. That would be as fair."

"Pour." Rhoenne replied.

He watched as the knight fumbled for the other tankard to fill it, making him realize the truth. Montvale was well into his drunk. He wasn't going to be able to fight him for some time.

He reached out with the sword and knocked Montvale's

tankard off the table. They both heard the sound of metal hitting the stone floor.

"You saying something with that move?" Montvale asked.

"I'll drink. To even the contest. You . . . do not."

Harold winced. "Unchivalrous," he replied.

Rhoenne lifted the full tankard and gulped it down, feeling the familiar buzz to his head before he was half finished. He knew it was a mistake, but he was making an awful lot of them ever since he'd found her again. He amended that thought before he was finished. He was making a lot of mistakes since he'd found them. Together. Betraying him.

"You certain you want to drink all of that, Ramhurst?"

The empty tankard dropped to the floor, making the same sound the first one had.

"Now I'm human. Get your sword."

Montvale shook his head. At least, that's what it looked like he was doing with it. He was also wavering and a bit blurry.

"I probably should've warned you. That's the best your aleman has. Excellent brew. If you ever hire out his services, the Highlanders will pay well. They love their drink."

"You truly were with them?" Rhoenne pulled out the chair that was opposite Montvale. He either had to do that or resort to showing how much the drink had already affected him by wobbling where he stood.

"Four months. This mark here?" He moved forward and pointed to the bluish streak below his right eye. "Moon carving. New moon. Their choice. I earned it."

"How do you earn a mark?"

"By besting savage people. Savage people, Ramhurst. Possessing lusty women. Beautiful, full breasts; large hips. They want a man between their thighs and they're very open with their wants and needs and appetites. It was heaven. I was in heaven." He licked his lips. "Heaven," he repeated.

"What . . . of Aislynn?"

"What of her?"

"You were wed to her. You were faithless? Are. You are faithless."

Harold smirked a bit. "I asked her to wed. She refused my suit. I dinna' ken why. The lass is daft."

"She refused it?" That didn't make sense. Rhoenne smacked the side of his head with one hand. He'd heard it wrong.

"She dinna' accept it. That was more the story."

"But . . . you wed with her. You told me you were wed."

"I told you we may be wed. You believed it a fact. I said 'may.' Always."

"What?" That made less sense. "Why?"

"Because you're a beast. I was afraid for her."

"Of what?"

"You. More specific: the beast that is you. Someone had to protect her. Someone had to make certain you knew she had a champion, so you could na' just take out your rage on her. Damn. I should've drunk more. I have na' managed to save her. Why dinna' you just be a good vassal and follow a king's orders the first time? Barring that, why were you na' better with that hunk of steel you call your Pinnacle, so you could slice my head cleanly when you had the chance? Instead of her hands? Well?" He licked his lips. At least, to Rhoenne, it looked like he was licking his lips. "Barring that, why could na' you just take the lass, tell her you love her, and heal all this mess?"

"Because I don't love her. Not anymore."

"And you call me a liar? At least, I only lie to others. You lie to yourself. That's worse."

Rhoenne sat straighter. His head sung with a quick note

about the movement and then it dimmed. "Did you just insult me? You?"

The knight rolled the amusement through his lips. "I've been insulting you since you discovered me attempting to look like I was having your woman. I just canna' get you to finish the challenge and lop my head off! If you'd do that there would be no more reason to drink myself into an early grave, because you'll have already put me in one!"

"You *want* me to kill you?"

The knight sighed. Rhoenne watched his shoulders move with it. He thought it was a sigh. It certainly couldn't be anything else.

"I've wanted you to kill me since I set this up. You are uncannily dense, and thick-headed, and slow-witted, and a terrible swordsman to top it off."

"Terrible? If you hadn't put her in front of you, you'd be rotting beneath the soil instead of having to smell up the earth while you rot atop it! I barely stopped my swing in time."

Montvale threw back his head and laughed heartily, so heartily he had to wipe at the tears when he looked back. "If I dinna' ken what your words were going to be a-fore you speak them, I'd never understand them, Ramhurst."

"Why not?"

"Because you slur them. Already."

"Bastard!"

"Wretch!" Montvale shouted back.

"Cur!"

"Swine!"

"Whoreson!"

Montvale sucked in on his cheeks as he considered that label. Then, he nodded. "I like that. Whoreson. That's me. I agree."

"You can't agree."

"Why na'?"

"Because I'm insulting you."

"I fancy the word, though. Find another."

"I'm trying to challenge you!"

"The only challenge you're up to, oh, great laird, Rhoenne Guy de Ramhurst, is one of who can stand steady . . . and who can na'."

Rhoenne scrunched his forehead and sucked spittle into his mouth to wet it. "Why do you lie and fool with words, and make everything all mixed up and misunderstood?"

"I dinna' mix words. Your head mixes them for you."

"Is there more of that ale?"

Montvale lifted the wineskin and peered into it, earning a slight trickle of liquid into his eye, which he cursed at. The question was hammering at the back of Rhoenne's eyes, making them burn. It was something Montvale had said . . . something. Rhoenne frowned, licked his lips, and then, just asked it. "You truly aren't wed with Aislynn?"

"She would na' have me. She has her sights set higher."

"Your meaning?"

"God, but you are a blind fool, Ramhurst."

Rhoenne launched up, and tried to kick the chair from beneath him while pulling Pinnacle out again. All that happened was the chair rocked backward and then righted itself, while the sword seemed melded into its scabbard and wouldn't come out. He had to give it up.

His antics had Harold laughing again. Rhoenne had to swallow the reaction. He'd known not to drink a full tankard as quickly as he had. He'd been stupid. Again.

"She does na' have eyes for anyone else. She had her pick of the Gallgaels. They're descended from the Picts, you ken. That's a tongue basher, that."

"What?"

"Pick of the Picts."

"Her eyes, damn you! What of them?"

"I should set that to verse and song. I could be a minstrel.

I'd have a song. Pick of the Picts! Pick of the Picts. The Picts! The Picts!"

He was slurring it discordantly. Rhoenne scrunched up a shoulder to halt the assault on his ears. It didn't help. His head was buzzing and ringing and echoing with Montvale's voice and the words he was singing.

"Cease! Silence! Stay your song!" He was louder, but Montvale had spoken the truth—the words were slurred.

Then Sir Harold did something strange. He pounded his chest, reached for Destiny and was on his feet with her, pointing her at Rhoenne and gesturing with the blade for him to do something.

"Get up, Rhoenne."

"What? Now?"

"You saddled me with a wench possessing a vicious tongue and a shape akin to a water pig. For months. Get up."

"I saddled—"

"You made me take her! You made me do it. All of it."

Rhoenne stumbled to his feet, losing the chair for ballast since it fell onto its back, and then he had to grip the table for a replacement. That structure shuddered. That was bad.

"So . . . you admit taking her? From your own lips! You, God-damned, soulless liar!" Red was coating his vision, and making it easier to grab up Pinnacle, although his arm wasn't steady enough to hold her up.

"I had to take her . . . *with me!* Fool! Any other woman would have been clinging to me, teasing my ear with lovewords and warming my frame with more as she begged for me. Na' her. Oh *nae*. She's spike-tongued and weepy, and even impugned my honor by saving me from them! God-damned wench! I could na' even get killed by them. A whole clan of them—blue-painted and ungodly, and wanting my head, and what does she do? This witch of

yours? What does she do? She saves me. Again. Damn
her. Damn. Damn. Damn."

"She's not a witch!" Rhoenne swung. The blade arced
through space, and nothing else, and took him with her, as
well. He stumbled three steps, then four, then slammed
against a wall, knocking a bit of dust from it, and little
else. Rhoenne shook his head to clear it. It still looked like
a wall. He had to turn back around. He couldn't decide
which way to go to do it, though.

"That's right, Ramhurst! Fight a wall! You'll have better
luck than against me. You ken why?"

Rhoenne was still shaking his head. Montvale took it
for an answer.

"Because a wall has more mercy than I'm going to
show you!"

"At least a wall stays silent! You curse a man more than
he can stand with the endless words you spout!" Rhoenne
lifted the sword again, and swung to his right, using the
motion to rotate away from the wall. He made it too wide
of a swing, however, and stumbled, kicking one of the
empty tankards right to a table leg, where it bounced back,
hitting his shin. The instant pain had him almost to a knee,
which had Harold laughing harder.

"You fight like you dance! Poorly!"

"And you fight like you sing. You can't!"

"She's a witch, Ramhurst. A witch. A witch. A bloody
witch! You've lost your heart to a witch!"

"Cease calling her that!"

"Nay!"

"Why not?"

"Because it's the only word getting you angry enough
to kill me! Come here, Ramhurst. Find my chest! Stick
Pinnacle straight through it! Here, I'll help you! Now!"

Harold had shoved the kilt band off his shoulder, baring
his upper torso and a vicious-looking scar. Rhoenne lifted

the blade high over his head, and then he went backward with the motion, stumbling and fumbling and lurching to a halt that arched his back as the sword tip stuck into the floor. Harold thought that was uproariously funny. Rhoenne felt the reaction all the way through him, making muscles bunch with anger and his throat swell with the rage. That emotion he knew and could use. Everything went cold. He swiveled, put both hands on the hilt and yanked the blade free.

"Have you ceased playing, yet?" Montvale teased.

"As God is my witness, Montvale, I really am going to kill you."

Something about the words, said as calmly as they were, stopped the knight's smile.

"I swear it," Rhoenne finished, and bent his knees for stability.

He watched the other man gulp. "Well, you're going to have to do it a sight better than you are now. That's all I can say. I wish you'd do it quicker, too. Hell needs me. Hell needs me a lot more than anyone else on this God-forsaken world does!"

"Cease moving, then!" Rhoenne tried to find spittle in his mouth to swallow. It was impossible. His mouth was dry as dust. Yelling wasn't helping it, either.

"Cease moving? I'm doing all I can to put my body in your blade's path! Why dinna' you cease moving, put your sword straight out and let me impale myself on it! That will kill me quicker than you are!"

Rhoenne frowned. "Why would you want to do that?"

"Because I've tired of this! I've tired of her saving me. She does it even when I've set it up so she can na'. How can she save me from a murderous band of Gallgaels bent on taking my head? How? By turning into a wild banshee and frightening them out of their wits. She even made me hold her up, parting her shift so everyone can see her mark, and then when they're all under her spell, she claims me. Vicious wench. She shows off that lovely body of hers and never once lets me taste it. Never. I hate that about her, Ramhurst. I hate that about you. She wants you. Only you. You."

"Then . . . you forced her? You bastard!"

"That's it, Ramhurst. Use it. Use the anger. Use whatever you can. Of course I would have forced her. It's the only way I can get a wench that you've ruined first. What woman ever leaves Rhoenne de Ramhurst for me? They have to be forced. Fiona even had to be forced. I still have the rakes she gave me to prove it. Look at what she did to me!"

He stood, shoved a portion of his kilt aside, showing a long, jagged mark scoring the tanned flesh above his knee.

"Fiona did that to you?"

The knight frowned, and then shook his head. "I can na' think. Mayhap it was a Highland woman. God love them . . . those women. They're lusty. Did I tell you? None of your fancy words for them. Hell. I could na' even speak the language. They dinna' care. They liked me. They loved me. Well and good, too. I could na' walk. They must have done this to me. Nay. Maybe it was that wench down Londontown way. She really liked me, too. You recollect that, Ramhurst?"

Rhoenne stood from his stance. His legs were starting to shake from holding it. "What are we talking of?"

"Women. Curse of the earth. Women."

"Women?" Rhoenne shook his head to clear it. It didn't work. The room spun and wobbled, and what light there was dappled on Montvale's bare, streaked thigh. Nothing made sense.

"I hate them," the knight said.

Rhoenne blew the snort over his lips. "Liar! You love women. They love you. All of them. I've seen it."

"She dinna' love me. She dinna' even want me. Damn

her hair and luscious limbs and those green-brown eyes. What would I want a wench that dinna' want me for? I have wenches wanting me! I dinna' need her rejection."

"She didn't want you?"

The knight shook his head.

"It doesn't make sense."

"It never made sense. Think."

"Then . . . you forced her."

Harold sighed heavily. "Are you getting angry?" he asked.

"You forced her to betray me!"

"Angry enough to find my heart this time?" Harold taunted. "Because I'm getting tired of your failure to kill me! I want to die and you're going to help me do it! Raise your sword! Now!"

"Why do you want to die?" Rhoenne knew the words were slurred, but he also knew they were understandable as Harold's face crumpled for a moment. Then, it cleared.

"God's blood, but she's a lovely wench, Ramhurst. Curves like warm oil; a face like a dream; hair like midnight; and those eyes. . . . Eyes like that? They see deep into a man. Verra deep."

Rhoenne growled, deep and low and with a menace to it that had his own hair whispering of it at the back of his neck.

"The Highlanders wanted her, too. Near every man about wants her. Brent. His knights. Me. I wanted her."

Rhoenne lifted Pinnacle, using both hands, to make it easier and bent forward to make the charge.

"Good. Bring it! Do it, now! Now! Blast you!"

Sir Montvale went to his tallest, baring his flesh with his arms spread wide apart. He had Destiny hanging from one hand, and he was thumping on his chest with the other, making a target for the blow.

Rhoenne lunged, and the knight must have moved, because the next thing he knew, he was slamming Pinnacle

into the seat of the chair he'd vacated. That had his
stomach smashing into the hilt, sending him somersault-
ing over the whole. He didn't have the breath to howl the
disgust because the floor was as hard as it looked and he
hadn't let go of Pinnacle, so he'd brought the chair with it,
and worse. It was atop him.

Then Montvale added insult to it, by striding over,
bending his knee, and putting a foot on one of the chair
legs, pinning Rhoenne right where he was. The knight
folded his arms over his bent knee, leaned forward, and
shook his head.

"I canna' get you to kill me, and I canna' get her to
cease saving me. I canna' die. What a tangle."

"Get off me."

"Will you kill me better next time?"

Rhoenne sucked in breath, tried to pull his sword from
where it was embedded in the wood, but the chair was
moving with it, and all that happened was Sir Montvale
rocked a bit.

"Is that an aye?" the knight asked.

"Let me up. If I was sober this wouldn't be happening.
You'd be dead."

"I'm about ready to give it up, Ramhurst. I canna' die
by your hand or anyone else's; you're unable to kill me;
and that merciless wench of yours keeps saving me. That
leaves me only one recourse."

Rhoenne steeled himself for what it would be. "If you
touch her—"

"I'm na' going to touch her!" Harold interrupted him.
"I'm going to do what I should have done a long time ago."

"What?"

"I'm going to get drunk enough to fall onto my own
sword and end this myself. *That* I can count on."

"You wish to die that badly?"

The knight turned such a look of agony toward him,

Rhoenne's eyes watered up. He had to blink rapidly to clear them to his own disgust.

"Aye," the knight finally said, with a hoarseness that made it worse.

"But why? You had the woman. You had everything! I know. You took it from me."

Harold pushed with his foot, making the chair a crushing weight. "I dinna' have anything . . . save the ability to kill everything I valued. I had the ability to turn my best friend against me, ruin the love he had for his woman, and turn everything into a whole existence of hate and disgust and vengeance and loss. And then I get to find out it was all for naught. Oh. I had everything, all right."

"You should have thought of all this a-fore you . . . seduced her."

Harold shoved at the chair, cutting off Rhoenne's air before he got the last word out.

"You ken, I rather like you like this. Under my power. Unable to sway it. Unable to leave."

"Get . . . off." Rhoenne had to say the words in two huffs of breath, since that's all the air the knight gave him.

"This must be God's will, too."

"God's . . . will?" The words were whispered. Rhoenne thought he might faint if he didn't get some air.

"If you were sober, I'd na' have you pinned like this, and able to tell you exactly what I'm going to tell you. I owe her that much. I owe . . . you that much."

The knight's voice was breaking. Rhoenne moved his free hand, bending it at the elbow and lifting the structure enough to suck in a breath. Montvale didn't notice.

"I dinna' want to do it, Ramhurst. Swear. It almost killed me. God . . . but I wish it had."

"Every man wants to do it."

"She tried to tell you of it. You dinna' listen. You never listen. You're going to listen now. There's na' much time, but you're going to spend it listening. That's what you're going to do."

"We've got time."

"Nae. We dinna'. Your son is going to kill her, she's going to leave this world, and she's going to die with your undeserved words of hate ringing in her ears. It's going to happen soon, too, Ramhurst. Soon. You ken it. I ken it."

The knight's eyes were glowing. Rhoenne gulped and kept gulping. He didn't know why his body had to curse him with a surfeit of spittle now when he least needed it.

"That lass is all that's good and precious and right in this world, Rhoenne. I ken it. I've seen it. I was blessed by it."

"Montvale!"

The chair pushed against Rhoenne's chest again. If he hadn't had his arm holding it up a fraction, Harold would have had the result he wanted and cut off all his air. He watched as Montvale realized it. Then he watched the knight smile.

"You're going to win, Ramhurst. You always win. Always."

"I'm on my back . . . my sword is stuck in a chair that you're using to pin me, and I'm winning?" Rhoenne asked.

Montvale gave a half-smile. There was a tear trail on his face, caressing the slight curve of his moon mark. Rhoenne sucked in the shock at seeing that. He'd never known the knight to show such weakness.

"Aye. You've won. I'm going to die a coward's death, impaled on my own sword by my own hand, and reeking of my own fluids. She's going to die bringing your son into the world. And you? You're going to have what you want; what you've always wanted. You're going to have your vengeance. You're going to win. Again. Always."

"Get off this chair and let me up. You'll not die a coward's death. I vow it."

The knight shook his head. "This is much better, I think. Besides, Pinnacle is stuck so far into that wood you may never get her out. You canna' even cleave open a chair right. It's a good thing I love you like I do."

Rhoenne groaned. "Can't you just taste your blade and let me up? Do I have to listen to words first?"

Harold sighed. He shook his head. He sighed again. "She is na' what you think, Ramhurst. She only did it to save you. Us. She agreed to meet with me to save all of us. That was her lone reason."

Rhoenne grunted with all his might, trying to get the chair to topple with the one arm. His arm ached with the effort, and all that happened was Montvale rocked upward, and then back.

"She dinna' want to. She fought me when I first suggested it. You should have listened to her, Ramhurst. I dinna' want to, either. We did it to stop a siege. That's the lone reason we did it."

"You . . . still did it." The words were hissed through his teeth.

Montvale shook his head. "I must be a much better actor than a minstrel. We had moments before you found us. Mere moments. You ken that. You were at her heels. No man is that rapid. Even me. Especially me. My women receive pleasure from me, not rabbit quickness. Think, Ramhurst! Do what you should have been doing from the moment it happened. Think!"

Rhoenne tasted the bile at the back of his throat and swallowed around that, too. He didn't answer.

"She saved me again when she took your blow instead of letting me have it. I deserved it! I'd earned it! And what happens? You sliced her. If I'd taken it then . . . none of this would have happened. I'd already be in my grave and I wouldn't have to put up with myself for another God-forsaken moment. Do you ken what it's like?"

"What?" Rhoenne asked.

"Losing trust? Losing everything you hold most dear?"

"I lost her."

Montvale's lip lifted and he nodded, as he considered that for a bit. "Close. You still able to look at your reflection, Rhoenne?"

"What are you talking of now?"

"Self-hate! Listen to me, you cur! I hate myself. I hate what I did. I'd take it all back if I could. I'd lay open my chest and let you cleave it in two if it will take some of your pain away, and if you could manage to find it. I still canna' do what every other man takes for granted! I canna' look myself in the eye! Do you ken what that's like or na'?"

"You never touched her?"

The knight shook his head. "Never. She was yours. She's always been yours. Ever."

"Why didn't you tell me sooner?"

"Back when I was a liar, you mean?"

"You could be lying now."

Montvale nodded. "True. You ken I'm na', though. Deep in your gut, you ken it."

"Why are you so certain?"

He sighed heavily. "Because you always win, Ramhurst. Always. I dinna' question it any longer. There's *nae* need. Here. Get up. You already got your revenge on me. I lose. I am a man who longs for death, because it would be more merciful. There. I said it. All of it. Get up. Go. Do what you have to."

The chair rolling away gave him an instant of pain before it was followed by the relief of gaining full lungs of breath.

"Dinna' make her suffer this any longer. Go to her. Before it's too late. Tell her of it. I'll do myself in without your help. You need na' even stay and watch. I vow it, although I may need more of your fine ale first."

The knight reached out his hand and Rhoenne took it, and then in the silence, came the muted, far-off wail of a newborn's cry.

Chapter Twenty-Five

This dream world was different; not as distinct, nor as otherworldly. It had to be a dream, though. Aislynn didn't question it when she opened her eyes, and was immediately drawn to where Rhoenne Guy de Ramhurst was sitting right beside the bed in his chamber that she was lying in, watching her. The look in his eyes and on his face would never have seen the light of day, it was too beautiful. It was peaceful and content, as if he'd found his own heaven.

Aislynn smiled shakily. She hadn't known death transported one to a space like this, although some of the Rune writings from the Norsemen hinted to it with their tales of *Valhalla*.

"Good morn," the Rhoenne of her dreams said, and he smiled slightly, making small lines show around his eyes.

"What are you doing?" she asked.

"Watching you . . . breathe."

That was a strange answer. She licked her lips, and her tongue skimmed over the chapped, dry feel of them. She'd never experienced such a thing in the other dreams. Death was very strange. Very wondrous.

"Why?"

His smile deepened. "Because you breathe. It's the most wondrous thing I can imagine."

"I had a son?" she asked.

"Aye."

"He's healthy?"

He lifted his eyebrows, left her gaze for a moment and then returned. "You definitely had my heir," he replied.

"Where is he?" she whispered.

"With Rosie. And before that, Harold."

Aislynn struggled with that. He was calling Sir Montvale by his given name. That would only happen in a dream, but the distinct feel of the bed linens against her back wasn't dream-like at all.

"Har . . . old?" she asked, splitting the name in two.

He nodded.

Her eyes flooded with tears. She watched as his features changed; distorted; blurred. . . . And then she begged the gods to take her before she had to see the hate-filled specter take over. She slammed her eyes closed, put her hands to them, and knew this was the most horrid dream she'd yet had.

"What is it?" The mattress dipped slightly as if he was entering it. "Rosie told me not to move you much, but I think a bit of this . . . wouldn't go amiss. Let me know if I hurt you."

He was slipping an arm around her shoulders; jostling her just slightly, as he moved to fit one of his shoulders behind hers. Then he was putting a finger beneath her chin, rolling her head against his chest, and tipping her face up to his. Aislynn knew it by feel. She didn't dare open her eyes. Nothing about the man holding her, and breathing on her, and putting his lips against her forehead as he spoke, felt like a dream or anything other than absolutely, physically real. She didn't dare breathe as she waited to awaken.

"Harold tells me you wish my firstborn named after him."
She nodded.

"Are your eyes brown?" he asked.

She opened them, blinked, and looked into tenderness that existed in her past. He must have seen what he wanted to, for he grunted.

"I've forgiven him, but I still had to check. The man has a glib tongue. It is difficult to tell when he lies, and when he doesn't."

"You . . . forgave . . . Sir Montvale?"

"He has a very persuasive manner, if one is forced to listen to him long enough. As I was."

Aislynn blinked. His expression didn't change. She took a breath, dared herself to reach for him, and although her hand hesitated when she reached his face, she curved her palm to it. Other than a swift intake of breath, he didn't move. He didn't yank away, he didn't give her a glare of hatred, and he didn't send scornful words at her.

"I think I shall like this realm that is death," she whispered.

She watched his eyes glaze over with a film of wetness, making them shine, and felt him shudder. "You . . . didn't die, love."

She frowned at the endearment. "I dinna'?"

He shook his head. "And this is not death."

"I dinna' understand. It is too . . . wonderful . . . to be real. You hate me. I have deceived you. Betrayed you. Taken your love and turned it to hate. I dinna' understand. Has a son made so much difference to you?"

His entire face went into a frown, making a bruise stand out near his temple. Aislynn moved her fingers to the spot and cupped the swelling. "You're hurt," she whispered.

"I'm not hurt anywhere, Aislynn."

"You have a bruise . . . here. And here." Her fingers were drawn to the lump that was hidden beneath his hair.

It was even larger and more angry-looking than the one at his temple.

His face cleared. "Oh. Those. I was fighting a wall. And the floor. I believe I even fought a tankard and a table at one point. I'm a terrible swordsman. I did poorly."

"You are na'!"

"I am when I've had a tankard of ale first. Trust me. There's nothing safe. Pinnacle is, even as we speak, buried deep in a chair bottom. I don't think we can get it out. I'm too abashed to take it to a blacksmith or wood-carver and Harold won't assist me. He's keeping it as a trophy. I'll have to order another sword smelted and designed."

Her lips twitched; then she was smiling; then it turned to giggles, and then it calmed into a sigh of pleasure as he tightened his arm on her, holding her like she was precious to him, rather than something he needed to destroy.

"Sir Montvale . . . told you the truth?"

She felt him nod.

"That is good. I can die knowing it's right. Everything is right. You must promise to keep drink and women from Sir Montvale, though. He is trying to kill himself with them. You have to stop him. His is a death wish. He has nothing to die for."

"Neither do you."

"But . . . you have a family curse."

"And you have just broken it. When Brent takes a wife, they will be grateful. If Richard ever decides to take a woman, he will also thank you."

"This is real?"

"Doesn't it feel real?" He pulled her against him, and then sucked in a breath when her elbow hit one of his ribs.

"You're injured there, too?"

"I already told you. I have no pain. I feel nothing but warmth and contentment and love . . . yes, love. That is what I feel."

"Right here." Aislynn skimmed her fingers along his abdomen and connected with two lines of bruising. She knew it as he tensed. "How did you get those?"

"Chairs have backs to them."

"You let Harold Montvale beat you with a chair?"

He pursed his lips. "Will you still claim me if I say 'aye'?"

She giggled again. "I shall have to learn Sir Montvale's tricks. He never wins you. Never."

"You know, I always wanted a son named for me. You should have checked with me a-fore promising such a thing to one of my knights."

"Perhaps . . . we can name him Rhoenne Harold?"

"It's not an issue. Harold Montvale de Ramhurst it is. Firstborn."

Aislynn couldn't contain the joy. It flooded her eyes, looking like extreme sorrow, but feeling like her heart was full to bursting.

"I grant your request and you sob? Why? What have I done now?"

"I—I love you, Rhoenne. What's happening doesn't seem possible. It's an emotion I canna' contain. That's all."

"Oh." His arm tightened, putting her nose against his neck and keeping it there. She heard the next words through his throat.

"I suppose I should confess that I'm not being entirely unselfish here."

"You're na'?"

"Of course not. I got my wish, too. Rhoenne Guy de Ramhurst. Second born. We shall call him Guy to avoid confusion. Until he's larger. A lot larger."

Aislynn's eyes flew wide. He was ready for her reaction as her head moved and he had her shoulders to make it impossible to go anywhere.

"What did you just say?"

"Twins. Identical. Sons. Two. You have made me the proudest father in the world. Wait until you see them."

"Dinna' make me wait another moment! Call for them! Bring them! Twins? You're certain?"

"Unless Old Rosie has a penchant for magic, and can wizard two identical babes into being, I'm more than certain. Harold!" He pulled back from her and said the name loudly, making it pulsate through the room.

"My Liege."

Harold was there, and he went to his knees beside the bed, in deference as he bowed his head to Rhoenne. Sunlight glinted off hair that had been cleaned and barbered to a well-groomed length, and he was dressed in a Ramhurst-blue tunic and gray chausses again.

"Rise."

He was clean-shaven, too. Aislynn looked him over, and could see why many a maid would swoon into his arms. Just not this one.

"Have you . . . been here long?" she asked.

He stood straight, and then winked at her. He had his bearing back, too. Aislynn couldn't believe how it felt just to look at him and know the change that had taken place. She knew it was Rhoenne who had effected it, too. It was worth the cost of a sword.

"Answer the question," Rhoenne said.

"I'll admit to being near."

"Were you listening?" she asked.

"I can hear, aye."

"The entire . . . time?" Aislynn was turning red with the blush, and she couldn't believe it. She'd lived with this man for months and never had the problem.

"I take offense to keeping me from women and drink. I think that's a bit stern."

"You argue with your punishment?" Rhoenne asked.

Harold sighed. "Nay. I but beg a time limit put to it."

Aislynn giggled. She watched Sir Harold Montvale redden beyond the neckline of his tunic. He was looking over her head as he waited.

"It will be up to Aislynn. Well?"

"I dinna' believe the women of this world could survive such a penance. Nor have they done anything to deserve it. I believe a full moon sufficient."

He winced. "That long?"

"Montvale." Rhoenne said his name in a stern fashion.

He stood straighter. "My Liege?"

"Where are my sons?"

"They are with their wet-nurses. They appreciate a woman with a bountiful bosom, too. Harold will do his namesake proud. Yours is a trifle stubborn. I believe he is named correctly."

"Montvale!"

Aislynn was giggling again. "Let me see them! Oh, Rhoenne, please?"

"You heard. Sir Harold? See to it."

The knight dipped his head and was gone, in a swirl of dark blue cloak and gray hose, and he had a long broadsword at his right hip. Aislynn frowned at that.

"He has his Destiny back?" she asked.

"In more ways than one," Rhoenne replied.

They hadn't long to wait and they could hear the procession, due to Old Rosie telling everyone exactly how to carry babes, and how they should be handled, and then the door was opened, two bundles were placed in her arms, and Aislynn was looking down at very small, black-haired babies. One was sleeping. The other was whimpering.

"You see? My namesake slumbers. He knows what is good in this life; got it, and now he sleeps. Yours? He fusses. Continually. He squalled throughout the morn, too, and for what?"

"He had a right to be angry. He had to wait for his

brother to get out of the way first. Powerful angry he was about that, too, and fast. On the other's heels. I've never seen the like, in all my years of assisting at births."

"You ever assist with twins?" Montvale asked.

"Don't get all smart with me, Sir Knight. I'll have you know a babe just wants to get birthed. Having your brother in the way is enough to make any lad angry. You'd be angry, too."

His brows rose. "There's no way to make that one content. He had what he wanted, he had what Harold got, and he still fussed. He doesn't ken what he wants, just like his sire. Exactly like his sire."

"He dinna' have me." Aislynn picked up the babe that was whimpering and held him to her cheek, and he immediately calmed, and started rooting about on her cheek.

"He's my namesake, all right," Rhoenne remarked.

"How will we ever tell them apart?" Aislynn asked.

"That part's easy, My Lady." It was Rosie speaking. "They're not exactly, perfectly identical, although you'd never know it from a casual glance. The women discovered it when we bathed them, and it was very crowded in the nursery, because we had this knight overseeing everything all night, as if he's supposed to be in a nursery, overseeing that sort of thing."

"I was guarding them," Harold replied.

Aislynn smiled. Her heart was too full to put word to it. "From wet-nurses?"

"From large, loud-mouthed, overbearing women, who think they have the power of the household. These are future lairds of Ramhurst, they're not melons to be handled roughly. I was making certain the care and feeding of them was handled by fit persons."

"What? I'll have you know, I'm not large. I'm just a buxom lass. The other men all say so. You'll say so, too. I'll visit with you later, Sir Knight, and I'll show you large."

Sir Harold pulled back. "I'll have to decline. Sadly. My abject apologies. I've been given a punishment. No women."

"Truly? You accepted that? You?"

Harold cleared his throat. "I deserved it."

"For how long? Tell us it's not long." It wasn't Rosie asking it, it was one of the wet-nurses.

Aislynn opened her mouth to answer it. Rhoenne advised her not to, with lips near her ear, and a voice that belonged to her very best dreams. She leaned toward it and missed the next part of the discourse taking place in front of them. She watched Montvale struggle with trying to conceal the truth from Old Rosie, while flirting with both the other women at the same time. That was amusing.

She cupped her arms to cradle Bairn Rhoenne, and crooned to him, and watched as he settled against her, and slept.

"This one is exactly like his sire," Rhoenne commented at her shoulder. "Save for the black hair."

"If they gain your eyes . . . and keep this hair, they'll be the most striking, handsome men birthed," Aislynn whispered.

"They already are. Look."

"I tell you it's for months. I'll be on a drought for months! Months! Years! Tell her, My Liege." Sir Harold had a line of sweat on his upper lip when they looked up. That was amusing, Aislynn thought.

"I'm not stepping into your woman-troubles at this point, Harold."

"Then hand me my namesake. I need a buffer, and all women go misty-eyed and loving when you have a newborn in your arms." He looked down at the bundles. "Well? Which one is he?"

"I thought you could tell him immediately, even without looking at his mark," Rhoenne teased.

"Open his bundle. I'll see."

"My babes . . . have a mark?" Aislynn couldn't keep the dread away.

"Rhoenne Guy has a mark on his arm. Left arm."

"Nay. Please, say it's na' true."

"It's not large," Old Rosie spoke up. "There's only four linked portions on Bairn Rhoenne, while Bairn Harold bears the brunt of five of them on his upper arm; also left. See?"

Old Rosie was unwrapping the slumbering one Rhoenne was supporting. They could all see the darker pigment.

"Oh, Rhoenne . . . I'm so sorry," she whispered.

"What? They have a god-mark and you're sorry? If you weren't recuperating, I'd shake you. It makes them unique, like a cross of both worlds. Which is exactly what they are. They're going to be handsome men. They're going to be strong men. With any luck, they'll have the gifts that accompany it. They're going to take this mark, and make the world take note. They're my sons, the Ramhurst lads. I like the sound of that already."

He wasn't the actor Harold was. Rhoenne's voice had caught several times during his speech. He'd been right when she met him. He was a troubadour. They were interrupted by a knock at the door, and everyone looked in that direction.

"Answer it, Montvale," Rhoenne said, breaking the strange silence.

"There are wenches about, my lord. Servant wenches."

"These women are wet-nurses, sir! They were hired for one purpose, and one only," Rosie replied.

"As I got a very good view of, all night. They can open doors."

"Montvale. Answer it."

The knight looked over at Rhoenne. Then he bowed, and did as he was requested.

"It's the sheriff, Richard. Apparently there's a belief that if twin sons are born into the Ramhurst family, then all in the clan must congregate to the chieftain rooms forthwith."

Aislynn giggled. She watched as both wet-nurses had the same reaction, and knew by the looks they were both giving him, that Montvale was going to have a difficult time with his punishment.

"You have a royal emissary. He's been spotted at Leistonshire. He'll be here before nightfall." Montvale stopped and looked across the chamber at both of them. "Whatever it is, My Liege, I'll stand at your side. I'll not waver. I swear. I have learned my lesson."

"He doesn't have any other children, Harold. It's something else," Rhoenne replied.

"Perhaps Brent has dissatisfied His Majesty and he wishes you to see to it."

Rhoenne shrugged, lifting Aislynn and Bairn Rhoenne with her. "Whatever it is, we'll see to it. We'll all see to it. Together. Understand?"

Montvale nodded, and when the chamber door shut again, he had gone out with it.

Chapter Twenty-Six

"I'm so afraid, Rhoenne."

Aislynn whispered it to him as she held his hand. She woke up afraid. She went to sleep afraid. She'd been living with fear ever since the emissary had arrived at Tyneburn Hall and given the edict that not only was Rhoenne Guy de Ramhurst ordered to Edinburgh Castle, but he was to bring the woman he was holding, known as Aislynn, with him.

It had taken five weeks to prepare . . . five weeks to arrange the path to escape for the twins, in the event their parents were seized; five weeks to arrange credit with every other influential family should it be needed; and five weeks to get her healthy enough to travel.

Old Rosie had been behind the effort. It showed. Aislynn had sleek muscle where her legs had once been wasted and thin; she had stamina that could have her racing every step in the castle and every floor, for any length of time she needed to; and she had every bit of her shape back. All of which was very appreciated by the Ramhurst laird.

He smiled down at her from the advantage of his height and squeezed her hand at the same time. Aislynn returned the smile. She was still afraid. There was only one reason and one event when the fear left her completely. Rhoenne's body and the pleasure he gave with it figured prominently. She ducked her head and blushed at her own erotic thoughts.

The court at Edinburgh was a crush of men and women, seeming to vie with each other for expensive fabrics and costly jewels. Ornate, rarely used weaponry adorned the sides of men, while women primped and simpered behind embroidered, fragranced handkerchiefs. She didn't know why anyone would want to be around people who reeked of pretentiousness, arrogance, and pomposity.

"Is he there?" Aislynn stood on her tiptoes, using Rhoenne for a bulwark so she could see better. "Has the king arrived?"

"He's in his receiving chambers, on the throne. We'll be granted an audience soon enough."

"We will?"

"Unlike most everyone else, we're not here to request an audience. We have nothing to request and nothing to ask. We're here because he sent for us and we have to be."

"But he doesn't know we've arrived."

"Aye." He nodded. "He does. He saw you last eve. That's what made me so certain he'd see us this morn. That's why I had you dressed in my colors and nothing else. It's effective."

She knew what he meant. Her underdress was of silvered material, while the bliant covering it was Ramhurst-blue velvet, and belted with a silver girdle at her hips. She had a caplet of silver atop her head, while blue ribbons were threaded loosely through her hair, to make a mesh and keep it orderly and modest. Compared to the other ladies, she was understated and very different. He'd put it in perfect words when he'd seen her. She was elegant and refined. It was even more noticeable in the Main Hall of Edinburgh Castle.

"He'll see us this morn? Why?" She pulled his head lower to whisper the question in his ear.

He turned his head and smiled. "I just told you. He saw you. He was overcome. He was speechless."

"I dinna' meet a king yester-eve."

"There was a man standing at the steps when you arrived. He greeted you and then you asked him directions to the Ramhurst rooms."

Aislynn gasped. "Him? That was our king?"

He nodded.

"Nae," she replied.

A little man pushed his way through the throng toward them, and it must be an honor to be the one he was looking for. Aislynn caught several envious looks tossed their way as the man bowed before them.

"Laird Ramhurst?"

Rhoenne nodded.

"You are to follow me."

Fear made her hand grip him tighter. He smiled down at her before turning back to follow the man. They were going to see the king, and her belly was threatening her with a wave of sickness at the thought! She was so afraid! She missed her babies, she missed the comfort of Tyneburn Hall, and she missed Old Rosie. Aislynn reached up and wiped at a tearless eye. She even missed Sir Montvale. He had to stay behind. He had to make certain the twins made good on an escape in the event their parents were imprisoned . . . or worse.

There was a contingency of Ramhurst men just inside another room. Aislynn stopped. They hadn't been granted an audience, they'd been escorted into an antechamber to wait, and given a dozen Ramhurst knights for an escort. She watched as Rhoenne reached out and clasped hands with his men.

Aislynn knew their time was out then, when the large

double-doors at the other end of the antechamber opened, and a drum was sounded. Everyone quieted and then everyone was bowing.

"His Royal Highness, King David of Scotland, requests Lord Ramhurst, Earl of Tynebury. Rise! Rise and greet your sovereign."

Aislynn hung back, trailing Rhoenne as he strode through the lines of fancy-dressed men and women, and the rows of expensively dressed men that must be courtiers, and then they were in front of a wooden throne, with a man in brown hose and a brown tunic seated on it. His throne wasn't even on a podium to make it higher, larger, or more impressive. She peeked from behind Rhoenne at him, and then ducked back as he caught her at it.

"Ramhurst. My once loyal earl . . . and friend."

Rhoenne bowed his head and then raised it. He was pulling his hand free at the same time. Aislynn nearly snatched it back, since it felt like she was being pushed away. She watched him walk forward, go onto one knee before the throne, and then he said with a depth that made the words rise to the ceiling, "Your . . . *always* loyal and true friend, my king."

"Rise."

The king wasn't an old man. Aislynn noted that. She had no choice but to meet his eyes. There was no large man to hide behind. There was nothing. Rhoenne stood, looking incongruously large next to the seated man. It wasn't how she'd expected a king to look, but she didn't truly know how a king was supposed to look.

"You took your time agreeing to a betrothal with my daughter."

"True . . . but I did agree to it."

The king sucked in a breath and let it out. His entire frame moved with it. "Too late to matter."

"You would rather I had Fordingham Castle to my possessions as well, Sire?"

"I would rather you ceased disrupting my kingdom. I need knights at my control, armies I can command, not regions I cannot rely on. That is what I expect of an earl. That is what I tasked of you."

Rhoenne nodded.

"This is not an easy country to rule. You knew that when I brought you here. You know it now."

Rhoenne nodded again. Aislynn was afraid to blink. Her mouth was ash dry and her palms were cold and sweaty. Rhoenne had a tight look to his jaw at hearing what sounded like charges that were going to be leveled against him.

The king sighed again. "I try to bring the clans together. That's what the Battle of the Standard did. That's the first time all of Scotland fought together against one enemy—not just each other. I even had the Highlanders at my command, for the first time ever! You know the importance of such a thing. You know we cannot build a country without a strong union. I need all the people; be they Celts, Gallgaels, or Normans like yourself. You know this!"

Aislynn forced her throat to swallow, although there wasn't anything in her mouth to warrant it. She was afraid she was shaking. The king had a weakened, older voice that one had to lean closer to hear. That made it more frightening for some reason. She was very near tears. Was Rhoenne going to be charged with treason—and if so, why did they want her? Why?

Rhoenne didn't reply, he simply bent his head in a full, slow, nod again. He was being silent for a reason. Aislynn suspected it was to prevent the retort he might not be able to take back.

The king sighed again. "Then how do you explain this?"

He waved with a hand, and the crowd behind them

started separating. Everyone turned around and watched with baited breath and some gasps as it looked like the entire clan of the Donals was striding toward them; covered in blue paint; wearing their plaid cloth across their shoulders and over their loins, and little else; and with looks that forbade an argument with them, for it would have but one end.

The twins were at the head. Aislynn started smiling. It wasn't returned. Her expression died away. There wasn't a sound in the entire series of rooms except for bare feet moving on flooring, and the sound of spear shafts hitting the floor when they stopped, making a semi-circle about the throne.

"Well?" The king asked in the stillness that seemed to be sucking up the sound of everyone's breathing with it.

"I believe I'm looking at Donal clan," Rhoenne replied.

They recognized the name if not the words. She watched as they watched Rhoenne. Everyone seemed to be watching Rhoenne. He wasn't shy over it. He had his arms crossed, his own Pinnacle strapped to his side, and was a head taller than any man facing him. He also had a quizzical expression on his lips. Aislynn moved a step closer to him.

"You know them?" the king asked.

"I know of them. Aislynn knows of them . . . more."

"Ah yes. The woman, Aislynn. This is the real reason I brought you here. You suspected as much?"

"Your edict was clear, Your Majesty. That's why she accompanies me. Aislynn?" He put his left hand out toward her. Aislynn moved the few steps to his side. She was still shaking when she got there. He wasn't. His hand was warm, strong, and solid as he fit her at his side.

"This is the woman, Aislynn, then?"

Rhoenne nodded.

"You should have brought her to my court sooner."

"I wouldn't have brought her at all, if it hadn't been

required of me to do so . . . Sire." He'd paused before the title. Aislynn held her gasp. King David didn't take offense. He considered the words and then shook his head.

"You would keep such beauty from my court?"

"I would keep such a woman safe."

"My court is safe."

"For a woman of beauty, there isn't a court in the land that's safe."

King David chuckled. "True." Then, he lifted his head and spoke to the clan standing in front of him. "Is this the woman you requested?"

Aislynn's eyes widened as she realized he spoke perfect Gaelic. That was a surprise.

"This woman belongs to the Donal clan. She was stolen from us. We want her back."

"*Nae,*" she whispered it, but it still sounded loud.

They opened their ranks, and a small, wizened woman stepped through. She was wearing a rich *plaide*, with feathers all along the neckline and sides, and a very large, gold sun-disk at her breast. She was also covered on one side entirely in paint. Aislynn told her body not to recoil. It didn't work. She leaned into Rhoenne. He released her hand to put his arm about her, and helped calm the desire to run that had made every other thought secondary. She didn't want to listen.

"The Donal clan has several enemies. They claim Beck, Dunichen, Aberlem, Galway, Freid. Names to some, enemies to some." The woman had a beautiful voice. There was also something familiar about her. Aislynn couldn't decide what it was.

"I am Donal clan, by way of Galway. I was taken as a young girl. I became Galway clan. I never forgot. I had a granddaughter through my Galway Laird. She was stolen. Years past. None thought to search the Lowlands. No clan gives one of us to anyone other than another Highlander.

Until now. My granddaughter was given to one. She stands before you now. I want her back."

Aislynn was swaying in place. Rhoenne's arm about her was the reason none of it showed.

The entire speech was translated. Rhoenne tipped his head a fraction and regarded Aislynn as the words became known. She couldn't move. The words died out and Rhoenne lifted his head. He looked over the Donal clan. He looked over at the king. He looked back at her.

"Nay," he said.

The word didn't have to be translated. It started a flurry of head bobbing and shifting, and then the old woman raised her hand and started speaking again.

"The Donals traveled north, to tell me of this lass. She has the god-mark, like mine." She parted the material, on the unpainted side of her frame, exhibiting a chain-streak just above her knee. Aislynn's heart was beating faster, taking over every other sound, until it was a throb of noise. She didn't realize she was holding her breath until the words had finished the translation and the king spoke again.

"Ramhurst?" he asked.

"Nay," Rhoenne said again.

The woman put her chin down a fraction and glared over at Rhoenne. "My granddaughter was in the Highlands with her husband . . . a Norman. He is a warrior but he is a man who puts other women before her. I will not tolerate such disrespect. She sorrows. I was told this. I want her back."

There wasn't another sound to be heard, except for words as they were being translated. From what Aislynn could see, the only reaction from Rhoenne was he looked like he was trying very hard not to smile.

"Ramhurst?" the king asked.

"The man she was with was not her husband. He's a

knight; my second-in-command. This woman has no husband," he said finally.

Aislynn moved her glance to the Donals, and saw the confusion, especially on the faces of the twins. She knew what caused it. They were deciding that Rhoenne couldn't possibly be Montvale.

"You sent a maiden into the Highlands with only one knight to guard and protect her?" The king was asking it, and his voice showed how appalled he was at the thought.

"The woman was safer than with me at the time," Rhoenne answered.

"What? Why?"

"I was suffering royal interference . . . at the time."

There was a gasp from the assemblage of fancy-dressed men and women and it seemed to run the length of the hall.

"You dare much, Ramhurst," the king replied.

"Knights?" Rhoenne said the word and Aislynn's eyes went wide as the row of Ramhurst knights stepped from behind him. She hadn't known they'd followed them. They formed a row, with six on either side of where Rhoenne and Aislynn stood, their hands on their swords, and their stance showing how ready they were for whatever the situation warranted. Rhoenne was moving, too, flicking his cloak free of his right shoulder, so he could rest his hand on Pinnacle's silver and gold hilt.

"Rhoenne Guy de Ramhurst."

"My Liege?" Rhoenne said the words in deference, but he didn't move his head to do so.

"This woman has a valid claim."

"Nay," Rhoenne replied.

The Picts knew what the row of knights facing them signified, and the spears weren't resting on the floor any longer. Aislynn heard a whisper of movement, and then each spear tip was tilting toward them.

"You cannot do this. The Gallgael have a valid claim."

"Nay," Rhoenne replied easily.

"You defy me?"

"I'm a very powerful castellon, my king. I command legions of knights, strongholds, land . . . and allegiances with other powerful barons. You know this. It's why you forced my hand to a betrothal with your daughter."

The king sighed. "You swore fealty to me. You vowed to remain my loyal servant."

Rhoenne swallowed. Aislynn watched it. She couldn't move her gaze. "Aye," he replied, finally.

"And yet, you'd defy me now?"

Rhoenne moved his head, pinning his gaze on Aislynn. "I would defy the devil himself for this woman," he said. And then he lifted his head, turned to look toward the king and finished, ". . . Sire."

There was a louder gasp. Aislynn didn't hear it over the one she made. Ripples of shivers were trilling all over her body, making her eyes moist and her throat pain her with how many times she had to swallow to keep the emotion from reaching her vision, so it wouldn't distort or change anything she was watching.

King David sighed, long and heavily. "What would you suggest I do now, Ramhurst? Order a bloody massacre to take place in front of my eyes?"

Rhoenne turned back to look at the Highlanders, narrowed his eyes and glared at each of them in turn. Aislynn looked with him, and could see that he was intimidating them, for the entire grouping backed, almost imperceptibly.

Then Rhoenne started talking again. "If I were a king, and put in the position where I wanted unity among the peoples of my country on one hand; while on the other, one of my most powerful earls was in danger of defying me . . ." He stopped as if for effect and then turned his head to the king to finish, ". . . I believe I would order a scribe, My Liege."

Someone was translating what was being said to the Highlanders. Aislynn could hear the soft words.

"A scribe?" King David asked, with a confused tone.

"So that this thing you want could be accomplished, and your vassal could be punished for his daring at the same time."

"Punished . . . you say?"

"I would instruct that another royal edict be drawn up. One forcing the hand of my vassal, the carl Rhoenne Guy de Ramhurst. I would force him this time to take as his wife, a daughter of the Galway clan, named Aislynn. I would nullify any dowry because of his defiance, and I would make the ceremony take place this day, at Saint Margaret Church, right here beside your castle, on Castle Rock. This is what I would force on my earl for his crime. Aislynn?"

He was waiting for her answer. King David snorted. Aislynn didn't think her feet were on solid ground any longer. She couldn't feel it, if they were. Everything felt warm and clear and very real. She nodded and knew he felt it.

She watched the Donal clan listen through the translation, as everyone else seemed to be. Then the old woman with the chain-mark stepped forward, hesitantly at first, and then with more assurance. She stopped in front of Aislynn and Rhoenne. She was Aislynn's height, and was forced to look up to where Rhoenne was watching, with the slightest smile touching his lips.

The old woman smiled back. Then she nodded. "I agree to this edict. He will marry my granddaughter. This day," she said.

And that's exactly what happened.

Discover the Romances of
Hannah Howell

__Highland Barbarian	0-8217-7998-2	**$6.99**US/**$7.99**CAN
__Highland Champion	0-8217-7758-0	**$6.50**US/**$8.99**CAN
__Highland Destiny	0-8217-5921-3	**$5.99**US/**$7.50**CAN
__Highland Lover	0-8217-7759-9	**$6.99**US/**$9.99**CAN
__Highland Savage	0-8217-7999-0	**$6.99**US/**$9.99**CAN
__Highland Honor	0-8217-6095-5	**$5.99**US/**$7.50**CAN
__Highland Promise	0-8217-6254-0	**$5.99**US/**$7.50**CAN
__Highland Vow	0-8217-6614-7	**$5.99**US/**$7.99**CAN
__Highland Knight	0-8217-6817-4	**$5.99**US/**$7.99**CAN
__Highland Hearts	0-8217-6925-1	**$5.99**US/**$7.99**CAN
__Highland Bride	0-8217-7397-6	**$6.50**US/**$8.99**CAN
__Highland Angel	0-8217-7426-3	**$6.50**US/**$8.99**CAN
__Highland Groom	0-8217-7427-1	**$6.50**US/**$8.99**CAN
__Highland Warrior	0-8217-7428-X	**$6.50**US/**$8.99**CAN
__Highland Conqueror	0-8217-8148-0	**$6.99**US/**$9.99**CAN

Available Wherever Books Are Sold!

Visit our website at **www.kensingtonbooks.com**